For Jul

with tha

warm wishes

Dine

MOONDANCE

DIANE CHANDLER

blackbird

First published in 2016 by Blackbird Digital Books

Blackbird Digital Books
2/25 Earls Terrace
London W8 6LP

www.blackbird-books.com

Copyright © Diane Chandler 2016

The moral right of the author has been asserted.

A CIP catalogue record for this book is available from the British Library
ISBN-978-0-9954735-2-2
[eBook ISBN 978-0-9954735-3-9]

Cover concept by Maddie Chandler
Cover design by Mark Ecob
www.mecob.co.uk

Printed and bound in Great Britain by Clays Ltd., St. Ives PLC *for Madeleine Rose*

PART ONE

PART ONE

1

When I was six years old I used to torment the family cat. I'd dress it up in bloomers of white broderie anglaise, strap it into my doll's pushchair and race around the garage. When it leapt out, streaked across the floor to hide behind the Raleigh bikes, I'd slip a hand around the wheel, submitting to the claws and needle teeth. Then I'd lug it across the room and stuff it back in the pushchair.

I don't know why I was cruel to my cat. It's an isolated episode, well, pretty much, in the grand scheme of my life. But I do know that it's why I've ended up in the bowels of a swanky clinic in Knightsbridge, hands clenched on the arms of the chair, eyes fixed on the door. Because the past always catches up on you, eventually. The door is purple of all colours, rich and velvety, more regal than clinical – which is why they chose it, of course, but it doesn't do the trick. Even the shelves are a dusky lilac, their neat rows of perforated boxes ripped open to expose vials and bandages. And they've scrubbed the lino to a chalky white, in reassurance that the service I'll be getting this morning is indeed private.

So there I sit waiting for the nurse to return. Each breath, deep and jagged, sucks medicinal wafts into my lungs and down into my belly, bringing on those quivers. Of course, there's a part of me that wants the door to open, to get it over with; the part which has always comforted myself through tough times with the reassurance that in x hours this would all be over and I'd be out the other side. In one hour, this filling will be done and that drill will cease; in two hours, this meeting will be over and that obnoxious

MP out of your hair; in one hour, it will be acceptable to escape your self-obsessed mother. In this case, however, I know that it won't be a matter of hours, this one will be ongoing and so mostly I want to flee from that room.

The door opens and the nurse enters, with a kind smile for me which I return avidly. She busies herself, explaining how to prepare the syringe, while her fingers work the packets and the foil wrappers, tossing debris into the pedal bin. Its lid closes softly, with an *oof* sound, as if it too has a soothing role to play, but that sets me off again and I clamp the tears back. I've always wondered whether some feather-voiced therapist might absolve me of that cat, might point to Mum's shrieks which punched through my bedroom floor, to the scratches on Dad's arms the next morning. I'm even called Cat, short for Catriona, so maybe there was a hint of self-flagellation in the mix. Whatever, I am paying for it now.

The nurse hands me the syringe with a gentle smile. "Take your time, there's no rush."

Her voice is somewhere faraway, as I take it from her, glance down at my bare midriff and pinch a fold of my stomach, studying the flesh which appears to belong to someone else. Silently, I tell myself, you have to do this, you have to do it. There is no point delaying the moment, especially given that I'm usually one to seize it, so I grip the syringe between slippery thumb and forefinger and hover over my belly, as if preparing to throw a dart, just as she has instructed me. Still it takes me a good minute.

One hundred and eighty!

I plunge the needle in, hearing the presenter of *Bullseye* from my childhood, and I see my little brother, Billy, and I playing darts in our new house. The yellow feathers, the black cork slab against the wall, the draught excluder we'd lay down for a line. Of course, I always allowed him to stand well beyond it, even let him creep up and screw his dart into the triple twenty, cheering for him when his face lit up. So I wasn't all bad as a child then.

2

Slowly, I push the stopper and watch the clear fluid disappear into my stomach, wondering what alchemy it will craft when it reaches its destination. Two hundred units of Gonal F, a drug that they tell me is tried and tested. And perfectly safe.

Dom flew in from Japan tonight. I sprint up from our basement kitchen, taking the steps two at a time. Normally I don't mind a week alone, but this time the days and distance have fed the jitters already running ragged inside me. He drops the briefcase onto the tiled floor of our hallway and we stand together for a long time, my cheek scuffing his chest, his chin resting on my head; the steady reconnection. I breathe deeply against his shirt, he smells of travel; a little stale, a hint of suit fibres.

"Missed you," I say.

"Me too." He pulls me closer.

When they see us kissing, people often smile, because Dom ranges well over a foot above me, and it always involves a stoop on his part and tiptoes for me. As we kiss now, I reach to take the sides of his head in my hands, knitting my fingers through those tight locks of greying blond, and I can sense the poignancy of this reunion coursing through us both. Then he stands back and looks at me, his eyes gleaming. With exhaustion, yes, but there is something else there too, a wonder at what we're about to achieve.

"How was it?" he asks.

"Fine," I say, delaying the moment. "I'll tell you over dinner. Five grand on the credit card though."

He shrugs. "What's this, if not a rainy day? Let me see."

He shimmies the T-shirt up and out of my jeans, squinting at my stomach as if scanning his PC for share prices.

"Bit lower." I unzip my fly and place a finger beside my navel – I've removed the diamond stud, which seemed respectful somehow.

3

Slowly Dom drops to one knee, then the other, and sits back on his haunches. "Did it hurt?"

I shrug, but feel the tears threatening as my husband closes his eyes and presses his lips to the flesh, sliding his arms around my body.

After some time, he gets to his feet and reaches for a paper bag. "I brought you something back."

I see the pink leather peeping out from a fat package of tissue paper and, smiling warmly at him, I take it out. It's a laptop bag. "That's gorgeous, thank you."

I hate pink though, I'm more of a chocolate brown girl; anybody else and I'd probably let them know. Dom always brings me a gift home and it's rarely something I want – he'd be hopeless on that programme, *Mr and Mrs*. But then, he'd get the questions that matter right, like, 'What would you say if your wife shaved her head bald?' (He'd laugh). Or, 'How would you react if she told you she'd murdered somebody?' (He'd hide me away). And in answer to the question, 'How would you react if she became unexpectedly pregnant?' Well, he'd be ecstatic.

I cook us a steak – I knew he'd be craving red meat after all that raw fish – and we eat in the garden, which is spilling over with an abundance of whites. We decided together on an all-white scheme just after moving in and the gardenia, iceberg roses and even hibiscus have now swollen out and up, overwhelming our beds and walls with a cushioning mass of foliage. Funny how our garden is so fertile and yet we as a couple are not.

The evening is a balmy one. They say July 2006 will be the hottest month on record, the nights still seem to be drawing out and several playful swallows are wheeling high up through the wisps of cerise. I serve us both a heap of salad leaves and I wonder how to tell him about the clinic, whether I should reveal all, or leave the worst bits out. The memory of that purple door alone is making me flush with angst.

"How was the trip?" I ask.

4

"Manic. Told them I'm staying put for the next month."

Dom nods at the family organiser I've propped up against the water jug (he too has given up wine). The rest of this month is blank, apart from the column for our Golden Lab, Silkie, which holds a vet's appointment and her monthly flea treatment.

"We need to focus on this," he adds.

I watch him while he speaks, frowning into his plate, struggling with his own emotions as he saws the meat, spears and jabs it at his mouth. His cheeks, though peppered with a day's growth, are still taut enough. Once again, I think how he might just make it to fatherhood before his fortieth birthday next year.

"Have they given you the timing?" he asks.

I smile to myself, we both live by structured time. I guess it's what happens when work and hedonism have been your life for fifteen years; the pockets of activity perfectly honed to squeeze the maximum out of each day.

"They said it should take about two weeks for the eggs to grow."

"OK, that takes us to end of the month."

"Have to go back every other day for a scan though. They won't start developing for a week or so, but the clinic needs to monitor me, make sure I don't hyper-stimulate from the drugs."

Dom motors on, taking swift stock of my words. "We read about that in the bumf didn't we? I'll have to keep an eye on you, so you don't swell up like a balloon."

We exchange serious nods and reach for our water glasses, which puts that risk to bed. If you talk authoritatively enough about something you will set it in stone, that's what we're used to, even if, in the silence that follows, my thoughts are darkened by a shadow of myself in an ambulance should the drugs wreak havoc. From across the table, a fat bee flies between us, hovers a while and makes for the jasmine that climbs our garden wall. As I watch it land, I wonder if Dom too feels this signals a happy portent, but he is still immersed in his thoughts.

"And then the op?" he asks.

"Yeah."

Under my first ever general anaesthetic, to harvest as many of those eggs as possible. I clasp his arm, my vision blurring on his skin which crinkles into papery lines with the flight's dehydration.

"You'll look after me, won't you?"

His calm blue eyes find mine. "I want this more than anything, Cat, you know that."

"I'm scared I want it too much."

"It is going to work."

"Yeah," I say, adding with fake brightness, "First time."

"First time. It'll pass in a flash and when it's over we'll have forgotten all about the shitty bits."

"You're right." Not sure I'll ever forget that injection though.

His eyes are still fixed on mine. "Cat, we're in this together."

*

I'm sitting at the kitchen table, my face bathed by the early morning sun, about to prepare the syringe. By fussing Silkie, I manage to delay the moment. She sits expectantly, lead in mouth, while I stroke her velvet head, our mournful eyes locked in mutual sympathy. Our morning routine of a jog in Kensington Gardens is broken today. "We'll go soon Silkie," I assure her, with a final kiss to the nose, and turn to the boxes awaiting me.

First, I have to dissolve two ampoules of powder into one ampoule of solvent. The fine glass vials of powder have tapered heads, which I snap off, leaving hairline trails of blood and crystal on my fingers. Then, with a large-bored needle, I draw up the solvent into the syringe and flush it out into one vial of powder. The two mix

6

instantaneously and I draw the resulting liquid back up into the syringe to repeat the process with the second powder. Holding the full syringe vertical, I change the needle to a much finer one, making sure not to spill the liquid even though my hand is shaking. Actually, my whole arm is shaking. I feel like I did on my first day at school, my fear at the sight of children and chaos in the playground, the knowledge that any minute my mother would let go of my hand and press me forward, and I would have to lift a wobbly leg and put it down into a new life, one that filled me with dread.

Dom is still in the shower, I can hear water pounding in a distant room of the house. I stand and hold the ready syringe up to the sunlight, which is now streaking onto the oak floor, and I study the large air bubble lodged at the bottom of the plastic tube. A few sharp taps of my nail on the chamber will force the bubble to the surface, at which point I will have to inch the stopper up, painstakingly, to push the air out, without wasting any of the magic fluid. A good ten minutes lapse until, finally, an air bubble the size of a peppercorn emerges from the spike of the needle and hangs there. Visions of a Hammer horror movie spring to mind, and I am both mad professor who will inflict this potion and unwilling victim who is to receive its mutant powers.

Dom appears in his towelling robe. Still jet lagged, his hair is wet and a sliver of reddened toilet paper clings to his chin. He looks over at the syringe I am brandishing, stark against the benign light.

"Oh. You haven't done it yet then." He opens the fridge and buries his face in it, even though the milk is wedged as always in the door.

The sun is now filling the kitchen, turning the sage green walls to a dusty pastel. I sink back down onto the chair, tug at the belt of my own robe and let it fall open. I gaze down at my thighs, at the tuft of pubic hair, at the wispy grey bruise from the previous day's injection, and I pinch a roll of flesh to the other side of my navel. Visualising a dart before me, I hover once again, telling myself to do it NOW. Nothing happens.

"Not sure I can do it, Dom."

Over my shoulder, he is busying himself at the island in the centre of our kitchen, pouring milk onto his bran flakes. Our backs are square on to each other.

"They told us you could get the GP to do it, didn't they?"

"What about the weekends?"

Silence. He's already made it clear that he couldn't possibly manage the injections for me – I didn't even ask, because he's off with the tweetie birds whenever he has a simple blood test. And I still haven't told him what the nurse said as she bundled up my supplies; how most women have no problem self-injecting. So all these women all over the UK are injecting themselves daily, without anxiety or the slightest compunction even. And yet I, managing director of a major Westminster lobbying firm, am petrified of this simple action. I wonder what further secrets I might have to hide from Dom, what emotions I'm about to experience that he will not share.

A movement in the garden catches my eye; next door's ginger tom is jumping from the wall onto our lawn. Behind me a frantic scuffle of claws clatters on wood, and Silkie launches across the kitchen like a cartoon dog, her paws spinning in mid air, failing to find purchase. As usual she hasn't registered the closed patio door and the collision is pitiless.

Dom is already behind her with pats of sympathy, and a friendly, "Daft dog," as he unbolts the door, allowing her the dignity of renewed pursuit.

But I have been watching that cat, with its one eye raised at me. Knowingly. Standing its ground until the last moment, when Silkie is freed, before it leaps back up to the wall, making it perfectly clear why we have to endure this, why we can't just shag our way there like all of our friends have. I am being punished for my cruelty of thirty odd years ago.

Dom turns to me with a smile and a glib, "Good job it's double glazed."

I smile back, then look down, taking his eyes with me. Flicking my wrist back, I fling it at my belly. The needle pierces my skin and I hold it steady, before I slowly pump in the second dose of my fertility drug.

Because we're in this together.

2

Dom and I met years ago, while travelling in Vietnam. It was the summer of 1993. I was out there with a guy called Simon who worked for a rival firm of lobbyists. We'd met on a joint campaign to persuade the European Union against their proposals to ban herbal remedies, and as we came up with the arguments, the precedents, the key players, I was impressed by Simon's sharp mind. So we each wangled a month's holiday over Parliament's summer recess and flew into Ho Chi Minh City, the former Saigon. The problems began on our first day at breakfast.

"This hotel's too expensive, Cat," he said, his *Lonely Planet* splayed on the table.

"It's twenty quid a night, Simon. Clean sheets, hot water, and we're only here for three nights."

That morning, while I drifted, soaking up Saigon, Simon was off into the backpacker's quarter. He returned at lunchtime with a 'find' at a tenner a night.

"So we're both on thirty grand and yet you've just wasted a morning to save a few quid?"

"It's the principle, isn't it?"

"Ah," I said, "the principle."

That afternoon, nose in guidebook, he traipsed me round with a checklist of sights, the Post Office, the City Hall, the Cathedral – all of them French. I stopped for a beggar, smiling at the war veteran in his green fatigues, while Simon grimaced.

"Why are you giving him money? He's just an old man."

"Because he's poor and I'm not."

In an effort to lose him I took a sharp turn towards a local market, but he scuffled after me. Inside the market was the Asia I wanted, the sting of spices, the pungent dried fish, the pyramids of limes and lychees. None of this was on his list, of course, so I did manage to shake him off eventually, and wandered against the tide of scooters into the botanical gardens. I sat down beneath a tree and watched young men doing Tai Chi, wondering how I could have misjudged Simon so dramatically. It wasn't just his manner, he looked so different in his shorts too – I'd been attracted by the suited version, which hid those puny legs and added a woven silk tie.

However, we'd agreed to hire a car with driver to reach Hue, the midway point from where the roads give way and you have to train it up to Hanoi, and we continued with our plans. Was it the potential squall of a mid holiday break-up? Or perhaps trepidation at travelling alone? Whatever, life in the car was fortuitously silent, our faces buffeted by the warm air as we looked out on the paddy fields and aubergine mountains.

In Hoi An, an early town on the banks of a slender river, I wandered alone through the old quarter, a wooden jumble of temples and homes, and was invited into an old lady's house. At dinner, I began to tell Simon about the rooms darkened by walls of teak, and the wisps of incense.

He yawned at me. "Templed-out myself, been down by the river all day."

"Getting stoned?"

He shrugged a yes, and I gazed at that blond hair, at the freckled, peeling nose. "Anybody ever tell you, you look like the Milky Bar Kid?"

In a beat he came back. "And you're the spit of Betty Boop."

We soldiered on, the days taking themselves forward easily enough, the sights so vivid they stay with me today. I remember the salt fields, where a tiny woman hoisted heavy pans of white crystal across her shoulders; the

11

outdoor sweet factory, where the cane moulds trapped bees within the molten sugar; and the girls planting grass shoots by hand onto a tourist golf course. But of course, it was after Hue that my memories of Vietnam are most vivid.

That day, while visiting a mausoleum, I'd almost trodden on a stringy, lime-green snake that had flashed across my path. Still distressed at dinner, I craved the company of a genuine friend that evening, and was in foul humour as we sat under the fluorescent lights of the cramped restaurant. He ordered chicken with ginger and garlic – which he did every night – and as usual I was disgusted by the way he stuffed rice into his mouth, dipping his head to shake any rogue grains back into the bowl.

"What's up with you?" he asked.

"Can't you try something else for a change?"

I was silenced by the arrival of my silkworms. Also fried in ginger and garlic, but unmistakably silkworms, each one a ridged inch of slimy creature. Wielding the chopsticks, I brought one to my mouth far too skilfully, and whimpered silently, unable to slip it between my lips. As I dropped it back into the bowl, playing for time, I was vaguely aware of a couple squeezing into the table beside us.

"Yours looks disgusting." Simon's eyes taunted me.

"Yours is probably dog anyway." I slipped a silkworm into my mouth and bit. It popped.

Think of snails in garlic, I told myself, and forced a further load down, swallowing them whole to prevent the gunk squirting against the roof of my mouth. I could sense that the guy at the next table was staring at me, and that riled me. At first, I refused to look up, incensed by this intrusion into my discomfort, and I fixed my vision on the table, cheeks stretched in the grimace required to glug the creatures back without chewing them. But then, mouth empty, I looked across at him with the nastiest of scowls.

There are moments in your life that you recall forever, with absolute clarity, so that you can re-live them at whim.

His eyes were the purest blue, translucent even, and for a moment they held mine in a steady, almost leonine gaze, while the pupils dilated. Then he smiled at me with a sudden kindness – which is what did it for me. Dom has told me that it was my feisty glare – that and my guts with the silkworms.

"Mmm, yummy!" His strong Northern accent took me aback.

I smiled. "Would you like some?"

"I'd rather stick hot needles in my eyes."

For several moments we simply smiled, locked into the intimacy of our banter. Odd to capture, but in my mind I actually saw a rush of images from our life ahead, as if I were flipping through photos on a computer. It was then that I sensed the girl who was sitting opposite him watching me, and I turned to meet her scrutiny. She was of Indian origin. Her silken hair was even blacker than mine – she could have wound it twice around her lithe body, whereas mine sat snug in its bob. Instantly I knew that I would take her on.

"So where have you two been so far?" I asked. The opener for everyone you met along the trail, travellers didn't bother with introductions.

Dom jumped in, allowing me to focus on him again, those tight blond curls, the luminous cheeks, smudged with a flush I've come to know so well. "Saigon, Nha Trang, Hoi An. Only here for ten days, so bit of a whistle stop."

I watched his lips work around the words and then looked up at his eyes again – he had omitted any 'we' as he spoke.

And she'd caught it too. "We live in Hong Kong," she added in triumph, squirrelling Dom away from me before I'd even begun on my life with him.

"We're on the train to Hanoi tomorrow," Dom said. Glumly, I swear.

"So are we!" I cried.

Our meal that first evening was brief, as if we all needed to head back to our own camps, to regroup and figure out how this situation was to proceed. When we stood to leave, Dom suggested we meet up at the train station. "Let's get a compartment together, shall we?" I watched him shrug off Harinder's glare before adding, "Better the devil you know."

In those days, the Reunification Express from Hue to Hanoi took twenty-four hours to wend its way north. We boarded mid-morning, hassling our way past the livestock, the food vendors squatting in the aisles, and found a couchette with four berths. Dom swung his rucksack up onto one and I bagged the top bunk opposite his.

We stood as a group by the open window, the rice paddies and rubber trees trundling by in the green sunshine, and shared anecdotes, battling to outdo each other with the remarkable life we'd all witnessed in Vietnam. Having manoeuvred myself to Dom's side, my heart quickened whenever our arms brushed, but we were all four still behaving nonchalantly about what was happening. As if somehow we were just a group of backpackers having the usual transitory encounter on the road. Although Harinder, I noticed, had slipped her hand into Dom's jeans pocket and held it there clamped to his buttock.

Dom entertained us with his tale of breakfast at a roadside café. "It looked clean enough, a few Formica tables, old woman shuffling around. So we sat down, Harinder facing outwards and me in. Then a flash of movement caught my eye and the metal racks on the back wall came to life. Rats. Only small ones, almost like overgrown mice really, but masses of them, leaping over the plates, in and out of the cups, over the cutlery."

"Jesus Christ." I pulled the shocked face he wanted from me. "So did you get up and leave?"

He shrugged. "Seemed a bit rude, so we just ordered bananas."

"We gulped them back though, didn't we, babe?" Harinder added in a froth of laughter.

At her punch line, Simon and I laughed far too heartily; Simon in search of an ally, I in search of a disguise. Beside me, Dom's arm grazed mine once again.

The train's frequent stops brought colourful appearances by the locals. We would purchase finger bananas, or chunks of sugarcane, from the kids smiling up at us and, once, Dom attempted a thank you – 'Cau mon' in Vietnamese – to a girl in a conical hat.

"You just told her to come on!" I laughed, nudging him, while the girl and her friends dissolved into cupped-hand giggles.

He reacted to my sarcasm with a mock throttle, his hands around my neck in our first open gesture of skin contact, which caused us to share a surprised smile. Harinder had clocked it too, and she glowered at me, removing her hand from his pocket and slipping it beneath the waistband of his jeans – down onto that soft skin.

In the afternoon, we all settled down to read. Dom opened a copy of *The Quiet American*. Lulled by the click-clacking of the lazy train, we fell quiet. I chanced surreptitious peeks at his body, my eyes flicking up and then back down with snatches of intelligence gained – his height, the way he lay one leg casually across the other, the way his forehead split into furrows of concentration. He appeared to be so together, so self-possessed.

"Have you *read* this book?" Dom let out a snort of derision. Now, of course, I'm used to Dom's caustic reaction to the ridiculous, but that first time it thrilled me.

"Yes," Simon and I chorused.

"The bit about that naff religion, Cao Dai?"

I smiled to myself, Cao Dai was an absurd mixture of Confucianism, Taoism and Buddhism. We'd visited the cathedral outside Saigon, just as Graham Greene's character, Pyle, does. Simon had enthused over the altar, a

15

paper globe painted with a human eye emitting rays of sunshine. "It's a really cool concept, isn't it? Take the best bits of each religion and roll them into one – makes complete sense to me."

Now, I waited to see if he reacted.

"I know," he said, "it's all a bit cobbled together, isn't it?"

His glasses jutted out like girders to protect the little boy lost behind and, finally, I felt sorry for him. He disliked me too, but no doubt thought we'd muddle through the last week together – as had I up until then.

Oblivious to this moment, Dom was nodding. "What a load of wank. You can't just cream the best philosophies from ancient religions and mould them into a totally new one." Simon and I nodded back, the last time ever that we would act in unison. Dom went on. "I mean, how could such a timeless nation like Vietnam buy such crap?"

"Especially when you think how they worship their ancestors," I added.

"Yeah. Mind you, bit like our family that, we still have a knees up for my Gran, every year on the day she died."

I smiled. "Are you a close family?"

"Yeah." He smiled back and I was tweaked by a twinge of envy, together with a sudden sense that I'd like to meet that family, maybe even have some of it for myself.

During this exchange, Harinder had remained silent. But I felt her gaze and raised my eyes to meet those inscrutable brown eyes of hers, the skeins of hair lit by the sun slanting between the mountains. Her eyes held mine for several seconds; she knew I'd shaken Simon off, but she was holding on with crampons. It was me who looked down first, in a flurry of embarrassment or guilt, I suppose. Whatever, it was a momentary flurry.

Later, when the train lights were dimmed, Dom and I glanced up at each other, just as the bulb faded, with what must have been primitive reflex.

"Time for beddy-byes." He bent to peck Harinder on the lips before swinging himself up onto the top berth. "Night babe, night guys."

When I returned from the filthy toilet, Simon and Harinder were in their berths also, eyes closed. Startled by a mouse, I climbed up quickly into mine, pulling the thin grey blanket over my clothed body. On the bunk opposite, Dom smiled sleepily at me and closed his eyes, drawing my gaze to the lashes resting on his cheek. I watched him silently, until finally his eyes opened once more and they smiled again. Then we slept, side by side in an oversized bed.

In Hanoi, Harinder announced they were staying at the Metropole and I followed them off the train. A whistle from Dom brought bicycle rickshaws to the kerb and we were off, Simon beside me searching for the hotel in his guide.

"Very clever," I muttered, when we arrived; he hadn't thought to check the luxury section. This was the release we both needed.

"I'm off, Cat." Simon jumped down from the rickshaw.

"OK. Think I'll stay here."

"See ya then." Rucksack on, he sidled off into the cacophony of Hanoi. It was months before I set eyes on him again.

Turning back to the hotel, I saw Harinder's tight little bottom jerking its way up the steps, while Dom hovered by the kerb, waiting for me with a grave look. We both knew that what I was doing was abnormal, bizarre – call it what you will – and then I followed him into the only swanky hotel in Hanoi.

In my room, I immediately tossed the contents of my rucksack onto the bed, rummaged for my bikini, and headed down towards the vantage point of the swimming pool, only to meet them in reception. Clearly she'd whisked him out of the room.

17

"We're going to hire bikes, Catriona," Dom said. "Maybe see you later?"

He followed his girlfriend out, smiling at me over his shoulder – a sure signal that he wanted me to find them. I hired my own bike and staked out at a pavement café by the busy lakeside, with a sweeping vista of the road. Within the hour they had cycled into view.

"Hi guys!"

The yell brought startled looks my way, but then Dom was dismounting his bike on the other side of the road and wheeling it to a scarlet poinsettia tree. As he waited for a break in the relentless bicycle parade, his face was illuminated by a mass of those blood-red petals. Still today, come December, I find myself staring into the Christmas rose on my desk, seeing Dom by that tree. Harinder of course dragged her feet behind him, scowling at me when they reached my table, then sitting at the one beside it. I ordered three more cokes, while Dom attempted to straddle the distance between our two tables.

"Thought we'd head out to the park," he said hopefully, "there's a B52 bomber they shot down still lying there."

"Great," I said. "Count me in."

I was behaving as if we were just three backpackers on the road together. True, couples do become morphed into the ragged groups that form between travellers but, let's face it, the frissons between Dom and me must have been bouncing off the pavement. Yet still, at that point, she said and did nothing.

A truck pulled up beside us, and a wiry youth manhandled a block of ice off it and down into the gutter, while women scuttled out from the café and began chipping off chunks into a bucket. In synchronisation, all three of us examined the ice in our drinks.

"Think there's a tarantula's leg trapped in mine," I said.

Dom laughed. "Got his head in mine."

Harinder was silent, just staring into her coke.

On the way to the park, she led and she rode fast, her legs a sandy blur. We headed out along the wide colonial boulevards, where the poinsettias merged into the scarlet banners strung up for Ho Chi Minh's anniversary. Then, from out of nowhere, a storm hit us, the rain falling in sheets, pounding us with a sensuous warmth. All around us, the Vietnamese stopped to pull on their plastic capes and became a mass of primary reds and blues, while we rode on in our shorts and T-shirts. Eventually, Harinder spotted a café and pulled in, so we followed her, and all heaved our sodden selves off the bikes.

On the bar of the café was a large jar, the sort that used to hold lemon sherbets at our childhood corner shop. Inside was coiled a mass of snakes; thin ones, thick ones, all of them pickled orange-brown. While Dom wandered over, I made for the back of the cafe and sank into a chair which faced the wall, the rain now trickling down my body in cold ribbons. Harinder pulled the chair beside me a few sullen feet away and sat down. Her T-shirt clung to her chest, outlining two pointy breasts.

"This'll warm us up, we'll have three glasses please," Dom said, and with a silent squeak, I turned to see the barman ladle out shot glasses from the snake concoction.

In a panic, for some reason I swung round to Harinder, who took that chance to throw me the coldest of sneers. "You, are the bitch from hell," she said.

And it's strange, I know, but that shocked me. I was still kidding myself that, like Simon, she too would realise there had been a coup de foudre and would eventually lope off.

"Here we go, ladies." Dom shuffled over with the tray. "Bottoms up."

We chinked glasses and I threw the snake wine back, feeling it explode against the top of my head. "Wow, better than sex!" I grinned at Dom, digging in for battle now.

And then came a moment in that café that I will never forget, in fact I still find it spooky today. Sneaking a glance at Harinder, I shot my eye to the side, only to see that she

19

had slid her own eye sideways too. The result was alien. In my line of vision was a triangular sliver of her iris, right at the corner of her eye. She would have caught the exact same reptilian view of my eye, before I hurriedly looked away.

The next day, I saw nothing of Dom and Harinder. She'd given me the slip, and I traipsed around Hanoi alone. That evening, I dined in the hotel hoping glumly that they might splash out on their last night. Just before midnight, I was sitting by the swimming pool, some way into a second bottle of expensive French wine I'd tossed onto my credit card. The turquoise pool was lit from within and encased by the dark night, forming a cocoon for me. I sat slumped in my wicker chair, staring into the candle flame on my table.

"May I join you?"

I looked up. He was dressed in a white muslin shirt, which billowed out of smart khaki shorts. There was no Indian beauty behind him.

"Where's Harinder?" I asked.

"She's not well, ate something dodgy, she's asleep now."

My heart leapt. "That's a shame on your last day."

He shrugged, nodded at the waiter who had brought over a clean glass and I poured the Sancerre for him, the sound of my thumping chest blocking any thoughts I might have been able to muster.

"Do you live together in Hong Kong?" I asked finally.

"Just moved in together, actually." He shucked his head. "Funny, when you think about it."

"You meet out there?"

"Yep. She was born there, my firm sent me out. It's not a permanent thing, just a couple of years."

"The job?"

He shrugged again as we both allowed the silence to linger.

"So what do you do there?"

20

He seemed grateful for the question. "Training to be an investment banker."

"Ah. So what do you actually do?" I smiled, dipped a little closer, and he smiled back.

"Basically, I gamble with other people's money. What about you?"

"Training to be a political lobbyist."

"Ah, so what do you do?" he mimicked.

"I bribe politicians. Basically."

"We've a lot in common then, both a bit shady."

We laughed briefly, before then retreating to gaze down into our wine. His hand cradled his glass so close to mine, and I felt it drawing me in, as if the hairs on our knuckles would bristle and touch.

"I think you're my soul mate," I said suddenly. Pathetic, but it just fell out, and he didn't flinch, simply lifted those eyes to mine. Shrugging off my embarrassment, I slipped a business card from my pocket onto the table. "If ever you're in London."

He studied the card, then pocketed it and pulled out a pen, took my hand – for the first startling time – and wrote on its palm.

"My number in Hong Kong, if ever ..."

I was buzzing to take him back to my room and swathe myself over that velvet body, but we sat together and stared into the pool, silent and still. Out on the open water, a large black moth was in peril, fluttering and then motionless. The pool pump had clicked on, swirling currents around the insect, gradually pressing it towards the edge. When it was close enough, Dom knelt down at the poolside and scooped it out with his cupped hands, placing it safely onto the concrete slab. For a long while, we watched as the moth rested, static with exhaustion, its wings lifted by the odd burst of energy. Eventually, Dom reached for my hand and squeezed it, his fingers shaking. I held his look, let him know, if ever there was still any doubt.

"Cat. It would be so … so delectable. But, I can't. Not now."

He stood up and kissed my cheek, his lips brushing the corner of my mouth, and then he was gone.

Bizarre choice, but delectable has become our word – and I still rib him about the 'not now'.

Not now. But later.

3

Egg collection. Conjures up an idyll of the bobble-hatted farmer slipping a weathered hand beneath feathers and sliding out the smooth newly-laid warmth, with a comforting coo at his favourite hen. Far from the reality of it. My first ever surgical intervention. Although the only giveaway that this is a hospital and not a hotel is the high steel-sided bed with its cables and parade of switches. That and the ominous smell of antiseptic. I'm sitting cross-legged on the bed in a white paper gown, my exposed buttocks fused to the blanket, waiting for Dom who's gone to fetch the bottle for his sperm. Despite having strained to fasten both ties of the gown behind me, a draught is weaving through the gaps like spooks between wisps of mist, and although the heatwave continues to pour itself through the window, I am shivering.

From my elevated position, I survey the room, which naturally is carpeted in lilac, with a single winged chair and a sterile bedside table. Beside the door there's a watercolour print of lavender fields with a tree-lined path, poplars or cypresses, and a smudge of grey where they meet in the distance, promising a stone manor house in France or Italy. Somewhere far away from here.

The door is flung open and bounces back onto the outstretched hand of a tiny Hispanic nurse, who drops it shut behind her with a frown.

"Hello, my name is Anna," she says, defiantly it seems to me.

After tossing my notes onto the blanket, she rips the wrapper off a plastic thermometer strip and aims it at my mouth. Any other place and I'd scowl back at her, precious little cow, but instead my anxiety offers her both a smile and a ventriloquist's, "Uvley day."

"Mouth shut please."

She bites at some masking tape and clamps my engagement and wedding rings to my fingers, then splays my hands and scans my toes.

"It is good, no paint."

They'd advised me that nail polish could interfere with the procedure, though I've no idea how.

She tugs the plastic strip from my mouth and scans it, before slinging it at the bin. Then, with a flamenco toss of her ponytail, she gestures towards the scales on the carpet. Some bedside manner, it's as if she resents the fact that I'm not actually ill. When I'm weighing in, the chill air mocks my naked bottom and I grip the gown behind me, guarded against her scrutiny. Even though she is now writing in my notes. Finally, I give up an arm to the blood pressure cuff and succumb to its tightening vice.

After she's gone, I climb back onto the bed and flick on the breakfast news. Where the hell is Dom? The door swings open once more, and a middle-aged woman breezes in, her long skirt swirling as she makes for the bed, beaming at me. She sits down beside me and opens my notes. I draw my knees up protectively to my chin.

"Good morning to you … Mrs Wyatt?"

I nod. "Catriona Wyatt, yes."

"I'm your anaesthetist today."

When her eyes meet mine I shoot her an intense smile, hoping for a hint of warmth behind that brisk manner, and for a moment those eyes do linger.

"Is this your first time?" She leans towards me, so close that I catch a fine spray of hairs above her lip. "Nothing to worry about, you're in good hands."

"Thank you."

Desperate for her to see the human being, rather than the case on her list, I consider engaging her in conversation, letting her know that I too am a professional woman, but I can tell that this would be of no matter. Already she's leaving me far behind.

"Now, I have some questions." She rattles them off. Do I know my blood group? Am I allergic to penicillin? Have I had any major operations?

I watch, more than a little smug, as she ticks only the 'NO' boxes, because I am a healthy woman who never before has lain in a hospital bed.

"Do you have any caps?"

"Sorry?"

"In your teeth?" She makes as if to examine my mouth but I compress my lips together and shake my head.

"Good veins?" She raps the back of my hand. "Excellent," she says. I wrench the hand away like an injured paw and clasp it with the other one.

"You're first on the list, so we'll come for you soon." She smacks the bed in a last gesture of support and is gone.

When the door has clicked shut, I take a look at my good veins, the blue strings beneath the flesh on the back of my hand; they are juddering.

It's 7.45am and Dom is still not back, I wonder if maybe he's decided to do it by himself after all. Stretching out my legs, I unfurl my back against the blanket and feel for the band of bruise which swathes my lower abdomen, the result of sixteen daily injections. I administered them all myself, and it didn't get any easier. Pilates will help, I think, and I draw breath in deeply, letting my back sink heavily into the bed. I breathe out, and there is a moment of calm. Then my body stiffens and rails against the mattress. Grasping at the thin blanket, I scrunch it into my fists, wrenching it back and forth, and scream silently at the world. How can this possibly be happening to *me*?

I've always been in control of my life. Even as a teenager, I worked out that Manchester was best for political sciences, crammed for the grades to get in – and, let's face it, the first class honours was a slam-dunk. I went

25

on to bag a job with the best lobbying business in Westminster, and these days I actually run the place. Then there was our home. I dragged Dom round more than forty houses before we bought our Georgian townhouse, with its white stone steps and ironwork at the windows. Nothing has been left to chance. None of the memories I call to mind from the slots of time that have made up my life include failure, only calculated success – unless you count my first driving test, which I failed for speeding. That says something else about me, I guess. So how come I'm now lying here?

Again, the door opens and I heave myself up to a sitting position, fixing a smile in place; this has to be Dom. Instead, our consultant, Olu, glides in, all six foot six of him, and stands planted at the end of the bed. Shiny, safe Olu, with the indelible white smile.

"Hello Cat, how are you?" he asks, the deep African diction so comforting, and I feel myself blush.

"Bit nervous." I turn off the TV.

"Do not be nervous, we are going to take good care of you."

His forehead creases into furrows of reassurance as he takes a pen from the pocket of his baby pink shirt, drawing my eyes to the embroidered polo jockey. I watch him reach for the notes on the bed and I realise that, of course, he is also here to process me.

"What time did you have your HCG shot on Saturday night?" he asks.

"I did it at ten." I want Olu to know it was me who managed the injection, which prepares the eggs for extraction, rather than Dom. Lately, I find that few opportunities for sympathy are going wanting.

"Good girl, the eggs should be nice and ripe for us." His words warm me – that lyrical emphasis on the 'us'.

"Now, I must ask you to sign this consent form. It is routine for me to point out that, while it is not a major intervention, the egg retrieval procedure can cause damage to blood vessel, bladder or bowel. But this is extremely rare, the operation is straightforward and you are in good hands, my dear."

I take the ballpoint from those large smooth hands. Swiftly, without allowing myself to visualise precisely what he means by damage to my 'vessels' or internal organs, I sign the disclaimer.

"Good, now do not worry about a thing."

He scans a graph in my notes, the chart of my two-week journey to produce as many eggs as possible, turns it towards me and, taking back his pen, taps at each X plotted across the grid, the links of a gold chain jangling on his wrist.

"I will do my best to obtain every single one of these eggs for you, Cat, but as I have told you many times, it takes just one egg for us to make a baby. Just one. Now, I will see you again after the operation when you come around."

I throw him the girlie smile he wants from me, hunching shoulders to chin like some sixties film icon. After resting his eyes for one last time on mine, the pink shirt billows out of the door, leaving a trace of aftershave. Inhaling steadily, I am able to prolong his calming impact.

It is nearly 8am and there is still no sign of Dom, so I switch the TV back on. On the news, the MD of a company which experiments on animals has had his home fire-bombed, apparently while his young children were asleep upstairs. As I take in the burnt-out bay window, it strikes me that my own mother could have been involved in this. Animal rights, that's her latest fad. We're not really in touch any more, but I did see her on London Tonight a few months ago, behind a trestle table on some high street, brandishing a poster of a cat's head embedded with wires. I mean how many women in their sixties still wear their hair down their backs? It looks like grey candyfloss. And she still calls herself Lizzie, at her age.

Of course, I shouldn't have let her anywhere near my thoughts this morning, I know that, but she's already in there. Funny how when I'm at my lowest I need to torment myself with the memories, but here they are, all lined up for inspection. She left my dad for a man brimming with latent aggression, which she mistook for zeal. Whisked us off to a scruffy two-up, two-down, near Willesden junction, where the garden was a yard with the remains of the outside loo. To reach the bathroom he had to walk through the bedroom, which Billy and I shared, and each morning he'd head past us for his shit and his shave, no shower, leaving the door open to air it when he left for work. Lizzie thought him erudite because he'd spout stuff like, 'union recognition' and 'repression of the workforce', but I hated the way his nicotine-stained finger would jab the table top, fag clipped against his thumb, dropping ash when he made a point. That treacly table had succumbed to a thousand ringed stains from the mugs of comrades, and once, in the early days, Billy and I had crawled beneath with a vegetable knife and carved *You Bugga* into it. What satisfaction, knowing that those words were on the underside of contact with Nasty Norman's finger. After junior school we called him Norman Bates.

A bizarre peal of laughter spills from me. "Good work, Cat," I say out loud, "you're feeling really shit now, aren't you?"

The door handle dips and I sit up, this has to be Dom. Whoever it is hovers outside, murmuring to a hidden somebody, tantalising me. Then four tanned fingers appear around the rim of the door and my nurse enters the room. I flop back onto the bed.

"We are ready for you, Mrs Wyatt," she says.

"But, we still haven't produced the sperm sample."

"That is for your husband, no?"

Maybe her grin is an attempt at sisterhood, but a chill quivers inside me, rendering my voice hollow. "Yes, but we wanted to do it together."

"Oh, I see." Her forehead furrows in apparent surprise. "You will go second then."

Once again, I am left alone. Instinctively, my finger and thumb seek out my rings, to worry them, as always when I'm anxious, but they brush against the rough alien tape which has them pinned down, untwirlable. So instead I pump the remote, until I come across a pink and green stripy creature with a pot belly, which is skipping around a magical garden of tissue paper. It asks me if my fingers are twinkling and my nose wrinkling. How can Dom have left me alone like this? Making me miss my slot on the list, because he wants me to help him do the job, rather than some porn video in a fetid box room. I try to settle back on the bed and watch the creature dancing chirpily to some nursery rhyme, my eyes darting back and forth to the clock.

It is a further five minutes before the door is flung back once more, and Dom's flushed face appears. In one hand he has a brown paper bag, which I know secretes a sample bottle, and in the other, a *Do Not Disturb* sign.

"Where the hell have you been?" The rattlesnake coiled in my tummy lunges at him.

And for the briefest of moments my husband stares at me in surprise, before he then tries to trump me. "Fucking hell, Cat, I nearly died of embarrassment down there. That blonde girl on reception was literally waving the bottle around, shouting my name, while the waiting room was full to busting."

Bewitched by his histrionics, I want to scream back at him. In half an hour's time I am to have a needle inserted through the walls of my vagina to aspirate ten eggs, which I can feel hanging like grapes off my ovaries. I'm aware, however, that if there is one thing I can control this morning, it is this critical stage of the process, and empathy is the only option. So instead I smile at him.

"Nightmare," I say, slipping off the bed to hug him. "Come on then let's do it. Lock the door, will you?"

"Can't. No locks. But that Spanish nurse has sworn blind that nobody will come in if we put this notice up."

Dom hooks the sign on the outside handle then closes the door, pressing it for good measure. In a few strides he is by the chair wedged between bed and window. He unzips his jeans, shimmies them and his boxers down, and sits on the chair. I kneel before him and reluctantly scroll the white paper gown up to my neck. With a neat little pat he places the sample bottle on the windowsill. I'm struck that its neck is rather narrow for these kind of antics. Wrapped around the bottle is a label with my name and date of birth – WYATT 21/3/68.

"Think that's indelible ink?" I muster up a sexy smile.

"Not going to miss, am I? Gonna fill it to the brim. But not with him watching me." Dom clicks the remote, dispensing with the stripy creature, and bends forward to kiss me. He reaches for my breasts.

Within minutes he is scraping the last beads off against the bottle rim before screwing the cap on.

"Don't contaminate it with your hands, Dom." I smile, relieved that we've managed it.

"Well, it'll have saliva in, won't it?"

Our eyes meet in a burst of laughter, and I sense the relief in Dom too – he is all man. Then the door opens and a woman wearing a pinny walks in.

"What the?" Dom cries, while I swivel to the bed, burning my knees on the carpet.

"Have you filled in your lunch order, love?" The woman takes the sheet of paper from the table on the other side of the bed and studies it. "Tuna with sweetcorn. On white or brown?"

She looks at me in question and I clasp my hands together on the blanket, the gown still bunched up around my neck like a choirboy's ruff. I must look as if I am in prayer. Behind me I know that Dom's boxers are still around his ankles, paper bag grasped to his crotch.

"Brown please," I mutter.

"OK, thanks love." She leaves the room, the slight shake of her head our only confirmation that she has clocked the situation.

Dom is bewildered. "Jesus, Cat, she could have seen us at it ..."

Worse than that, two minutes earlier and she may have wrecked our chances of collecting any sperm to fertilise those eggs. We both jump to our feet, scrabbling to cover our bodies and I head for the bathroom. Leaning back against the closed door, I look into the mirror above the sink and contemplate the apprehension I see there. Without make-up, my lips seem to fade into the pale wash of my face, and in my eyes there is not a glint of chestnut; it seems that only my hair is its normal lustrous self.

On the ceiling of the pre-theatre room they have painted a mural, presumably to ease my transition under the anaesthetic. It is a Latin American scene, of a couple dancing in a garden beneath the stars. You can feel the heat in that midnight sky, sense the joy between them as they kick with abandon, her turquoise skirts carried high, a mass of scarlet hibiscus petals grazing his trouser leg. Above the lovers – for they are clearly lovers – an oversized moon hangs in the sky, luminous and full of promise. Is that the clinic's quirky way of helping me along?

A short while ago, I kissed Dom goodbye and handed him my new silk dressing gown, together with the slippers I've had to buy especially for the lift ride to the basement. Then they wheeled me off into the sterile underbelly of this clinic, flat on my back, the mottled ceiling tiles skimming by, counting me down. I'm lying there, dreaming up a life for those dancers in some sultry Latin village, when the anaesthetist slides through the swing door from theatre and stands over me. Her breath smells like the water from the flowers I threw away last night and I turn from it, fix my eyes on the lovers above me, imagine myself dancing beneath the moon. And begin silently singing our song.

31

"Oh, those naughty veins of yours have tricked me."

The unease in the woman's voice jars me. I feel a needle jabbing at the back of my hand, surprising me with the pain, and again further round, tearing my skin, then it scratches the base of my thumb while a hand fumbles at my wrist. I screw my eyes shut – please, just get the sodding thing in – and sing louder.

Moondance. It was playing one night during the summer we met up again, as we drove around London with the roof down, the balmy night brushing our cheeks, the mellifluous mix of sax and piano. The word has to be a euphemism for sex, doesn't it? And so is IVF, if you think about it.

"So … now you'll soon feel yourself go."

I sense the woman relaxing. Her voice floats somewhere above me, while a prickling gnaws inside my arm, then it stalks my shoulder. I crawl onto the springy grass beside the dancers and curl up on its feathery cushion. And sleep finally saves me from this lunacy.

Feet first, the trolley rattles me back into my room, where Dom is studying his Blackberry, the share price index rolling across the telly. Well, what did I expect? That he'd be poring over a photo of me on our wedding day?

He springs up from the chair. "Hi darling."

They roll me onto the bed, Dom strokes my cheek and I begin to weep.

"Does it hurt? Try to sleep again," he says gently.

"Can you shut the blind Dom?"

I hear my voice, small and childlike, then the slatted sunlight on my pillow is folded into grey and I drift away to kill off another portion of this horrendous day.

It feels like much later when Dom is calling my name. In my dream, he was reaching from his bunk across the whole width of the train carriage in Vietnam, brushing the hair out of my eyes. I open them to see his lazy smile.

"Dr Akande is here."

Olu stands at the foot of the bed, his smile now muted out of respect for the private moment of my waking, even though a few hours ago those huge white eyes were staring into my fanny.

"There is good news, we can use nine of the ten eggs we retrieved."

"Is there bad news then?"

"The sperm sample was not optimum." His emphasis is on the 'mum,' which softens this word, makes it sound benign even.

Beside the window, Dom draws himself to his full height and pronounces the word with its rightful meaning. "Not optimum?"

"The count was good, well over 100 million sperm per millilitre. But motility was poor at only 40%, and we saw 90% abnormality." Olu's voice is gentle.

I gape at Dom, how can nearly all of his sperm be abnormal?

His own eyes are challenging Olu. "But I've had two samples done before, and both of them were ... were excellent," he says.

Olu remains placid. "There is often volatility with a man's sperm count, the next one could be much improved. But we are looking today at the need to perform ICSI. Do you both know what that is?"

"It's when you select an individual sperm and you inject it directly into an egg to give it a better chance of fertilising," I say, vaguely recalling the paragraph in the clinic's glossy brochure. With all Dom's blather about his prowess, I've never once imagined that this procedure would apply to us.

Olu nods. "We are more likely to produce some embryos for you, if we proceed with ICSI."

When Olu has left the room to let us mull this over, Dom slumps back onto the chair and stares at the carpet. I reach over and take his hand, awash with sympathy for my husband.

"It's OK, we'll still get there, Dom." I watch his jaw twitch, as he struggles with emotion, and I squeeze his fingers tighter. "It must be all that stress you're under at work."

But it's obvious what both of us are thinking. Is the problem with him?

4

It was 1994. Square Ambiorix was a neat little square park. I loved its boundary of trees knitted together and pruned flat by gardeners I used to smile at each morning on my way to work. They took great pride in their shrubs too and, even back then, were experimenting with a blousy crimson flower I now know to be amaryllis.

On one side of the park stood my penthouse studio flat, an extravagance I'd allowed myself for my two-year secondment to our European office. It had been ten months since I'd met Dom in Vietnam and I'd heard nothing from him. At first, on my return to London, I'd somehow hoped, even expected, him to make contact; so smitten had I been. But as the weeks and then months fell away, I began to tell myself that he'd clearly not felt the same way, that too much wine must have skewed my take on that last night in Hanoi. By Christmas, I had put in for a stint in Brussels, a promotion that would test me professionally, but which I was rising to nicely. I felt that I had moved on. Still, he lingered in my mind.

At that time, Brussels was already buzzing with lobbyists who were getting to grips with the arcane workings of the European machine, and there were six of us at Westminster Policy Advisers, competent, fired up and having a ball. Our boss was based in London but we were shepherded, more than we realised, by our Belgian office manager, Sylvie.

I remember that Monday 13th June was another hot one. While we'd sat that morning beneath the crystal chandelier, sipping coffee and sharing the specialist European press around our boardroom table, Sylvie had announced that the heatwave was to end in a storm that night. A sexual tension was always palpable in the office, what with three girls and three guys all still in our twenties and single, but that morning the close air was clamping our bodies and we were restless. When my junior colleague, Ash, and I headed upstairs to our office, we exchanged glances; sometimes we nipped back to my flat at lunchtime, for sex. We weren't an item, nobody had come anywhere close since Dom, but we often 'sorted each other out', as Ash put it.

However, that day as I recall – because you do remember the hours before everything changes forever – Geoffrey, the Great White Chief, was bringing over the Chairman of our latest coup, a construction company which had offered us a lucrative retainer. And their account manager was to be twenty-six-year-old me. No time for a quickie then, however randy we both felt, however suggestively Ash slid the tip of his tongue between his lips in question at me, because I had to prepare. And the job always came first.

In the mid-afternoon, I answered the front door and turned my professional smile onto the portly face of a Sir Stanley something or other. Behind him, Geoffrey, trussed up in his usual belted raincoat despite the heat, beamed at me – I was his 'petite protégée' as my colleagues enviously ragged me. Today, of course, their prophecy has been fulfilled, but still I find it curious that I was so driven from that young age, already the consummate lobbyist. That day, I was perfectly prepared as always. I had analysed all upcoming EU legislation, which would have an impact on the construction business, had discovered who was in charge of each policy, and already made contact to assess how lay the land. My client had received an ample file, alongside a full itinerary for his first visit to Brussels, and I was feeling more than a little smug with my proficient self that day.

Geoffrey opened the meeting, rolling out his usual spiel for new clients, with the emphasis on all at WPA being 'helpful', which was the buzzword of that time.

Sir Stanley responded. "I was most impressed with your overview of EC legislation and its potential impact on our business, Miss Black. Clearly we need to keep our ear to the ground out here, even if we'd rather be out of the damned Common Market altogether."

"Thank you Sir Stanley, I think we are well placed to educate the European Commission about the ways of your business."

They loved it when you implied that they knew better than the Eurocrats, even though the whole EC thing was way over their heads. I went on, bamboozling him with technical detail.

"Of course, since the Single European Act, the Parliament has a say in all major legislation, and we've arranged a lunch with four MEPs, all of them key players."

Then it was time to back off. I was also learning how to play people and knew that he might become irritated by my superior knowledge. After all, lobbying is ultimately about persuading, cajoling, flattering – that's just the nature of the business.

So I threw him a smile and tossed my hair, which I'd now grown into a fuller and glossier black bob. "And tonight, we have dinner with the senior British Commissioner."

"Ah." He smiled and sank back into his seat.

"At the best restaurant in Brussels," I added.

Then I stood and turned to the photocopier with the Commissioner's biography, keen for him to note that I was not above a menial task. I could feel both pairs of male eyes on the back of my legs. My grey checked kilt stopped above my knee, adding a childish touch to the black silk shirt, which was another less threatening touch on my part.

"Are you limping Cat?" Geoffrey asked, watching me walk back to the table.

"Sprained my ankle playing tennis yesterday. Do you play, Sir Stanley?"

I knew he did, because I'd read his CV. And sure enough the man held forth about the recent match he'd won at his club, while I listened with rapt attention, clocking on the periphery Geoffrey's bead-eyed admiration. For sure, my boss taught me everything I knew.

Later, as Sylvie saw him into his cab, Geoffrey winked at me. "Good work, Cat. And how did you really do your ankle in?"

I winked back and began to clear the tea tray. My kindred spirit knew me well – I'd fallen off a table in the English pub, Twickers, a Brussels legend near my flat. My new Scots friend, Jackie, and I had been belting out *Hi Ho Silver Lining*, and I'd lost my footing on the chorus. Too drunk to feel any pain, I'd stumbled home with her through the early hours of staid Belgian slumber.

Jackie worked for BBC radio. She'd called our office about a feature on lobbyists during my first month in Brussels. Her cropped pink hair had thrilled me when we'd met in a bar for the interview, but I'd eyed her Dictaphone warily.

She'd begun with a platitude. "I hear that Commission officials are hardened to lobbyists, no longer flattered by the attention?"

She was right, I was finding it challenging enough to extract information about new legislation, let alone manipulate these Eurocrats into making changes to it in favour of my clients.

"It's tricky yes," I responded, "but proficient lobbying is all about two-way traffic. They're often keen to learn more about the industries we represent, so at WPA we give as well as take."

In a beat she'd come back, pressing the pause button before she spoke. "And does that two-way traffic mean you have to wine, dine and shag?"

That threw me and for a moment I gazed at her, this complete stranger with her eyebrow curled at me, but then I rose to the frisson of danger. "Only if they're Italian," I said. "Oh and some of the Greeks are quite hot."

Play resumed, and we continued the interview quite formally, but that spike had bonded us and we soon became inseparable. Twelve years on, and Jackie's still my closest friend.

Sylvie floated into the meeting room with a piece of paper. "Cat, a friend of yours called. A Dom, from Hong Kong?"

The tray slipped from my hands and I grabbed at a china cup which was spilling its dregs across my papers. "What did he say?"

She read her note. "He's in Brussels, at the Hotel Schuman, room 209."

My heart was thudding, he was just streets away. In what felt like a single wash of movement, I took the note from her, gathered my papers and glided upstairs, where I reached for my briefcase, turned off my computer and turned again for the door. Across the room, Ash was smiling quizzically at me, his eyes half-seeking, half-realising the relevance of this moment.

Downstairs, I assured Geoffrey that I'd make it to the restaurant on time, and I left the office. Then, in slow motion, a chaos of thoughts and emotions skidding towards me, I crossed the park – why was he here ... ten whole months of silence ... he must have been thinking about me too ... Gazing at the amaryllis heads as I went, the jump from one flower to the next was the sole confirmation that I was actually walking. Their scarlet petals leapt up at me in turn, and I was back in Hanoi, basking in the warmth of Dom's smile when he parked his bike under the blinding poinsettia tree.

In the hotel foyer, I asked for Dominic Wyatt, room 209, and the receptionist reached for the phone. Only when it was answered did it strike me that he was actually here and

I began to shake as the woman spoke to him, as his physical presence became real. And then he appeared, standing before me, those large blue eyes searching mine, any trace of trepidation squashed by the overt joy he must have seen in my face.

"Hello Cat."

"Hello Dom."

What else was there to say? Everything and yet nothing at all.

"How've you been?" he asked.

"Good. You?"

"Good." He smiled. "Would you like a drink?"

I nodded and he reached out to me, electrifying my shoulder while he guided me to a leather sofa, before he turned back towards the bar. I watched his back as he ordered the wine; he was taller, broader than I remembered, the tight blond curls less unruly. He turned with two glasses and a bottle of Sancerre, the wine we'd shared that last night in Vietnam, and my eyes lingered at his air force blue shirt before I braved another smile at him. He sat down beside me and poured the wine. I watched the imperceptible shake of his hand, and that calmed me, I remember.

"How come you're in Brussels?"

"I hear the beer's good here," he said smiling. "What about you?"

A dumb question, given that he'd obviously tracked me down via our London office.

"Well I work here. Just for the moment." If he'd left Asia for good, I didn't want him to think this stint was forever. "Are you back in London?"

He nodded. "Contract didn't work out. And I missed the UK."

"Is it good to be home?"

"Could be." He fell silent for a moment. "Thought about you, Cat."

I swallowed. "So why didn't you call?"

40

"Why didn't you?"

"You had a girlfriend."

"Not for long after Hanoi." He took my palm between his hands and I could hear my heart thumping, as if through a stethoscope. "Are you free for dinner?"

"No, sorry, I've got to work tonight."

"Bribing politicians?"

"Something like that." We watched each other and I could feel the inevitability sweeping through me. "I'm free for a night-cap after, though."

"Great. I'd like that."

Then I needed to get out, to regroup, to control the situation, as I always did. So after a last sip of my wine I stood up.

"Better go. I'll call by the hotel, shall I? About eleven? There's a great sports bar round the corner if you want to explore?"

*

La Maison du Cygne dates back to the sixteenth century and is the kind of restaurant where the stacks of hand towels in the toilets are emblazoned with its name. I had one on show in my bathroom, and I was on a mission that night to nick one for Jackie. We four sat down at a table beside tiny lead windows, which looked out over the Grand Place, and had been thrown open to lure in any lurking breeze.

"Magnificent isn't it?" The British Commissioner turned back to Sir Stanley, who was tasting the Chateaux Margaux he'd selected.

The waitress poured the wine and we all took appreciative sips, my own murmur much softer than the testosterone grunts around me. By then, I'd learnt that, having impressed our client in the office, my role at such dinners was to play the gentle female. Perhaps I was also already aware that confident women like me can come

41

across as aggressive, can spoil such evenings, and that night I was particularly happy to be left on the margins of their discussion. With one ear alert, I allowed my thoughts to drift.

Behind the Commissioner's head, the wood-panelled wall was draped by a vibrant tapestry, with a lush scene of a medieval prince playing the lute for his princess, surrounded by orange trees and lambs. I gazed into their faces, both of which held an enigmatic smile, clearly captured before they had first made love. My stomach flipped; our first time would be tonight. I'd lived it already, so many times over the past year, even though I thought I'd never see him again.

"Well, of course the French blighters are the worst."

My thoughts were snapped back to the Commissioner's pompous words.

"Our innate sense of fair play means that most of the Directives become law in the UK, whereas those buggers force things through and then ignore them, you see."

"Quite." Sir Stanley was relishing his new friend's company as much as the red wine.

Smiling, I nodded at the men, took a sip of my own wine and drifted off again, glancing round the restaurant at table after table of suits on expenses. Except, in the far corner, a young couple sat at a small table, holding hands around a candle. Each of them was intent on the other's lips when they spoke, offering the selfless, bewitching revelations of a brand new relationship. I saw again Dom's smile as he'd turned from the bar, and knew that I myself was on the brink of this too.

"What do you think, Cat?" Geoffrey pulled me into their deliberations.

"Oh yes, very tricky." The retort flashed with the promise of a catch-all.

And for a moment, the three men considered me, then appeared to decide my comment pithy and reached for their wine. Clearly, I'd been overly winging it. "Take that disk out, Cat," I told myself, "slot your work one in."

Our meals arrived, milk-fed lamb for our two guests, cassolette of lobster for Geoffrey, skate in champagne for me, which seemed somehow symbolic of the night ahead. We began a long conversation about the construction industry, where Sir Stanley was on home ground and I knew that my cue was some way in, allowing me the luxury of imagining Dom naked, as I'd done so often in bed at night.

Several bottles of claret later, Geoffrey picked up the bill and we left the restaurant. The Commissioner waddled to his waiting limousine and a content Sir Stanley, patting his own paunch, announced he would take a stroll and sauntered off across the Grand Place in the general direction of the red light district. Geoffrey threw me his little boy pout at my refusal of a last drink in the ancient Chaloupe d'Or opposite, but I pleaded a throbbing ankle and left him to it.

Just before midnight, I emerged from the Schuman metro station to an almighty sultry deluge. Sylvie's storm was here. His hotel was a two-minute clip away and I set off with a slight hobble, my stilettos catching between the cobbles. After a few yards I yanked my good foot too vigorously out from a crack and the heel of my shoe snapped right off. I contemplated the spike sticking up from the pavement and began to laugh, a giddy laughter, nourished by the rain, and of course by nerves, then I pulled off both shoes and wrenched the broken heel from the pavement. Above me the moon was nearly full, and I stood gazing up while the rain pummelled me in sheets, taking me back to that downpour in Hanoi. Then I began to take barefoot fairy steps across the slippery cobbles, savouring the anticipation. In the hotel lift, I wiped at the smudged mascara with the pilfered hand towel. Then I stood at his door, my chest soaring and diving.

And there he was, laughing at me, his beautiful open face, his tender eyes. He ran his hand over my dripping cheek and spoke in his best Yorkshire French. "Plus ça change, eh?"

Dom pulled me inside the room where a blast of air con hit my wet skin and I began to shiver. He drew me into him and we kissed, for the first startling time, then he folded me into his arms, his chin resting on the top of my head.

"Come on, we need to warm you up," he said, and peeled the sodden black dress over my head, dropping it on the floor.

My hand firmly in his grip, I trailed Dom to the bathroom, where he opened the glass shower door and flipped the tap, releasing a cascade of water from above. We fumbled at hooks and buttons, and then we were naked in that immense shower, the searing water streaming between our faces, splashing off the seal of our lips as we kissed. Dom lifted me up and on to him, pressing me back against the marble wall. The minutes were a haze of steam and craving, until finally a jagged current surged through me and I slumped against Dom's shoulders. Then he sank to his knees and we sat enfolded, pounded by the scalding rainforest monsoon.

The following Saturday night, we lay on our backs on the balcony of my penthouse, smoking a joint. Our legs were hooked over our drawn up knees and my foot lolled against Dom's thigh. The moon was now full and it hung heavy in the sky, creamy and pendulous; in those days it was ripe for the taking.

"Favourite film?" I asked him lazily.

"*Deer Hunter*. Yours?" He passed me the joint.

"*Killing Fields*." I inhaled and handed it back. "What about band?"

"REM, or maybe the Stones."

I smiled to myself, the doleful *Angie* was drifting from my living room.

"I went to an REM concert in…must have been, oh, 1986," I said.

He turned his head. "At Wembley? I was there too."

"Really? Who knows, maybe we even smiled at each other across the stands."

"Bet you were already gorgeous then weren't you? Bit scary for me, mind"

I grinned sideways at him. "Cat or dog?"

"Dog. No-brainer."

My smile broadened, I took the joint from him and inhaled deeply.

"OK, my turn." Dom slid his hands behind his head, swapped his leg over and rested the sole of his foot against mine. "Favourite novel?"

"Difficult, there are so many. *Pride and Prejudice* is up there, of course."

"Why?"

"She's such a fantastic character, feisty, outspoken. Before her time."

"Ah, bit like you then."

I kicked his foot, he kicked back.

"How about favourite food?" he asked.

"Silkworms."

He snorted. "They were so gross, Cat." He reached for the joint, took a long drag and exhaled with a sigh. The sound of complete contentment.

"Delectable," I murmured.

"Yeah, delectable."

We lay in silence for a few moments, contemplating the moon, then he steadied the ball of his foot against mine and pressed.

"Do you want kids?"

"Of course." A mild panic rose within me. "But not yet."

"I'd like four."

In sudden need of a prop, I reached for the joint from him. I can still see myself taking several drags on it, giving myself time as the appalling vision of a screaming baby sprawled across my office desk hit me. Then I spoke quietly.

"Later though, yeah?"

He plucked the joint from my fingers, laid it on the paving slab beside him.

"Need to get some practice in though."

He'd ignored me, but I had told him what I wanted. Way back then.

5

It is 2am and I've just woken from the craziest of dreams. A glass dish on a counter was bubbling with a mass of transparent spheres. Tiny balls, all jostling for position. They were glowing lilac from within – bursts of purple light pulsing from them, as if they had beating hearts. The balls began popping out of the dish, jumping like popcorn, before rolling off the counter to be dashed on the floor. I come to with a jerk, sweating, unable to blink away the image, and I lie still until my heartbeat has lessened and the vision has gone.

Behind me, Dom's snores are puttering like a distant pneumatic drill. I lift his hand from my waist, place it gently behind me onto the mattress and swing myself out of bed. At the open window, I look out over sleeping London. Only this is still the height of summer, the corker of 2006, and the city is not asleep, but vibrant, with the revving of car engines and stray pub-goers laughing on Gloucester Road behind the houses opposite. Beyond them, beyond the mass of Imperial College, the duck egg bricks of the Natural History Museum and the holy pillars of Brompton Oratory, not so far away, in the basement of a Knightsbridge clinic, nine of my eggs lie in a Petri dish. Precisely nine of Dom's sperm – hopefully none of the abnormal ones - have been sucked up into a pipette and injected into these eggs. In one of the many books I've amassed, I have read that they are immersed in a culture medium, which includes some of my own blood. The dish is safe and warm inside an incubator, where conditions reflect those within my body – embryos need to be nurtured until settled in their natural habitat.

The balmy air ruffles my dressing gown against my skin. I stand and observe the moon, full and hanging harvest-like in the dusty sky, taking me back again to that night in Brussels. This will be our moon, this will be the one we will draw down for ourselves. I close my eyes and visualise the glass dish, isolating each of the eggs inside the flat vessel in turn. I imagine tiny spheres, not purple but iridescent orange, like iced kumquats I once saw on a Christmas card, and I send them vibes. One by one. In the morning, we will know how many have made it through to fertilisation.

It is 9am and I am sitting at the kitchen table on my second coffee. At my feet, Silkie has given up on her walk and lies flopped with her head in her paws, lead by her side. The phone sits precisely midway between my balled-up fists on the table. Every so often I span my hands out in measurement to ensure it is exactly halfway, nudging it back to the perfect location if not. I gaze down at its buttons, the eight is fading more than the others and I begin to run through everyone we know, ticking off with a flick of my fingers those who have an eight in their phone number; my mind has to be busied, it cannot bear the state of leisure. When I get to ten, I give up and shunt my thumbs and fingers back into fists to concentrate on that call.

The phone rings once and my fist opens, reaching for it. It's Jackie.

"Hi sweetie. How did it go?" Her voice is unusually soft.

"Jacks, get off the frigging phone will you? I'm waiting for them to call me." I press the red button and then ram the handset to my mouth again. "Sorry. I'll call you back." But, of course, she's gone and it rings dead.

I stab at the green button to check if I've missed their call, but there is no message tone, so the phone takes up once again its ominous position on the table.

It's 9.22am when the clinic calls. "Hello, Mrs Wyatt, how are you feeling this morning?"

"How many have fertilised?" My question snaps itself out at her.

"We have five embryos. Still at the two cell stage, but we hope they will develop into three or four cells by tomorrow morning."

"Five? But we had nine eggs."

"That's actually a good result, Mrs Wyatt. We normally expect only half the eggs to fertilise." So I've got half an egg more than normal. "We'd like you to come in tomorrow at 10.30am for the embryo transfer please. You'll need a full bladder, half a litre of water an hour before should do it."

After I hang up I punch in Jackie's number.

As always, she's cut me some major slack. "How ya doing?"

"Five embryos." My voice is flat.

"That's fantastic!"

There's a gaping pit in my stomach and I'm blinking back the tears, but still even I smile at this. Of course she has not the slightest notion; I could have said as many as twenty – or just two, and she'd still be on the end of that phone buoying me up.

"How can you drop a huge dollop of sperm onto nine ripe eggs in a confined little dish and not have all of them fertilise, Jacks?"

I don't tell her that the sperm have actually been injected into the eggs. Not for us some cute tadpole wriggling its little heart out to get there first, Dom's sperm have received the ultimate leg up, head first into the core of the matter. And yet still four have failed on their mission; a fact so incredulous that it's still whirling around my mind. I think back to Dom's tender kiss and the way his knuckles

49

brushed my cheek before he left for work at the crack of dawn. Tonight he's taking me out for dinner. I already know that I won't broach my disappointment with him.

"But Cat, you only need one embryo, don't you?" Jacks is still there.

"Yes, but we need to have a choice, we only want the best. Anyway, they insert two embryos into the womb, not just one."

"So, you've got five, from which to select two. Sounds fabulous odds to me."

For a moment we are both silent. I struggle to feel positive about the two in five, and then she says, "What happens to the others then, Cat?"

I frown in question at the phone. "Well. We'll freeze them, I guess. If they're good enough." I pause. "And if not, they just … well they just … perish." Who cares about the dud ones? The question has never crossed my mind.

There is a beat before she speaks. "Well, they're not really babies yet are they?"

The word 'babies' – already a trigger to my emotions these days – takes on a rosy glow from her Scottish accent and it tweaks me inside, in that squishy spot just behind my breastbone. "No. Anyway, I imagine they'll freeze them and then we can use them for the next go."

"Might not be a next time. PPT sweetie – power of positive thinking."

I hang up, and realise I've forgotten to ask how she is.

It was earlier this year, still winter, when Jackie told me, in a coffee shop on the Aldwych. I was in the middle of the clinical investigations, and had been holding forth about the medley of gruesome blood tests and ultrasound scans – all that torture to make absolutely sure it wasn't going to happen naturally. As I'd been blabbing on, Jackie had caught her breath at all the right places for me, even covered her mouth with the odd gasp, but I could see that she was preoccupied, and finally, dissatisfied with the depth of attention I was getting, I'd sat back and asked for

50

her news. Conspiratorial then, she'd leant across the table and dipped her head with a grin. I'd even mirrored her actions, waiting for some juice. And then I'd caught a sense of it, before the first word was out.

"It's still early days, but I'm pregnant, Cat."

I'd tutted. Actually tutted. And it wasn't just a semi-silent click of the tongue, it was a clear kiss of the teeth heralding utter misery, so loud that in my head it bounced off the walls of the café and back at me.

I'd snatched at her hand. "Sorry Jacks, I didn't mean that."

But the treason was out and she'd gawped at me. "Aren't you pleased for me?"

"It just came out, I'm so sorry."

She'd studied her hand, which I was kneading between both of mine. "Cat, you're my closest friend in the world, I haven't even told anyone else."

"Jacks, it's fantastic news, really, I'm so happy for you. It's just that I'm in such a state over what's happening to me, I'm sorry. I'm sorry."

I'd willed her to come round with my eyes, pleading, beseeching, while I continued to pummel her hand with my thumbs. And it had taken some time, but finally, she'd pulled my hands into hers.

"No *I'm* sorry," she'd said. "It must be hell for you. But you'll get there too I promise you, Cat, I bet you're pregnant before I even have my first scan."

For days I couldn't get over it. She'd only just married Henry – I'd been her maid of honour for goodness sake, me who'd been married by that time for nearly nine years. She must have conceived only two months after the wedding, and that meant they'd only had two stabs at it. Two piddling little windows. Whereas, by then we must have been going at it for a skyscraper full of windows.

At my office, a townhouse in Smith Square, which our founder Geoffrey had the presence of mind to purchase in the early seventies, my secretary Ellie has gone through my emails and printed out the important ones. Several yellow notes are stuck to my PC and the voice mail flashes six messages. Ellie waits until I'm seated, then brings through a leather document folder of letters to sign, I like her to organise them so I can scoot from page to page.

"Get me a coffee will you?"

"Yess'm boss and don't whip me!" Ellie's little gag lately when I don't say please.

"Please." I speak through tight lips and don't bother to look up at her; please is totally unnecessary when you've known someone nearly ten years.

Parliament has broken up for the summer, but my clients see the silly season as a time to tidy up their loose ends, or even float ideas my way, offloading, before they head off themselves. One of the messages is from a recent coup, an energy giant, which has switched its public affairs base to us from a rival firm. Their board are ready for us to present the position paper we've drawn up on renewable energy sources. The draft sits on my desk, awaiting my comments and I sweep through it with my trademark green pen, adding potency to the arguments, panache to the language; these days I can work a five-page document in as many minutes. Once they'd approved it, we'd push the paper around Whitehall and Westminster in a co-ordinated campaign to change hearts and minds – just as our slick website says we do. Our database includes the background, interests and foibles of all 650 MPs in the House, and we use it to ingenious effect.

I buzz for Ellie to send in Geoffrey's granddaughter, who is our work experience student this summer, and overtly scan her from toe to top as I ask her to check a detail. I've told Tim, our finance director, that she's useless, no initiative, though he said she was just nervous around me. Which is totally ridiculous.

52

Just after one, I meet Ash at the Inn in St James Park. I've been shouting him lunch every month since he left WPA to became an MP. I knew that he would be distraction for me today, so I decided to keep our date before he heads off to his gite in the Dordogne for the summer. He is there first, in shorts and smoky blue polo shirt, the hair flopping over his forehead as he beckons me. Ash still smacks of raunchiness, even though it's been eons now. He kisses my cheek and I breathe in that aftershave, the same he used to wear back then – Obsession – which always reminds me of sex. Dirty sex.

"This is very lovely of you, Cat. I've got no snippets to divulge today though, they've all scoffed their tuck, packed their trunks and gone home to nanny." He lifts a bottle from the ice bucket, with its smattering of perfect droplets, and pours me a glass.

"Always enjoy your company, whatever." I sip the wine, ice-cold and tart, and sigh inwardly with the pleasure of savouring my first drink for over a fortnight. Today will be the only day in the whole IVF cycle when there are neither eggs nor embryos inside my body, and I'm looking forward to being cast adrift for a while.

We both turn to look out over the lake, a glistening haven amidst the dust and rumpus of central London. Beside it, civil servants in ill-fitting suits are lounging on benches and chomping crisps, while the pelicans exaggerate their white waddles for sandwich scraps from the ever-growing masses of tourists.

"How long are you away for?" I ask, taking another slug of my wine.

"Month. I so need it too. They do my head in, all those Sticky Toffee Puddings, you'd find more talent at my kids' nursery school."

Ash was elected five years ago, in 2001, and since then he's been on a mission to tackle social injustice. A passion ingrained in him from an early age, having grown up on an estate in Vauxhall and witnessing all that anger. Last winter, for example, he launched a campaign to slash the number of teenage pregnancies in Britain; nothing too challenging of the Prime Minister – he has to keep him sweet – but emotive enough for the nation. I enjoyed ribbing him over the mantra he'd made his own: Keep our Youth Young!

"You're a Minister-in-Waiting, you'll soon be free of those pesky backbenchers." I smile at him and pour myself another glass.

"Hope so, I can't keep up this sham of being so earnest for much longer."

"Earnest is not what springs to mind from your performance on the box last month, you should be raking in royalties from that."

The footage of him heckling the opposition leader, causing the Tory toff to fluff his lines in a unique moment of dithering, has been aired endlessly on TV.

Ash smiles and shucks his shoulders, basking in my flattery. "Anyway, I can divulge that the Sticky Toffees continue their plotting, from the depths of their pudding bowls."

He continues, telling me all about the pressure on the PM to name the date for his resignation, and I sip my wine, finding myself watching his mouth moving around his words. There's always a dark shadow of stubble outlining his jaw; always was back then, even first thing in the morning when he'd just shaved, and I feel a fleeting urge to reach over and stroke it. Instead, I put down my glass, realising that the wine has shot to my head; amazing how quickly your body adjusts to a period of abstention. We often flirt mildly, but today it is out of the question. My babies with Dom are coming into being,

Ash must have noticed my glazed look. "Jesus, I'm even boring myself with this crap," he says. "Maybe I'll step down at the next election, get back to the real world. You still got a job for me?"

"No I haven't. Your country needs you, young man."

He smirks at me, I suspect he still views me as his senior in many respects and he loves it when I massage his ego. I pour the last of the wine into his glass, upending the bottle, and change the subject.

"Are your kids excited about France?"

"Twins are too young really, and Jake's pissed off at leaving his friends, who are all off at their own country shacks anyway."

"Oh, that's why I love London in the summer, deserted streets, no live clients, the whole city's taken off and I'm left with weeks to catch up on all those articles and papers."

He lets out a soft snort. "Always were a workaholic. Best in the business too."

It's my turn to shrug his comment off, but as ever it does feel good. He sinks his wine, plonks the glass on the table, and lifts those brown eyes to mine. For a brief moment they seem loaded with memories.

"So when are you and Dom finally going to get round to it then?"

"What? Kids?"

"Yeah, kids."

"We're working on it."

My stock response. It slides out automatically now with a cheery smile, but still I feel the heat in my cheeks, and I find myself folding my napkin into four concertina wads and placing it on the table as a buffer.

"It's been twelve years since you left me for him, just walked out on me and my aching balls."

"I didn't leave you, we were just friends who shagged. Fun buddies they call it these days."

"Fuck buddies, actually. Today's youth have no need of euphemism."

The word sweeps me back to those sybaritic lunchtimes, sprawled naked and shameless on my silk sheets, and a charge surges through my thighs. It pulses bizarrely against the dull throbbing, which still hankers low down in my belly after the operation, and I shift uncomfortably in my seat in order to quash it. The last time Dom and I had dirty sex was probably in the last century – for the past two years it's been a ritual on day fourteen and day fifteen of my menstrual cycle. Oh, and we had it on Dom's birthday recently too.

It's now the evening and Dom and I are sitting by the window in a Lebanese restaurant on Knightsbridge. I wanted to be close to my little ones, let them know I'm rooting for them to go forth and multiply. After champagne cocktails, Dom orders an expensive bottle of St Estephe and raises his glass to me.

"To the patter of tiny embryos."

I chink with him and take a long slug of my wine. After lunch, I didn't return to the office but tubed it home to sleep off the Chablis, a delicious afternoon doze on the dappled sunlight of my duvet. So I am starting with a clean slate, and the chance for more alcohol to ease the soreness. Tonight I can relax, wallow a little in the glory of having got so far. I reach for Dom's hand across the table.

"Delectable." I smile warmly at my husband.

"Delectable." He gives my hand a squeeze.

"It is one more hurdle crossed, isn't it?" I want to savour our moment.

"Probably the toughest one too."

Dom is always the optimist, I think he gets it from that ever-smiling family and sea air of his childhood. His parents ran boarding houses in Scarborough; his two older sisters manage them now.

"Think of it as Becher's Brook at the Grand National, they don't come more punishing than that." His eyes gleam at me. "I'm well proud of you Cat. You've gone through hell, I know that."

His words feel good on my shoulders. My little brother Billy sometimes warns me about self-pity, because he just got on with his life despite our shitty childhood, and I know that he does have a point. But I have been through a challenging time, well the whole of the past year has been tough if you include all the tests, so I feel entitled to at least a hint of self-indulgence. And it is making me magnanimous.

"You're part of it too, Dom," I say.

I mean the ups and downs of the last two weeks, the way he's supported me, rubbed my feet, bought me body creams and flowers. But my clumsy words seem to draw us both back to the dodgy sperm sample of the previous day, and our eyes dip to our wine. I contemplate again my discovery of this afternoon.

After waking from my snooze, I was still baffled by the fact that not all of my eggs had fertilised. So I dug out the test results of the two sperm samples which Dom had produced earlier this year. Our consultant Olu's letter had been reassuring, confirming that both samples were within range. So I was surprised to find in our files that there was an appendix to this letter, which Dom hadn't shown me back then. This gave a detailed breakdown of data for his sperm, and it signalled both low motility rates and high abnormality. In one of my reference books, I read that at least 50% of the sperm must be moving. Well, 51% of his sperm appeared to be moving, so fair enough. Then I was stunned to read that it's quite normal for up to 40% of sperm to be abnormal. Still, Dom's figure stood at 35%, so again he was marginally within these criteria.

However, just as I was slipping the papers back into the file, some words hidden amidst all the figures jumped out at me: 'poss impaired fertil.' Possible impaired fertility? Had Dom known this back then too? And been so proud and defiant that he continued to make me believe that I was the sole root of the problem? The discovery shocked me, but I've worked it out of my system. Or at least buried the unease. I've decided not to mention my findings tonight – I'll probably never need to.

But while the silence hangs between us and I'm conjuring up some positive reinforcement of what I've just

57

said to him, he reacts to the awkward moment with a non sequitur.

"I am under a lot of stress at work, Cat. I haven't told you this, but I've had to sack a woman recently."

I frown at him, why is he telling me this? The evening is supposed to be momentous, to be all about us. Dom's nearly forty; he's a manager, he hires and fires, just like I do. I've no need to know the detail.

"Dom, let's not backtrack, we've got our embryos, it's all fine." I take a hefty gulp of the wine and survey the restaurant, implying boredom so that he'll change the subject.

"Thing is that, well she's claiming compensation for unfair dismissal."

"What? Against you?" My eyes dip back to his.

He shrugs. "Against the company. We've got insurance, but she's a mardy cow, and it's me she's after."

"Why?" A shadow of unease flits through me; why would this woman feel scorned by my husband?

"I didn't follow procedure. Apparently."

"What procedure?"

"You're supposed to give verbal and then written warnings. I know I gave her both, but I can't find the emails, or her appraisal reports."

I study his look, which is guileless. He wouldn't have an affair would he? Surely not Dom, and surely not while we're trying for a baby.

"She's just chancing it, isn't she?"

"Hope so." He shrugs and gestures to the waiter. "Let's order, shall we?"

We reach for our oversized menus. I order the stuffed red chilli peppers, wondering why I would jump to that ridiculous conclusion, when Dom's love for me is so blatant, when we've told each other honestly that neither of us have ever strayed in nearly ten years of marriage. Closing my menu, I beam over at him. I know full well that my reaction is simply the hormones from those crazy drugs coursing through my system.

"Only a few hours to go now," I say.

He beams back at me. "Love you, Cat.'

"Love you too."

My hand reaches for my belly and I shift my thoughts back to the five pure, frosted kumquats in my dish, which at that moment are each dividing into four cells of life.

6

Dom and I were married in May 1997, the week after Labour came to power. Those heady days when the country was awash with cash and expectation.

Our wedding was held at a country manor house. My mum, Lizzie (as even I was expected to call her) had been gathering brochures on venues in North London, where we'd lived after she'd left Dad – and so I decided on Surrey. I'd barely bothered with her since I'd left home for university. You could say we were almost estranged, and whenever she did wheedle herself into my life she still didn't seem to comprehend the consequences of her actions. But then, at twenty-nine I couldn't have unpacked it all either, that was only to become apparent in stages. Was it a lack of self-esteem – the effect of her endless reproach – which created the control-freak in me? The need to shut any weakness down before it might reveal the depths of truths hidden even to myself?

Dom and I had bought a small house together south of the river and, on the day itself, I told her not to arrive there until two hours before the service. Dom felt that was cruel, that a mother would want to be fussing around her daughter on her wedding morning, but I imagined her feigning interest, pinching at my hair, pulling at the veil, while she jabbered on about herself, and my shoulders locked like some rusted-up machine. Meanwhile, my dad Frank, perma-tanned and beaming like some football pundit, flew in the evening before from Portugal, where he'd long since carved a new life as an IT consultant. Dom secreted him at the pub well before Lizzie arrived.

In she swept, like a prima ballerina, in tiers of purple bohemia and a matching velvet cap with feather. I'd barely closed the front door when it began.

"Too much eyeliner, Catriona," she said. And the smile that followed was one of satisfaction, tinged with relief that she'd actually been able to find something to criticise. The sting smarted, fanning its pain out.

"It makes my eyes stand out." I took a deep breath, already cross with myself for justifying it, turned and walked away from her.

"Bridal make-up should be subtle." She followed me into our living room.

"Sit there, Lizzie, I'll get Jackie to make you a cup of tea, I've still got to find something blue."

I wandered out of the room, but she was already recalling her own wedding day and her voice trailed me. "I was married barefoot on a lawn, in a short white dress with flowers in my hair."

Dad had told me once what a twat he'd felt on that grass, his pale knobbly feet lapped by cream linen flares, under a horse chestnut festooned with loops of white ribbon and carnations. I stopped short, swallowed hard and stepped back into the room.

"Maybe you would have taken your vows more seriously if you'd got married in a church, Lizzie." I had to have a pop at her.

She eyed me shrewdly. "A church is just a picturesque backdrop too, isn't it, Catriona?"

She was right. I'd worn my own atheism boldly since an early age, but Dom had visualised our ceremony within the Catholic chapel beside the manor house. The pews dented by the weight of ancient bottoms, the cool stone floor that dipped from the paths of royalty gone by. I'd happily gone along with it, and not only to please his parents, who were still regular churchgoers, even if their son had lapsed.

Jackie, my only bridesmaid, settled Lizzie in the garden, pouring her a schooner of sherry and winking at me to disappear upstairs. She had spent the night in my bed (I'd banished Dom to stay with his best man) and we'd whispered and giggled through our shared memories of a young, but already precious friendship. Always a thrill seeker and ever popular, yet Jackie had chosen me as her closest friend, which still today makes me glow – and sometimes also wonder why.

As she sat then with Lizzie in the garden, I lingered at our dressing table mirror in my lingerie of duck egg blue, removing some of the eyeliner. I gazed into the tiny brooch my mother had brought with her, unable to avoid the creeping childhood memories. A garnet heart set in gold, it had belonged to my grandmother. I've seen a photo of her wearing it, sitting straight-backed with her husband, just before the war, his hand fondly at rest on her shoulder. They had stayed together for all of their lives. I slipped on the string of pearls Dom had delivered that morning and gazed into them, mesmerised by the promise they gleamed at me – of a smooth, silky future. Dom and I would stay together too. It was just Lizzie and Dad who broke the chain.

A foolish match from the start, the humour that had delighted her when she'd first served him in the Covent Garden café had soon become an irritation. "Your dad's a buffoon," she'd say. Which to my seven-year-old self sounded like a fond description, like a warm woolly animal with a big heart, which is kind of how I saw my dad – still do really. But I'd looked the word up and discovered that she didn't mean that at all. Towards the end, I heard her screech far worse at him, the wails of a dervish coming at me through the pillow over my head. And this was a woman who campaigned for peace.

It was 1977, in the middle of June. We'd sat with our usual trays on laps in front of the telly, and she'd told us. "Your dad and I are splitting up."

Nobody's eyes had left the images on the six o'clock news, of a killer perch called Jaws that had finally been

62

caught after years on the rampage in a goldfish lake. We'd all continued eating, sinking forks into potatoes, placing food in our mouths and, in my case, down a throat struggling not to chuck it up again.

"I want you to pack your things together. I'll bring some boxes home from the café, and we'll be moving out on Sunday."

I could still hear the very words. Lizzie had assumed that Billy and I would be going with her. On the telly, I saw a vast net and a stun rod – the perch had put up a fight – and then goldfish had swum through a blur of watercolours.

Smiling at my reflection in the mirror, I clipped the garnet heart brooch onto my bra, and shook the memories off. Dom had blown me away, I loved him so completely and this was a bride who had not one qualm, not one flutter of disquiet about her wedding day.

Jackie knocked and entered my bedroom. "Come on sweetie, we've got a wee job to do." She tugged at the duvet cover which hid my dress on the wardrobe door, and ruffled it up to the hanger. "Ach, Cat it's so beautiful."

"Do I have to put it on already?"

"Yes you do! The photographer will be here any minute and this bodice is going to take me an age."

We pulled the dress on, slipping the svelte creation of cream silk over my head, and then Jackie stood before me smoothing down the neckline and remarking on the new pearls. I could smell the sweet sherry on her breath and smiled at her.

"You hate sherry, Jacks."

"Aye, but I'll wash it down with champagne before I take your mum off in the car. She's had a couple, she's out there deadheading your jasmine – talking to it too if I'm not mistaken."

"Thanks, Jacks."

I threw my arms around her and we stood locked in embrace for a long moment, rocking and savouring the warmth which flowed between us. Then she drew back, her eyes a tad misty, as were mine, and she span me round to tie the laces. Feeling her fingers scrabbling against my spine, I was compelled to speak.

"You'll get there too, I just know you will. Maybe you'll meet somebody today, weddings are notorious for that, aren't they? Some distant relative of Dom's, or maybe one of my clients."

Clients there were aplenty at my wedding, and I spent much of the reception ensuring their glasses were charged and basking in their attention. Dom's allocated portion of the numbers, however, was mostly taken up by family.

We sat down for the meal, and my dad, by then cheery with champagne, made the extra effort when my new father-in-law bid the room to bow their heads over their buffalo mozzarella and began to say Grace.

"Bless, O Lord, us and your gifts,
Which from your bounty we are about to receive ..."

I, however, was alert to Dad's bowed head, waiting for the twitch, and when it came I glanced up myself to catch his wink across the table. Smirking, I turned away and looked at Dom beside me, my new husband whose name means *of our Lord*. Eyes closed, he was immersed in the meaning of his father's words and for some moments I savoured the peaceful sight of him at prayer. He believed. I didn't. But our differing takes on God had never been an issue between us – not back then anyhow. Beside him, though, Lizzie was having none of this religion lark, her proud pagan chin up, defying Dom's parents into a potential spat, with her at its epicentre.

As I bowed my head again for the remnants of Ray's sermon, I remember smiling to myself – I was leaving all of that behind, the mess of divorced parents, the uncertainties of being single. I'd now dumped my past, packaged up the anxieties of my childhood and stifled them deep within the bubble wrap which was Dom. It would take forever, for even the sharpest nails to burst the million air pockets he'd cushioned me with. Now, of course, I'm realising that one million is still a finite number.

Maybe it was that early recognition of having been saved by Dom that allowed me simply to sink into his body for our first dance together. Despite our Latin dance lessons, where we'd perfected each switch of our hips so that we could shine to our song, when it actually came to it, we just stood and shuffled to *Moondance*.

Afterwards, we pulled apart reluctantly to take new partners and I sidled over to wrench my brother, Billy, away from the bar. He refused, of course, and clung to his pint; he's not the lover of attention that I am, so I took a glass of champagne and leant back against the bar with him.

"Do you know how stunning you look, sis?"

"Heels are killing me, Billy." I hitched up the dress to flash the stilettos.

"Blimey, thought you looked tall." He laughed and hugged me to him, in that rough chummy way he has.

I drew back and tugged at his floppy grey lapel. "Thanks for wearing this, Billy." The morning suit drowned his slight frame, and he'd had to pad out the top hat with cotton wool so it didn't slip down over his eyes.

He shucked his neck in the stiff collar and cocked a leg. "Nice and roomy round the old balls, even if I do feel like Coco the Clown."

"You look fantastic."

He'd even dragged a comb through that mass of dirty blond hair, the wiry jumble he'd inherited from Lizzie.

"Top wedding, Cat." He raised his glass in a gesture to the room.

Billy's reassurance felt good. Looking back, though, I'm amazed now that he'd been so relaxed about my refusal to have his young daughter, Daisy, as my bridesmaid. I didn't even invite his kids to the wedding, and his wife, Maggie, had huffed a bit. Now, I kind of get it that four-year-old girls yearn to be bridesmaids, to wear that satin frock, to scatter rose petals in the aisle. And apparently Daisy had sobbed over it. But while, after what was to happen later, my niece is now always lingering somewhere painfully in my mind, like the smart of seawater on the eyes, back then she hardly ever crossed it. I wanted to do it my way.

I drank in the scene of my sophisticated wedding, raising my glass to a couple of clients. Dad rolled up to my side, his tan florid against that silver skunk head of hair – I still swear he blow-dries it. With a smack of his lips, he plonked his empty glass on the bar and whisked me off for a slow waltz, even though the band had launched into that ubiquitous wedding track about a girl with brown eyes.

"That was a lovely speech Dad, thanks," I murmured, as he hummed tunelessly into the top of my hair.

"Meant every word of it, Catriona."

"Was my graduation really the most outstanding moment of your life?"

"It was." He paused and pulled me closer to him, shifting us round in a rhythm of sorts. "Cat, if I could turn back the clock, I'd do it all properly, get it right this time."

A shiver ran across my shoulders. The world was miniscule, just we two floating together across the floor, while around us everybody jumped and bumped to the chorus. This was the first moment ever that Dad and I had connected, and it felt as if his words had fizzed up a magic dust which seeped down through us, melding us into a mass of golden honeycomb, all sweet and light.

"Of course, another outstanding moment was when Wycombe Wanderers went up from the Conference in '93."

I smiled to myself; he couldn't bear the solemnity. As he squirmed away from what might have sucked us further in to that sticky sweet place, I squeezed his arm and let out a chuckle, wondering what response might ease his discomfort.

Then Ray's bulbous eyes loomed at my side, like one of those jumbo faces which rose over the table edge in *Land of the Giants*, just as the miniature hero was preparing to abseil down the leg with a safety pin and string.

His beery breath blasted me. "May I have the pleasure?"

My new father-in-law pushed me into the centre of the dance floor and over my shoulder I watched Dad being drawn away from me, our eye contact severed by Ray's bulk. He grabbed my hand and, as if spinning a Frisbee, he cast me away from him, reeling me then back into his chest, and I realised that he was attempting to propel me into a jive. Maybe at nineteen, Ray had quivered in a sexy fashion, maybe he had jabbed his feet in time to the music, but at sixty he shuddered as if under electric shock, jowls a tremor, shoulders in spasm. Despite my tight dress, he then tried to spin me, and stood on the fishtail, which is when he came out with one of his specials.

"Ooh, you're as much use as a chocolate teapot!" His Yorkshire accent was the kind that people mimic.

I threw him a scowl. Ray has always put me down, he can't handle me any other way, but that's his problem, and after nine years I'm well used to it now. But they say if you treat somebody like an imbecile they become one, and these days I've transformed myself into a flopsy-mopsy who doesn't challenge him. Takes a vast effort, but then we don't have to see my in-laws that often.

Later, upstairs on our four-poster bed, Dom and I lay naked, making silken snow angels on the sheets, which Jackie, the keeper of the key, had strewn with crimson rose petals and – bizarrely – Smarties. We were buzzing with memories of the day and, like elated children after a trip to the zoo, we chatted endlessly about small moments with our guests, just as you'd share anecdotes about the animals and their antics – the chimps, the tigers, the elephants. It had been a fabulous wedding day, not least because I had paid minute attention to every last detail: church, reception, flowers, cake and music. According to the best man's speech, I'd even 'controlled' the sunshine, an emphasis which had raised a few male guffaws – which struck me as a bit over the top.

Even the presence of Dom's two young nephews had been tolerable. In the run-up to the big day we'd actually had a row over that, a spat which Dom had won. There they had sat, in their miniature Liberty floral waistcoats, beside Dom's older sisters – the bitchy Josephine and the bossy Charlotte. And, as I saw it then, had taken up precious table settings, forcing me to drop two of my clients from the list.

There had, however, been one unpleasant moment. After the speeches, I'd looked down to see two-year-old Johnny tugging at my lap with a toothy grin, holding aloft a silver horseshoe. My immediate reaction had been to jerk the crêpe de chine from his fingers, but with a forced smile I'd graciously accepted the plastic tat, snatching a glimpse at the chocolate smudge on my dress.

"He's like a cat with you," his mother, Josephine, said, also clocking the stain.

"What do you mean?"

"Everybody knows that cats slink towards people who don't like them."

I dropped the smile. "Aren't even *you* supposed to be nice to me on my wedding day?"

I didn't tell Dom any of this as we lay widthways on that vast bed, hewn from centuries old oak.

"Think the parents enjoyed it, don't you?" He raised his eyebrows at me.

I nodded. It had been such a momentous family day for him, even if I couldn't rid myself of the vision of my mother dancing to Mary Hopkins at the end of the night. In stocking feet, and up on tiptoes, she'd swept like a fairy between buttercups, plucking at imaginary petals, warbling lines about some café and days gone by. I shook the image off.

"So is it true what they say? Did you marry your mum?"
I asked him.

"Well, you've got her sense of humour. And her looks
too, of course, she was a scorcher when she was young. But
you're far more sarcastic."

"Takes one to know one." I kissed him.

"Did you marry your dad then?" he asked.

"Oh, Dad's really quite a weak man, you know.
Whereas you, you're my Hercules."

Disloyal after my dance with Dad, for sure, but it had
always been at the heart of things. Lizzie had trampled all
over him, and they might never have split up if he'd stood
his ground.

Dom laughed. "Maybe now we're married I won't have
to pump myself up to fight any lions though, eh?" He rolled
over and curled himself up into my chest, his spent balls
flopping against my thighs. "I'd rather sink into you like a
pussycat."

7

It is the day of embryo transfer. August has brought with it the end of the heatwave, but the morning is still bathed in sunshine, alive with birdsong and traffic. In the waiting room we sit on a sofa, forming a square with three other couples, each of them rigid, scanning magazines, or the floor, or the telly. The soft cool leather beneath me heightens the chill in my thighs and belly, even though I've been assured by the chat rooms on the web that this stage is not painful.

Nobody has spoken a word in the ten minutes we've been sitting there. I wonder if they are all thinking the same as me: that only one of us will take a baby home out of this. Those are our odds, one in four. I feel the bile rising in my throat at the thought and distract myself by sizing up the competition. Directly opposite us an Arab couple sit silently, she in full veil, and I lower my eyes before they might catch hers behind the slot. To our left sits a tall skinny woman in jeans, with a bare midriff, the sight of which makes me pull my stomach in. She must be right at the start of it all; surely she too would have bloated after all those drugs – I can't even squeeze into my jeans now. Her husband is in a power hunch over the *Daily Telegraph* on the coffee table between us, and he's so slickly turned out you could check your eyeliner in his shoes. They both look distressingly determined to succeed, so I slide swiftly on to the couple on our right, an older woman who, reassuringly, must be in her late forties. Her blonde hair has lost its gloss (not much oestrogen left in that body) and I reckon my chances must be much higher. Beside her, a guy in red socks sits with his legs crossed, seemingly mesmerised by the pinstripe in his trousers. He is some celebrity, I'm sure of it, but now is not the time to ask Dom, who is hidden behind his *FT* beside me.

Sighing, I turn away from it all and read again the twee poem of thanks, in cross-stitch and framed on the wall by the window:

At first we were two
But now we are three
And it's all thanks to you …

It is eight minutes to my appointment and my bladder feels empty, even though I've slugged back a half litre of water in the cab here. Apparently, a full bladder will facilitate the insertion of the tube though my cervix and into my uterus, but I try not to envisage this as I nudge Dom and nod to the water cooler beside him. Silently, he closes his paper, takes my bottle and fills it for me, clearly embarrassed by the gurgling sounds which are drawing eyes in our direction. He slots it back into my hand which grips the plastic as if it's a stress ball.

At 10.30am a nurse calls out the surname of the celebrity couple and their relief is palpable as they sweep out of the room with a waft of cloying aftershave. I frown at Dom in question – it *is* that man who presents those documentaries – but his nod of confirmation is imperceptible. He's desperate to avoid any sudden movement that might attract attention. I take another long slug of my water and consider how brave the man is to show his face at this game, but then I guess, like us, he'll go to any lengths for a baby.

At 11am my bladder is a sack of pain, and they still haven't called us. My distress takes shape in words and I lean to hiss into Dom's ear. "If I kept one of my clients waiting this long I'd lose them, it's so inconsiderate."

He reassures me with a brief smile, his cheeks smudged with a flush. He hasn't turned the page of his *FT* for at least five minutes.

71

"Mrs Wyatt?"

A young nurse I haven't met before stands in the door with a cheery smile, which I return even more fervently. We rise to our feet and trail her, much further down the corridor than I've ever been before, into a treatment room with a small bathroom en-suite. I eye the toilet through the open door and toss the empty water bottle into the bin, I am bursting for a pee and relief is now so agonizingly close.

"Please undress from the waist down and climb up onto the bed for me, Mrs Wyatt." The nurse is at least ten years younger than me, but she is instructing me like a school ma'am, and my pain lets out a silent schoolgirl retort in my head.

I discard my skirt and knickers and clamber up. At the end of the bed are stirrups, into which I slip my feet with their freshly painted toenails – lollipop pink. I've opted for a long white shirt this morning and I furl it down over my stomach, but immediately the nurse asks me to shunt it back up, though at least she does then tear off a wide strip of paper and place it over my thighs. Dom can sense my nerves, I know, and he smooths some strands of hair away from my face. I smile at him and have a momentary flash of myself lying there in labour, preparing to give birth rather than awaiting IVF treatment. Even though it's his hand which is bathed in sweat and not my forehead.

A hatch in the wall thrusts itself open, and a curly-haired woman pops her head through, like in a scene out of a sitcom from the 1970s. I see Hattie Jacques shunting Sid James' dinner through a hatch from the kitchen, and him gurning at the congealed gravy and tight Brussels sprouts on the plate. My dad used to love watching those and I adored curling up on the sofa with him, one arm clasped through his, basking in his laughter – the large yellow teeth, the bunched up cheeks, the way he wiped his eyes with the back of his hand. Often it would be just we two at home of an evening, after Billy had gone to bed.

72

"Good morning Mrs Wyatt, good news for you." I recognise the voice of the embryologist from yesterday's phone call. "We have two excellent embryos to transfer today. They have both already divided into four cells and are grade two in quality."

"Not grade one?" I hear my voice, small and hollow as a child's.

"The grades are just a guide to the degree of fragmentation, nothing more, I'll put them up on the screen for you soon so you can see them." Her head disappears.

Dom takes my hand in his own and calls over to the hatch. "What about the other three? Can we freeze them?"

Her head pops out again, its comic quality accentuated by the paper mop-cap she's wearing, as if she is touring a cheese factory. "No, the fragmentation was too marked, they would not be suitable for freezing, I'm afraid."

Dom grips my hand, a clumsy reaction which only intensifies my own dismay that I might have to endure this all over again, but I turn to smile at him and mouth, "This one's going to work."

"Just confirm your name and date of birth for me, please."

"Catriona Wyatt, 21st March 1968."

Dom attempts some humour. "Make sure you've got the right ones! We don't want to end up with a black baby..."

He trails off as Olu punches his way through the door with a broad smile and a presence which knocks us all into little girl mode. Apart from Dom, of course, who is still angry with Olu about the dodgy sperm sample, and now also embarrassed by his seemingly racist comment. But he is only referring to a recent story about just such a mix-up, where a white woman gave birth to a black baby after IVF treatment. It has become a running joke at home, a kind of reach for when we can sense ourselves sliding.

Olu stands, hands on hips, shirt sleeves rolled up, and beams at me. "Hello Cat, how are you feeling?"

He nods at Dom and, when he offers him his hand, I swear I catch a flash of power in his smile, almost as if he is magnanimous in victory. And yet what is this combat? That he can make me pregnant while Dom cannot? I watch my husband meet the challenge with his own brazen smile, and I draw both men back to me and my pain.

"I'm fine Olu, bladder a bit full." A vicious flush has now spread upwards from my chest, engulfing my cheeks in fire.

"That is good, we will be able to see what we are doing," he says.

While the nurse pumps the examining bed to its full height, he sits down on a stool between the stirrups, his face an inch from my splayed vagina. In fifteen minutes this will all be over, I tell myself, eyes clamped shut, fingers reaching for my rings.

"I have a bit of housekeeping to do first," he says, distracting me nicely. Judging by the exactitude of his intonation, he must have borrowed that word from an English colleague, perhaps when he first set out on this odd gynaecological path many years before.

Then Olu inserts an ice-cold instrument inside me, to clean out the cervix, he says, and I feel liquid seeping down between the crack in my buttocks. It's at that point that my usual tactics desert me and I resort to my last recourse, of pretending it is happening to somebody else. Whilst I myself float somewhere above the action watching some other woman suffer, I drift back to those times with my dad, giggling on our sofa, and I try to recall his favourite sitcoms. *Love thy Neighbour* was one of them, of course, and I smile to myself, wondering what Olu would have made of that show when he was growing up in Nigeria. Those two idiots trading insults over the garden fence – Honky and Sambo, I think it was.

A sharp snag jolts me. I fix my gaze on Olu's head between my legs, then on Dom who is watching me steadily. He smiles gently, Dom is very much au fait with my raft of strategies for the unbearable.

Olu raises his head, his expression one of absorption. "OK, we are ready now," he says. "May I have the catheter?"

"Yes, all set," the embryologist calls out from behind the hatch.

Olu smiles at me. "Up there you can see your potential babies, Cat."

Hanging from the ceiling is a TV monitor displaying two large bubbles, each of them split clearly into four, roughly equal quarters. I am looking at the embryos, which might divide into a foetus, which might develop into a baby, my baby. I turn euphorically back to Dom. His eyes are shining, he is already building sandcastles with them.

"They are very good embryos, Cat. There is a slight fragmentation, as you can see from the tiny bubbles around the edges, but this is of no matter for a fresh transfer. It is only an issue for freezing." Olu speaks as if they are peas.

My babies disappear off the screen and the embryologist appears with a thin white tube which she gently threads through the hatch to Olu. Careful, I think, holding my breath, don't let them slip out.

With his own measure of reverence, Olu takes it from her and holds the tube aloft.

Now, Cat, if you look at the screen, you will see your embryos as they appear in your womb."

He nods to the nurse, who spurts a dollop of freezing jelly onto my belly and presses down hard with her ultrasound node, sending a spasm of pain into my bladder. I cry out.

"Good, your bladder's nice and full," she says, and I wince at her.

Olu contemplates the ultrasound screen, the tube still cradled in his vast hand. "Your womb lining is nice and thick, a good nine millimetres, very inviting to a pair of embryos seeking a new home."

I know that he must use these words many times a day, and yet he makes me feel uniquely special for being already such a nurturing mother.

As he sets to, I feel the catheter slipping in, and am sure I can sense the straw-like tube scratching inside me. And then, up on the screen, I see two specks of white amidst the fuzz of grey shadows. The room falls silent and I focus on breathing, while Dom's hand remains clasped around mine.

"OK, I have injected them." Olu withdraws the tube and passes it back through the hatch. "Check the catheter please."

The woman's voice rings back. "All clear."

Olu smiles broadly up at me. "Good. Now, you may go to the loo, Cat."

With a kick of the heels, he pushes his stool back and I am off that bed and into the bathroom, grateful for the long shirt now covering all that has been on display as flagrantly as a baboon's bottom. On the toilet, I am so scared of propelling the embryos out that I pee ultra slowly, taking a good two minutes to empty my bladder. Afterwards, I sit breathing deeply, savouring the bliss of relief. I can hear Dom commenting too loudly on the wonder of watching our embryos actually go into the womb. In response he receives a blank silence and I close my eyes in sympathy, but still he pipes up again.

"We're disappointed that the other three can't be frozen, though."

I hear Olu reply. "Hopefully you will not need them, let us think positively."

"So … what happens to them?"

"Did you sign the papers allowing for research on discarded embryos?"

"No." We have not. This is a self-centred venture, these are our embryos and nobody else is getting their hands on them.

"Well they will soon stop growing."

I cock my head at the door, but hear no more from Dom. After scanning the pan for any sign of baby embryos, I flush the loo. Back in the room, I make for my husband and kiss him, pulling him to me.

"OK?" He smiles and hugs me back.

Olu pushes a clipboard at me. "I should have asked you to sign this form before the transfer, Catriona, I need your consent to put two embryos into your womb. The law is becoming stricter and I am afraid that soon it may allow us only one embryo. But that will not affect you." His smile is so white against that perfect skin, taut as a chestnut.

Beside him the nurse takes my arm in hers and leads me towards the door. "You go home and rest, Mrs Wyatt. Get your husband to do the housework." She eyes Dom, clearly still riled by his black baby comment.

Ignoring her, I slip my arm out of hers and turn back to Olu. "Can I drink alcohol?"

She jumps in, raising her eyebrows at me, "Well you are technically pregnant, so best not."

But he lets out a boom of a laugh. "The odd glass of wine will not hurt you, the next two weeks are going to be tough, very tough. The waiting will feel much longer than it actually is. You must call us if you have any concerns at all, about anything." He rests his wide eyes on mine.

"When can we test to see if it's worked?" Dom is in there again.

"Not before day thirteen. In the ideal, you should come here for a blood test on day fourteen."

"And this is day one?" I ask.

Olu nods. "Good luck Cat. Dom." He slides past us, shakes both our hands, thanks the staff, and is out of the door with a flourish.

"Almond Crisp or Pecan Melt, now that's a tricky one," Jackie murmurs.

I've decided to take the rest of the day off, and she and I are lounging on the sofa, feet up on the zebra ottoman. Our living room is a serene sanctuary which runs the whole length of the house, with high-ceilings and white marble mantelpieces sourced by Dom when he did the place up. Jackie arrived with lunch just as I stepped out of the cab home, a svelte velvety box, which I stroked a few times before opening.

"It's all about serotonin and endorphins," she said when I finally unwrapped the chocolates. "Hormones require happiness in order to sustain pregnancy, and today we may both scoff the whole box with impunity."

"What about caffeine, am I allowed a Coffee Praline?" I ask her then, my index finger trailing the smooth oval shell, teasing the raised nubs of dark chocolate.

"Yep, eat it though, don't shag it."

I pluck the chocolate out and push it whole into my mouth, allowing it to sit there and melt. Hands cupped gently over my belly, I curl the wodge slowly around my mouth, the sweetness spreading over my palate, and I sigh as the chocolate gradually thins. Then I reach for the box again, eyed by Silkie, who lies on the rug drooling.

"What's left then? Mint Medallion, oh that's got to be yours, Jacks. Remember that guy you met on holiday? Greece was it ... or Tunisia?" I scoop the green-foiled praline from the box and plonk it on her bump.

"All hairy chest and gold chains? Think that was Tunisia." She unwraps it and nibbles it. "1995. Remember how he danced, shirt open to his navel?"

I throw my arms into a *Night Fever* pose. "The spit of Travolta."

She laughs, surveys the box. "Anyway if we're playing at that malarkey, where's the Extra Dark Truffle?"

"The black guy? Stop it, will you? I'm not supposed to laugh, I might shoot the embryos out."

"Rubbish, laughing reduces stress hormones. Where was it you had him? Come on!"

She picks out a dark sphere dusted with cocoa, and reaches up to pop it between my teeth. I bite into the chocolate, smoothing the ganache over my tongue, and allow her a gummy but prim reply. "You know where it was, the Gambia, Easter 1994. Before Dom."

"Ah yes. He was only a boy really, wasn't he? A lamb at the altar."

"Well more like a stallion really. Couldn't stop smiling at me, it was just one big game to him."

Jackie turns to me. "Was to us all then, wasn't it?"

"Yeah." I smile at her.

Spurred by the jollity, Silkie gets to her feet and waddles over to me, tail wagging.

"Nope, afraid this stuff's toxic for you, Silkie, but you can have one of yours," I tell her, rummaging in my handbag for some of her treats. I feed her a mound of chocolate buttons from the palm of my hand, and the dog we named after a plate of silkworms hoovers them up, her tongue slurping at my fingers. I pat them dry on a tissue and groan, stretching out my body. "I'm stuffed, Jacks."

She closes the box and stretches with me. "OK, but finish the rest for your dinner."

I find my hands drifting again over my belly. It is still flattish, if bloated by the drugs, but it is quite tender. Olu has said that I would experience a vague cramp for all of that day as the embryos settle themselves in, and it does feel like the onset of a period, but I have to know that it is not. I look at Jackie's stomach beside mine, rising into a perfect pink T-shirted mound of blancmange.

"How many weeks are you now?" I ask her lazily.

"Thirty-two today. Look, she's moving."

I fix my eyes on the stretched fabric which is showing not the slightest movement, and then it ripples. Jackie takes my hand, places it over the bump and my palm is pummelled by what must be the extremity of a limb.

"Gosh." For a moment that's all I can say. "That's amazing." Clearly I'm not able to better it and Jackie grins at me – for my best friend the simple reaction will suffice.

"So when will yours be due, Cat?"

"Let's see."

With a curious mixture of reluctance and relief, I remove my hand from the strange sensation and reach for my diary.

"Apparently, you take the date of embryo transfer and count thirty-eight weeks." I begin to calculate the months. "So, that takes us to …Wednesday May 2nd. A spring baby."

"And when can you do the test to see if it's worked?"

This is the first time either of us has verbalized any hint of uncertainty and I quash it, finding today's date, then counting forwards by the day. There it is: 20th August. Day twelve is when I will do the test, not on day thirteen as Olu has advised; I know from the online chat rooms that loads of other women test early.

"Week on Sunday." I say, tapping my finger on the date.

She smiles at me, a chocolate smudge below her lip, and watches me give the open page a pat for good measure before closing the diary. Then she takes my hand and squeezes it and we lie back again, resting our heads with synchronised sighs.

"It'll be fantastic to be mammies together, Cat."

"Won't it? Just think, they'll be in the same school year."

"I'm thinking more of pushing prams in the park first."

"Or jogging with them," I add. "Just imagine them both on the swings."

"Down the slide."

"In the rocket."

"Do they still have rockets?"

"No idea."

We both let out a chuckle and then sit in silent contemplation of our babies.

"Think that serotonin's kicking in, Jacks," I say finally.

We turn to each other, her breath chocolaty against my face. "That was my goal, sweetie. And somebody's kicking me in the bladder."

She heaves herself off the sofa and toddles from the room. Seeing her chance, Silkie gets up again from the sunny rug and ambles over to me. I fondle her ear and reach for my mobile; there is just one text, from Billy, in reply to mine of earlier. *Well done! Will keep everything crossed for you.* Nobody else knows, certainly not from my family. Billy said Lizzie has been trying to get in touch with me recently, but she must have needed something – I seriously doubt she's finally ready to make amends. I shudder at the thought of her, she is the last person I'd want to know about all this. And Dad, well I couldn't take his bluff jolliness at the end of a phone, willing it to work for me. The burden of my own hope is enough to bear.

As Jackie returns to the room, there's a key in the front door. Our dog-walker trills, "Siii-lkie," and the dog reels out to the hallway. With a glance at Jackie, I raise a finger to my closed lips; the woman doesn't need to know we are there.

"Good girl, let's go."

A lead jangles, the boot room door closes, then I hear another voice coming from the front step; my niece Daisy's.

"Is Cat home?" she asks.

My heart sinks and I groan at Jackie, who screws her nose up and whispers, "It's OK, I have to get back anyway."

"No, sorry dear she's at work, who shall I say called?" Our dog-walker is laying on her telephone voice, even though Daisy's speech is not at all educated.

Hoisting myself up from the sofa, I call out to them. "Yes, I am in." I shuffle stiffly across the parquet floor, sensing Jackie giving me the once over.

"Why are you walking like a robot, Cat?"

"Have to hold them in, don't I?"

In the hallway, I assume my professional smile. "Hi Daisy. Thanks Mrs P." I gesture for Daisy to come in and for the woman to leave, which they both do and I close the front door.

My niece stands in the tiled hallway, gripping a handful of stiff carrier bags, her smile bright. "Dad said you're not well, and I've been shopping on the Kings Road, so thought I'd drop by and cheer you up." Not yet fourteen, and yet she has the gravelly voice of a radio DJ.

"That's really kind, Daisy. Have you been shopping alone?"

She shrugs. "With a mate, but Mum thinks her mum was with us."

"Ah."

Jackie emerges from the room, her mac already on.

"Oh, hi there Jacks." Daisy shortens her name as only I am allowed to do.

"Hello Daisy. Wow, you've grown." Jackie rolls her eyes at me and takes me into a bear hug for our habitual rocking. "Take care, sweetie. And let me know how it goes."

I close the door again, and rest my forehead against it to compose myself; the last thing I feel like is playing aunties. This girl, however, has a hold over me, we both know that, and I turn radiantly to face her. She really has grown, the transformation in less than a year is breathtaking.

"Like a drink?"

"Love one please."

I follow her down to the kitchen focussing on her legs, slim and tanned below the mini skirt, telling myself not to look at her hand. Then, as always happens, my eyes seek it out. Today she is wearing a short-sleeved crimson blouse; in defiant mode then. She slouches against the granite island and observes me taking the last few steps, perfecting the arthritic shamble that is cushioning my embryos from sudden movement, but she makes no comment.

"Tea? Or something cold?" I ask, a hand brushing my stomach.

For a moment her eyes linger on mine. "Tea please. Supposed to cool the blood, isn't it?"

My niece, though barely a teenager, has always been old for her age – whatever Billy and Maggie claim.

"What's the matter with you, Cat?"

"Just time of the month." My lie is a nimble step onto common ground – it was me Daisy told when she had her first period, not her mum.

"Oh, poor you."

She groans, pushes herself up off the granite with a spring, approaches me arms outstretched, and presses her slight frame to mine while those long blonde tresses fly against my cheek.

"Let's see what you've bought then."

"Bikini, look." She pulls out a tiny piece of lycra, black with red dots, and holds it out to me.

"Now that's an itsy-bitsy teeny-weeny, if ever I saw one." I lift the string between pointed finger and thumb and dangle the bikini with a conspiratorial look.

"Used your holiday money for it."

I'd secretly given her fifty pounds.

"Good choice." I hand it back to her before lifting the boiling kettle.

"I've got a boyfriend, Cat."

I'm pouring while she speaks, my back to her, but I'm expected to swing round in delight, so I place the kettle down and do just that. "Wha-hey!" I shout, beaming at her. And my joy is not at all fake, I'm more than happy, in fact, because she is not being held back, she is up there with the others, when she might have been blighted after what happened.

"We're going swimming tomorrow. All my mates fancy him, and it was me who got him." She prods her chest, her smile revealing the brace on her top teeth, and flips open her mobile. "He's gorgeous, look."

I see a blond scruff pot sticking his tongue out. "He's hot," I say, leading her out to the garden, where I'm relieved to sit down and ease any pressure on my pelvis.

After she's left, I feel in high spirits and pad back down to the kitchen to check our family organiser. We've pretty much blanked out the month of August, and there's not the usual jumble of lunch or dinner dates at the weekend, so we'll be able to drive down to Poole, for distraction at our favourite hotel and beach. I reach for the phone and leave a message on Dom's mobile. The Japanese markets will have closed ages ago, but he is out with the brokers tonight, and I guess he's left already for wherever it is they take him.

8

Back in May 1999, two years to the day after we were married, I brought in a major client, which would secure the remarkable future of Westminster Policy Advisers. A new supermarket chain, Dinwoodie's, had been formed from a series of small outlets. There was one just by the tube at Gloucester Road where Dom and I used to pick stuff up for dinner on the way home from work. They fed the mounting hunger in Cool Britannia for organic and fresh produce – spit-roast chicken, hummus, line-caught sea bass – and they counted some fifty retail units throughout the UK.

I'd met the chairman, Stewart Dinwoodie, a slightly built Scot in his late thirties, at a conference and had cornered him over coffee. He was gay, hence no point flirting as I normally would have done. Instead, having genned up on his clan history, I regaled him with a quirky analysis of his trademark tartan tie.

Geoffrey, the Big White Chief, let me handle the follow-up pitch, so Ash and I tubed it over to Clerkenwell for a meeting with Dinwoodie and his management team. I remember Ash clocking Stewart's tight leather trousers, and recoiling slightly when the man himself swept out to greet us in reception. It's hard to imagine now that it was all so informal; these days even I have to cut through at least one layer to speak to Stewart.

As I'd expected, his offices were minimalist, all dazzling white walls and moody splashes of paint on canvas, which I surveyed as he took a call – doubtless to keep us waiting. When he spoke on the phone, there was a force to his voice which bordered arrogance, and that fired me up, sizzled through my chest. He was defiantly in control and I saw him then as a bit of kindred spirit.

He hung up and turned to us with a shudder. "Deals. Make me so horny!"

I beamed at him; if work didn't turn me on, it was for sure an addiction, a need which clenched me up inside. Impressed, I flashed my eyes at Ash, but he just rolled his back and followed me through to the boardroom. The oval table, carved from a single piece of teak I noticed, was laid out with lime silk placemats, which sported mini-packs of shortbread, sleek porcelain cups and individual baby cafetieres. A line of glass tubes, each containing a single pink gerbera, divided us from Stewart and his acolytes across the table; this man had taste to go with the millions he'd inherited from his father, a veteran in the whisky industry.

Once seated, I scrutinised the row of three canvases behind Stewart's head, one a smooth pattern of bulbous purples, the next a muddle of jade and magenta cubes, the third a chaos of chocolate spikes. I felt him watching me and realised he'd probably arranged the paintings in order to analyse his prey, depending on where their eyes strayed; it was clear that this man required a multilevel intellectual challenge beyond the rudiments of a meeting. To feed his game, I allowed my eyes to flit between the canvases, even though the bristly brown pattern was clearly me, while beside me, I sensed Ash gazing innocuously at the violet lava lamp design – he's always been a much less complex beast.

When finally my eyes rested on Stewart's we shared a knowing look.

"So," he began, "the clock's ticking."

I nodded back. "So," I echoed.

And Ash and I began our well-honed double act. I was skilled at the business side – had recently been enrolled by Geoffrey on an MBA at London Business School – while

Ash, by then already an aspiring MP, was intimately familiar with Westminster.

"You know your business, Stewart," I said, "and you know what kind of policy environment you need for it. At WPA we will develop with you a strategic programme to influence that policy environment." I'd sussed him as the kind of guy who enjoyed hearing the word 'you'. "We can help you get your messages across to the right people, in the right way and at the right time."

He eyed me with that piercing appraisal I've come to know well, and then he threw me. "In Uganda, there's a tree called the balanites, and its seed can only germinate once it's passed through the digestive system of an elephant."

My heart began to race, but then so did my mind, skidding through his words. Looking back now, I realise that Ash was right when he claimed that Stewart was a complete tosser from the start, but I was thrilled by this twist and I'd soon grasped his meaning. I smiled at him.

"I assume you're referring to the symbiotic relationship that must exist between lobbyist and client?" I asked, excited by the mask of calm which hid my turmoil.

"Correct."

Inside I pulled a victory punch, but he didn't smile, remaining perfectly still, hands resting on the table. High as I was, I did very nearly ask him if he was the seed or the elephant, but my instinct warned me against humour (rightly as it's transpired). I do remember Ash saying on the tube home later that Dinwoodie was neither seed nor elephant – that he was the shit.

I went on. "Working closely with you, we would bring ourselves up to speed on the main issues your business faces and identify areas where government policy is not optimum for you. I'm guessing your concerns include food labelling, packaging, and distribution, also retail ownership as you expand?"

"Very astute." He allowed me a half nod.

"Then we can identify the key decision-makers we need to reach across Westminster and Whitehall. Brussels will be critical too of course, it churns out so much food policy, and our European office is ten strong. Ashley, here, is our institutional expert and he's extremely well-connected."

Dinwoodie appraised Ash as if he'd suddenly materialised, and I swear his lip curled before he swept his eyes back to me.

"You would manage the account though?"

I nodded.

"And you're not going to spawn on me?"

"Spawn?" I blurted. "Have kids, you mean? No!" I was shocked as much at the prospect of falling pregnant anytime soon, as at his choice of verb.

"Hope not," he said, and for several moments he considered me, twirling his pen between his fingers.

I held his look, adding some steel to my own, and then I continued as if we had him in the bag. "We will monitor developments, gather intelligence on your behalf and intervene with strategic approaches tailored to the issues."

This was the language of the day: intelligence, strategic, tailored. Words that seem glib to me now whenever I reel them out, which is still often; the business hasn't changed that much, if more heavily regulated. But that day, at the age of thirty-one, each time I heard myself utter one of those buzzwords I felt the greatness of my profession, I felt its drug ooze through me and I myself buzzed. That day also, a canny young Stewart Dinwoodie, with his vice-like handshake and shrewd grey eyes, had also liked what he heard. I was appointed Account Director for WPA, and we were taken on under a monthly retainer of £10,000, a sum that soon doubled, then tripled. Dinwoodie's were not yet the household name they are today, but those days were heady ones for me and I was loving it.

*

Dom too was caught up in those giddy times, a star performer reaping the yield of his Japanese technologies fund, ploughing his fertile expense account, and much sought after by the brokers. Occasionally he would mention starting a family, but amidst the flurry of corporate events and fine restaurants, where the truffles were shaved and the wines had great legs, there was no pressure on me to conceive. However, the matter of babies did raise its chubby little head on Millennium Eve.

Dom and I had by then bought our house in Kensington. Dom had fallen for the iron filigree frontage that spanned the two bay windows, as it held a hint of the exotic East, which always beguiled him. It was he who transformed the house with a palette of taupe, petrol blues and at least six shades of cream; he's always had an eye, whereas I consider interior design a frivolity. Dom's colleague and closest friend, Ben, had opted instead for an apartment on the Thames, facing up river towards the Houses of Parliament. On Millennium Eve, he and his new wife, Laura, threw a party. We were invited to claim our own piece of history; prime views of those once in a lifetime fireworks and that river of fire – a flame bank as high as an office block they promised – that would burst along the water towards us and, it seemed, only for us.

Ben had devised a drinking game for the evening, an habitual pursuit of Dom's and his cohort, and each time the word 'millennium' was mentioned on the TV or radio, we each had to knock back our drinks. Ben had two TV channels and three radio stations on the go in various rooms and he'd hired students to keep us in champagne, which we were downing like lemonade. If the word was not heard for a while, somebody – often Dom the life and soul – would fake a mention, "The millennium's arrived in Ukraine!" And an hour later, "It's millennium in Spain!" A cheer would go up and mouths would sucker themselves to the rim of a glass, then one of the guys would take to the floor as a Cossack, or a flamenco dancer, and we'd all follow, dropping to our haunches, kicking wildly, or stamping and tossing hair, delighted with our drunken hilarious selves.

I can remember at some point stumbling through to the kitchen in search of water, and coming across a young woman leaning against a counter. She had her blouse open and bra hitched up and I stopped short at the sight of her. Clamped to her breast, an incredibly flappy one I noticed, was a transparent plastic cup, which was pinching her flesh. In and out, screeching like a ship's siren as it went. While I stood gawping at the machine, she turned sheepishly to me and shrugged.

"Tits are so full. No point wasting it, is there?"

I watched squirts of green-tinged milk hit the bottle which was attached to the cup, streaks of it dribbling down the plastic sides. And my disgust let itself out in an audible, 'Urgh,' before I turned and lurched out of the kitchen. In the bathroom I screwed my face up at the mirror. "Urgh!" I cried again. "Don't ever let me get like that."

As midnight approached we all lined up at the plate glass windows, twenty floors up, throwing condescending royal waves for the thousands of tiny revellers below, who swarmed onto the bridges or clung to the embankments. Dom sidled up to me, his hand around my waist and I leant against him. When the fireworks began, scattering jewels that descended into magical froth against the night sky, we whooped like toddlers. And when the river of fire fizzled out, with just one flash of white flame, we whined with disappointment.

"That was a damp squid," Dom muttered.

I laughed and kissed his cheek. "It's damp squib, silly."

Soon after midnight, people began to drift off, eager to soak up this unusual London, afraid that those below were having more fun now the moment of our vantage point had passed. At around four in the morning, Dom and I, having bagged the spare room, were snuggled down on a sofa opposite Ben and Laura, sipping coffee and gleaming at each other.

"So what does the New Year hold for you guys?" Ben asked us, cradling Laura's head on his lap.

I spoke first. I'd already made my list of resolutions – could visualise it in bullet points:

- Complete my MBA
- Pull in two new major clients
- Secure my appointment to the board
- Take up archery

"I'm going to take up a new sport," I said brightly. "Archery."

Dom eyed me, glazed with fatigue and booze. "Wa-hey, fur and feathers in the bedroom, that's my New Year's Resolution."

Ben let out a knowing laugh and cried, "Am-zon-Woman!"

I smiled, well aware of my scary reputation amongst Dom's mates. "How about you guys then?"

Ben looked down at Laura, who nodded to him, and he smiled at us, eyes misty. "Actually, we're going to have a baby next year, aren't we Laura?"

"Are you pregnant?" Dom jolted back in his seat, knocking my head off his shoulder.

"No." Laura turned her head lazily across. "But we're going to start trying now."

"Already?" I snapped at her. She was only thirty-two, barely older than me.

Laura caught the glare and rambled her justification. "We want to get them out of the way, I mean before I'm made a senior partner, I can just about afford maternity leave without any real damage if I do it now." She shrugged. "Twins would be ideal of course."

In bed later, Dom curled himself around me. "How about we make a baby this year too, Cat?" he murmured as he was drifting off.

"Ha ha, not sure you're up to it right now, darling." I patted his arm.

But my words were enough of a challenge for my husband to flop on top of me, his cock as soft as dough.

"I will now impregnate you!" he roared.

It was the cry of the invincible. And then he sighed and sank down onto me, a dead weight, and I grinned, heaving him off and succumbing to my own slumber.

9

It is Friday afternoon, only fifty-one hours after Olu slid the embryos into my womb. I'm on the web, scanning the abbreviations used in an online IVF chat room. I've already worked out what TTC means – trying to conceive – and some of these women have been at it for years. DH has to mean darling husband, and amazingly there is not a trace of blame in any of these postings.

I don't join in the conversations, I just observe, glean my own comfort from the experiences of others without offering any. I've still told nobody, apart from Jackie and Billy, and I don't want to engage with anyone – even anonymously. So I enjoy the way they all send each other 'sticky vibes' to urge the embryos on to implant into the womb. I take faith in the support they offer whenever somebody posts a BFN – bye for now: a failed cycle, and I smile whenever I see mention of a positive HPT – home pregnancy test. It is a whole new world.

As for me, I am three days into the 2WW, which means the two-week wait, to know whether it has worked. In school history lessons, 2WW used to be my shorthand for Second World War, a perfect euphemism for the turmoil within me. At the very start of our cycle, the two-week wait had been out of sight, over the other side of the mountain, and I imagined it as the easy bit, all downhill after our slog to the summit. However, it's a headlong plummet that I've taken down that mountain. And it is endless.

I'm still working at the office, burrowing into my day, just as those two embryos are supposed to burrow into my womb. They've told me to look out for a sharp pain after a

93

few days, which could be an indication of implantation. However, period cramps have hit me several times daily, and each time I've thought, this is it, this is where it ends. At work, my run of the mill grist won't engage my brain. So I'm forcing myself to tackle those in-tray runts, which are normally too demanding for immediate action and left to ferment; a tricky call to a stubborn MP, an analysis of banana skins in a piece of new legislation. In the evenings, I wrap myself up in a plaid cashmere blanket and eat chocolate. Dom isn't sure what to do with this invalid and he sits quietly with me watching reality TV, not once flicking over to Sky Sport.

Later that evening we are driving down to our favourite hotel in Poole, having left Silkie with the dog-walker. Dom was held up at the office by the woman's dismissal case, because the lawyers were in to thrash it out with him. Apparently, they still can't find his written warnings to her. He tells me about it on the drive down the M3.

"I gave her loads of warnings. She was useless, a gormless back-room analyst, no gumption. Fed us shit for research."

He speaks as if trying to convince me, but I'm barely listening to him. I'm contemplating my reflection in the side window; my cheeks do seem more radiant tonight, plumper somehow.

"I just can't put my hand on the emails, and her appraisal notes have disappeared from the file. You know what I think? I reckon she's taken them."

I realise from the lengthy pause that a reaction is needed. "Would she dare do that?" I'm turning my face this way and that; there's definitely a glow about me.

"She's barmy, this woman. I'm not going to let her shaft me with some freaky discrimination case." He slams the steering wheel.

"It'll be alright, I'm sure," I reassure him, smoothing my hand over his thigh, giving it a pat.

94

As we drive on, I sense him throwing me the odd glance, but I refuse to turn from the window to face him and his problems. I want to be alone with the fact that I am a few hours off being a quarter of the way through my two-week wait, and at this moment in time I am on one of my upward swings. I'm feeling distinctly pregnant.

It's Saturday evening. After a lazy day of the papers, of pottering and positive thoughts, we've strolled down to the sea front for a fish supper. Dom, who is still limiting his own alcohol intake on my behalf, orders a half bottle of Sancerre. The sight of the name on the menu alone sets my mouth off, watering in tart anticipation of the grassy pleasure it will have to forsake tonight. But as the wine arrives, and Dom nods at the waiter, I'm alerted to another sensation, a cramp is advancing on my pelvis, has slunk up on me. Panic flutters through my chest; is it a real feeling? Or just my imagination? Rigid, I sit and stare through the wine bottle, trying to pin the ache down. Slowly it spreads itself across my lower belly. I seek out the sign for the ladies, compelled to go and check for blood, but my body won't move. Clenching my fists, I sit tight, a flush of fear engulfing my face.

Our starters arrive. Two half pints of prawns. Dom sips his glass of wine and beams at me with the delight he's been raining on me all day. "How about we think about names?"

"It hasn't worked Dom."

"What?" His smile fades and I shrug at him. "But, the whole day you've been saying that you felt it *had* worked."

"Well now I'm sitting here with a period pain, OK?"

He reaches for my hand across the table, his eyes uncomprehending. "Cat, remember what they said? The ovaries are still swollen after holding all those eggs, and they messed around with your cervix. They told us to expect some cramping."

"Us? Us? How do you know how I feel, you're not inside my fucking body."

I snatch my hand away, twist a prawn head and tear it from its body. A couple of faces are raised at my language, and I waggle my eyes at them like a kid in the playground – 'who you looking at?'

Dom folds his arms, presses himself further across the table at me and lowers his voice. "This is hard for me too, you know."

I tut at him. "You haven't got a clue."

"Look, I want this baby just as much as you do, Cat. OK I haven't been through the physical hell that you have, but it's just as tough for me."

Glaring at him, I slice my nails murderously into the prawn's shell, split it from its belly and prise it off. "Oh yeah? Launching a needle at yourself every day for a fortnight, hanging wide open for all to have a butcher's? I don't think so."

"I wish I could have done all that for you, I hate seeing you suffer."

"Well you didn't have to, did you?"

He shrugs. I can see him wondering where to go next, and I'm gunning for him, daring him to put a word wrong.

"And all those hormones," he says finally, "they must be driving you crazy."

The tears come then. I jab my prawn at the mayonnaise in its porcelain pot. Is it just the hormones? I'm now onto my fourth new drug. Every night I have to shove a progesterone suppository inside my bum – to boost my chances of holding onto a pregnancy that might or might not exist.

Dom goes on. "Every time you have an emotional up, it boosts me too, I feel a real sense of hope, Cat. And then when you're on a downer, I plummet with you." He pauses. "It's like being one carriage behind you on a rollercoaster, I can only go on what you are feeling, it's completely out of my control."

96

I look up at him, my eyes pleading then. "It's out of my control too. I so want it to work Dom."

"It is going to work, Cat, it is."

I take the hand he offers again across the table and press it between my own. The cramp is gradually subsiding. I sniff myself out of my tears, while around us nobody takes the slightest notice; clearly this crowd is used to people getting in touch with their feelings.

"OK, give me a name for a boy then." I throw him a weak smile.

"Matthew, that's champion."

"Not Raymond, after your dad?"

Dom tosses a scrap of French bread at me. "Hardly a name for the noughties."

"Definitely not Frank after my dad, either. Anyway, it's going to be a girl, and I get to choose the girl's name."

"Come on then."

His relief at my instant mood change is tangible. And once again it strikes me how Dom and I have never been tested like this. We've been together for twelve years, married for nine of them, and it has all been a breeze thus far. No financial worries, lots of laughs, good sex – well at least up until last year. We are being buffeted by this external influence and I'm conscious that this very first cycle is going to have to succeed, because the alternative is inconceivable. Something I can see only as darkness ahead, a black mass which might even crush us.

I smile at him. "How about Hannah?"

"No way, I knew a girl called Hannah at uni, she was a right bitch."

"Emily?"

"Pretty. Too common though, been top of the girls' list for years."

"Oh you check them do you?"

He throws me a flirtatious look. "'Course."

"How about Phyllis then?"

"Syphilis? Are you bonkers, woman?"

"Phyllis is pretty, very delicate, like lace."

"Ooh you drive a hard bargain. OK we'll call her Phyllis for the moment then, but you'll have to come up with something decent by the time she's born."

Sunday brings fabulous sunshine and blue skies. The sea is a frenzy of yachts and jet skis skirting the hulks of ferries, which plough to and from the harbour, and Sandbanks beach is scattered with an impressive layer of singletons, couples and families. As we settle ourselves on towels and fiddle with our iPods, a man in flowery shorts approaches, dangling a young child from his hip.

"Oh to be childfree," he cries with a broad smile as he passes us. "I haven't listened to music on the beach in three years."

He sweeps on, feet grappling with the sand, and I can but stare after him, stunned by his audacity. What has made him speak to us like that? Can't he see that we are no spring chickens? Didn't it cross his mind that we might just *want* children? I hoist my knees up to my chest, hugging them for comfort, press Coldplay and gaze out at the beach. Everywhere there are small children, at every stage of their development. I watch a tiny girl in a pink gingham costume batting her spade against the crab-shaped sandcastles her father is building, destroying them in fits of giggles as he clutches his forehead in mock despair. I watch a toddler fetching water from the sea to fill the moat around the pirate castle his big brother is building, so proud to be needed on this mission. Alongside them, two twins are burying their parents' feet in the sand. And behind my sunglasses, as Chris Martin reaches the guts of *Fix You*, the tears freewheel to my chin. Copious. Warm. Stinging. Another necessary release.

Now it's Monday and I am positive again, my belly is peaceful and I am feeling with child. I'm also nearly half way through. Six more days until I can pee on a stick – well five and a bit really as it's nearly bedtime. By next Monday I'll know on what basis I'm to move forward from this ghoulish crossroads. I look one way and I see my heavily pregnant self, a protective hand at my tummy, I look the other, and I see myself at my PC, svelte and professional. Will I? Won't I? In the past, I would have considered the options, made a decision, taken action. But there'll be none of that in this game. I am suspended in time, hanging uselessly, under the control of a force which is so much more powerful than me.

I am working my way through a bar of Green and Black's when Dom, who this evening has decided, after all, to watch the football upstairs in the bedroom, strolls into the room with the phone.

"It's your mum," he mouths at me.

I shake my head at him in consternation, but he rattles the phone at me. When still I refuse it he covers the mouth section with his hand.

"Come on, she sounds nervous."

I snatch the phone from him with the mother of all scowls, ensuring that he's registered my rage before he leaves the room.

"Hi." My voice is a monotone.

"Hello sweetheart. Just thought I'd call and see how you are?"

"Fine."

"I've been ever so busy. I've been…"

And she's off. I hold the phone an arm's length away, drop it onto the sofa as if it is contaminated, and break off more chocolate. Clamping the square between my tongue and the roof of my mouth, I squash it flat, letting it melt. I can visualise the sweetness seeping into my shoulder muscles and relaxing them. On the telly, a woman is being chastised for spending over budget on tiles for the loo in her buy-to-let flat, when she should have put in a shower. I pick the phone up again.

"Hello? Hello? Are you there, sweetheart?"

"What do you want Lizzie?" My hand drifts protectively across my tummy.

"Well as I was saying, our group is developing a campaign for Parliament, and I told them that you worked as a lobbyist and I'd talk to you about how to go about it."

"What cause are you into now then?"

There is silence as she registers that I've not been listening to her, and in the hurt, childlike voice, which she always pulls out about now, she says, "Still euthanasia."

"Euth-a-nas-ia. Got bored with the animals did you?"

Will she ever see what a stupid, selfish cow she is? Will she ever focus on me for once?

"It's such an important topic, Catriona, such a slippery slope, you might have unethical doctors murdering their patients, children bumping off their parents."

I remain silent, now there's a thought.

It's as if she's read me. "Catriona, this is serious, life is sacrosanct."

Life. She gave it to me, the only thing she ever has given me. An image slides into my head: letting myself in after school, a chilly, soulless house, watching *Blue Peter*, huddled over the one-bar fire, heating up lentil stew. And hoping they didn't come home too soon.

"I'm busy at the moment, don't think I'll have time."

"Oh just a few pointers on what to do, Catriona, just a couple of meetings with MPs maybe? They're expecting it from me now."

"There's a huge pro-life lobby out there, you should be coordinated with one of the bigger organisations."

"I am Catriona, I'm part of a national body, but they encourage us to campaign on a local level too."

"Lobbying Parliament is not local level."

She falls silent. I know for a fact that both the pro-life and pro-rights lobbies have got Westminster stitched up, you can even trawl the web to discover how each MP votes on euthanasia. And the latest vote has already been taken some weeks ago.

"I'll see," I say. "Are you still at the same address?"

"Yes, sweetheart, above the hairdressers. Come and see me sometime?"

"Like I said, I'm busy at the moment."

"Oh." She sounds deflated.

"Look, I've got to go." I bite my lip, desperate to get away.

"OK, speak soon?"

"Bye Lizzie." I seize the moment and hang up on her.

She is stupid, the brain of a gnat. This is stupid. And yet I know that I will spend time digging out the information she wants, present it professionally, bind it in one of WPA's plastic folders with its portcullis and handshake logo in the corner. I will try to impress. Because somewhere deep down inside, I still want to please her.

10

"You mean you've already had lunch with her? Without telling me?"

It was September 2004, almost exactly two years ago. I was still digging my heels in whenever Dom mentioned starting a family, but that was all about to change. We were having dinner in the garden, I remember, the evenings already assuming that eerie end of summer light.

"She was nearby and gave me a call." Dom shrugged, snapped a breadstick in two.

"Nearby? Where does she live?"

"Guildford."

I held his eyes, took an overt sip of my wine and waited silently for elaboration.

"She runs her own interior design business and came up to meet a client."

It all sounded innocuous enough. Dom had told me about Suzanne, his girlfriend throughout university. How they'd spent the summers helping his parents manage their boarding houses in Scarborough. A few years after graduation he'd headed off to Hong Kong as a trainee banker, hoping to maintain it at long distance, but she'd left him and moved on. From friends, he'd heard that she now had four kids. Dom had told me that she was a bit like me – gamine, feisty.

"You're not getting the old seven-year itch are you?" I reached across the table and scratched the back of his hand, leaving a white scuff on his tan. We had been married for seven years and four months.

"Don't be stupid. She's not worn well anyway, looks much older than you."

"Oh, so if she had worn well you would have shagged her?"

"That's such a stupid, inane, female thing to say. You're being completely ridiculous, you know I'm still nuts about you."

It was good to hear, and I sat back mentally preening myself, but still I niggled deeper. "Can't be much of a businesswoman with four kids."

"They're all at school now, the oldest is twelve."

In the silence that followed, his thoughts were not only tangible but weighed down with a hefty dollop of reproach. Perhaps I'd even provoked him by mentioning the sprogs, because then, naturally, it came.

"Cat, when are we going to start trying properly?"

I see this moment as the catalyst. Maybe there was an imperceptible shift in the balance of power; I'd enjoyed nearly ten years of having that ever-so-slight edge, and was securely planted in the knowledge of it. But when a butterfly lands on a leaf, the flutter of its wing might unsettle even the deepest roots. I know that he saw Suzanne several times after that. Should I have flounced about with the displeasure of a medieval queen towards the knight she possessed? Well I didn't want him to think I even cared. And in truth, I did and still do believe that she was just an old girlfriend.

However, there was no denying that butterfly effect, and I took myself off to St James Park during one lunch hour and began a process of reflection. I was thirty-six years old and my feet were secure under the table after Geoffrey had appointed me managing director of Westminster Policy Advisers the previous year. However, I was still consolidating under the watchful eye of the Great White Chief, who maintained a stake, a desk and an advisory role in his baby, an outfit which now counted thirty employees and twice as many clients. And I was still pulling in the punters; I flitted around the country, back and forth to Brussels, spoke at all the public affairs conferences, and networked through Ash, who even then was a Minister-in-Waiting. Catriona Black (I still used my maiden name for work) was a well-known and highly respected name in the business.

That day in the park, the pelicans waddled around kicking up leaves, posing for photos with toddlers, who did look adorable in their miniature coats. Looking back, I know that I studied those children as they played, willing myself to want one of my own; the girls were cuter than the boys of course, in their pink hats and wellies. But they didn't move me. Not really. Not like the need to clinch a new client, or that sweet moment when you realise that government policy has been amended because of your input. I've never told anybody that though.

I had hoped to wait until I was touching forty, to give myself three or four more years before succumbing, but eventually I came to the conclusion that then could in fact be good timing. If we had the baby nine months later, I would take maternity leave over the summer, and be back at my desk by the following September. A neat year out of my life, that's all it would amount to.

Having processed this for a few days to be absolutely certain, I announced to Dom that we could start trying. The moment my next period was over, he was wreathed around me like a hot day, hand up my skirt, lips on my neck.

"No point trying until I'm ovulating," I said, basking in the attention.

"Aha! That will be day fourteen or day fifteen of your cycle."

"How do you know that?" I grinned at him.

"Research." He tapped the side of his nose.

"*Research*?" I pulled him to me again. "I thought you never had time at work to surf the web?" I'd seen the splash of screens around his desk and understood his stress well.

Dom was ever more the golden boy and his fund still enjoyed growth of over 30%, year on year.

He teased me back, all Long John Silver voice. "I knows all there is to know about how to get you pregnant, my lovely."

I found it liberating – symbolic even – to chuck my pills down the loo, plinking them one by one from their packet (now I wonder what I was thinking of, tossing all those hormones into the water supply). We began that month, armed with a new red basque from Agent Provocateur, jasmine-scented candles and massage oils. So zealous were we that we went at it every day throughout my cycle.

By the second month, when nothing had happened, I had spent hours Googling 'ovulation' and had already bought a book about infertility. I needed to look out for signs: ovulatory mucous when I peed, maybe some discomfort at the point of egg release, and apparently my temperature would rise immediately after ovulation. That month, I prided myself on being able to ascertain all three. The discomfort was hardly perceptible, but how come I'd reached my mid-thirties and never realised that, in the middle of my monthly cycle, there was goo a bit like egg white on the toilet paper? When that appeared, and the newly purchased aural thermometer spiked, we blitzed it over a period of five days, until I came down with cystitis.

By the third month, I was exasperated; it was nearly Christmas and the baby would then be due in late August, just before the busiest time of our business year. I considered asking Dom if we could leave it for a few months in order to take the birth of our as yet un-conceived baby to a later period, where things would ease off slightly. But my subconscious was probably already on the case of what was to come. And I never did ask him.

One Saturday during that third month, Dom awoke with his usual morning glory and nudged at my bottom.

"We can't Dom, it's only day twelve." I pulled away from him.

"Aw, can't we get some practice in?"

"No you've got to save it. We could have done it on Thursday, but the book says not within three days of trying, we have to get more technical about it now."

"But I'm so horny for you." He took hold of my haunches and made a few rutting movements at me.

"Better have a cold shower then." I tutted, flipped myself out of bed and downstairs to make coffee.

On the Monday morning, day fourteen, we set the alarm at 5am. It was still dark and the bedroom was freezing, with the heating not yet having clicked on. I scurried to the loo and then jumped back into bed, annoyed that he'd already turned on the TV as he always did on waking.

"Off with your PJs then," I said to him.

He whipped them off, then tugged at my silk camisole and pulled it over my head. I wriggled out of the bottoms and snuggled down deeper under the duvet, vexed by the muted share prices rolling across the screen in the corner. Dom shunted himself on top of me, pulling at himself a couple of times to restore the hardness the business figures must have softened. Surely he could have waited until we had done the act before filling his mind with work?

"Don't I get anything to warm me up then?" I frowned at him.

"Sorry." His head disappeared, but the only whirring I could feel was that of Japanese telecoms equities through his mind.

"OK, I'm ready." I yanked him up and we were off.

Forget shopping lists. I can remember precisely what ran through my mind as we shagged that morning: if this was to be the moment our first child would be conceived, then let me obliterate it from memory. I'd always imagined it would be wanton, balmy, silken.

That evening we had another stab at it. I was determined to make it romantic so I lit candles, struggled into the basque, put on *Angie*, the track that stirred memories from our lovemaking in Brussels ten years before. And while we humped around the bed in doggy position, and I came for the second time, Dom collapsed on top of me in heaves of laughter.

"I'm the one who's supposed to be having the orgasms, not you!" he cried.

*

By the following spring, after six months of trying, I'd reached the point where I needed to crack this, to find a solution. Because no problem was insurmountable. When I'd lived in Brussels, I'd had my own gynaecologist, and I decided on him as a starting point. Over the phone, I arranged an appointment with Dr Lacroix to get us both checked out. He would examine me and also perform a motility test on Dom's sperm, he said.

I then invited us to stay with an old friend of mine who worked at the European Commission, and on the Friday afternoon she led us to our room at the top of her large wisteria-clad townhouse. I apologised for our rudeness at having to dash straight out for a doctor's appointment – what I didn't mention was that we had to have sex first, so that, within the hour and after a sprint across Brussels, Dr Lacroix could assess the mobility of Dom's sperm inside me.

My friend's young child, who must have been three or four, sat on our bed chattering.

"We just need a wee-wee, Sophie. Can you go back down to your mummy?" I asked her sweetly.

"No, I will wait here for you." She gripped the duvet as if holding on.

I threw Dom a desperate look as we slipped into the en-suite bathroom and shut the door; which didn't lock. We dropped our jeans, Dom scrunched up my shirt and bra, and bent to take my nipple in his mouth. Then the door opened and Sophie's face appeared, screwed up in thought.

"What are you doing?" she asked.

"We're just having a quick wash, can you wait outside for us please?" I pushed her out backwards and shunted the door shut.

It wasn't sex, it was an exercise in how to get Dom's sperm inside me. We did it standing up against the door, with me balancing on the upturned wastepaper basket and Dom squatting awkwardly behind me, while Sophie pushed at the door giggling and I pushed back. The taxi driver had arrived, and we heard my friend's footsteps on the stairs as we zipped up our jeans, the ooze already trickling in my knickers.

We three emerged onto the landing, Sophie tripping over her words to get them out. "Mummy, Dominic was washing Catriona's boobies with his mouth."

I laughed. "No Sophie, Dom was just trying to get a mark out of my shirt."

My friend frowned a smile at me, but I threw her an enigmatic one back and left the house, not displeased for her to believe that Dom and I were still hot for each other after so many years together. Especially as by then, given all the mechanical sex, we were not.

Dr Lacroix ushered us into his office, a cosy study where a don might hold tutorials, with scruffy wood floors and a blackened fireplace. The walls were cluttered with children's drawings, his desk with papers, and yet he found my file – untouched for ten years – quite easily in one of the cabinets by the window.

"Ah yes, you have the polycystic ovaries, n'est-ce pas?" He scanned my notes.

"Polycystic ovaries, yes. You diagnosed them when I was twenty-five, but you said it was a minor problem, loads of women have them, you said."

His head rocked in consideration of my words. "We will take a look."

I watched the man as he squinted at the ultrasound screen by the side of the examining bed. He must have been in his sixties then, his remaining hair just two grey fluff balls, seemingly glued on each side of his head.

"Yes, I see that the left ovary has many, many follicles. Perhaps twelve or fifteen, all of them clumped together." He pointed to several black blobs against the fuzz of grey on the monitor. "This means that perhaps you do not ovulate. You see these follicles are sacs of fluid in which an egg may ripen and reach ovulation. But these many, many follicles could all be immature. It is possible that no dominant egg may be able to develop within them."

"You mean I'm not ovulating?" The prospect of failure did skid through me, but it slid straight out the other side. I wouldn't allow it any chance to take purchase.

"Perhaps not all the months." He smiled benignly. "In order to be sure, we must do more tests, to check for hormonal imbalances, but those you must conduct in England where you may be scrutinised."

"OK." I smiled back, already burying the idea; no hormonal imbalances inside of me, I was sure of that.

"Now." He turned to Dom. "We will take a look at the spermatozoa and see how they move." He was silent as he manipulated the ultrasound probe inside me. "Bon. We have a good number of sperm who moves. I would say…" he rocked his head in prevarication, "Yes, quite rapidly. And many of them in the good sense."

"In the good sense?" Dom asked brightly, the first time he'd spoken.

"He means in the right direction," I said flatly, irked that Dom's news should be more cheery than my own. And already digging in further – looking back, I can see that now.

After I'd dressed and we sat at his desk again, Dr Lacroix allowed me the kindly smile of my maternal grandfather. "It seems to me that you must simply continue. Vous avez quel âge maintenant Catriona?"

"Thirty-seven."

He nodded wisely, the smile not leaving his face. "Then it is time, n'est-ce pas?"

From the edge of my vision, I saw Dom also smiling quietly to himself; he'd found his first ally.

Afterwards, as we made for a nearby bar, Dom's hand wrapped tightly around my own, I grappled with those black blobs on the monitor. Surely if polycystic ovaries were truly an issue then Dr Lacroix would have imbued their fertility significance upon me all those years ago? But then perhaps he had done, and my immortal youth had just not registered it.

"So, do you think you should do the tests?" Dom interrupted my thoughts.

I frowned at him. "Why should it be me?"

He pursed his lips as if to hesitate, but still he came out with it. "Well because my sperm – "

"Your sperm *seem* to be moving in the right direction," I snapped.

We fell into an awkward silence and I sipped the cherry beer I'd always loved so much during my stint in Brussels. Briefly it took me back to a time long ago, when life was less complicated. Still, I allowed the thought to flutter again to the surface, that I might just not be as fertile as I'd simply imagined I would be. I considered myself attractive, ultra-fit, super-healthy – and how could I possibly not be all of those things on the inside too? Finally I broke the silence, albeit churlishly.

"He said simply to continue and that's what I think we should do."

Back home in England, I dusted myself off and we kept going on our frenzied mission. Until several more months had passed and we'd been at it for a whole year.

*

Then something happened which knocked me sideways. It was a weekend just last year, early September 2005 and my

110

brother's wedding anniversary. He and Maggie had booked a country hotel for the night and asked me, the aunt and godmother of their two children, to babysit. Dom always played hockey on Saturdays and so I asked Jackie to spend the day with us. I think, by this point in her life, Jackie was only pretending to enjoy singledom, like one of those celebrities in *Hello*, and she jumped at the chance for some company on a Saturday afternoon.

We took the kids to the park, where Jackie and I raced each other for the swings. In bluff competition with each other, we swung ourselves high, while twelve-year-old Daisy and her younger brother Scott had to wait their turn, lolling against the frame with their arms hooked around the rails, both of them fascinated by this display of the puerile adult. Back then, Daisy was still gauche, with dull blonde hair scratched back into a ponytail, squarish buckteeth already in a brace, and a face still searching for its correct proportions to accommodate the puberty which was just about to come upon her.

We kicked a football through the crunchy autumn leaves, exuberant in the glory of our goals against little Scott, whose freckled face scowled each time the ball slid past his rolled up sweater. Both Jackie and I were oblivious to the fact that we were not cutting the requisite slack for my niece and nephew and we laughed at each other knowingly, in a *what fun playing mummies and daddies* kind of way. But at the root of all those wacky tackles was our awkwardness; we were way out of our comfort zones. Let's face it, Jackie and I belonged in an office.

Back at Billy's small house in Hatfield, we settled down to watch a film. I remember that it was *Toy Story* actually, which Billy had suggested we would all enjoy.

"I'll go and make tea for us." Daisy left the room. I dropped to my hands and knees to seek out the DVD from the messy piles behind the telly.

"She's not supposed to boil the kettle." Behind me, Scott's whiny voice piped up.

There was a moment of hesitation, but it was only a moment; Billy and I, the original latchkey kids, had been warming our own dinner in the oven from the age of ten. And I was frustrated at my brother's messiness, *and* I was riled by a comment Scott had just made about my black eyeliner being so thick it was scary.

All of that in my defence then. Without even glancing behind me, I murmured back at him, "Don't tell tales on your sister Scott, it's not nice."

Then it came. A scream so primal, it was almost bestial. A drawn out wail of pain, followed by the clattering of a metal object onto the floor. Daisy had poured the scalding water over her hand instead of into the mug. I don't remember any more, although I'm assured by Jackie that I had her hand under the water within the minute, that the ambulance she called had arrived promptly, that the medics had dressed her hand.

What I do remember is sitting beside her as the emergency vehicle flung us at speed through the streets, yanking us around corners. And I remember too that, for the first time ever in my life, I wished that I could take the pain for another human being – for my own flesh and blood. Daisy's anguish turned my insides to slush, which then seeped icily out across my shoulders and dripped around my whole body, coating me with a chill. While futilely soothing the by then pathetic mewls of my niece, to whom nothing bad had ever happened in her life, I phoned my brother.

Finally, I tracked them down to a joint spa session, in the converted stables of their hotel, where they were wallowing in the hot oils being poured over their bodies. The irony of that spa treatment has never left me, as if bizarrely they induced Daisy into pouring all that water onto her hand, as if it was their fault. And somehow not mine. Yes, I'd had the hand under the tap within the minute, but the scald was deep and it wasn't quick enough. Today, the flesh on the back of her hand is still a puckered swathe of pinkish brown, resembling dirty skin. That skin has contracted, leaving the index and middle fingers on her left hand slightly clawed. A disfigured girl, today my niece is routinely stared at, often taunted, sometimes bullied.

"You stupid fucking cow!" Billy emerged shaking from behind the curtain at A&E and bellowed at me.

My stomach convulsed at his words, sending shock waves up to my chest and down into my wobbling legs. When Maggie followed him out, she simply sat and wept silently, having held it together for her daughter, whose blistered hand was now swathed in gauze and suspended in the air.

And instead of comforting them, I tried to defend myself. "*We* were making cups of tea when we were twelve, Billy."

"*We* weren't a normal fucking family!"

It was that afternoon that my desire to have my own child became a necessity. The compassion I'd felt for my niece was a new sensation for me – the strongest empathy I'd ever experienced thus far in my life. Witnessing her pain felt as if I'd been forced to watch Silkie being kicked in the face by thugs. Held back, helpless and distressed while she suffered. I couldn't shed the feeling from then on in, and it made me yearn for a child.

The following weekend, I was lying on my back with my feet up on the bedhead, waiting the by then habitual half hour for Dom's sperm to wriggle their way to that month's egg. Knowing then that they never actually would. It was clear to me that we'd been playing at it. Terrified that we might discover some major problem, I'd taken us off to a foreign country, to an old man with an imperfect science. I'd put us through some sideshow, ensuring that the outcome would have no impact on us.

Dom trundled in with the breakfast tray. I rolled my head back and watched him place it on the bottom of the bed, with its toast and boiled eggs beneath the *Humpty*

Dumpty cosies. His mum had bought us those, ever hopeful that somehow the nursery rhyme inference would spur us on to have kids. I waited until he looked at me, and locked upside-down eyes with him.

"Dom, I need to go and have those tests done."

11

It is now Thursday afternoon, and I have sixty-four hours to go before I'll know. Impossible to believe that I used to be one of those seriously efficient women who exploit every minute of every day. I'd cram toast at my mouth while checking my finances online and jotting a to-do list in a spare few minutes before work, or paint my toenails, with *The Economist* open on the floor and the TV news on, while I called Jackie. And now look at me, I can't bear all that time swilling around me, like some tepid mud bath, lapping up at the skin, smarting its oily way into grazes I didn't even know existed.

I'm working from home again today. It prevents me from snapping at the staff, and without the constant interruptions of the office I can find some distraction in the monthly report I'm working on for Stewart. But every few minutes, I pull up one of the web chat rooms, to see how others are faring – I've become a chronic lurker. And I've deciphered some superb acronyms this week, my absolute favourite being AF. It had me puzzled for a while, I could tell by the way women used it in their postings that it meant menstruation, but I just couldn't figure it out, and then somebody wrote it in full: *Auntie Flo*. Perfect! There are several euphemisms for sex too. One woman posted that she and her partner were topping up the IVF with a BD, which I was gleeful to learn meant *Baby Dance*. Another bright spark called it LO, which means *Love Olympics*. And there is no shying away from the announcement that they are having BMS, which is *Baby Making Sex*. Is there any other kind these days then?

Well, my husband would like there to be, that's clear. Last night I was on a high, feeling distinctly pregnant, and we spent some time together laughing about these various online postings. He's so chuffed when he sees me smile; these days it's as if I control his moods – as if I work his strings. But then he began musing about us having our own baby dance, his paw stroking my thigh, his snout at my neck. And that annoyed me. Surely he should realise that my belly is averse to intrusion by all foreign bodies at the moment?

Today, I'm feeling so positive that I've even strayed into the chat room for those newly pregnant to see what I can expect next. Although that only made me fret about the shellfish I ate in Poole. It also drew me back to a few days ago when, in one of my black moods, I stupidly took myself onto the postings about babies lost. Just to torture myself, I suppose. There was one message from a woman in her early forties. She's been through twelve IVF cycles, and finally she's pregnant, but they've just discovered that the baby's got Downs Syndrome, and she's going to abort it. Horrific to think that she's suffered so much only to then discard her baby – and yet I've not stopped wondering what I would do in her position. Because I too don't just want a baby, it has to be a perfect baby. Baby, baby, baby, the word resounds while an image plays in my head without respite.

My mobile rings. It's Stewart's private line, and I answer it with a frown.

"Just finishing it, now, Stewart."

Over the past few weeks I've felt as if I were a junior again, but the pressure to justify myself is coming solely from within me; it's a new phenomenon that goes with the new territory. Still, there's no way I can tell him what's going on.

"My team have just come across an interesting piece of draft legislation from Europe," he says.

"Really?" His team are a pack of hyenas. They've sensed my recent vulnerability and gone in for the kill whenever they can.

"Mm, very clever too. It's billed as an environmental step, but it's clearly not. They plan to limit the number of cows per square metre of grazing land throughout the EU. They say it's a move to reduce carbon emissions; you know, methane from cow's arses?" He snaps the words out. "Of course, what they're actually doing is…"

"Limiting meat production by the back door." I have to get in quick to salvage myself here.

"Correct. Quite critical for us to be on the case, wouldn't you say?"

"Yes. Sorry, Stewart." Even as I speak I'm telling myself, never say you're sorry. "I'll draft our position on it, and set up meetings for next week in Brussels."

He hangs up and I smash my phone down. "Smart-arsed shit!"

Suddenly exhausted and desperate for hot tea, I close my laptop. Back in the living room I set my mug and chocolate biscuits down, and Silkie climbs onto the sofa with me. I switch on the telly in search of regression, which I find in the form of an afternoon film, *The King and I*.

Two hours later, we are nearing the end, at the bit where Anna has angrily decided to leave Siam, and her boat waits in the harbour, the king is on his deathbed and all those cute little royal children come scampering in. I've got one arm around Silkie's neck and am blowing my nose with the other hand, when the doorbell rings. Naturally, I ignore it. On the screen, I see a blurred image of Yul Bryner's youngest princess, beseeching Anna not to leave them, she can't be more than four-years old. And just as Deborah Kerr rushes to the girl, both she and I then releasing our tears, a face appears at the window, making me jump as it slides comically across the pane. My brother, Billy. His cheeky boy grin disappears and he gestures to be let in, so I make a stilted dash for the front door, one hand on my

117

belly, then scuffle back into the living room, leaving him to kick his boots off.

"Jesus Cat, what's the matter?" I hear him trip over the boots as he follows me in. He drops a family-sized bag of Maltesers onto the sofa beside me.

"This film, it's so sad."

Billy stands gazing at the screen. "*The King and I*?" He takes stock of my face, then shuffles out of his paint-spattered boiler suit, dropping it in a heap on the floor and plonks himself down beside me, ruffling Silkie, who has ceded the way for him and now sits at his feet. On the screen, the teenage prince is strutting around in his silk frippery and bare feet, preparing to be the new king.

"Have they done that dance together yet?" Billy nudges my arm. "Dum-dum-dum, da-da-da-dum?"

"Shut up, he's dying."

The tears are bubbling down my cheeks, the violins have drowned all dialogue, straining themselves to a crescendo, backed by cherubic voices singing of love. Yul Brynner speaks his last words to Deborah Kerr, and then he lays back and dies, as cornily as ever they did in a 1950s musical. As she hurries over, kneels and presses her cheek to his hand, I let out a loud sob and release the grief, my shoulders heaving, vaguely aware of Billy's incredulity beside me.

"Cat, how can you take this seriously?" He says, sniggering. "The set wobbles, the actors are looking into the camera ..."

"They really loved each other." My head feels clamped in a vice with emotion.

Billy watches me. "Blimey, sis, you must be pregnant. Maggie always blubbered at funny stuff on the box, both times she was pregnant – that's how we knew she was."

"Really?" I stuff another wet tissue under my thigh and reach for the box.

"Straight up."

After an arduous struggle to compose myself, which takes the whole of the credits, I turn off the TV. Ripping open the bag of Maltesers, I offer them with a weak smile to Billy, who dips a grimy hand into the bag and stuffs a heap in his mouth.

"I'm fine, really I am," I say.

"Sure?" he asks. "Not in pain or anything?"

"No. Just this waiting, hoping. It's horrendous."

Billy leans in to kiss my forehead and wraps his arm around me, pulling me close to his chest, he stinks of sweat and turps.

"How come you're in Kensington, then?"

"On a job off the High Street."

"Business or domestic?" I grin at him, seizing my chance to focus on him. Billy's a decorator and sometimes gets himself into a pickle, as he puts it. Once, he bolted from a job when the Spanish wife of a famous footballer appeared in the kitchen doorway wearing only stockings and suspenders. I do believe him when he says he scarpered, because my brother is the ultimate in husbands.

"Business!" He digs my ribs with the skill he mastered at the age of eight. "Estate Agents."

I pull back to observe him, he looks like Stig of the Dump, with his matted hair and his vest and boxers, which is all he wears under his overalls. His pale thighs are thinner than most women's, but then some women prefer a slighter build. And, like Daisy, he has one of those voices which is sexy, (even if he is my brother) slightly hoarse with a hint of East London, despite the fact that we were born in the Home Counties. He found his own way of toughening up, I suppose.

"How's Maggie?" I ask. Billy and Maggie; they sound like a children's storybook. But then people often say that Cat and Dom has a comical ring too.

"Good. Looking forward to Cornwall." He adds no more. I've known Maggie since I was doing my A levels, and we rub along together nicely.

119

"Saw Daisy last week."

"Yeah, she said."

It is coming up for a year since Daisy's 'accident' as we all call it. Billy and I spent many hours going over what happened, and I know he'll always blame me, even if we are still joined at the hip. When I lie awake at night, going over it in my head, letting out whimpers to myself at what I did, deep down, I'm still convinced that she was old enough. Especially when you see how she's now suddenly become almost a young woman. I've concluded that he and Maggie don't know their own daughter, that they watch her with unseeing eyes.

"Maggie suspects she's got a boyfriend," Billy adds.

"Oh?" Of course, this I know already, but I won't rise to his digging. The closeness Daisy and I have shared since the accident is precious to me, it helps calm those night-time demons. Billy observes me for a few moments and then gives up.

"Any chance of a cuppa then?"

"Yes, of course."

I run my finger along the scar that lines the rim of his jawbone. He tells everyone a croc got him in the Australian rainforest, but really it was a school football accident. The one kindness ever shown by my mother's new man, Norman Bates, was to take Billy to hospital and stay with him that day. I give the scar a tweak, reasserting the balance between us, and push myself up from the sofa.

"Walk this way." I commence my robotic shuffle to the door.

Behind me Billy lets out a snort, which is part tease, part annoyance that I won't grass on his daughter. "Do I have to walk *this* way?"

He mimics my gait, rolling his body with a Quasimodo-like spring and a jerk across the wooden floor. And I'm pleading with brother to stop, cradling my belly to cushion the new life, I know for sure is inside me, from the reverberation of my laughter.

120

12

It was just before Christmas last year, the end of 2005, when we met our consultant, Olu, for the first time. Amazingly, Jackie got married shortly afterwards.

The Knightsbridge Fertility Clinic was supposedly the best in the country, claiming a 'take home baby' rate of 25% for thirty-eight-year-old women – as I would soon be – and it was just one mile from our house. I remember how Olu fixed his intelligent eyes on me. Despite this, I felt then that he was curbing a broad smile, that his family parties would be a hoot, but this environment called for muted enjoyment of life, in case it didn't go to plan. I also came to realise that he would need me to transfer my hopes entirely over to his hands but, at that point, I still believed that I was in control. My list of questions were typed and printed out, in small font to prevent them from being easily read by others. Beside me, Dom had a copy and was briefed.

"Could you unpack for me the high success rate you claim in your brochure, Dr Akande?" I began. In my analysis I had to be careful, as some clinics boost their take home baby rates by refusing to treat older women or handle the more difficult cases.

Olu rose to my challenge in fine fettle, jabbing at buttons on his PC then printing off a chart, which he laid on his desk with a smack of his hand. After whisking me through the various ways of reading the chart, he then seemed to tire and pushed it to one side – even though I'd been able to keep up with him. Instead, he ran through a list of questions, including how often did we have sex? As I answered, at least three times a week, I felt Dom glance sideways at me in a clumsy revelation of my lie. But Olu wrote my responses down without any hint of having caught the look.

"Good," he said. "You should not bother attempting to calculate the best time to get pregnant, couples who conceive naturally are those who maintain regular sexual relations." And without looking up, he added, "It does help if you have an orgasm too, Catriona."

Dom and I sneaked a mortified look at this impertinent intrusion into our private lives. Now, of course, I realise that Olu wasn't even brushing the surface, let alone scratching it. He put his pen down and rested his eyes on both of us in turn.

"First we need to assess the causes of your difficulty to conceive, and we will start with one month of follicular tracking on you, Cat."

Cat? I hadn't introduced myself as Cat. I balked at his audacity, but he flashed me a brief winning smile and went on.

"This will involve a series of ultrasound scans and several blood tests over one menstrual cycle. The scans will show us whether your ovaries release an egg, and the bloods will give us a hormone profile, so that we can assess the quality of that ovulation. A key indicator will be the level of FSH, that is follicle stimulating hormone, which will tell us how your ovaries perform."

I wrote this down in my new taupe suede notebook.

Olu continued. "FSH is like the fuel injected into your car engine when you press your foot on the accelerator. If the engine is in poor shape, then no matter how much petrol you feed it, it will just not perform. The ovaries are like that; high FSH levels will indicate to us that you are simply flooding the engine, as they say."

I nodded slowly, trying get my head round the ABC order of our car pedals: accelerator, brake, clutch.

"Oh, I'm with you." Dom jumped in with that jocular mode he'd now adopted for all matters IVF. "So, if Cat's

122

ovaries are in poor shape, they just won't respond to the drugs."

I glared at my husband, there had been no need to personalise it.

Olu caught my annoyance and nodded with a gentle smile. "We would expect that, at the age of thirty-eight, the FSH would still be a good number. Below ten is ideal."

I wrote LESS THAN TEN on my page and underlined it. That was my challenge.

"There will also be a small biopsy of the uterine lining."

"A what? You mean you're going to slice some tissue from my womb?"

"Don't worry, it is a minor procedure, painless, no worse than a cervical smear test. We must examine a small piece of the womb lining, to see whether it has been exposed to, and has responded to, progesterone. That would indicate a successful ovulation. Do you understand?"

"OK," I muttered, and jotted down BIOPSY!

Olu then turned his bulk on Dom. "We will also take a series of sperm samples from you Dominic, ideally over a period of three months which would allow for any volatility."

"Oh, we had a sperm test done in Brussels already, it was completely fine," Dom said, with a dismissive waft of his hand.

Olu flicked through our notes. "I believe you had a motility test, yes?"

Now, I realise that Olu had seen it all before; the husband who was content to let the wife undergo the raft of tests, including having a sliver of her womb scraped off, but was petrified of any medical intervention himself. Or, worse still, of any blame landing on him.

Olu went on. "Well, we will need to look at a range of aspects, in addition to motility, including the number and appearance of the sperm." He waited until Dom had nodded his acceptance. "And then we will meet again, we will discuss the results and we will decide together how to move forward. How does that sound?"

It sounded like me talking to a client, it was all so business-like, but then at £200 per consultation I guess it should be.

On day two of my next period, I lay on a gynaecological bed with my feet in stirrups waiting for the sonographer to arrive from the neighbouring treatment room. Apparently she flipped between the two in a drive for maximum efficiency. From the waist down, I was naked and covered by a white cellular blanket, which, oddly mindful of pubic lice, I was attempting to hold raised with a pyramid of my fingers. As I was rehearsing my habitual mantra – in thirty minutes this will all be over – there was a perfunctory knock and she was in the room, washing her hands before taking my notes and wheeling her chair to the end of the bed.

"Now, Mrs Wyatt," she said, with only a flutter of eye contact. "I'm going to scan you to check your menstrual evacuation and see how the womb lining is thinning out at the start of your cycle."

She slipped a plastic sheath over the ultrasound probe and put her fingers to my vagina. Then she tutted and pushed her chair back with a kick of her heels.

"Mrs Wyatt, you have a tampon inside you."

I recounted this to Jackie whilst we pored over her wedding photos the following weekend.

"I think she actually expected me to take it out in front of her, you know?"

"You're not serious?"

"Well, she was so cross with me, drumming her fingers when I came back from the loo."

Jackie made all the right noises, even bestowed a sharp intake of breath on me, as good mates should do, but of course she was enraptured by her own present. She'd met

Henry, a city lawyer, and married him less than three months later, in a small affair at Chelsea Town Hall with a posh restaurant jobbie to follow. Henry had moved into Jackie's townhouse in Fulham, but kept his own city pad, to rent out, he said (for which read bolthole). In addition to the wedding album, Jackie had had over fifty hefty photos printed, which she planned to frame for the house. As if, I thought, somehow this would prevent him from ever leaving, as if they'd secure him to the walls, to the mantelpiece, to the side table. These fears, naturally, I kept to myself, while she turned the pages of her album.

I studied myself in the photos. In my crimson velvet gown, beside Jackie in her golden silk, and together with our bouquets of draped ivy, we looked like Christmas at Harrods. My face was hardened, I was surprised to note, with a furrow between my eyebrows. My smile I've always considered disarming, but even that cannot hide what is happening inside me, and the tension of my new daily existence is laid bare. I wondered then if others had noticed it too.

*

Towards the end of my follicular tracking process, I was summonsed for an HSG – or hysterosalpingogram – to check for adhesions or polyps on my fallopian tubes. The doctor was a friendly Northern girl in her twenties and I chatted with her about Scarborough, where she'd spent her childhood holidays. She'd often played at the same amusement arcade on the seafront, where Dom had started his gambling habit, which had led him to fund investment. So engaging was she, that I'd hardly noticed I'd taken my knickers off and was on my back on a treatment bed, when I looked up to see a contraption hanging above me, all steel arms and tubes, some kind of medieval instrument of torture. I balked and scrunched my body up from it but, in fact, it was just the X-Ray machine.

As she wielded its arms, the doctor reassured me. "Now, when I insert the tube through the cervix, you will feel some pain, like the cramp of a really, really bad period. Don't worry though, the tube is actually no thicker than a stick of spaghetti."

"Before or after it's cooked?"

"Oh. Before. Maybe I'll have to revise my analogy." We laughed together at that, in another life we could have been friends.

And then the cramp hit me. It was as if my ovaries had been clamped in a vice, an alien and briefly agonising sensation, and for some reason I thought this is how it must feel to be kicked in the balls. Though when I described it later to Dom he said, no, that was far, far worse.

A week later came the grand finale: the endometrial biopsy. It sounded like something out of *The Lancet*, an experiment inflicted on sick people to gauge the extent of their disease. But no, it was about to happen to me. For the very first time I had become the subject of medical scrutiny. On duty that day were two young men – or rather boys – whom I eyed furtively and uneasily. Each time the pair of them emerged to retrieve another patient, I heard them jabbering on about sport. Laughing as if we weren't there at all, this mass of infertile, nervous, *strong* women sitting in bovine lines. I willed them not to call out my name, hoping instead for that brusque sonographer from my first visit. I scanned a magazine, and then another, slamming it shut at each turn of the page, barely registering the celebrities flashing past with their long legs and swimming pools. My mobile vibrated in my pocket and I dived for it, sneaking in the earphones. I muttered a surreptitious greeting to Dinwoodie.

"Stewart, sorry can't speak now, I'll call you back."

"You, lassie, are supposed to be available to me twenty four seven. That is why I pay you so much." And he hung up.

I fumbled with the earpiece, buried the phone in my bag, and heard my name being called; of course the next notes the two boy medics had picked up were mine. And in any other environment I would have stood up to them with a, 'No thank you I'd rather wait for somebody more professional.' Raising my head above the parapet, sensing the shock from the other women waiting, the annoyance of the youths, none of that would have bothered me – I have met the Prime Minister for Christ's sake, discussed the shortcomings of his transport policies with him. But in this game I was vulnerable, more so each day. So I stood up and followed them blankly along the corridor.

After I'd undressed from the waist down, I could feel their eyes on my bare bottom as I walked from behind the curtain to the bed. I clambered up onto it and clasped that blanket to my belly – lice-ridden or not. Then they started on me. It felt as if a knitting needle was being poked deep inside me, to a place nothing had reached before, where nothing earthly should ever reach. On my chat rooms, I've read that other women have found this procedure painless, but these juniors had the bedside manner of mechanics. They prattled on to each other, like a couple of guys testing engine oil with a dipstick, mulling over the best route for the south coast – 'I would take the A23 through Streatham...Yeah, but the M25 is less hassle...Think we're OK for oil, one last shove.'

I battled to reassure myself that this would all be over in a matter of minutes. When that failed, I struggled to pretend that it was happening to someone else, that I was floating somewhere overhead. After a couple of minutes, however, I began to hyperventilate. My breaths quickened until I lost control and they came thick and noisily from my chest. Soon I was heaving the sobs of a child. Just like the day I found my mother hitting my father with my skipping rope, the ladybird faces on its balled up ends smiling at Dad's back as they struck him.

But still, I didn't complain about them to the clinic.

I never told Dom about that incident either, I'm not sure why. Perhaps I was gearing up to tell him, but the following day he began his own tests. And, as he announced, it wasn't all plain sailing for him either – oh no, he had to wank off in a box room stuffed with explicit porn.

I was back in the office, finalising the presentation on food additives that Stewart had been hassling me about, when Dom called me from the unisex toilet in reception.

"Cat, this male nurse has just examined my balls. Could have done without that this morning I'll tell you. Anyway, apparently I don't have enlarged veins, so that's good."

"Of course you don't, I could have told you that."

"There are six of us and I'm number three. I've got a ticket, like at the meat counter." He laughed.

I laughed back. So they ran the same efficient production line for male fertility tests, then.

"The first one's just come out, and he took an age, number two's in there now, so I'd better go."

I hung up, thinking, oh if all I had to do to have this baby was lie in a room and masturbate. Still, I decided to buy Dom a gift, just as he had done – several times actually – during my month of follicular tracking, and I called the off-licence near his office to have some whisky delivered later that day.

"Bottle of *Glenlivet* please," I began.

"Twelve years old or fifteen?"

"Fifteen please." I bet it was his turn now. I imagined him flicking the pages of a sticky porn mag; he'd taken a naked photo of me in with him but I wasn't duped.

"Certainly Mrs Wyatt, and how would you like to pay for that?"

"Masturbate."

"Sorry?"

The pause hung between us, I hadn't actually said it, had I? "Mastercard, please."

I divulged all this to him that evening, as he lay stretched out on the sofa sipping at the malt, languorous in victory. I was lying on my back between his legs, which he'd hooked around me in protection. Oh yes, he was Master of the Universe all right.

"Tell me about it then?"

"Well. The room was tiny, no bigger than our pantry. There was a sort of camp bed against one wall, a bit like you'd find in a hostel for the homeless, and they'd got this widescreen telly. Plasma."

"Plasma? So they shell out on the telly but not on the furnishings."

"That's what I thought too. Anyway, I switched it on and pow! In my face was this woman's fanny." He paused. "Shaved." As if that detail would render it all the more stupendous for me.

"So what did you do?"

"I turned it off and got my photo of you out."

"Did you hell."

"No, you're right." He squeezed me with his thighs. "Wasn't sure how long I could spend in there, I mean the first guy had taken fifteen minutes, but the second only five at most. So I thought I'd split the difference and set the alarm on my watch for ten minutes."

"I cannot believe you're actually telling me all of this."

"I'm just so relieved I managed to do it, Cat."

"So you filled your pot?"

"To the brim."

He smacked his lips and sipped more whisky. And I lay snug between his thighs, thinking, you haven't got a clue mate, not a clue.

The second time we sat in Olu's office, a third of the pages in my suede notebook were full. Research was my career, my life, then I went on to plan my action and execute it, usually with success. I was going to crack this in just the same way. Having devoured several books cover to cover, stacked up IVF websites in my favourites, and pored over Olu's charts, I was ready for intellectual combat.

Olu began. "OK, ladies first. Cat, your follicular tracking indicated that, in that particular month, you appear to have ovulated normally. And your FSH is a good level for your age, only 8.5."

Ha – no rusty old engine inside me then. I beamed at him in thanks, and thought, yeah you can call me Cat, I'm the one that got the cream.

"These are the results from your HSG." He shunted a series of X-rays up into a screen by his desk, flipped the light switch and I saw my womb, my fallopian tubes, my ovaries appear.

Olu pointed at the sheet. "There is a slight spur here at the top of the right fallopian tube." I peered at the sheets and could make out what looked like a wisp of smoke drifting into one of the tubes. He went on. "I don't think that it represents a blockage. However, normally, the next step would be to offer you a laparoscopy to make absolutely sure."

I already knew what that was; a telescopic lens inserted through your navel to check it all out and I shook my head. "I've decided against, thank you." He raised his eyebrows and I continued. "I'm now thirty-eight, and I want to go ahead with IVF, whatever. If the laparoscopy tells me there's a problem, I'll opt for IVF, and if it tells me there's not, I'll still choose IVF." For a moment I had forgotten Dom. "Won't we, darling?"

Olu considered my logic, looked at Dom, who nodded blankly, and then our consultant too gave me a steady nod. "OK, that is probably wise," he said.

Then he turned his focus on Dom. "And Dominic, all of your sperm samples were reasonable."

For some reason I smiled at this; reasonable was not music to Dom's ears, but doctors always hedge their bets, I was learning that. Now, of course, I know that his sperm is far from reasonable, and I do remember that Olu paused, as if he was about to add something, but decided against.

130

He summed up simply. "I would say IVF would be a good route for you now."

And our meeting concluded with a formal ceremony, where we both signed separate consent forms for the use and storage of sperm and embryos. It reminded me of my wedding day when we signed the register, shunting it back and forth – only here Olu was the priest. Dom had to consent to the use of his sperm to fertilise eggs in vitro, and I to the use of my eggs. Without any discussion, we both scored though the options which would allow for our sperm and eggs to be used in the treatment of others, or in any project of research.

That was all in May, just three months ago.

13

It's 5am and I've needed to pee for over an hour, but I've held it in because my urine must be saturated with the hormones that will feed the test. It's definitely worked, I know. Every night this week I've woken in a sweat, needing to wee, and my breasts are bags of pain. Lying here, with my ear squashed into the pillow, I hear my heart pumping, the thuds reverberating through my head as it propels blood through my whole body – and on into the new body which is growing inside me. I think back to the horrendous tests, the hideous treatment, the hell of the past two weeks. It's over now, I've got there.

Yesterday was thirteen years to the day since Dom and I first met, and we celebrated at our favourite Vietnamese restaurant in South Kensington, enjoying our usual reminiscence of that time. Each year, one of us adds some new memory of the occasion – a detail of the train journey maybe, or of the bike ride. Yesterday, over our spring rolls and lemon grass chicken, it was I who mentioned the tiny baby on the back of the woman who'd sold us cones of sugar cane juice through the train window. Dom was smiling even before I'd finished recalling my memory; he'd remembered the baby too, and together we formed a picture of it, the wisps of black hair, the bead eyes.

Now, on this peaceful Sunday morning, I'd like to enjoy the anticipation. I flip over onto my back, slide both palms over my tummy, and hold them there, I'm tingling with the anticipation of a new beginning. Inside me a new life is budding, I am the Goddess Isis, the embodiment of nature and magic, I am all woman. I lie perfectly still and savour the pure new light, the sweet birdsong.

A glance at the clock tells me it is time. Beside me Dom is still asleep, I'll wake him up in a few minutes. I slip out of bed and glide into the bathroom. My hand shakes as I sit on the edge of the bath and peel off the plastic wrapping from the box. I should have done this last night, it's so fiddly and I've bitten all my nails down, so the stubs of my fingers rub blindly against the cellophane in search of an edge.

I sit on the loo and begin to pee. They say to test in mid-stream, so I wait a couple of moments before I slip the white plastic strip beneath me. I count to five and add a couple of seconds, just to make sure, and then take it out and dab it with tissue. A golden glow warms the limestone floor, which I feel is fitting for this salutary moment.

After two minutes, I hold the strip with its two squares up to the light. The blue indicator line is there, thick and clear in its own window, assuring me that the test stick is working. I peer at the other window beside it and hear the man from *Play School*, my earliest TV memory. 'What will we see through the square window today?'

If I twist it, I'm certain that I can already make out a faded blue line – it seems to come and go with the light. It is extremely faded, but yes it's there. I strain my eyes at it, and am sure it is there, but it's not getting stronger. Maybe I've tested a day too early and it's still only a faint positive. Heart thumping, I stare at it, willing it into being. Like voices in the head of a schizophrenic I see the line, it's a bold turquoise. It is the way I want my life to go.

After eight minutes have lapsed, I know that it's not there at all. I place the plastic strip on the floor between my feet and sink my head into my hands. The convulsions come from my slouched body and I scrape my fingers across eyelids and cheeks, every so often ceasing my sobbing to check the square window, just to make sure. It is white, a stark sterile white.

133

I guess half an hour must have lapsed when, finally, I stand up and tear off some loo roll to wipe myself. And there it is, crimson against the white porcelain. The blood.

PART TWO

14

Ray's teeth bare themselves at a turkey leg while he tells a family anecdote. Detached from the jollity, I observe my father-in-law, having switched him into mute mode. The orange paper hat has slipped down to his eyebrows, masking his baldness and confirming, I realise, that the Wyatt legend of his stardom as the face of Blue Ice aftershave in his twenties was probably based on fact; Dom got his looks from somewhere after all. Remove that stomach, lift the saggy cheeks, give him hair, and his dad could have been a stunner too. But, today he is oblivious to the savoury jelly hanging from those cheeks, having shared several pints with his boy at the pub after church this lunchtime. I stayed behind, raining my professional smile over the scraping of vegetables, chattering brightly – in the dumbed-down version I have perfected for this family – adding to the discussion about the hanging of rapists (there was an article in yesterday's *Daily Mail*). Beside me, Josephine, the bitchy sister, chopped carrots to the chant of, 'Chop – their – balls – off,' with each clunk of knife on wood, while Charlotte, the bossy one, stupidly removed the white wine from the fridge to make space.

Around me now, the table is in riot as Ray reaches his punch line; they've all heard it before, but they are a generous lot.

"That's a good one Granddad." Across the table, Dom's oldest nephew, John, throws a histrionic roll of his eyes, but his grin belies that even pre-pubescent he is loving it. Being part of a family, of this family, this loving dynasty – whose name will cease to go forward unless Dom has kids.

Dom is beside his father at the head of the cracker-strewn table, while I am yards away at the bottom beside his mother. I'm happy next to her, but it's true that when we're in Scarborough I do lose Dom a little, to his memories. He skims past me on his way to enjoy another part of his childhood, into the large kitchen with its greasy carpet tiles, or this over-heated dining room which overlooks the sea. I get the odd kiss here and there, but his eyes are shining in the past, one I believe he does not have to embellish either, the way most people do. On this visit, I seem somehow to have lost him a little more.

And when he's home, his Northern accent thickens too. He'll scoop up his mum's bulk from behind and joke with her, "Ee lass you're a beaut." This year he's bought Peggy a musical cake slice for Christmas – there's always one joke present, in addition to the hundreds of pounds he'll spend on a cashmere sweater, or a handbag. It was used ceremoniously last night around the fireside, when she cut the delicious Christmas cake she bakes every year, and everybody had to stop and listen to the melody, and laugh. It plays the can-can, which gave them the opportunity to include me in some banter, because I speak French.

"Have you ever seen them perform this in Paris, Cat?"

"The can-can? Yes I did once, traditionally they weren't supposed to wear knickers you know."

All adult eyes turned in reflex to the children. Often I don't even remember they're there and come out with risqué remarks like this, as if I'm entertaining clients. But how could I miss the children? There are five of them now, bringing home to me that Dom's siblings are prolific reproducers. Bossy Charlotte has three, while bitchy Josephine has two; the youngest is five and the oldest now twelve, and none of them flush the downstairs loo.

"I always have to wear my knickers, don't I mummy?" Julia, the baby of the family reacted first to my faux pas.

"Yes you do JuJu. And you must never take them off, not until you're at least thirty." Her daddy Jeremy jumped in with an acceptable, opaque adult reference.

As always, Dom saved me, by dragging his mum up to dance the can can, her flushed face a flurry of happiness while the boys goggled the huge breasts flapping behind her apron, and her husband and daughters clapped and der da da-ed the tune out. I joined in, feeling stupid and, as usual, mortified by them all being so silly, so together. Then all the kids were up on their feet, arms wrapped around shoulders, and crying, "Press it again, Granddad." Ray obliged and a row of little legs kicked the air, bouncing on the carpet, until finally one of Peggy's porcelain dogs vibrated its way off the hearth shelf and landed on the real dog's back, and everybody laughed and hugged each other. Family life.

Now, at the lunch table, Jeremy, sitting opposite me, has taken up the gauntlet and begun his own story. He has oodles of Wyatt family memories, because like me he's been around for years, but unlike me Jeremy is in the tent. Behind his head, the Christmas tree is stuffed with tinsel and baubles. Its fairy lights have been blinking at me throughout the meal and now I stare into them, glaze over, and use the few minutes of Jeremy's tale to wallow once again.

For the whole of that sunny Sunday I sobbed, opening a bottle of red wine and then another until I fell asleep, or unconscious, on the sofa. Dom tried to console me, but his words slipped off me. And I was cross with him, I don't know why, and I don't want to go there yet. When I woke, livid to see that the day still burned, he was out. At evening prayer, he said, on his return, and that enraged me even more. He's turned to religion to help him through this, and while I know it must be tough for him too, I find his quest vacuous. On the Monday, I made an appointment with Olu and went straight back in there, despite his advice to leave it a couple of months. If the first cycle was an emotional

Big Dipper, the second was a Chamber of Horrors. And that one didn't work either.

In the middle of it all, Jackie had her baby. A girl, which is just what I was supposed to have; I would have been five months pregnant now. I didn't visit mother and baby in hospital – I simply couldn't – but finally I did brave-face it round to their house and, having the babywear market covered these days, was able to present a gift of the perfect pink softness. When Jackie handed Emily to me, after sitting me down, enveloping me with cushions, and preparing my arms into just the right angles, the baby blinked up at me, her forehead screwed into fine lines, her milky scent crushing. My despair was shoved in my face. I haven't phoned for a few weeks, I can't even bear to hear Jackie say the word 'she'. It cuts me up in pieces.

A bolt of laughter jolts me back to the room. Thrilled by his reception, Jeremy is feeling warm and fluffy, his cheeks are florid and his shoulders twitch and reel beneath that snowman sweater. He reaches across the table with the bottle to fill my glass, the same one I've been nursing throughout the meal; I have to cut right down to maximise my chances for our third cycle in January. And although my unchilled glass of Chablis is now tepid, to the point where it tastes like cheap plonk, still I'm sipping at it, hoping for some sort of a lift to get me through this ordeal.

"No thanks," I whisper to Jeremy with a warm smile. He's my favourite, a lawyer, somebody I can talk to properly without having to play the little girl; I've no idea how Charlotte ensnared him.

Despite my soft voice, the whole table hears me because I've interjected a hush that somebody yet has to fill since the flutter of mirth died down.

"Are you not drinking, Cat?" Charlotte pierces the fug of gravy with the sort of voice that repels people from rooms at a party.

"Yes, I'm just pacing myself."

I try to make myself small, collapse my shoulders, dip my head, but I can feel twelve pairs of eyes on me. I turn to Steve beside me. It's his turn to pull a family story from the hat, one that may become folklore because it was recounted on Christmas Day. But he's not ready yet and frowns at me for attracting the eyes his way like a shoal of minnows; he's the shy son-in-law and clearly finds Jeremy a hard act to follow.

"That's not like you, Cat." Ray lets out a guffaw, which oscillates the length of the table. As usual, whenever he sees an opportunity, he presses my buttons. In normal life, I would walk round Ray, have nothing whatsoever to do with this idiot, but I can't because he's the father of my husband.

"Oh I'm, just, you know, trying to stay healthy," I say.

"You've not got something to tell us have you?" At the other end of the table, Josephine, her mood heightened by wine and excessive exposure to family emotion, has seen the light.

She digs Dom in the ribs and he attempts to maintain the jollity. "No, nothing to report, we're not pregnant."

Twelve-year-old John lets out a cruel laugh. "You can't both be pregnant anyway, only *she* can." The little shit points at me with his knife, pulling all eyes to me again.

Dom continues loudly, to draw them back to him. "But you'll be the first to know when we are, sis, after about, ooh, thirty other people."

His smile for me is so broad, so bright, and yet his eyes are pleading with me – don't create a scene, keep your sadness bottled up for just one more day and then I'll continue to heal you.

And that could have been that, it really could, but Josephine, stupid cow, has a go. Clearly she's rattled by my lack of engagement in the frivolity that is the Wyatt Christmas and her voice is brittle. "Are you trying for a baby though?"

My fury is a flash. "Yes, we are actually. Not that it's any of your business."

Peggy places her hand over my forearm and smiles kindly at me, she smells of her sublime cooking, and I attempt to control myself, to deflate.

"No, love, you're right, it's very private," she says, and in that instant I know that Dom has told her. How could he? We agreed only to tell Jackie and Billy. My eyes spear him across the length of the table, but his own eyes are now defiant, saying, why shouldn't I have somebody to talk to about it?

Beside him, Josephine is not happy to have lost the floor. "Well it will probably take you ages now, you career women leave it far too late. I know someone who took three years to conceive in her late thirties. Better to start young, I always say."

That bitch had her two brats in her twenties. I can feel myself smouldering, and Dom is down her throat. "Josie that's enough. OK, my turn to tell a story – I remember about ten years ago –"

"She had to have an operation in the end, to flush her tubes out. What was it, a leperok-sopy or something, something to do with leper. Have you considered that Cat?"

"Laparoscopy." I reel the word out with menace.

All adult eyes are now on me, while the kids look around in expectation and seem unsure whether to giggle. I guess it could be some sort of charades game we're playing – maybe I'm about to gesture whether laparoscopy is a film, a book or a song and then mime it out. I can feel Peggy and Ray searching each other for a way back, while Dom's eyes are beseeching me to shut up. But I am too furious, livid at the whole world and my voice rings out, strong and lucid.

"And what makes you all assume that the problem is with me?"

15

"Have you ever had a testicular injury, Mr Wyatt?"

Dom jerks in his chair as if it's given him an electric shock, and my eyes shoot from the photo crammed with five children on the desk up to those of the andrologist. Mr Cracknell-Smythe, tanned after his New Year break, has been perusing our notes for several minutes. He takes hairy nasal breaths in a room which is otherwise silent, but for the faint cry of demonstrators in the street below.

Dom smiles brightly at the consultant, desperate for this man with the chamois leather face to be his pal. "I've had the odd hockey stick in the balls, yeah, if that counts."

I can remember it happening myself, at least twice, in the early days when I headed home from Brussels for the weekend to stand on a touchline. I'd hold myself back from clucking onto the pitch at Dom's pained grimace. I'm sure there must have been cricket balls too.

"Ah, I see." He notes this down with smug satisfaction. "But no surgical intervention?"

"Never." Dom's eyes cloud, as if the suggestion shovels more doubt on his manhood.

Being in this room is tough enough for him, it's taken me weeks to finally land him here, albeit with his guilt as my ally. Given that we're already halfway through our next IVF cycle, however, it's doubtful any treatment will kick in by the time we need his sperm.

The consultant goes on. "I ask because you have a high incidence of antibodies in your sperm."

Antibodies? Surely those are a positive in nature? I frown at the man, but he refuses to engage with me. Clearly

143

his well-trodden path is to focus on the puzzlement of the male.

"Antibodies are usually caused either by surgery on the reproductive tract, or by injury to it," he continues. "An injury could cause a rupture and thereby allow the immune system access to sperm. These sperm, it will perceive as foreign invaders and swiftly strengthen itself, forming antibodies against them." His voice is pompous, but I must capture its abstruse message and my pen flies across the page of my notebook, its suede cover now mangy from constant handling.

"Surely a strong immune system is a good thing?" Dom's voice remains bluff, a notch too hopeful.

The consultant, however, shakes his head, rejecting my husband's schoolboy quest for friendship. "Antibodies attach themselves to sperm, making them sticky, or even immobilising them, rendering them unable to pierce the egg."

His smile emerges more as a sneer beneath the moustache, and I have a sudden vision of him in the playground, spitefully pushing the new boy around. I want to ask him about the abnormality, which Olu had pinpointed as the key problem with Dom's sperm, which is why we are here. But I know I must remain silent, so I gaze into the lilac carpet with its violet flecks and wait for Dom to react.

"Is there anything we can do about these antibodies?" he asks.

"Steroids."

"What?" Dom squeaks the word out.

Cracknell-Smythe nods, as if pleased that Dom has finally comprehended how awful it is. "Steroids would suppress the immune system, which in turn would reduce the number of antibodies in the semen. Drastic, most likely with nasty side effects, and probably not worth it, I agree. I would keep going with ICSI, if I were you."

My glare hits him square on; but you're not us are you? You've got five kids in this room with you, otherwise you wouldn't have the balls to do this job, would you?

He averts his eyes, shuffles the notes. "Erm, there are other issues with the sperm too. A high incidence of abnormality, sperm with two heads or no tails, for example."

"I'm not firing all blanks though, am I?" Dom's voice has now found its distressed level, a good few pitches higher than normal.

"No. We have observed that when we proceed with ICSI, selecting a robust sperm and injecting it directly into the egg, then you are able to generate embryos."

I fix my eyes on Dom – but not any that can produce a pregnancy. He turns to me, fully aware that I need to come out of this room with a result, something new that will improve our chances, an action we can control. I raise my eyebrows at him, if he won't dig deeper, then I will.

He looks back at the man. "Is there nothing else I can do to make my sperm normal?"

The andrologist smiles, bunching up those cheeks with their over-sized pores, now he really is the school bully, with his prey cornered in the cloakroom.

"You don't smoke, that's good. You're in good shape; excess weight can keep the testicles at a higher temperature and lower the sperm count. And I assume you wear boxers, not Y-fronts?"

"Yes," Dom replies. I scowl at the andrologist. Yes, and he's got a bigger dick than you too, you tosser.

"Any stress at work?"

Now slumped by the coat pegs, Dom just shrugs. "Who doesn't?"

"Well, stress can affect sperm quality, so try and reduce that if you can."

He might as well have advised Dom to join the next space mission. I take my husband's hand and squeeze it, let him know that we should get the hell out of here.

And yet, when we escape that office, somewhere within me there's a bubble of rage that Dom won't agree to try those steroids. Yes, the very word conjures up mutation, a bolt-necked *Frankenstein* even, but why should I be the only one bombarding my organs, now for the third time, with virulent drugs? When their long-term impact is still inconclusive, whatever they say.

In the lift down, my hand reaches for the painful bump on my thigh; I must have burst a blood vessel this morning because today's bruise is plum red and just as large. At least now they've given me an injector pen. Spring-loaded, I hold the plastic tube against my leg, press the button, and it fires the hidden syringe into my flesh. Far less traumatic than watching the needle pierce my skin, even if I do still have to prep the syringe with its drugs first.

Outside the clinic the demonstration is rowdy; some pro-life group rattled by the use of discarded IVF embryos for research purposes. A bearded man jumps forward at me and shakes his placard, which reads: HUMAN RIGHTS FOR EMBRYOS.

I scowl at him, shoving his board from my way, and mutter, "Pond life."

And beside me, Dom emits noises I've never heard from my husband before, he actually growls at the man.

That was a week ago, and I have been in for the embryo transfer this morning. Alone, because Dom said he was too busy. Back home again, I am greeted by Silkie, teddy in mouth, slipping and scratching across the hall tiles. I hear Dom's voice. He's on the phone in the living room, though he's supposed to be at work.

"She's a dirty bitch, Ben."

I linger in the hallway, he's on about that woman from work again. She's been gone six months now but she's still trying to shaft him for unfair dismissal.

"Yeah, well... she should know the score with these things."

I enter the room and catch a glimmer of alarm in Dom's eyes; he's been caught at home when he could have come with me. At least that's how my consciousness chooses to read it.

"Gotta go mate, see you later." He hangs up and chucks the phone across the room onto the window seat, walking over to embrace me. "Hi darling, had to come home for a file."

"The evil woman again?"

He nods. "It's gone to court now, couple of weeks time. Anyway, how are you?"

"Fine." For a moment I thought he had forgotten. "Olu put two top grade embryos in. Maybe your new diet is kicking in!"

Since our meeting with the andrologist, I've got Dom on a raft of supplements: zinc, Vitamins B, C and E, and an amino acid called L-arginine, which I've read helps mature the sperm.

"Had the water sussed too, I sank half a bottle in the cab, and it was much less painful this time."

"Great." He is scooping up files from the floor.

"Olu says hi," I add. A little dig to tell him his presence was missed; clearly Dom was quite content not to witness the wonder of our embryos being slipped into my womb today.

"Sit down, I'll get you a coffee." My husband never did recognise a gibe.

"Can't drink coffee Dom. Technically I'm pregnant, remember?"

"Oh. Anything else I can do for you before I head back then?"

"Kiss?"

He kneels down to the sofa where I am now prostrate, and slides his arms around me as if I'm made of eggshell.

I consider his preoccupied face. "You do want this baby, don't you?"

147

"Of course I do. That's why we're going through this hell, isn't it?"

We? But I let it drop and hustle him off to the office like a small child, because I want to be alone.

Later that week, Ash and I are on the House of Commons Terrace, along with a smattering of other hardy fixtures. It's a chilling winter's day, softened by a streak of sunshine from across the Thames, the first of 2007, which warms my face. Ash has his back to the river as usual, not out of chivalry so that I may have the best view, but in case long lenses might be protruding from St Thomas' Hospital opposite to snap up the bottles of champagne. All the sussed MPs do it.

He has just held a celebratory reception for his allies in Westminster Hall, to which a handful of my clients were also invited (not Dinwoodie of course). For me it was an hour's sanctuary from the reality of my two-week wait. I was Catriona Black the lobbyist, respected and relaxed among the cream of public life, feeling the dog's bollocks in a new grey tailored suit. Ash held himself tall and recounted the discovery, up in the beams, of leather tennis balls probably lost by Henry VIII. I stood observing him with a quiet smile, proud that he's just become one of the youngest ever Junior Ministers.

"Did you see me beside the PM yesterday at Question Time?" he asks, acknowledging the Chief Whip who strolls past our table.

"Couldn't miss you, he almost sat back down on your knee." I throw him a mock frown. "Is all this power going to your head, Ash?"

"Maybe." He rubs an ear. "Why shouldn't I have some fun? Time for the real Ashley Schofield to stand up."

He puffs his chest out. I clock the fact that his body under that waistcoat is still in great shape. So far Ash hasn't sunk into the morass of receptions that have done for so many of them. Nonetheless, I continue to tease him. "I think you could easily become a Sticky Toffee Pudding."

"I'll be more useful to you now though, won't I?" He dips his head, its brow furrowed, with a taunt of his own.

He's right, his promotion has already secured us two new clients, and I bow my head in reverence, which he acknowledges with a smile, then he downs his champagne, sighs contentedly and surveys the terrace.

"I brought your mum out here you know, when I met her last autumn with her gaggle. What a bunch they were, all crimplene and cold cream."

"Yes, I know you did, thanks again for that."

"Couldn't help her though, think I already told you, she was way too late for the vote."

"I know, I know, I'm sorry, I know she's an embarrassment, she's like a kid playing at doctors and nurses." I flurry my words, tugging my scarf around my neck.

"*And* she took a photo of the Home Secretary with one of those disposable cameras, *not* the done thing." Ash chortles, as if the memory of Lizzie is now a fond one. "Mothers, eh?"

While he fetches a second bottle from the Strangers Bar, I suppress an image of Lizzie basking on this terrace and survey my surroundings, receiving nods of acknowledgement from the odd dark suit. I'm fairly well known here myself. Ash returns and tops up my barely touched glass. He leans to kiss my cheek and I inhale my full hit of that aftershave.

"Anyway, how are you Cat? Still excelling professionally, I see."

His praise seeps warmly through me. "I'm fine, thanks."

"Not drinking much?"

"January detox."

"Well, you look amazing on it, gorgeous even. Cheers."

We clink glasses and I let the bubbles tickle my lips, then allow those lips to form a smile – a coquettish one even – at my former colleague across the table. When I'm in his world I can pretend life really is elsewhere.

*

It's Friday morning and my two weeks are almost at an end. I haven't bled and I've managed to hold off from testing until today, even though I'm still a day early and should strictly wait until tomorrow. Having peed on three sticks from different packs, I'm certain there is a blue line in all of the windows. It could just be imagination, could just be that I've gone stark raving mad with all that's been thrown at me over the past months, but there's definitely a hint of a shadow of a sliver of a line. And my breasts feel strange too. As if they're buzzing inside, as if one of those joke bow ties that whizzes round like a mini-fan is embedded in the core of each one. I've phoned the clinic and, although I could sense a trace of exasperation at my premature call, they've advised me to go in for a blood test after lunch. So I phone Ellie and tell her I'll work from home today.

Dom agreed with me about the blue lines. "You'll call me as soon as you know for sure?" And he left for his tribunal in a chipper mood.

Stupidly, I found myself choked up after he'd gone. Yes, his friends call me Am-zon woman, and yes I am a strong, resilient woman, but I could really do with him at my side today, whether it's going to be a yes or a no.

To kill the morning, after I've peed on a fourth stick and twisted it this way and that, I head up the road to my hairdresser's in search of soothing hubbub. He welcomes me with a kiss to each cheek, and I sink into the expansive leather sofa, grateful for the half hour wait he's mentioned which will keep me lingering there and not at home. The batteries in those bow ties are now stronger, but I'm desperate to suppress any hope, and so I busy myself, jabbing at magazine pages with a moistened finger. I've

150

skimmed four *Hellos* and an *OK* by the time his assistant calls me over to the sink, where I scrape my shoulders back into the porcelain bowl and scan the ceiling for some other object to occupy my mind. The chandeliers are a mass of scrolled glass shades, protruding from loops of thick wire. They remind me of that game I used to play as a kid, inching the hoop along the wire without touching it, without it buzzing. I begin at the edge of one wire and mentally work my way in to the centre of the twisted jumble, but my mind discharges a jarring buzz, and I'm back at the start.

"Doing anything nice tonight?" The girl washing my hair breaks my torment.

"Not sure yet." I close my eyes to cut her off and visualise again the blue lines.

At the Knightsbridge, those campaigners are gathering again despite the bitter February day. A scrawny woman in a parka steps across my way and I hold her back with my glare. Upstairs, the nurse on duty is my favourite, a young fresh-faced woman, who has just got married, and she sits me in one of those purple high-winged chairs and takes my blood, while she thanks me for our gift, then chats away about the others they've received from John Lewis. I join in, asking her manic questions about glassware and tablecloths.

Twenty minutes later, she emerges from the lab into the corridor, still bright-eyed, giving nothing away in public, and approaches the waiting area, where I sit with my sleek bob, twirling my rings. The other women, each at their own stage of IVF hell, glance up as the nurse beckons me towards one of the treatment rooms, and I'm up on my feet and off. In my haste, I trip over a stray leather strap on the floor. I've gone a few steps before I look down to see a woman tapping at my leg; I have dragged her handbag with me across the carpet. Bending to unhook it from my ankle, I mumble my apology and dart into the room.

"Sit down, Cat," the nurse says.

I screw my face up. "It's negative, isn't it?"

"Well… it is positive." My heart flurries its beat and I begin to rise and reach to hug her. "But I'm so sorry, it's too weak a positive, I'm afraid."

I stop mid-rise and slump back down in the chair.

"The HCG hormone levels should be above fifty and yours are below thirty. I'm so sorry, Cat, it's what we call a biochemical pregnancy." Her eyes mimic mine as they fill with tears and she waits a few moments then reaches to place a hand on my shoulder. "I'm afraid you can expect to start bleeding within the next day or so."

"Thank you," I mutter, "OK."

"I'm so, so sorry. Can I get you anything? Glass of water?"

I shake my head, desperate to escape. "Thank you." I leave the room, and sleepwalk my way down the stairs, the term 'biochemical' adrift in my mind. In reception, I head for the toilet, and there is the blood I can be expecting, just a faint pink swirl in the water. I knew really, didn't I? I was just trying to outrun the blood, to beat it by testing early. I flush quickly, unwilling to linger there.

At the front doors, however, I realise that I am not yet strong enough to leave the clinic, so I make for the empty coffee area and flop into one of the bucket chairs. The tears roll and I allow them full limelight, taking masochistic pleasure in the way they sting my cheeks, cling to the corner of my lips, in the itchy wetness that tortures me. I can't even bring myself to call Dom. I look up to see the woman from catering handing me a cup of tea.

"On the house, love, it's a cruel world." She places a plate of ringed biscuits on the table and I gaze into their pink icing.

Inside me a chasm is opening. The tiny life I saw going into my womb has simply vanished. For two weeks I was convinced that my baby grew inside me, while I protected it, talked to it, sang to it, gave it succour. And now it's been stripped out of me. It's as if my whole being is a shell, hollow and useless, a husk encasing nothingness. But how can you lose something that was never there? How can you mourn someone who has never existed?

Finally, I make it outside. There must now be forty of those hideous campaigners, they seem to be frothing at the mouth. And I bet each and every last one of them has got children of their own – they don't give a toss that I haven't, that I can't. My dad always used to tell me there's no such word as can't. But there is; I can't have children. See there it is – a ginormous word.

The woman in the parka lurches forward and shunts her sign into my face, it reads: IVF DESTROYS HUMAN EMBRYOS. My fury is instant. I hear a war cry emerge from my chest, and some primal force within me launches my arms into the air, charges at the woman, tears the wooden plaque from her hands and hurls it at the ground.

"You selfish fucking bitch. What the fucking fuck has it got to do with you?"

And then I've got the fake chinchilla fur of her hood in both hands and am grappling with her. I feel myself being yanked back by other campaigners who are grabbing at my arms, my coat, my hair, and I find myself spinning backwards. After a few stumbles I'm sprawling on the ground, hands out for protection. Immediately I scrabble back to my feet, spurred on by anger and adrenalin, and let out a series of screams at the mob. Guttural. Terrifying. Immensely satisfying. Then I swing away and set off home along Knightsbridge.

Swerving through the shoppers, I pick up a sprint past Harrods, jog past the museums, pounding the streets until I'm home. The loss is now gaping in my belly, a period pain is beginning to spread, and the gall of having been set upon is rising in my throat. I just make it to the downstairs loo before I throw up, then I shuffle through to the living room and collapse onto the sofa, pushing Silkie's wet nose

153

off my face. This morning, there was still a chance that my life would move forward, but just hours later, it's clear to me that I could possibly – will probably – always be childless. The prospect looms before me, like a vast leaden sky, and for the first time in my life I feel utterly useless. Catriona Wyatt is abnormal, she cannot procreate, she is an unnatural woman.

The phone rings and I consider ignoring it, but realise I've still not told Dom.

"Hi sis." Billy's voice is warm, hopeful. I'm glad it's him.

"It's not worked."

"Oh no! Cat, I'm sorry."

"Yeah."

"Shitty."

"Yeah."

"You're absolutely sure?"

"Bleeding."

"Shit, I'm so sorry." He's silent for a moment. "Don't know what to say."

"I just can't believe it, I really thought this time ..." The silence hangs between us. "It'll be spring before I can have another go."

"Don't you think you should give yourself a break? What does Dom think?"

"Don't know, but we'll be straight back in there. Got to keep at it."

He whistles. "It's five grand a pop, sis."

"It's only money."

"A quarter of what I earn."

My fury flashes. "Look, if you can't be sympathetic then sod off."

I hang up on him and stomp down to the kitchen to make tea, slamming the kettle into its slot. The phone rings again.

"What?"

"Sorry sis."

154

I'm relieved that he's bothered to call me back. "Yeah well, I'm sorry too, it's a bit raw right now, that's all."

"Bollocks for brains, that's me."

I sink onto a stool at the island and study my grazed palms, the blood still bubbling in places. "I've just had a fight with a bunch of protestors too, Billy. Outside the clinic. Ended up on the pavement."

"Blimey, you are having a crap day of it, aren't you?"

I nod at the phone. "The great unwashed they were, all smelly breath and stringy beards. And that was just the women."

He laughs. "Hope you gave them a run for their money?"

"Assault and battery, if I'm caught." I stand to pour the kettle, grab a packet of Hobnobs and rip it open.

"Was it like those scraps you used to get into at school?"

"They were only to protect you." I smile. "You know that."

"Yeah," he says, and I can feel him smiling back. "You used to give 'em hell."

I dunk a biscuit and tell him about my run-in, while he draws out the details in his jokey way, working his magic until we're friends again. I'm feeling much better, my mind already calculating the timing for my next round and visualising it working.

"Wasn't sure whether to tell you this, sis, but now might be a good time. While we're on the subject of protesters?"

"What's that?" I dunk another biscuit and pop it in whole.

"OK, see if you can guess ... Mum ..."

Instantly I get his drift, but struggle to gulp back the biscuit. "Don't tell me she's campaigning too?"

"You could have bumped into her. Though I did tell her which clinic, so she'd avoid it."

"You've told her I'm doing IVF?"

"Only 'cos you might have come across her."

155

"Oh Billy, you know I hate her being in on my business." The thought that Lizzie might be party to some weakness of mine horrifies me, it's as if she's got one over on me.

"She was concerned about you."

"'Course she was."

"No really. Said she's going to write to you."

"Believe that when I see it."

"Yeah, well, you just might."

16

Jackie's baby is dressed in a pink babygrow, with *I love my Daddy* printed on the front. My best friend is holding Emily, face outwards, one hand around her tummy and one under her bottom, as if she's jiggling a jar of sweeties to guess the weight. I am there to baby sit, and I've been at her house over half an hour already, while Jackie has taken me through bottles, nappies, soft toys, blankets and the mobile above Emily's cot. But still she's reluctant to hand her baby over to me. Emily is nearly seven months old now and she bestows on me a wide-eyed smile, showing two bottom teeth, just like the ones on the baby in the book I have bought for her. She is so cute now.

Finally, Jackie shuffles towards me and places the baby on my lap, then she actually takes my arms and wraps them around her daughter – you'd think I don't know how to hold a baby. I look down at Emily and am disgruntled to see her throw her mum a frightened look.

"All you need to do is hold her and then – hey presto! – you'll find yourself pregnant, that's how I did it, with my sister's boy." Jackie's voice has a slightly manic tenor.

I suppress any inklings of outrage on the inanity of this comment while she smiles brightly at me; I can see she's hoping I won't mention my woes tonight. Jackie hasn't asked, and I haven't told her, that I've just started my fourth IVF cycle. It is Easter, after Oestre the Goddess of Fertility, and I am optimistic again. Rallying Dom round, however, is proving difficult. He's up in Scarborough for the weekend, and I suspect he's having a good old heart to heart with his mum, because our last failed cycle hit him badly. He won his tribunal though.

My friend is now hovering over me, as I coo at her baby. "You know it's amazing the responsibility you have for them as a ..." Her voice trails off before the 'p' word, then she babbles on again. "It's not like any other responsibility you've ever known, it's about keeping her alive, she's so dependent on us for everything. We have absolute power over her life, and it's such a precious privilege, so really there should be a new word for it. Responsibility simply isn't adequate."

I stare at Jackie throughout this diatribe, comprehending none of it, and wishing she would move back, stop shadowing my hands with her own while I'm cradling Emily. The baby is now beginning to squirm on my lap, reaching up for its mother, and I fold her arms back to her sides again, pin them down with my own.

Jackie's husband, Henry, is at the door, his over-moisturized face too open, as if he's expecting to burst into laughter at any time.

"Yes, it's just like Spider-Man says, 'With great power comes great responsibility,'" he says.

Jackie laughs. "Oh you big kid."

Oh you big wanker. "What does Batman say?" I can't resist it.

Henry shakes his head and throws me the punch Jackie spared me. "As a parent, you understand these things."

I've never been sure why she married him. To me he's just one of those guys she used to tear herself apart over, the idiots who could never commit, but he's now in his mid forties, and balding, so he's panicked and committed. For now. And she panicked too – although she won't admit it – because she was forty when she met him.

Emily seems to sense a tension, her mouth creases and she begins to cry. Determined to hold on, I bounce her fitfully on my knee and sing *Humpty Dumpty*, but Jackie takes her from me. "Ach, she's tired. Time for bed, wee girl."

She and Henry disappear from the room. Clearly it takes two to put a baby to bed, or is it just that Henry, for all his wiles and conviviality as a corporate lawyer, cannot bear to be alone in a room with me? But then it would be awkward for me too, I guess, and I'm relieved he's gone with her.

I tuck my feet beneath me on the sofa, settle down and sweep through the TV channels, my night's viewing all planned out. It's 8pm and I remember my nasal spray, the first drug of the cycle which I have to take at the same time morning and evening. Four daily sniffs, which will shut my system down, tricking it into menopause, so that next week the egg-stimulating injections can take over my body with complete control. Although taken in a quick sniff, this drug has a particularly menacing feel – to think a nasal spray can be so omnipotent. I shoot a dose up each nostril, inhaling deeply, then gripping my nose to resist a sneeze; it has to take effect. The fluid tastes bitter against the back of my throat, like the polish my mother used to paint on my nails to stop me biting them.

I screw the cap back on the bottle, and think about Lizzie. She hasn't been in touch, despite Billy's hints that she would. Anyhow, as far as I'm concerned, I prefer to maintain our role reversal, with me an absentee daughter. I haven't seen her for over a year now, and that was by accident when I called at Billy's house.

I settle back down and survey the room, which Jackie had painted grey when Henry moved in. It's a tip. Cluttered with mugs, muslin cloths, soft toys, and Henry's gear, which I know Jackie likes to let grow organically around the house, believing that it makes him more permanent. My eyes linger on a messy stack of unopened *Economists* in one corner, which I find most odd, because Jackie's always been one to devour her current affairs.

159

On the mantelpiece, the baby monitor flickers green and I hear her singing to her daughter. "Hush little baby, don't say a word."

I smile at the monitor. She has a beautiful voice, so lyrical, even if her appearance has become scarier – these days the cropped hair is aubergine, and her features more pinched. She's been presenting *A Letter from Home* on the radio for two years now, a programme she conceived herself that deals with issues around family and loved ones. I listen to her online every week and love hearing her voice, which bubbles with Celtic warmth but will then abruptly stiffen, cutting through the crap with no-nonsense insight. She's known for pushing the envelope – my friend has won awards.

"Are you sure it's OK to leave Emily with her, Jacks?"

I catch my breath and stare at the baby monitor, each syllable of Henry's question is a stab of green light.

"Of course it is, I've known her for years, she's my best mate, Henz."

"She's weird though isn't she? Did you see the way she gripped Emily to her, the way she looks at her? So intense. Sure she's a baby sitter and not a baby snatcher?"

Jackie actually giggles. "She is a wee bit odd at the moment, you can understand it though."

I hear myself cry out, gobsmacked by the disloyalty of my oldest and dearest friend. The one I have pulled to my shoulder when she's been distraught, for a good old cry, the one who knows everything there is to know about me. I stare in disbelief at the plastic gadget, which is now silent, eerily so.

It's a good ten minutes before Jackie comes back into the room and then she hangs by the door. "She's gone finally, she won't wake up now."

I don't look up from the telly. "OK, see you, have a good time." My voice is hollow, I'm trying to give some normal shape to the words, but my quivering lips cannot close properly on the 'time'.

I sense her hovering by the door as if wanting to add something, then she thinks better of it and glides back out to the hallway. There is the click of heels on wood and the front door clunks shut.

Baby snatcher? Like one of those sad women who take kids from supermarket trollies because they can't have one of their own? How dare he? How dare *she*?

I'm still smarting an hour later, rehearsing the lines I'll snap at Jackie on her return, when the baby monitor comes to life with a gruesome wail. Shit, I thought this was going to be easy. I heave myself up from the sofa and climb the stairs slowly, hoping she'll just stop crying, but Emily has been sick. I lift her out of her cot, holding her away from my body to avoid any contact with the gunk splattered down her front, then lay her on the carpet and strip her off. Leaving her screaming, I search frantically for a clean babygrow. The thirty minutes of training Jackie put me through pay off, and soon I have her buttoned up in white, with a new nappy on to boot. I have to leave her on the carpet bawling again while I scrub my hands. Then I bring her downstairs and pace the room with her in my arms, trying to catch snatches of the film on the telly behind her head.

Thirty minutes later, she is still screaming and now puce, flinging her head from one side of my chest to the other in search of a useful breast, something which of course I lack. She refuses to entertain the bottle left in the fridge, even though I've heated it for precisely forty seconds in the microwave. The tension is railing in my shoulders, why can't she just go to sleep? Finally, in desperation, I call Billy, the only person I can trust not to mock me now. He's at home watching a film with Maggie, as I know he will be; my brother and his wife are young fogeys, much happier with their home comforts than out clubbing on a Saturday night. I can hear him leaving the living room, his socks shuffling against the wood, and I imagine him hoisting up his jogging pants as he sits on the stairs in the hall.

"Have you given her a bottle?" he asks.

"She won't take it, just keeps smashing around my chest for a nipple."

"You have to hold the bottle on end for her Cat. Make sure the teat's full of milk, otherwise she's just getting air."

I stare down at the apoplectic baby, whom I've now dumped on the sofa, where she's kicking her legs and arms like an upturned beetle. With the phone clasped awkwardly chin to neck, I lift her up and shove the upside-down bottle in her mouth. It works. She pulls on the teat as if she's just crawled through the Sahara, closes her eyes and now makes only snuffling piggy sounds.

"Ooh Billy, you're a miracle worker."

"Just a tip, sis. One you never forget once you've spent hundreds of nights trying to calm a baby."

I watch Emily's face. Her mouth can't work quickly enough round the teat and I find myself letting out a plaintive sigh.

"Billy? Do you think I'd make a crap mum?"

"'Course not. Look I didn't have a clue before either, you don't need to know these things until you have kids, and then you hit the ground running. It's about self-survival."

"It's just that, well, I look down at her, and I don't feel anything for her, not really. I just want to get back to the telly."

"It's completely different with your own, Cat."

Emily has nearly finished the bottle of milk and is making frantic squeaking sounds as she pulls on the last drops. With rising panic I watch her empty the bottle. Then she starts to cry again.

"Shit, Billy, what do I do now?"

"Try winding her. Put her to your shoulder and pat her back."

I fling her like a rag doll over my shoulder and pound her back, thinking the harder I do it, the quicker she'll stop, but the piercing wail continues.

"Do it gently." He pauses. "Cat, can you remember that day when Nasty Norman came home early? We were watching telly and he turned over?"

I smile. "We were watching *Wind in the Willows*."

"Yeah. I can still see the bastard, tossing down his *Sun* newspaper and marching up to the telly."

"So can I. Funny what you remember. What a shit that man was."

"You don't know the half of it ..."

Billy trails off as the phone slips from my neck and I ruck it back up. Emily is still sobbing.

He goes on. "Anyway, I burst into tears, and you turned the telly back over again. I must have only been ten, but I can still see it all clearly. He grabbed hold of you and dragged you away."

I'm nodding at the phone, reliving the scene in my mind. "He actually shoved me back onto the sofa, it was the first time I'd been scared of him."

"I know, I was petrified he was going to hurt us. Anyway, I came rushing over, and you put your arms around me and rubbed my back to calm me down. Can you remember?"

"Yes I remember that." Eyes closed, I'm visualising the memory.

"Well, try that on Emily, Cat. Try rubbing her back, really gently."

I open my eyes and find I'm already doing just what Billy is telling me. I'm rocking Emily, clasping her dear little body to mine, sliding my palm up and down her back.

"I know you were only two years older than me, Cat, but sometimes you were just like a mum to me. And you're gonna make a wicked one, you'll see."

The baby lets out a burp, which must have reverberated down the phone and Billy laughs with me. Then she sighs and snuggles against me. I feel the tension leave her tiny body, and it drifts out of mine too.

"Thanks Billy."

"And Cat. Those *Sun* newspapers? I used to cut the nipples out of the Page Three girls."

"What?" I'm shifting Emily into the crook of my shoulder while trying to catch what he's saying.

"Yeah, one day I'll tell you what I did with them. Take care, sis."

"Bye Billy, I'll be in touch."

When Jackie and Henry arrive home just before midnight, I am flat on my back on the sofa, fast asleep, with Emily sprawled chin down on my chest. I don't hear them come into the living room.

"Fucking Hell, Catriona, she'll fall on the floor!"

Her screech is like one of those alarm clocks with a huge clanking bell, slamming into the depths of my slumber.

"What the ..." I scowl at her as I come to, my arms reaching around Emily. "She's absolutely fine Jacks."

"You could have smothered her. You should never fall asleep with a baby in your arms." She shrieks at me again, her own arms flailing.

I gawp at her and snap, "Is the cab waiting?"

"Yes," Henry says, his hopeful look now one of scorn, although I can tell that he too is grappling to understand the gravity of my negligence.

I peel a very sweaty, still sleeping baby from me, hand her, with a pang of loss, to my best friend, get to my feet and take my handbag from the floor. Without a word I leave their house and head down the stone steps for the black cab waiting.

17

A fortnight later I'm kneeling on our window seat scouring the street below, for another taxi, which is late. It's 7.20am and we need to be at the Knightsbridge in ten minutes for my egg collection.

"Where the hell is it, Dom?"

"I'll call them."

He picks up the phone and shrugs at me when it rings out, as if he can't fathom what to do next. For a moment we stare at each other. His face is blank but I'm fighting back a scowl at his apathy today, which is beginning to incense me.

"We'll just have to get one in the street." I reach for my bag, packed once again with its dressing gown, slippers and the novel I always think I'll be relaxed enough to read before the op, but never do. "Effing tube strike."

Dom sniffs and takes the bag from me, his contribution to the crisis, tucking a packet of tissues into the side pocket; thus far I've refused to comment on the cold he picked up on the plane. He flew in from Japan last night, cutting it very fine as I've pointed out several times. If he'd been delayed we have no frozen sperm for a backup.

"They always make you wait anyway," he says.

"I'm first on the list, if we're late I'll lose my place." Why do I still have to spell it out to him that I want to get it over with?

It's drizzling. On Gloucester Road, every black cab sweeps by, full and contented, but I step out into the road to wave down an unlit one and it swerves around me, its driver tapping his head at my demented action. We walk down to Cromwell Road where the bus queues are five deep. At the sight of so much humanity and traffic I clench my fist, digging a row of nails into my palm, furious for lending Billy the car while his van's in the garage.

"Shall we just walk there then?" Dom asks.

"I've got ten tennis balls hanging off my ovaries, my tits feel as if they're squashed in a vice, and you want me to walk a whole mile?"

I slink down to the kerb. Dom sniffs yet again, in a bid to be my co-victim, and lingers over me before finally becoming decisive and stepping out to flag down a Volvo. He reels out the histrionics about needing to get me to hospital, and the woman driver tells us to hop in, so I push myself up, hampered by the congestion of those tennis balls, and give her a weak smile.

I have missed my slot, and I blame Dom. I even make him trot off and have a wank in that stinky room to produce the sperm sample, I'm damned if I'm going to give him a blow job this morning. Finally, in theatre, I sink, for the fourth time in my life, under the scene of that euphoric dancing couple amidst their lush garden and their overripe moon, into a sweet and heavy false slumber.

In the early afternoon, I am back in the room feigning a prolonged sleep, while Dom is clocking share prices on a mute Bloomsberg, when Olu arrives to announce how we've fared at this hurdle.

"Good news, Cat, we can use all ten eggs."

"Fantastic."

I relax back into the pillows, taking an image of Olu's face with me as I close my eyes again. I've been researching his country, his culture, on the web and I've discovered that Olu is short for Oluwa, which means God. If anybody can help me procreate, it is he.

"The sperm sample was not of its usual volume though, Dom?"

166

My eyes flick open and I see Dom frown at Olu, but there is also a smudge of a blush on those pasty fatigued cheeks of his.

"You are quite sure that you have not ejaculated within the last three days? I know that you have been in a different time zone."

"No." Dom shrugs. "Must be the jet lag, I guess."

I glare at him. He's been wanking to Japanese porn. "Can you extract some decent sperm from it though, Olu?"

"We will try our best." Olu nods and with the kindest of smiles for me he leaves the room.

Once the door is shut I rip into my husband. "You tosser, Dom. Literally!"

"It's not my fault, I'm just knackered."

"Spring was supposed to be our best chance, it's Easter!"

He eyes me as if I'm mad. "You don't believe that superstitious crap, do you?"

"I believe in giving it my best shot. Have you any idea what I've had to go through again this month? That's my *fourth* general anaesthetic now. Some people don't even wake up from those, you know. And you go and destroy our chances by tossing off to bloody Geisha girls or whatever."

"I didn't Cat, it's just the jet lag. And I've got a cold."

"Oh, poor baby, why don't I give a shit?"

It's the first time ever that I've been vicious to my husband, and he gazes at me in despair. "Cat –"

"Just shut up and let me sleep." I roll over, allow the pain in my lower belly to overwhelm me and sink back into the pillows.

When I awake, Dom has been careful to ensure there is a minicab downstairs to take me home.

*

Thirteen fraught days later, followed by as many troubled nights, I am one day away from knowing if it's worked. But right now I'm sitting in Ash's office with Stewart, buried deep in my luxurious parallel world of escapism. A Minister's office is just what you'd expect it to be: wood panelling, a lavish chandelier, and muted lighting from a green glass shade sitting on the tooled oak desk. There are wall-to-wall books too, embossed with titles such as, *A History of Agrarian Reform*, but behind his head Ash has also laid out a few on fencing, to illustrate that his interests stretch beyond his new remit. As a Junior Minister for Food, Ash now has responsibility for the powerful Food Standards Agency, and Stewart has finally decided to request a meeting. My client has never deemed him useful before.

Stewart speaks first – he always chairs, whether he's hosting the meeting or not. "Congratulations Ashley, for once they've promoted a winner and, I suspect also for once, purely on merit."

Both Ash and I know that, despite the broad smile, Stewart's praise has emerged through gritted teeth. I observe him, eyes flicked to the side; today he is stiff, stripped of his usual Dinwoodie panache. He recently joined the Fortune Top 100 and the trademark tartan tie is now sported in an array of designs – this afternoon a fluorescent lime and fuchsia. Still single, he's linked with all manner of partners in the Sunday papers, some of whom I've met during his annual Christmas shindig at the castle on Loch Lomond.

"Thank you, Stewart, what can I do for you?" The voice is rich, but as Ash speaks he checks his watch, rucking his sleeve back to take measured stock.

Across the desk from him, I find myself suppressing a shocked smirk. To compose myself, I glance briefly behind me at his American researcher, who sits motionless in the corner, fixated on her notes, her lithe legs crossed at the knee.

168

Beside me, Stewart ratchets himself into steely mode, one tawny pitted cheek sucked in, his crow's feet flinching in a momentary frown. "Part courtesy call, Ashley, but I do have something pressing on my mind."

"Jolly good." Ash's false smile embraces both of us and, with a frown of my own then, I hand him the file I've prepared. Emblazoned on its cover is a symbol of traffic lights scored through with a heavy cross.

He scowls back at me, adding his cheeky boy glint to the mix; clearly he wants to have some fun with this man now that he has the upper hand. I continue my rebuke with a matronly scold that says, don't screw it up for me. And in response, Ash does something he hasn't done for thirteen years, not since we shared an office in Brussels, not since Dom walked back into my life. He slides the very tip of his tongue between his lips; the signal he used to send me from his desk, when he was up for a lunchtime roll in the hay. An instant flush hits my cheeks and my eyes drop to my own file, from which balls of green, amber and red jump up at me.

Meanwhile, Stewart has clearly been gathering his thoughts and decided to maintain what is patently a painful expression of bonhomie. "We go back a long way, Ashley, so I'll come to my point."

I sneak a peek at my client. Yes, a long way with no actual contact other than the odd snipe.

"You will know that the FSA is press-ganging our industry into adopting the traffic light labelling system – red, amber and green, to show levels of fat, salt and sugar in foodstuffs?"

When Ash nods smugly even I want to punch him on the nose.

"I'm hoping that you will agree, Minister, that the system is overly simplistic?"

Ash flicks his fingers dismissively. "Couldn't be clearer, in my view. You're standing in the supermarket aisle in front of the ready meals and you're faced with two options, you look at the coloured labels, you make your choice. Genius really."

I watch Stewart taking in the fingers, now splayed flippantly in mid-air, before he tries again. "A man of your intellect will agree, however, that you cannot simply tag food as unhealthy – or bad – by slapping a great red blob on it. The consumer is canny enough to understand the more sophisticated labelling system of GDA – Guideline Daily Amounts."

"No, no, I'm not sure that they are, you know."

Ash now makes a pyramid of his fingers and presses it to his lips, apparently off on his own train of thought. It's down to me to speak up and my voice rings confidently as I tap my file.

"We have the figures, it's all in here. 70% of the population understand GDA labelling."

"So 30% don't." Ash shrugs, his eyes locked on Stewart's. "And those 30% are the ones who most need the guidance. As Minister, I have my finger on the pulse of the consumer. People want to feel in control and this traffic light system allows them to be just that."

"Come, come, Minister, surely you credit your minions with more intelligence?" Stewart attempts to lock horns like some stag on his estate, beads of sweat now clinging to his forehead.

"Maybe you'd rather hide the high levels of junk, is that the real issue here, Stewart? Conceal all that salt and sugar in your Dinky Dinwoodie meals for one?"

My gaze has dropped to my feet, out of shame for my client, but I lift my head to interject again. "Ashley, we're not playing games here, this is serious stuff."

But Stewart knows full well that it is a game, that he is a rubber ball being pawed around the carpet by a tomcat. He pulls out his best Glaswegian and rises to leave, his cheeks now as puce as his tie. "We dunna sell deep fried Mars Bars by the way, Mr Minister. Thank you for your time, I'll raise it with the PM when next we dine."

You get the impression he means the issue of Ash as well as food labelling.

"Ach, have you not got a wee beastie anecdote for me today, Stewart? I was rather looking forward to it." Ash, always an excellent mimic, has his accent spot-on.

As Stewart makes for the door, I'm on my feet too, with a conspiratorial smile at my most lucrative client to reassure him that I'll deal with Ash and meet up with him outside. Meanwhile, Ash's young American casts a half smile at her boss while she escorts Stewart from the office. She knows that MPs detest being lobbied and has enjoyed this spectacle, believing it clever, rather than the childish skit it has been. Stewart's outraged back disappears and the door clunks shut with all the heavy history it can muster.

"Thanks Ash, that was stupidly puerile!" I glare at him. He shrugs back at me, still giddy with delight "Finger on the pulse, indeed. And since when have you ever said 'jolly good'? You're from Vauxhall."

"Oh, he's always been a wanker, Cat." Ash stands from behind his desk and makes for the window, looks up at the sky.

I continue to harangue his back. "Have you been waiting all these years for a superior moment? Well I hope it feels sweet, because now I'm going to have to grovel. It'll take me months to pull back from this."

"Rubbish. It was me that just shat on him, not you."

I continue to glower at him, even though behind my incredulity I'm struggling to contain another smirk at the scene I've just witnessed and – let's face it – at the humiliation of Stewart by my good friend.

Turning from the window, Ash instantly perceives the chink and his face softens playfully. "You're right, I should have thought. I'm sorry, Cat."

He leans back against the sill with his arms folded. That chestnut hair now peppered with grey frames a face which has aged but still oozes sex and mischief.

"I'll make it up to you. Let Stewie stew a while and come for a drink with me in the Strangers? I could murder a whisky, spent the morning skipping round a bloody maypole."

I'm tempted by the idea of remaining in his world, but I maintain my stern appraisal. "Oh so you know how to skip then, do you?"

He performs a comical hop and shuffle. "County shows kick off at the weekend too. Bulls snorting for rosettes. Bollocks bigger than mine."

I allow him a slow shake of my head. "Men. You never grow up do you? You're still that flopsy-mopsy kid I once knew in Brussels."

"Wish I was, Cat, wish I was."

As I bend for my briefcase, I let out a mock cry of frustration, unwilling to let him see my smiling face, and I leave the room with a dismissive wave over my shoulder.

Of course, Stewart has not waited for me, and once out of the building, my present engulfs me once again. I decide on a walk across Parliament Square, and meander between the statues of former grandees. Winston Churchill growls down at me, his bronze coat caught in a perpetual flap, and I wonder if his behaviour was ever infantile, if the gravitas of Parliamentarians was mythical even back in his day. What does it matter? Who cares whether they use traffic lights or percentages of daily allowance? If a contemporary of mine can make it to the pinnacle of government and still arse around in front of a captain of industry, then what does anything matter? For me, it was all once of such great magnitude, so of the essence; Cat the bright young thing swishing her pigskin briefcase through the lobbies of power. More like one-dimensional Cat blinkered by her career, I see that now, with a glance at the briefcase now trundling at my side.

A deep breath of the freshly mown grass brings me momentary comfort. I've always loved spring – I am a spring person. But then, as I stand and inhale deeply, I cannot help but take stock. Today is May Day. Tomorrow is the day my baby would have been born, if that first IVF cycle had worked way back last summer. Tomorrow is also when I'll test to see if the fourth cycle has got us there – even though I know it hasn't. From my vast tally of ten eggs, only three fertilised, thanks to Dom's substandard, sticky sperm, with its two heads and tails. Our embryos were of the poorest grade and there really is no hope – I even sank a couple of glasses of wine this lunchtime at the café in Tate Britain.

Back at my office, there's nobody on reception and the phone is ringing.

"Where is everybody?" I yell up the stairs of the sprawling townhouse.

Our latest receptionist scuttles out of the meeting room and back to her position. I toss her one of my finest dirty looks and climb the stairs to my office, barking at one of the new graduates emerging from it.

"Sorry Catriona, I needed a quiet desk to work from, didn't think you'd mind."

"Well I do!"

He has been at my top drawer, which stands open. Staring up at me is a double pregnancy test pack. These boxes pop up all over the place now, like lipsticks I leave around the house and forget about. My misery is such that I want to hurt myself badly, to really do some damage, so I remove a white strip from the box, stuff it up the sleeve of my jacket and head for the ladies.

Inside one of the cubicles, I pee on the plastic and place it behind me on the toilet cistern. Then I put the seat lid down and sink onto it, elbows on knees, cheeks in hands. Outside I can hear police sirens, the bustle of commuters, white van man swearing his way home through an open window. I wonder when Olu will let me try again, I know he's going to insist on a three-month gap this time, advising me to get myself some R&R, as he puts it.

The door to the ladies opens and I hear footsteps, two pairs of them, then shuffling and the smack of plastic make-up containers on the sink.

"She's such a bitch. I was only taking tea in to a meeting, I must have been gone two minutes, tops."

"Don't worry, we've all been on the receiving end. She used to be nice enough, but these days we call her Medusa." It's my secretary Ellie.

The receptionist giggles. "I've heard she's trying to get pregnant."

"Mm, supposed to be a secret though."

"They shouldn't let aggressive women like that have babies, should they?"

"Probably just needs a good shag." Ellie giggles now too.

"Up the arse! Give her some of her own medicine."

Amidst their laughter, their feet click clack across the tiles, the door squeaks open and then it flaps shut.

In the silence that follows, my world has stopped dead. I feel as if I'm perched on a mountaintop, deafened by the crashing noise of nothing against my ears, stung by the whip of static air on my cheeks. I had no idea. All those years Ellie's worked for me, I've bought her perfume at Christmas, taken her out for lunch on her birthdays. True, I have been ranting around the place recently, especially when I'm super stressed, but I thought she found that amusing. And I'm mortified too, because I remember a few months ago walking in on a conversation and catching the end of the Medusa thing – only I thought they were talking about a client. So I'm both resident bitch and laughing stock then.

A long while later I'm still sitting there, unable to comprehend how the world has shifted, when the door swings open again and I hear heels, different ones, entering the other cubicle. I get to my feet, rub beneath my eyes and smooth my skirt down before I unlock the door. I'm half way out of the cubicle before I remember the test stick.

174

And when I turn to reach for it, my world shifts again. I'm pregnant.

18

I am with child. The joys of motherhood are within reach. Humming softly, I pad through the house, find myself in the nursery, currently our junk room, and linger there over colour charts of rose mallow and summer lichen. I moon around the kitchen, swaying to the foetal-developing piano concertos of Chopin, nourishing myself with fruit-crammed smoothies, gazing at online furniture of powdered ivory. Filling my soul with what lies ahead. At the newsagents, I pluck a pregnancy magazine off the shelf and lay it smugly on the counter, glowing at Mr Patel. Some years ago I helped his daughter with her personal statement for uni and I'm already a favourite, but today he clocks the cover and breaks into that munificent beam, the one he reserves for the important women of this world: the mothers-to-be.

"Your husband must be a happy man," he says.

Indeed. My husband flew through the door on Tuesday evening and swept me up in the air, whooping, "Who said Dominic Wyatt shoots blanks, eh?"

I thought that odd as a first reaction but basked in his joy. We stayed close with excitement for the rest of the evening, nudging and holding.

"It'll be due just before Christmas, won't it?" Dom said.

I nodded. "I can't believe it. I have to keep pinching myself."

"Always knew we'd get there, mind. You clever girl."

"All those months of trying though, it feels unreal that it's worked."

I stood naked for us at the cheval mirror, breasts and tummy held in a Demi Moore pose, even if my stomach is still flat.

"Delectable." His eyes shone as he took the photo.

"Delectable," I echoed.

Life has finally given us a break. Serendipitously, it's coincided with our tenth wedding anniversary next week, which I feel is a nicely rounded achievement for my mind to slot away. We'll come to view the last eighteen months as a glitch, a blip against the lifelong backdrop of marriage. We've decided to throw a party, and most of our friends are coming over, though I haven't announced our news, as the books say you're supposed to wait until the first twelve weeks are up. Both Jackie and Billy have emphasised this too.

I did even consider calling Lizzie. A postcard arrived from her last week, one of those freebies, with a naked couple running away from camera through a golden field of wild flowers, their bums glowing against the rape and cowslips.

Dear Catriona, I feel you are angry with me. Please don't be, anger is a negative energy. I hope you can find it in your heart to call me. I would like us to be friends. Love from Mum x

The card is in my knicker drawer, but I've decided not to call yet.

It's Saturday afternoon, and I'm with Jackie on the fifth floor at Harvey Nicks, tucking into stuffed tomatoes on linguine pasta and surrounded by stiff bags of baby clothes for Emily. Henry is at the football and Emily's now finally asleep beside us, though Jackie jumps each time a waiter sweeps past the table in case he nudges the buggy. When we arrived, two women were smoking at the adjoining table, so I turned my best scowl on them, informed them I

177

was pregnant, and they each stared pointedly at my stomach, before deciding not to take me on. One of them stubbed her cigarette out too softly though, and a whirl of smoke is now rising in my direction, so I reach over to their table and grind the cigarette into the ashtray. It'll be banned soon anyway.

When I called Jackie to tell her my news, she did apologise on the phone, for what she termed, 'Henry's behaviour' that night. I didn't press her to include herself, because my present benevolence embraces all of mankind. In fact I insisted that it didn't matter a jot, it was all forgotten, I was ecstatic.

Today, however, she has annoyed me with her lack of curiosity about my pregnant state, and now that her daughter's asleep, I'm hoping she will show some interest, allow me to hold forth about how I feel. But we're barely half way through our meal, and have hardly even begun on her news, when Emily wakes up again. Sixteen hours a day, that's what the book says they sleep in their first year, but this one has been out for half an hour at most all morning.

In a single sweeping movement, Jackie pushes her plate away and reaches for Emily and a bottle of milk from her bag, which she then waggles at a waiter. When he brings it back heated, my friend manages to contort body, arms and head so she can feed Emily on her lap and also eat. One wrist is curled, while the other hand saws at the tomato skin and linguine with the edge of her fork. She reminds me of a circus act.

"I've joined the birthing class, like you said to do," I say.

"Already? How far are you again?"

"Nearly six weeks. You said they get full."

"Aye, they do." She nods, shovelling food down with hasty glances at the bottle.

I decide to finish eating in silence, and survey the restaurant, taking in the slender bodies, the bobbing heads in full chatter, aware of my special status among these women. My breasts are still a-buzzing, though luckily I've not yet felt queasy at all. Plate empty, I push it away and begin rummaging through my bags to savour the one pregnancy purchase I've allowed myself. A black maternity sweater, which I hold up against me. In the shop, the woman had given me a bump-shaped cushion to stuff up the jumper, and I looked ginormous, as wide as I am tall, like one of the Seven Dwarves – Happy, judging by my grin in the mirror.

"What do you think? Natural mother-to-be?" I ask now.

"You're going to make a brilliant mother, Cat." She juggles Emily over her shoulder to wind her. "Come on wee girl, give mummy a burp."

When she reaches behind for a soft toy from her bag, her chair leans back at such a precarious angle that I fear she might even pull off a backwards somersault, while Emily clings on like a baby koala.

"Have you decided how long you're going to take off?" she asks.

"At least three months. Hopefully I'll have the baby in a routine by then, onto the bottle, sleeping through. The book says if they wake up then you shouldn't make eye contact, and you should never take them downstairs, that's –"

"Shall we snuggle down with bunny?" Her rudeness startles me, but she continues oblivious. "You can always ask me for advice, can't you?"

"Sure."

She is annoyed herself now, so again I delay talking about myself until she's finished fussing. "So how's it been back at work?" I ask

"Let's clip wee bunny onto your cardie." She prods Emily softly in the ribs. "Fantastic. I get to drink a whole cup of tea without it going cold."

"Have you got any new programme projects lined –"

"Somebody's got a smelly bum-bum haven't we?"

A sudden fury hits me. It's been like this all morning, she can't finish a sentence, every shop we've been in, and now here, it's as if she's mocking me.

"Jackie do you think we could manage five minutes of conversation without you having to coo at Emily?"

"I'm awful sorry, Cat." She throws me a sarcastic look.

"She's happy, just leave her be."

"You wait on." As my friend pauses, Emily receives a soft jab on the nose from bunny, and then Jackie turns on me. "You're in for a shock you know, it's tough. I was at home with Emily for months, did you not think to come and visit me? At weekends? After work?"

I gaze at her. I hadn't. Jackie was simply out of circulation, as if struck down ill – well that and my inability to be anywhere near her baby. Often I'd called her from work to entice her out for a drink up in town, but that hadn't ever come off, and I was beginning to think I was losing her as a friend, that she'd ridden off into the sunset of babydom.

"Have you any idea how boring it is for an intelligent woman to be at home with a baby all day? How mind numbing? You cannot even finish a *thought* without it being interrupted."

With a mute shake of my head I concede that I haven't.

She hurtles on. "I'll tell you what it's like. Imagine, you're sitting at your desk, working through some new idea, something that grips you, sucks you in it's so fabulously creative. While standing beside you, some idiot is spouting incessant nonsense at you, jabbing your arm with a finger to get your attention, constantly, jab, jab, jab, so that you can't even begin to think straight. And it's not as if you can shake them off 'cos that's not allowed, that's not in the rules."

While she pauses for breath, joggling Emily wildly on her knee, I gawp at my friend. The women at the next table have also stopped chattering and turned to size her up.

180

"Do you know what you do? You give up trying to think, you sink into a mindless state, where you simply jerk in reflex every time she needs something of you ..."

Jackie waits for my reaction, but I am unable to respond. Surely she can control her baby better, this doesn't seem normal at all.

"And do you know what it's like not to sleep for more than three hours at a time? You're so dog tired, so dead to the world, and then CRASH!" Around us a sudden silence falls, apparently spurring her on to repeat herself. "Crash! You're bolt upright, because she's screaming. And that happens every single night. In the morning, you're so fatigued, it's like the worst jet lag ever, but you can't go to sleep, because she's there, and she needs you. Every moment of every day."

Stunned, I wait for more. Then, realising she's done, I fumble for a reaction that might sound reasonable. "Doesn't Henry get up at night to help?"

"Ach, he doesn't even hear her cry. It's a woman's job anyway, so he says." Jackie now glares at the women beside us until they wither and look away.

"Jacks, if I'd known."

"You could have asked, Cat." She juts her face up, eyes widening to bring the message home.

"Yes, you're right. I'm so, so sorry."

"You think my life is a ray of sunshine, because I've got a baby and you haven't. But do you know what? Sometimes it's hell. There I've said it, never thought I'd dare. And to cap it all, I've lost you. You weren't there, you simply were not there."

I stare at her. "Jacks, I-"

"You've become so self-obsessed, so caught up in this ... this mission, but you've no idea. So, do I really think you'll make a good mum? Well I'm not so sure, really I'm not."

Clutching Emily, she stands, gropes for her changing bag and strides off to the ladies. In her eyes there are tears –

181

in mine too, and I blink at the tablecloth, grappling to absorb all that she's thrown at me.

When she returns, I reach for Emily. "Here, let me take her, you have a pudding."

She smiles, but I can see that the smile is at me, not with me. "I'm sorry Cat, I didn't mean anything by that."

She hands Emily over to me and I jiggle the baby, scooping plate, cutlery and water glass away from the uncoordinated chubby hand which reaches out for them.

"No, I'm sorry. I can't believe I've been so selfish."

For several minutes she refuses all eye contact. When finally she allows me to look her in the eye, to try and reach her soul, to begin rebuilding our friendship, to restore the years of trust and empathy, I see that her eyes are dull, blunt even. And I'm well aware that this is not just sleep deprivation.

*

On Sunday evening, our living room is fragrant with flowers. Lilies and gerberas, peonies and lisianthus from friends and family, plus a hundred and twenty velvet red roses from Dom, one for each month of our marriage. Before our first guest has arrived we have a little dance to *Moondance*, pulling off a kind of salsa come waltz; we are neither of us accomplished.

"You sure you don't want to announce it?" he asks me.

"Nope. Tempting fate. The twelve weeks will soon be up, and then we can."

"Won't people know if you're not drinking?"

"I'll plant a glass somewhere and put my lips to it every so often."

"Ah, every eventuality covered."

As we kiss, the doorbell goes.

Soon our living room is a flurry of guests and I stand taking it in, inhale the heady scent of lilies and smile compassionately from one face to the next, imagining that my own must be bathed in a golden glow. Billy – life and soul in private but recluse in public – is hanging round the door, which offers him the prospect of a quick getaway. As I hand him another beer, he asks after my health again; tonight only he and his wife, Maggie, know that I'm pregnant, even though I'm dying to broadcast it.

"I'm euphoric, Billy. Can you believe I've finally got there?" My hand drifts across my belly.

He cups my cheek in his hand. "It was always going to happen, sis."

I take the hand and kiss the rough palm, before turning to make for Maggie, who I can see is boring my old boss Geoffrey. Topping up their glasses (we have caterers, but I like to have a prop) I listen to her drumming home her mantra on the evils of sweet machines in schools – as if the Great White Chief will help get them banned because he was at school with the Education Secretary.

At the front end of the living room, which looks out over the Japanese cherry blossoms now creating a fluffy pink shagpile in our street, Dom and a posse of his banking mates are rowdily holding up the mantelpiece. The house is crammed with Dom's friends – on the sofas the cricket contingent, by the table the hockey mob. My friends are also mainly clients, or work related in some way; Jackie cried off, claiming Emily is teething, as I knew she would. I mingle amongst them all, enjoying the banter, winking at Dom as I reach for my glass on the mantelpiece and wet my lips.

On the window seat my niece, Daisy, sits listening in to the buddy-buddy jokes. She has hoisted her knees up to her chin and, even though she's tucked her skirt in beneath her, I bet I'm not the only one who can see her knickers. Maggie is still enraptured by Geoffrey, though he himself is snatching blatant looks over her shoulder. At the door, Billy sports the benign smile of the uncomfortable and I make my way back over to him, topping up glasses as I move.

"Have you seen your daughter over there, Billy?"

183

He follows my gesture. "Yeah?"

"Well, should she be sitting like that?"

"She's just a kid." He shrugs.

I observe my brother, leaning casually against the doorframe with one hand around his beer, the other in his pocket, then I turn to study Daisy again. Now highlighted, her long hair caresses her shoulders, while the tip of her thumb is lodged in her mouth as she listens to the anecdotes of Dom's friends. Fourteen going on twenty, I'd say, and I wonder if Billy knows that she's now on boyfriend number three. I've had the usual text from her – with photo – and I've responded, as usual, something along the lines of, *Treat 'em mean, keep 'em keen*. Tonight she showed up with a love-bite below her collarbone, which shocked even me when I was granted a furtive peek. My pregnant state has rendered me particularly protective towards her. I beckon her over to help me prepare the champagne toast. Knowing I'll let her have a sip, she slips her legs to the floor and strides like a model across the parquet towards me.

"Enjoying yourself?" I lead her out into the hallway.

"Very much." She has an adult air about her tonight. "Hope my future husband will love me as much as Dom does you, he's all soft and gooey tonight."

She's right. Dom traipses out into the hallway and scoops me up into a kiss. "Ready?"

"Absolutely." I'm suddenly exhausted – or perhaps it's just that I believe I should be at this stage in my gestation.

When he gathers people together to make his speech, I lean lightly against my husband and watch him, chin tilted like an Oscar winner's wife. His timing and humour are perfection, he's so alive, so vital again.

He closes with a tribute to me. "Cat, my beautiful wife and best friend, has been the source of my every happiness over the past ten years."

184

Mock groans resound and his best mate Ben heckles. "Apart from beer, hockey, cricket, beer, Leeds United, and beer!"

Dom has factored in the required pause for this barracking. "Well maybe not every single one ..." As if he has just won that Oscar, he slides an arm around my waist and kisses my temple. "She's my soul mate. Has been since I came across her eating silkworms all those years ago in Vietnam, and tonight we both of us know that the best is still to come."

19

On the following Friday morning, we cross at the lights on the Cromwell Road, hand in hand. We've decided to walk to the clinic for our first scan and the day is bright and clear, the cobalt sky picking out the bricks of the Natural History Museum where the birds are flitting between the trees. Even the traffic horns seem less discordant.

"What if it's twins?" he asks me.

"Perfect, ready-made family." I squeeze his hand.

"Triplets?"

"Can't be, they only put two embryos in."

"One could have split."

"Hmm, not sure I could cope with three."

An article I've read, on something called selective reduction, flits through my mind. It's where they abort one embryo by inserting a needle, directly into its heart if possible, and inject a toxin to kill it, leaving the other – or others – intact. The very idea of this is horrific, barbaric even. But still, I wouldn't want more than two.

"Won't be triplets." I am decisive in my response.

In the waiting room, I can't help but feel superior to the other couples and I actually make eye contact with some of them, even smile at one woman, before her eyes drop from mine. Maybe, it's that I want to tell them, 'We did it, you can too.' Or maybe it is just a smug, 'We won't be seeing you again in a hurry.' It's a self-centred game. I feel as if I've climbed out of an enormous stainless steel pot, which is seething with infertile people, all of them either unable to find purchase on the polished sides, or else scrabbling up bodies to reach the brim, before tumbling back down.

186

While still in it, you feign happiness for people who tell you they've got there, but really you're cross that one more has escaped from the pot, leaving you still floundering.

The sonographer calls us in, and I'm naked from the waist down before she's even locked the door. I climb onto the bed, while Dom, in his charcoal suit and crisp blue shirt, sits down beside it, folds my trousers across his knee and clasps my lace knickers.

"How are you Catriona?" she asks.

"Fine, breasts really sore." I smile at her and cup them with a grimace. I've come to really like this woman with her brisk efficiency and, now we're much higher up the food chain, she has told us her name is Ros.

Smiling back at me, she slips a sheath over the probe, smothers it with jelly and slips it inside me.

"Right let's see. OK … There is just one foetal sac, so it's not twins." She points to the tiny white blob amidst the grey fuzz on the screen, and Dom and I throw each other a soppy smile.

And then she is silent.

"How far are you Catriona?" Ros turns to scan her notes as she asks me.

"Six weeks and two days." Our three voices ring out in harmony, and then Ros falls silent. I turn my eyes on hers. They are fixed in fierce concentration on the screen, while beside me Dom takes my hand and grips it.

Finally, she speaks. "I'm so sorry, I'm afraid I can't see a foetal heartbeat."

The black iron mass has dropped in front of me with such an ear-splitting crash that I know instantly it is impenetrable. Still I persist.

"Sorry?"

"I'm afraid there's no heartbeat, Catriona."

"But surely it's too early for the heart to have formed, I only found out I was pregnant two weeks ago."

She shakes her head, and I can see that there's no point, that she knows her science, but I have to pursue her. "Can we just keep looking for a while?"

"Yes, we'll give it a little longer."

Her eyes remain glued to the screen, as do Dom's and mine. Within the tiny blob there should be a solid flickering dot, if you blink you could miss it, so I don't. She waits for what must be a full five minutes. When she has given us enough time to absorb the news, she clicks at buttons and plots two Xs on the screen.

Then she says gently, "It's not good Catriona. The foetal pole is just two millimetres long, it should be three times that by now."

Foetal pole. What a sterile, technical term for a baby. My baby.

They take me out of that room sobbing like a widow at a funeral, with Dom having to support me as my legs are giving way. And for some bizarre reason, I glance again at the couples in the waiting room. Every single one of them raises their head and makes eye contact with me, to scrutinise the misery they are so desperately hoping to avoid themselves. The woman I smiled at just fifteen minutes earlier locks her frightened eyes onto mine, trying to gauge the level of horror. Then the tears blur my focus and she's gone.

*

That was a month ago, one excruciating month ago. It was tough coming back to the Knightsbridge today, but I was ready for the counselling they offered me, and it's on a different floor, so I don't have to face everybody.

I suppose it's unusual to have reached the age of thirty-nine and not to have experienced grief. Both my dad's parents died before I was born, and on my mother's side they went when I was young, but in childhood dying was something grannies and granddads did. I heard once of an

188

old university friend who had been killed in a car crash, a few years back, but I decided against writing a card to her parents and never dwelt on it. Now though it's been on my mind, and I wish I had taken that trouble, to offer words of comfort, I bet they needed every single one to get them through.

A year ago I would have scoffed at the idea of counselling; it was the new salsa, everybody with no partner and too much time on their hands dabbled in it. But over the past year I have been humbled. Humbled by a realisation that in my life I control nothing that has any worth. Humbled by the misguided self-importance of my career. And now I'm humbled by my grief.

I can't talk to Dom. He doesn't seem affected by it, and I wonder if, for a man, perhaps it only kicks in when you see a scan of a baby *shaped* like a baby, or maybe even only when you put your hand on your partner's belly and feel it kick for the first time. Oh, he asks me how I am, he's very attentive with cups of tea, glasses of wine, he's even tucked me up in bed at night a few times. But he won't talk about it, he just skates around me offering niceties, like chocolate biscuits, when an intravenous drip is what I need. I know that he's not gone through the same physical experience as me, it wasn't inside him and he doesn't feel the loss the way I do, but surely he should be sad? Because it was his baby too. I even heard him laughing on the phone with Ben the other night. Laughing, what's that all about?

I enter the room, lilac as ever, and introduce myself to the counsellor. With a gentle smile she bows her head and points to the sofa, offering me coffee, her large blue eyes looming behind frameless glasses to assess me and my case. After I'm settled in, and she's allowed me to absorb the room, with its box of tissues on the table by my side, she begins.

"How do you feel in yourself, physically, Catriona? After the D&C?"

189

The D&C, that was another thing. The dilette and curettage, in French so dainty, but on the invoice so grotesque: The Evacuation of Reproductive Contents. Dom did come with me for the operation, though he didn't hang around. He was there waiting when I was wheeled back after surgery, and he held my hand as I slid back into the relief of slumber. But when I came to properly he had left the room. On waking, my body folded itself in two, to protect the place deep inside me where my baby had nestled until they'd removed it from me, and I needed him more at that moment than any other. For me, it was imperative that we say a final goodbye to our baby, together, but I was left alone facing the definitive end. He wasn't there, and I won't ever forget that.

I blink myself back to the present and the counsellor's question, and take a moment for my own analysis of her. Typical therapist, she has crinkly hair, she lingers too long on the sibilants, and if I wanted I could run circles round this woman, give smart responses to her probing, outdo her with superior intelligence. But I won't fight her, I've stopped fighting.

"I'm OK, thanks," I say softly.

"Good," the woman says, "And how are you feeling emotionally?"

Where to start? Bereaved. Empty. Dead.

An unexpected sob leaves my chest. "I can't believe she's gone."

"She?" Her voice is extra gentle, but the 'sh' grates.

"I was sure she was a girl, we had a name for her – Helena. I keep thinking, if only I'd stopped work, if only I'd lain down more, I could have held onto her."

She is shaking her head. "It wasn't your fault, Catriona. One in four pregnancies end in miscarriage. And half of all early miscarriages occur because of chromosomal abnormalities, so it was most likely genetic."

Her words slip past my skull without absorption. I am thinking back to our party, to Maggie's look of disapproval

190

when I raised my champagne glass during Dom's speech. I did take a sip or two.

"I had a drink too, at a party."

She shakes her head again. "Many women don't even know they are pregnant until five or six weeks, which is well after you found out, Catriona. They keep on drinking, smoking even, but healthy embryos can survive all manner of onslaught. Your baby was probably not developing normally, right from the outset. You must not blame yourself."

What is she blabbing on about? I scrunch a tissue, push it under my thigh into the wet mass already crammed there and reach for another one.

"I just feel so tired, I want to sleep all the time. Nothing matters."

"Those are all normal aspects of the grieving process, you have been through a harrowing experience. Time really is the great healer."

"And people, they're so insensitive, I don't know how many times I've been told how common miscarriage is. Is that supposed to comfort me? My husband's sister, she said to me, 'At least you know you can get pregnant now.' How fucking cruel is that?"

She doesn't balk at my language. "Does she know you were pregnant through IVF, rather than naturally?"

"No. No, but still …"

The woman nods a few times, nice and slowly, allowing me to process that thought, before she goes on. "Sometimes people don't know how to cope, they find another person's loss very difficult, they feel uncomfortable, helpless even."

I'm taken back to the death of my university friend and my cold, careless stance, the way I'd thought, well she had a sister so at least they still had one child. How could I have lived my life on such a shallow plane?

The counsellor goes on. "IVF and miscarriage are both distressing experiences, but when we suffer them together, our feelings can be overpowering."

191

We? Since when was she suffering with me? I wish she'd just let me talk.

"Even my best friend, even she said, 'Well at least it was an early miscarriage.'" I'd been stupefied by Jackie's reaction. She'd harped on about the size of the foetus, how it had hardly formed, was no larger than a grain of rice. As if that had anything to do with it. We haven't spoken since.

"It was your baby though, wasn't it?" The woman asks.

And now she's pierced me and I'm nodding, the tears freewheeling down my cheeks. "It was my *baby*."

It's funny how a toilet cubicle can take on a life of its own, how it becomes familiar to you – and familiar with you. I have visited the one in reception so many times now, each time in a differing state of emotion, and each time the room has had a different impact on me. As a new patient, still impervious to what lay ahead and eager to crack on, its aura was objective, simply clean and functional. Then I saw the first blood of a failed cycle there, and the room's walls, the lino floor, the door, they all rose up to me, engulfed in their own sadness. I've had a congratulatory pee there, after the blood test which confirmed this pregnancy, and at that point the cubicle encased me in a benign lilac glow. Today when I flush, the room is melancholic; it's a place which has come to symbolize my life.

I shuffle back out into reception to see Olu coming down the stairs, swinging one large hip after the other. He spots me and in a few strides is beside me, his face already sad and tender.

"How are you Cat?"

"OK."

"I am so sorry, my dear."

As I make for him, he lifts his arms stiffly, enfolds me gingerly and uncomfortably. I sink into the fresh linen of his pink shirt, comforted by the padded muscle of his chest, by his powdery smell. My shoulders relax and I push myself in further, feel myself letting go, as if he is draining toxins from me. Is this the start of my healing process? An overwhelming relief floods its way through me, a lightness of being – it is over, and we are free to try again. Fertility is considered a gift from the Gods, I tell myself silently, and Olu means God. This man is my miracle-maker and he will know instinctively how to move forwards.

Finally, hands on my shoulders, he pushes me gently away and stands back a little. "Cat, there are positives we can take from this. The fact that you have been pregnant is a good thing, it means that your chances are now slightly higher than those of a woman who has never before conceived."

"I need to try again, Olu."

"You must wait. At least two months, give yourself three. Take a holiday, you must allow yourself to become completely relaxed. And when you are feeling strong again, then come back and see me. Are we agreed?" His eyeballs are large, bulbous even in their sockets, his forehead furrowed while he aims to bring his message home.

I give him the weak nod he wants, and mutter, "OK."

Olu releases my shoulders and I feel his hands smoothing the bob of my hair, then I turn to leave the building. I'm so exhausted, I just need to go home and sleep.

"And Cat?" he calls after me, "take good care of Dom too."

At home, Dom has been out walking Silkie, and is cleaning her paws off in the boot room. I push open the door to the tiny space and, overwhelmed, I raise my arms to him, like a small child who's tripped over on the pavement. Silkie steps towards me, nuzzles my thigh, and Dom rights himself from his bending position, clasping the muddy cloth.

"Hey, what's all this?" He folds his arms around me, but there's no grip to his embrace. It's as if he's hugging a frail grandparent, and I know he's timing the moment until he can extricate himself.

"Dom, we need to talk about this."

"You just need a nice long bubble bath, come on I'll run you one." His hand strokes my back and I grip him to me tightly.

"I don't need a frigging bath, I need you back. All we do, every night, is search for some stupid innocuous subject, and talk politely about it."

Last night at dinner, it was our dog walker's holiday plans in Cornwall. Dom took me through a description of the Eden project – we had a whole discussion about how they grow bananas inside the domes and even market them.

Dom lets go of me and sits down on the bench. Fondling Silkie's ears, he refuses to look at me. "Do we need to be so morbid about it?"

"Morbid? We're grieving the loss of our child." He frowns up at me, apparently unable to grasp what I'm saying to him, and it strikes me. "You're in denial, aren't you?"

"No I'm not. I'm just really busy at work these days." He has coaxed Silkie to put her paws up onto his knees and is now roughhousing her, to delighted growls.

I stop for a moment, confused by his non sequitur of an answer. "Yes you are, you're in denial, it's the first stage of grief. Look, come to counselling with me."

He gives me one of his best derisory snorts. "No chance." He heaves Silkie down, stands up and tries to push past me, brushing against the coats on the wall, but I'm blocking the doorway. Finally he looks me in the eye.

"Look, I'm fine. There are far worse things happening out there, you know, men are *dying* in Afghanistan, blown to pieces, children are *dying* of hunger in Africa, my mum's best friend is *dying* of cancer. What's our little problem compared to all of that shit?"

He shoves me out the way and escapes the room, leaving me hearing myself pleading. "Dom, you can't just

194

bury what's happened, we have to get through this together."

I watch him take the stairs two at a time, and am left standing in our hallway while Silkie licks the salty tears from my fingers. Where do I possibly go from here? We've had blazing rows before, but we've always resolved them by sex – not that either of us feel like that anymore. And in any case, this is not a spat, this is a vacuum.

20

August is the hottest month to visit the Algarve, but my dad
has reminded me that he hasn't seen me since last spring,
and the chance to lose myself beside the pool at his villa
wins me over. Dom is head down at the office these days,
some Japanese mobile phone company has taken off big
time and he's riding a crest of investment. We've had the
odd weekend away with friends, but neither of us has
mentioned a holiday together as that would involve too
much time alone. There's not even a tension between us,
it's just that we move around each other, shadow dancing, I
sense his recent presence in an empty room, but our
encounters are rare, and any conversation perfunctory.

At Faro airport, I collect my hire car and head west
along the motorway, cutting through hills and plains baked
the red of builders' tea. Wire-like trees are dotted about, as
if they've all been scrunched into a Lego board and
produce nothing. The occasional white block sprouts from
the landscape, stark in the brilliance of the late morning
sunshine and, sweeping past in the fast lane, I wonder who
might live there. Dad has told me that when they first built
the motorways the peasants protested, took to the bridges
and pelted cars with fruit, or even stones. On the back
roads, he says, you might still find yourself stuck behind a
stubborn horse and cart, piled high and wide with melons or
carob sacks. And this is where my father has chosen to
carve out a life for himself, sixteen years of it now. It's
certainly a good place to convalesce.

I pull into the tennis club and park beneath a tamarind
tree, breathing in its herby scent. Strolling past the huddle

of clay courts, I hear the thwack of the ball, which sends a judder of anticipation through me; I haven't played for years now. Dad doesn't appear to be on court, so I continue on to the bar area. Hearing his voice I hang back to listen, fingering the papery orange drapes of bougainvillea.

"I missed the shot because there was a spider driving a soft-top Mercedes across the court and I was distracted." He's had a couple of beers – and he'll still play another set after lunch.

There's laughter from his friends, and somebody teases him. "Beats the sun in your eyes, Frank!"

Smiling, I emerge from my hiding place and make for where he is sitting: my dad, excellent tennis player and popular man who oils the wheels of expat life.

"Catriona! Princess, you're here." As he stands and hugs me to him, my cheek scuffs against the rough fabric of his white polo shirt and I catch the smell of fresh sweat, mingled with beer and peanuts.

I know all his friends well and greet them warmly, while Dad pulls a chair up beside him and presses me down into it. The large wooden table, shaded by an oversized green canopy, is scattered with empty beer glasses. A waitress arrives with a tray of full ones, the foam frothing over their edges. Beside me, a woman pushes hers my way, ordering another, and I sink it gratefully and begin to relax. Losing myself among these people comes easily, and they treat me – the visitor from home – with a semi reverence, as if they're trapped in a time warp. For a while, they'll insist they loathe London – the cold, the crime, pollution – but then they'll scrabble to learn about new theatre productions or restaurants. Dad throws me a knowing look while they list their memories and I smile back at him. I've told him it's like that game we used to play on the drive down to Dorset for his two-week stint each summer, Grandmother's Suitcase, or something. Dad could never remember the items in alphabetical order and I, who would have been about the age when I realised my father was not omniscient, would be excitedly prompting him from the back seat.

After lunch, he tells me to get my racket and I cock my head and grin at him.

"You have brought it haven't you?"

"Yes, but I've had at least four beers."

"Let's work it off then, come on, chop, chop." He smacks my bottom, sending me off to the car for my gear.

When I was doing my O Levels, I used to partner my dad at his club back in the UK, and we did get through to the finals of local tournaments a few times, even won a couple. So we take on husband and wife, Ron and Mavis, formerly of Sheffield, in the soporific afternoon haze.

I serve last, hoping to get into the flow of it, but my first ball drops beside me after I swipe and miss it, which gives me the giggles. I manage to get the next few serves in, even pick up some speed on some of them, while my dad is jumping sideways like a crab at the net.

"Chalk dust!" he shouts at one of his shots that's clearly inches out and Mavis wags a flirtatious finger at him.

When we're at 40-30, I serve a corker, it's come off the sweet spot of my racket and I feel sure it will land just within the service line, but instead it hits my dad at the net, smack on the back of his head, with the comical sound of rubber on skull.

"Oi!" As Dad pretends to see stars, and wobbles around the court like Charlie Chaplin, I drop my racket and double up in laughter, the slapstick moment surprising me with the welcome release, priming me for more.

Ron and Mavis take the first set, but we begin to find our past form and we're three-love up in the second set, when the collision happens. A ball is dropping in mid-court. My dad stumbles backwards for it and I rush forwards, both of us crying, "Mine!" We crash full on, trip over ankles and end up face down in the clay. Sniggering like kids, we lie there smothered in red earth.

"Always wondered what this stuff looks like close up." Dad peers into the ground.

And with that I find myself curled up like a jellybean against the cool, sandy surface, succumbing to an immense, lurching belly laugh. Each wave snatches at my stomach, producing heaves of laughter I haven't felt or heard from myself for months, probably even years. It renders me helpless, and it feels so good, so necessary.

After the game, we shower at the club, and I find myself still sniggering as I rinse out the red clay from my tennis whites, the silliness catching me again just as I've composed myself. Then, avoiding the main roads and potential police encounters, we drive in tandem back to Dad's old farmhouse in the hills. The surly pool attendant is just leaving and nods at us as he finishes winding up his apparatus. Dad plucks a lemon from a tree on the terrace and ambles inside to fix me a gin and tonic. Leaning against the railing, I look out over the land below. Here it's less barren, the earth is still baked but sprinkled with rows of lush citrus trees, there's even a river snaking through the distant valley.

He bounds out of the patio door. I turn and smile at him, my dad the big kid. He still looks so young, the hair which turned silver in his thirties remains thick and layered, and his body is fit – if now weathered to a hide. Behind his head the house looms, with its crumbling walls swathed in purple bougainvillea and crinkled terracotta tiles which tumble down the roof, tripping over one another to reach the edge first.

"Life's good then, Dad, is it?"

He reaches where I'm standing, kisses the side of my head. "Life's golden, princess. It will be for you too, you'll see. A whole week of nothing will recharge the old batteries, do wonders for you."

We clink our glasses and turn back to the view. The sun is setting in a red blur behind the hills. In the near distance, a stork sits on top of a redundant brick chimney in a nest

199

the size of a rubber dinghy. It's been there since he bought the place, it must be fifteen years now.

"Sorry about that blessed stork over there, Catriona." His voice is still infused with amusement, but of the gentler kind. "Tried to shift it, even went down there to light a fire, but she wouldn't budge, stubborn madam."

I have to smile, my dad has always taken an upbeat approach with me when I'm down, chivvying me along rather than letting me wallow. "It's OK Dad, live and let live, eh?"

He slides his slender arm around me and pulls me into him awkwardly. "I am really so sorry about your baby, Catriona."

"Yeah." I let myself sink into his chest. "I'll get there though, Dad."

Dad works in the afternoons, servicing the PCs of his regular clients every few months, plus any trouble-shooting. Mornings are fresher for swimming or tennis, and everyone has air con so afternoon work suits him. More to the point, he often ends up socialising with his clients over a sundowner by their pool. He's never remarried, but if it's a lonely life for him out here it doesn't show.

On the evenings I'm visiting, we receive several invitations to dinner, and also eat out, with someone or other from Dad's gang, in the handful of local restaurants where he is well known and warmly welcomed. They too are all on his client list, as are a heap of British companies with offices in the Algarve. On one evening, Dad entertains; he's a dab hand with the barbecue and packs me off with a shopping list of fresh prawns, sardines and sea bass. At the market, the salad vegetables are neither shiny nor well formed, clumps of dirt clinging to their skin, while the supermarket fish counter is smothered by frozen sheets of salted cod. It's a simple world, drifting somewhere in the past, and it's doing its job nicely on me.

While Dad's at work, I lie by the pool and read or laze to my iPod. Allowing the days to merge into one, I reach for another of Dad's crappy novels whenever I sense the danger of reflecting on my life. Over the course of the week I also sink into a state of sleeping sickness, waking late, only to be dragged down again by heavy paws of slumber padding over my head and shoulders. At night, Dad and I chat into the small hours, and as usual we discuss everything and nothing; jobs, family, next season's prospects for Wycombe Wanderers. It's like meeting up with a friend only twice a year, and having to catch up on the mundane before knuckling down to the nitty-gritty, except that, with Dad, we never make the nitty-gritty. I cannot recall a single profound conversation with my father, ever, and I'm happy to maintain the status quo on this visit.

On my last evening, we sit together on his terrace with a nightcap. We slaughtered Geoff and Betty at doubles earlier this evening and enjoyed dinner on them as our prize. Dad has gone inside to fetch the bottle of white port and I am staring into the turquoise pool. Lit from below, it's luring a horde of insects to their death, and it reminds me of when I first met Dom. When Dad comes back out, I know he will reach for the net and scoop the flies out, just as my husband did in Vietnam. With a rueful smile I think back to Dom's question on our wedding night. "Did you marry your dad?" Well the jury's still out on that one.

"It's been lovely having you here." My dad is by my side, kissing the top of my head as he puts the bottle down. Then he reaches for the net.

"I've had such a great time, Dad. Need to drop the booze again when I get home though, your expat livers must be shrivelled to walnuts." I'll have to turn my mind to many things when I get home, not just abstinence, I think, watching him run the net on its long pole smoothly through the water.

201

"What's next then, Cat?" He shakes the moths and flies out over the railing and lays the net down.

I shrug and turn my gaze over the black valley below, its feral dogs yapping and a motorbike whining against the white noise of cicadas.

"We go back in there, I suppose."

He nods, clinks his glass to mine. "To your success, kiddo."

I smile at him, saddened by a momentary melancholy that he's not going to dig deeper, and then I gesture to the oleander bush he's planted beside the pool, which in the daytime is a fabulous frosted pink with spiked grey-green leaves.

"Did you know oleander leaves are poisonous, Dad?"

"Really?"

"Deadly to children."

"Well then, princess, I'll have it chopped down for the next time you come." He performs a violent slice of his hand, lest the moment should linger.

*

On the Sunday I land back at Heathrow, Dom has a cricket match and although it's a home game often he doesn't finish till late, so I've pre-booked a cab. The nights are drawing in and I arrive home in darkness to see a light on in our bedroom. I dump my case in the hall and head upstairs, calling out Dom's name; I have missed my husband.

In the bedroom, Dom is kneeling on the floor beside my open wardrobe, his back to me. Surrounding him are a mass of open boxes spouting flurries of tissue paper, and dozens of carrier bags struggling to contain cellophane packets. I stand and gaze at the scene. Inside the packets are cot sheets, teated feeding bottles, miniature hooded towels, tiny vests, babygrows. Having taken it all in, I then look at Dom's back in horror. He waits until I have gauged the situation then turns to me, his eyes full of a pain I have

202

never seen before. Red and sore, they well up again as he speaks to me and I realise that I'm looking at grief.

"What were you thinking, Cat?"

Unable to respond, I glide to our bed and sink down onto it, my eyes fixed on his.

"There must be a hundred items of clothing here."

I shrug and feel my eyes prickle. "I just …"

"Pink … they're all pink."

He sounds bewildered, as if the colour of these tiny garments is the key. Then my husband's shoulders shudder and he begins to sob like a child. I drop from the bed to my knees and move across the floor to him, take him in my arms. He clasps me to him and I thread my legs around his middle, wrap my arms around him, clamping my body to him, providing maximum succour. We settle into the same position as in that shower the very first time we made love in Brussels, rocking gently.

Eventually, Dom opens his eyes and seeks out my lips with his own, his breath hot and salty as he pushes me back to the carpet. We haven't made love in such a long time. I would say it's been two years since it steadily became…well what exactly? A technical necessity? But our lovemaking tonight is not as before, it is not an expression of happiness, of seeking to give pleasure, to take pleasure, the one in the other. It's now infused with sadness and loss, a yearning for something that we are no longer able to give the other. We thrust our limbs, stretch our needy bodies, snuffle into each other, in desperate search of something neither of us possesses. At this moment, I know that it will never again be the joyous, frivolous love it once was, and I wonder if a marriage can be sustained on a union of misery rather than contentment.

Afterwards, we climb onto the bed, crawl under the duvet and lie on our backs, staring up at the shadows flitting across the ceiling.

"You should have told me, Dom, you seemed so … so blasé about it."

He lets out a soft snort. "I was supposed to be strong wasn't I? People only wanted to know how you were, nobody ever asked about me."

He's right, Olu was the only person to mention Dom. "I'm sorry, I should have realised."

We fall silent and I'm thinking about the last couple of months, absorbing the fact that he's been suffering so badly too, that he's been unable or unwilling to let me in.

"I felt so alone, Cat," he says eventually.

"You could have told me, though." I'm frowning despite myself. "I tried to reach out to you, but you shut me off."

"I know. I'm sorry, I guess it became too difficult even to talk to you about it."

"Even to me?"

"I just buried it."

"But I felt alone too, Dom, I felt you'd left me to it. I mean, I really needed you after the D&C, you know."

"Oh that." He blows his breath out. "That was dreadful, I couldn't bear to watch you. You were crying in your sleep, you know, actually weeping. I just had to get out of that room."

I turn my head. "I had no idea."

"I felt so useless."

I roll onto my side, kiss his temple and slide an arm and leg across his body. "We've both been silly, haven't we? We need to talk about this. Get it all out. We need to heal together, Dom."

He nods. "The fact that it was all my fault didn't help, either. I mean it's because of me that you had to go through that hell, isn't it?"

"Of course it wasn't your fault, Dom." My words are hollow; secretly I have always believed that Dom is the cause, haven't I?

"My sperm is shit."

Yes, I think, before I can stop myself. "Well we got pregnant with that sperm, didn't we?" Even if it did probably cause the miscarriage.

"True," he says blankly.

"Look we'll give it another month, let's get ourselves together, maybe grab a weekend in the country. And then we'll try again, yes?"

"No."

I've barely heard him but I feel the panic rising. "What?"

"I can't, Cat."

"What do you mean, you can't?"

"I can't go back in there again."

I stare at his head, unable to grasp why it's shaking in refusal, even if my subconscious twigs instantly.

Through the darkness I whisper to him, "Dom, we have to."

"I'm done."

"But we were so close this time."

"No more."

"But our chances are so much higher now, Olu said so. We can't just give up."

"I said I can't do it anymore. It's over."

He turns his head and looks at me, his eyes sad but unyielding, and a ripple of fear flurries through me; I've never witnessed such resolution in my husband. I lock eyes with him and I wonder if he can see that fear. But we have to, I urge silently, we *have* to.

21

In the weeks since that night, we have both become withdrawn, contemplative. I know that Dom needs time to work through his grief and come round and I'm giving him space. And yet I'm trying to fathom what that lovemaking, those words were all about and how I can bring him back on course for another stab at it. At the moment, there is a sorrow about us, an emptiness. It's so alien that we're ignoring it, and I can sense that he, like me, is hoping it will slip away from us, that with time the old Dom and Cat will win through. But who were the old Dom and Cat? We flitted through the years, with our healthy finances, our cushy jobs, our shared friends. And we laughed. Laughter was our essence, that quality of a relationship you mentally tick in a magazine quiz on marriage at the hairdressers, smug that the woman before you has penned in the answers and yet left that box blank.

Did we just assume then that we were good together because we glowed on the surface? Should we have spent more time on weighty discussion about our needs and wants? Were we shallow because we communicated only about which kennels to put Silkie in, about what shaped pasta we preferred, about whether to trade in the car? Surely, all relationships snuggle down into that kind of comfort, it doesn't mean they lack profundity, it's just that the important values that brought you together have long since been aired, resolved and then packed away. To ask Dom now what he feels about the big issues – family, honesty, politics – well it would be embarrassing, like a couple of gauche students finding their way. These values are intrinsic to him – to us. Maybe it's just that you accept what you dislike about each other, knuckle down to it, bury it, and move on – providing all is well with the world. But what rankles lives on, in fissures that hollow out beneath the surface, and any serious test will wheedle its way in, will undermine the structure and might even erode the foundations.

Most couples don't have to face this kind of trial; they have sex, they have a baby. If we could just get there soon, if say I was pregnant by this time next month, then we'd stuff our joy down into those fissures, plug our foundations again, and re-lay our surface. But I haven't yet dared mention another go at it, I need to wait it out.

*

On a Monday evening in mid-September, after another startling Indian summer's day, I return home from the office to the phone ringing. It is my mother, she's been arrested.

"I'm just around the corner from you, at Kensington Police Station." Her voice is small, not Lizzie-like at all.

"Why?" I roll out the flattest monotone I can muster.

"They've said if somebody comes to fetch me I can go."

"Why've you been arrested Lizzie?"

"It was a fur protest, London Fashion Week."

"Ah, back on animal rights are we?"

"Please, Catriona."

It's just before seven. Dom isn't home yet, lately either his work is burgeoning to fill the hours, or his expense account needs using up. I leave my mac on and head out to the police station a fifteen-minute walk away.

She sits on a bench in reception with two other women. I'm certainly not taking them home with me, they resemble the shabby lice-ridden specimens Lizzie used to shack up with for the weekend at Greenham Common. That was one of her more adventurous exploits to bring purpose to her life, we had photos of her with the protagonists up on the fridge at home. At least she waited until it was Dad's weekend before she hitched off there, give her some credit for not leaving us alone with old Norman Bates, I suppose.

Lizzie's face is pale, but the well-nourished skin is still luminous, she does look much younger than sixty-three. Before I make eye contact, I give her the once-over with careful deliberation, my head slowly taking in the plastic sandals on her pop-socked feet, sliding up past the polyester trousers, to the baggy T-shirt, which is topped by her walking jacket. Clearly this latest fad shuns all notion of natural fibres, cruelly produced or otherwise. Her hair is infuriating. A mass of electric wires spilling from a plug cable, the mere thought of dragging a comb through it stressful. When my eyes reach hers, I'm surprised to see them glued to mine, like a deer's, wide and static, preparing to dart if the hunter should as much as twitch. Only where would she flee to?

The policeman behind the desk throws me a sympathetic look, then aims a well-practised filthy one at Lizzie, and I realise that of course she is actually free to go, that she's wanted me to come to her. She reaches for her bag and peers back at her pals with an expression which says, 'Sorry, you can see how she is.' It's like a kid hoping her mum will let her school friend come home for tea, knowing that today she won't. The officer hands me a leaflet on crime prevention, as if he needs to formally hand her over, and I tuck it into my handbag then nod at the goods I am to collect. If she believes there is pathos in the scene it is lost on me.

She half trails me home, her diminutive form a semi-step behind my clipping heels. When we round the corner I see Dom at our front door. He turns and gives her a startled smile.

"Lizzie, how lovely to see you."

He waits for her to climb the steps to him then kisses her cheek – ever the well-brought up boy who is comfortable

208

with himself. Maybe that's why I married him, so some of it would rub off.

In the hall, I observe him while he hangs up her jacket and says, "You look like you need warming up." Did I hope some of that kindness would rub off too?

Without a single questioning glance at me, Dom shepherds Lizzie down to the kitchen. I follow them, cross that she's got away without the lecture I was rehearsing.

"Just had to fetch Lizzie from the police station." I make a show of unfolding the crime prevention leaflet beside the kettle.

Dom pours water into a mug and pointedly turns away, but I know he's got my drift; in more conspiratorial times we've joked about how she'll get herself arrested one day.

"You sit and drink this, Lizzie. You know what they say, a nice cup of tea can solve all your problems."

Does he mean the arrest, or me? I turn my back on them both, pour myself a hefty slug of wine from the fridge, and the nine-year-old in me slams the door shut. I try leaning casually across the island, my elbows at an awkward angle on its granite surface, while Lizzie tells Dom about her day.

"It was at the Natural History Museum," she begins. "We weren't doing anything really, only waving placards, it's just that these supermodels they have bodyguards, you know, big burly types."

Lizzie deepens her voice and puffs up her chest, with a brief glimpse at me. She often attempted humour to bring me round, maybe she saw how, as a small kid, I used to laugh with Dad and always wanted some of it for herself. I reward her with a blank stare and she takes a sip of her tea.

"Anyway, Maureen must have got in the way of one of them, he was built like a brick shithouse, as your Granddad would have said, Catriona."

Again the hopeful smile, again the silly humour, plying the same joke for Christ's sake. And still I stare her out.

She shrugs. "Maybe he thought she was going to attack one of the girls, but she's not exactly agile, Maureen. Well you saw her at the station didn't you, sweetheart?"

"So they locked you all up did they?" I ask.

"I had to go to her aid, didn't I? I mean, he had her in a half-nelson."

I notice Dom stifling a grin. In former times, I would have too – the thought of sixty-something, fifteen stone Maureen with her arm up her back.

"Well you're very welcome to recover from it all here, Lizzie. How about a lovely hot bath for starters?"

You'd think there was no guile to Dom the way he handles her, reeling out his cure-all remedy. But when she's gone upstairs, he scrapes his stool back and snarls at me. "Do you have to be such a cow to her?"

"She's stupid."

Dom grabs a bottle of beer from the fridge, snaps the top off and heads towards the stairs. "And you think you're ready to be a mother?" Barely muttered, but he fails to hold it in.

"What's that supposed to mean?"

"Grow up, Cat."

"Me grow up? *Me* grow up?"

He stops and turns to me with a placid stare. "Yes, you grow up."

I reel upstairs, shoving him out the way, grab my coat and slam the front door behind me. In a bar on Gloucester Road, I order a large glass of Sauvignon Blanc. I shouldn't be drinking at all again, but tonight I'm ready to do myself some damage. I climb onto a bar stool and stare blankly at the jollity around me. I've always considered myself grounded, so why can't I deal with her in an adult manner? It's as if, whenever she pops up in my life, some handle wrenches my innards, ratchets my gut round into puerile mode. The moment she's gone, it springs back, and I'm in control again, regretful even. I recall her frightened eyes at the police station, her recent attempts to call me, the postcard I've kept. Tonight she seems so meek, and Dom's right, I am behaving like a bitch. But still her behaviour doesn't square with the mother I've always known; the endless criticism while strapped into the straightjacket of childhood. This is a woman I've barely seen for over ten years, and it could be that she finally is contrite, that she wants to make amends. Still, deep down, I'm pretty sure it's just a ruse.

When I arrive home, I find Lizzie and Dom back in the kitchen tucking into a stir-fry, my mother all bundled up in Dom's towelling robe. Silkie lies at their feet, which smarts like a betrayal. Muttering that I've eaten, I pour myself yet another glass of wine and head back up to the living room, where I flop on the sofa, flick on the TV and hope to lose myself in dross.

Some time later, I hear Dom settle Silkie in her boot room bed and go upstairs. After a few moments Lizzie comes through. At first, tentative by the door, she then decides on the window seat and climbs up onto it, tucking her tiny feet beneath her. I take a fleeting glance up at her from the old sitcom I'm watching. In the oversized grey robe she looks like a furry dormouse, one which is clutching a glass of whisky. This does tweak me, despite myself; she's never been a drinker. From the corner of my eye I catch her taking in the expansive opulence of our living room, the marble mantelpieces and zebra ottoman. Naturally, it is me who has the power here, but she does seem smaller somehow, vulnerable almost. Is it age? Has she genuinely mellowed? Or is she just play-acting to bring me round so she can slink back into my life again?

Prepared for confrontation, I take a sip of my wine, press the mute button and study the silent actors while I wait for her to speak.

"Dom's told me about the miscarriage. I am sorry, Catriona."

On the screen, a guy in a velvet smoking jacket throws his head back in silent laughter and I feel the prickles behind my eyes. Christ, don't let her see you cry. At least she knows better than to cross the room and slip a comforting arm around me, although I guess my hackles must be pretty spiky.

She goes on. "You know, there are other things that would help you conceive."

"You mean sex, Lizzie? Yeah we tried that, funnily enough."

"No. No, I mean natural therapies."

"Oh, why don't I go and dance naked under a full moon on the chalk bollocks of the Cerne Abbas Giant?"

I snort my derision at her, something I have perfected from my husband, and her head dips to the side, recoiling at my vehemence. It occurs to me that Dom would never deploy this weapon on such a feeble target. I'm confused by this behaviour. She's even swept the hair back into a ponytail. Frail does not sit well on my mother, who once called me a bloody bitch when I was twelve years old for refusing to fetch Norman Bates a pack of cigarettes from the corner shop. That one still stings.

She opens her mouth to speak, and closes it again, so I leap into the gap. "Do they get you to preach natural therapies as part of your 'Ban IVF' campaign then?"

"No, I've stopped all that." She pauses. "I realised how important it was to … to some people. It's the only chance some couples have."

I resist the urge to snap that she could have clocked the bleeding obvious before she joined those interfering busybodies. Instead my mind trawls for some change of subject, for platitudes to take us swiftly through the evening and on to bed and oblivion. I consider enquiring about her camping holiday in Wales, which Billy has told me about. Then, well I don't intend to voice it, it hasn't even drifted through my thoughts this evening, but for the first time ever it's out.

"You didn't really want me, did you?"

"Of course I did, sweetheart." She's quick, I'll give her that.

"I got in the way didn't I?"

"That's not true, I cherished you. And Billy."

"Auntie Kate told me when I was thirteen. 'You weren't planned, you know, you were a mistake,' she said to me once, when you were out gallivanting. Well some auntie she was for telling me. They're supposed to be kind – the word auntie *means* kind to most kids – but she hated me, didn't she? I was the difficult child, the sullen one."

Lizzie watches me, a dangerous spark now in her eyes and I smile to myself; that's more like the woman I remember. She takes a slug of her whisky, her decision clearly made.

"No, it's true, you weren't planned. Things were already going downhill with your father, and I was only twenty-four years old, Catriona."

"What's that got to do with anything?" It's as if the bell has gone for round one, and we're off.

"It was the sixties, so much change, so exhilarating. And I was caught up in it all, of course I was, you would have been too. But then I had to sit and watch it all fly from my reach."

"Should have been more careful then, shouldn't you?"

"Perhaps." Her head dips in acknowledgement. "But when you were born I was smitten, I fell totally in love with you. I used to sit with you for hours, just watching you. You'd bat your tiny feet against my hand, and I'd pat back, and oh, you'd chuckle away."

At this she herself chuckles, and I find myself visualising the picture she paints, yearning for her to go on, but I snap again. "Funny, because I never actually felt any of that love. When I used to tell you things, about school, about friends, about anything, you'd just stare into the distance. You made it patently obvious you wanted to be elsewhere."

213

She lets out a sigh. "Did *you* want a baby at twenty-four Catriona?"

"No, of course not."

"Why is that so different?"

"Times have changed." I frown at her.

"Not really. I wanted something sensational to happen, just like you. Do you think it was easy for me to leave my life in that London café behind? Move out to the Home Counties?" Her eyes are blazing now. "One day, I took you and Billy to a Punch and Judy show, kids screaming, a gaggle of tedious mothers. I can still remember sitting there thinking, is this it?"

She's thrown me with that. Because I too remember that day, yet my take on it is wildly different. I see her slumped, sour-faced, while I longed for her to be like the other mums, arms around their kids, delighting in a wooden crocodile snapping at bug-eyed puppets.

She goes on. "Of course I loved you both, but I thought I was made for an exceptional life. Lizzie Stevens wanted to change the world. Why can't *you*, of all people, understand that?"

"Because I was your daughter, and I needed you there for me! Why can't you understand that?"

"Can't have done too bad a job, can I? I mean just look at you. Look at the job you do, the life you lead, the freedom you have. You've got it all."

"That's insensitive!"

"I'm sorry, I didn't mean it like that. But would you be ready to give it all up to have a child?"

"I wouldn't have to."

"Oh, something, somewhere, has always got to give, Catriona."

"Yes, and with you it was us that had to give, me and Billy. You should never have had us, why did you even get married if you weren't going to look after us properly?"

"Life isn't always how you plan it, is it?" She takes a sip of her whisky while she thinks about this, and I too glug

214

back my wine. She scrunches the robe tighter to her. "Anyway, I did my best, I stayed at home until you were both at school, you know that."

I scrutinise her face, with its entreating look, manipulating me as ever to extract my sympathy. And I won't buy it.

"You couldn't wait to get away though, could you? Were your causes so much more rewarding than us? Snatching at issues out of the air, willy-nilly? Oh, let's run off to Greenham Common and embrace the base. Oh, let's save the seals 'cos they're cute and dinky."

"It's healthy to get involved, Catriona, God knows the world out there is selfish enough."

"You're the selfish one!"

"I hoped you'd be spurred on by what I was doing, take an interest, channel that volatile energy of yours. I mean you seemed an angry young lady..." Her voice trails off. "Still are, I think."

"Angry? What did you expect? Did you ever think about Billy and me, when you dragged us away from home and installed us in that shitty house? With that fetid man?"

"Norman was a man of action, he cared about things. Your dad ..."

"Dad cared about *us*!"

Silence. Clearly she knows better than to take that one further and she withers from my glare, sips her whisky and surveys the room again. Still gunning for her, I watch her clocking the photo on our mantelpiece of me with Tony Blair, and wait for the moment she'll speak up again.

"Have you ever thought you might be a bit like me?" she asks finally.

I let out a howl of frustration. "Oh here we go, back to you. No I'm nothing like you, Lizzie, for a start I'm far more responsible."

"OK," she murmurs.

In the lengthy silence that follows, I grapple with myself, smarting with memories. Why can't she acknowledge what a bad mother she was? She's slipped from me like a snake shedding its skin. On TV, the smarmy actor has sidled up to a girl, one rakish eyebrow raised, and my focus blurs, turning his jacket into a prism of colour. But then, why can't I make peace and move on? I am nearly forty years old. Surely parental fuck-ups must have a shelf life?

"I've always been proud of you, Catriona. I wish we could be friends."

She appears undecided whether to leave me alone, and for a few moments we are both fixated by the girl on the screen giggling over a cocktail. Then, finally, Lizzie makes a move to rise from the window seat, and, surprisingly, I don't want her to go.

"So what natural therapies did you have in mind?" I ask.

She relaxes, sinking back down as if onto a defused bomb.

"Well, there's reflexology, for example."

I shrug. "That's just foot massage."

"Some hospitals have done fertility trials on it. Or how about acupuncture?"

"I'm done with needles."

"Homeopathy?"

"Aren't they just placebos?"

"Many people would disagree."

I guess I shouldn't have asked her, I don't believe in any of this and I'm unsure what to say next.

"Have you had yourselves tested for nutritional deficiencies? Hair analysis, for example?"

I shake my head. Come on Cat, get this conversation onto an adult footing.

Finally I force something out. "We do eat healthily, I only buy organic veg, we have bottled water, and Dom drinks green tea every day." At least I think he does, maybe he just extracts five tea bags from the box and dumps them in the bin at work.

"That's good. All I'm suggesting is that you consider some of these options. I came across a book about it all last week, I'll buy it for you and post it, shall I?"

She wavers, wondering if her final attempt will be rebuffed. I am touched that she's bothered with some research for me, I can visualise her in a bookshop at the wellbeing section, and I really do want to thank her. And yet I'm trapped in a childhood world of non-forgiveness and the best I can manage is a muttered, "OK."

On the silent screen, the credits are now rolling. Lizzie knocks back the last of her whisky and unfolds her legs to stand.

"Mum?"

Our eyes meet in surprise; I've not called her that since I was nine.

"What, love?"

"Dom doesn't want to keep trying anyway."

She stops in the awkward position she's reached, leaning forwards to place her glass on the side table, legs halfway to the floor. And then she surprises me.

"He's just lost a baby too, love, give him time."

22

"These are for you Daisy, can't get in them anymore."

My niece, just turned fifteen, is sitting on her bed painting her toenails lollipop pink. She pushes herself up and dances from one foot to the other beside the Harvey Nichols carrier bag; she knows how to please me. I have folded the jeans, the designer tops, and the one dress I have allowed her and packaged them in tissue paper, and Daisy is thrilled enough to extract each garment from its gift wrap with ginger reverence. She is also polite enough not to mention my weight gain.

"Cat, these are amazing, thanks so much."

She throws her arms around me, wafting up a cloud of perfume, and drawing my attention to the rose blusher on her cheeks. Daisy has now blossomed into a beauty. Her brace is off, leaving straight white teeth, she wears her blonde hair with confidence down her lithe back and her body brims with sexual awareness. The long cuffs that are now in fashion, as if for her personally, flap over her hands, partially secreting the ugly scar as she glides across to close her bedroom door then sits me down on the bed.

"Cat, I need to talk to you about Jack."

She's been seeing this sixteen-year-old lad from school for over a month now, a serious length of time in teenage years. I've seen his photo. Tousled hair a fraction too long, which the teachers would have overlooked because they too secretly fancied him; tie and shirt only slightly askew, in a sexy, morning after the night before sort of way. And that smouldering look, which Daisy would have been shocked to learn was no doubt practiced in front of the mirror. This one really was the dog's bollocks – as I'd texted her.

Smiling, I wait for her to begin. I adore this girl, and crave her continued forgiveness even more now she's older.

"I think we're gonna do it, Cat."

"Do what?"

"You know. Do it." She nudges me with her elbow, her eyes conspiratorial.

"Have sex?!"

"Shush my dad'll hear you." She scowls at the door and then at me.

"Daisy, you're only just fifteen, you can't have sex at your age. It's illegal for one thing."

She throws me daggers. "Well how old were you then?"

"Much, much older."

In fact, I was sixteen, in the back of an Austin Metro with a C&A sales assistant from Ruislip.

"How much older?"

"Eighteen," I lie. "And I was in love." No I wasn't.

"Well we're in love too."

Even before my snort is out, I'm regretting it. A skilful negotiator such as I knows that setting the atmosphere is vital, so why have I just pulverised it? I take my niece's hand, wincing as she snatches it away.

"You're just like them downstairs aren't you? You don't understand me at all, you've no idea what it's like to really want to be with someone."

I give myself a few moments to rehearse my next lines, and then speak tentatively so she'll see how seriously I'm taking her. "Daisy. Darling. The first time is special. Why don't you wait, just a few more months even, make sure he's right for you?" I know they will have split by then, she's dumped all the others niftily enough. "You can do other things to show your feelings for each other, can't you?"

"Yeah, this gives a pretty good hand job." She whips her left hand up in the air and the silk sleeve flops back to her wrist, exposing the disfigurement.

I gaze at her, incredulous. That she's been giving hand jobs already? Or that she's just displayed such slick cruelty to me?

"*You've* been egging me on, Cat. If my dad knew the texts you've been sending me ..." She snaps her head back, giving that hair a haughty swing, reaches for the nail polish and bends over her toes again.

She's right. I've been so euphoric that the niece I mutilated has been able, not only to find boyfriends, but to sweep up on the best, that I've stood skittishly on the side-lines whooping her along. What am I supposed to say next?

"Look, OK, if I'm honest I probably wasn't really eighteen when I lost my virginity, think I was more like sixteen. What's the harm in waiting just a little longer?"

She shrugs begrudgingly. "Why bother if I think he's the one?"

"But what if you got pregnant and then discovered he wasn't?"

"He'd stand by me." Her eyebrows rise in challenge.

"He might do, yes. But what if say, later, you met someone else, someone you fell so much more in love with? What then? You'd be stuck, wouldn't you?"

"That wouldn't happen."

"It might though. With me, it was much later when I met Dom, and fell much more in love with him." I'm coming out with far too many 'muches' – perhaps I'm convincing myself here too. Still, I reel more of it out. "The love of your life is worth waiting for, and I had my career under my belt too. Why not focus on uni and becoming a vet like you want to, before you settle down?"

Her look rummages inside me for evidence that Dom is the love of my life. And then she whacks me again. "I'm not gonna wait *that* long until I have kids though."

"No. No, I have been a bit foolish there."

I must roll with her punches if I'm to salvage anything from the trust she once bestowed upon me, and she knows she's beaten me down. Her voice softens.

"I am gonna do it, Cat."

She waits for me to challenge her again, but I just scan her face for a few moments. Then, with a weary sigh, I push myself off the bed and kiss the top of her head, inhaling deeply on the scent of her eponymous perfume, Daisy. Once upon a time, not so long ago, it would have been the scent of Johnsons Baby Bath.

"Promise me one thing then, Daisy?"

"What?" Her wide eyes now have a childlike lock on mine, she seems apprehensive for our encounter to end.

"That you'll use a condom."

She shrugs and bends further over her big toe, turning it a deeper fuchsia.

"'Course we will."

Downstairs in the living room, Billy is finishing a lewd joke about financial investment and exposure that he's clearly rehearsed for Dom, and my husband allows his brother-in-law a guffaw as I enter the room.

"Good one, mate," he says, and clamps his jaw to his glass of beer.

Sinking down onto the shabby sofa next to Dom, I place my hand on his thigh and he glides an arm around my shoulder. That's the way we've always done it, but these days there is no pressure from my palm, it's resting lightly on his jeans, just as his arm is hovering against my sweater. The love of my life, I said to Daisy. Well I still believe he is, but that we're presently in a lull. Just like the year itself before it gears up for Christmas, a dull and muted period, and one which I'm convincing myself is reflective and necessary.

With a wink, Billy offers me a conical glass and I take it, my mouth watering in withered anticipation. He does concoct a wicked margarita, if he says so himself. I've now

221

decided that, in the absence of either IVF or sex, I can relax on the booze at weekends – though I'm well aware it's becoming a bit of a crutch.

"Daisy like the clothes?" Cocktail in hand, Maggie smiles over at me from their old leather armchair by the bay window.

"Loves them." I smile back brightly, my mind fizzing over what this woman's daughter has just told me. She clearly has no idea, and I doubt if Billy does either. Should I tell them? I do feel conflicted, but already know I won't snitch on her.

Daisy's head appears through the living room door. Stunning in her diaphanous shirt and skinny jeans, she throws us all a weak smile, and I want to recall memories of her romping in her nappy on this rug, but all I see is that hand jerking off a boy's dick.

"Off then Mum, see you later."

"OK, enjoy yourself. Back by ten." Maggie seeks but fails to make eye contact with her daughter. It's me who receives a loaded gaze, and inside I wince at the way she thrust her hand up at me.

"Where's she off to?" I ask as the front door closes.

"Cinema round the corner. Didn't she tell you?" Billy's observing me, head cocked on one side.

I ignore him. "Can't believe how fast she's growing up. Feels only like yesterday when I was reading her a bedtime story."

"Did you ever do that? As I remember, you used to bury your face in the newspaper when you came over, it was us who used to put her to bed." Billy can't resist a pop at me when I've been in secret conference with his daughter.

Dom laughs with him, reinforcing the gibe, so I ignore them both and knock back my cocktail, relishing the bite of salt on my lips. "There was one about jungle animals," I say, "I remember it well."

"They were *all* about jungle animals." It's Dom who won't let it drop. He's being a shit.

222

I shrug and hold out my glass. "Any chance of another, bro?"

Later, already nicely oiled, we mooch through to the small kitchen. The table is set with a faded crimson cloth and lit from above by long candles in an iron holder slung up to the ceiling. The work surfaces are crammed as always with rickety piles of letters, magazines and exercise books for marking. They still own the same kettle. Turning my back on it, I sit down at the table, unable to prevent the image of Daisy's accident from flashing at me, followed then by one of her hand around that boy again. Maggie dims the lights and plonks an open bottle of red down on the table – to my dismay not one of the expensive ones we brought with us. Pushing Daisy out, I reach to pour myself a large glass and eye the fat jug of tap water Maggie also brings over.

"Would you have any bottled water, Maggie?"

Paranoia about female hormones in London tap water has now engulfed me. According to Lizzie's book on natural fertility solutions (which arrived the day after she'd left) it has been through five human bodies when it springs from the tap, and is suffused with unimaginables. My request is met with a vacant smile from my sister-in-law, who reaches for a half-full bottle of mineral water from the floor, which heightens my anxiety. This could have been standing around for months and for all I know the plastic will have become carcinogenic.

Our dinner conversation flutters like bees on honeysuckle over the usual films, books, and then work. Dom tells them about his success with the fund, how he's just won an award. They never grasp what he's on about. As the alcohol kicks in on evenings like this, Billy strives to get to the nub of what Dom does, goading him with playful questions (so, people invest their pension in your fund, and then you play poker with it?). But tonight he congratulates Dom on the award and asks us about the ceremony. I shrug, I didn't go, wasn't invited actually, and

I'm focusing on how animated Dom is as he holds forth; he's never like that with me these days.

After a watchful pause, Billy fixes his gaze on me. "So what animal magic has the Gay Gordon come out with recently, Cat?"

Clearly he's wondering why I'm not holding the floor as per usual and I conjure up a smile, dredging the anecdote I've prepared earlier. "Well, this week I was at a meeting with him in Whitehall and afterwards he came out with a beaut."

Billy leans into the table, Maggie takes a slug of her wine and smiles in anticipation, while I gather my thoughts.

"OK. When a poisonous snake strikes its prey, it must release its venom at the very instant its fangs pierce the skin." I wait for them to visualise this. "It's tricky for the snake. If its timing is out even by a fraction, then the venom is wasted."

I sit back, eyebrows raised at my brother and his wife, ignoring Dom beside me, who is sawing at his steak assiduously.

"So what do you make of that, then?"

Billy jumps in first. "Were you out lobbying with him at the time?" I nod smiling, he knows what this is about. "Well then, I'd say that he was praising you. He was saying something like, you need powerful arguments to throw at MPs, but you also have to time them right, otherwise there's no point."

I give my brother the thumbs up. "That's just what I thought too. You see, bastard though he is, he does value me, just in his own opaque and mysterious way."

And then I feel Dom's head lift towards me and I sense instantly, by the way the jaws have stopped chewing, by the heavy dragging arc it makes, that this movement has a malign purpose. "Maybe he was just saying you're a snake."

A flush prickles my cheeks and I balk at my husband, unable to comprehend this attack. He returns my blank look

224

with defiance, then shunts his chair back, leaves the kitchen and heads upstairs to the bathroom.

"Not quite sure how you'd draw that conclusion ..." My eyes meet Billy's and I see in them the hurt I'm feeling myself, but still I let out a hollow laugh.

Within a beat, and far too heartily, he and Maggie are laughing with me. Billy stands to take another bottle from the rack, with a nod at his wife to keep the conversation going. Maggie sets off on her own contribution, about school funding, something I can readily follow despite the competing turmoil in my head and clamour of my heart.

After a few minutes, Dom returns to the table without a glance at me, and turns his rapt attention on Maggie, who's now ranting on about the ratio between kids on free dinners and school budgets. Her cheeks are flushed, she's spearing her vegetables, jabbing them at her mouth, and apparently believes that she's moved us on successfully. Clearly I can't just sit here and let Dom know he's won, I have to contribute to the discussion somehow. So I wait for her to pause, and jump in, fork halfway to mouth.

"I love the way you're so passionate about your job, Maggie. You see, I think the only people who are still enthralled by their work at forty are teachers and doctors, the rest of us tend to lose the passion. I mean, there's so much bollocks around work, isn't there? Tedious meetings, office politics ..."

I'm waving my fork around as if engrossed by these thoughts and not at all wounded by Dom. And Maggie appears to be taken in, pleased to be able to develop her own ideas.

"I am passionate, yes, but I'm also angry about many things in the education system ..."

I tune out from her blathering, while opposite me Billy waits for his wife to wind up her diatribe, then tries to bolster me further. "But your job isn't tedious, Cat, you run your own outfit, you control the shots."

225

I catch Maggie's glare at her husband; clearly she was just getting into her stride. But I smile gratefully at him and am about to reply, when Dom interjects. "Shame you've only just realised your career doesn't matter. If you'd found that out earlier, maybe ..."

My fury is instant. "Maybe what? Go on, say it! Maybe we'd have kids by now?"

He shrugs. I feel the fireball rise inside me and I breathe it out in one great flaming blast.

"I see. Are you using this ... this forum," I sweep my hand across the table, "to air all that shit you've been bursting to chuck at me? Announcing in public what you don't have the balls to tell me in private. Is that it?"

I want to jab his biceps with my fork, to force him on, but I see that he isn't about to continue, so I turn to my horrified audience of two.

"Dom has decided, for reasons known only to himself, that he doesn't want to do any more IVF."

"Cat, this isn't the time or place." Dom back-pedals with a shake of the head.

"Oh, but you just made it that." I glower at him. Maleficent has nothing on me.

Maggie and Billy are frozen in their seats. "Come on guys..." my brother says, which spurs his wife up to her feet, muttering about pudding.

"Maggie!" I breathe my witch's fire on her and she slumps back down with a roll of her eyes at Billy.

Dom clearly senses an ally, and lunges for me again. "IVF is not natural."

"Oh spare me! Are you pulling the religious card on me?"

"It's interfering with nature, even Einstein said science is blind without religion. Sometimes you should just let nature take its course."

"Is that something your mum told you? The only time you set foot in a church is when you're with her."

226

"It's something I've come to believe, since you've turned into this demented harpy!"

"Didn't bother you earlier this year, when we got pregnant with IVF did it? You were perfectly content to go along with it then."

"Can't you see that we've done enough, that somebody is telling us to stop."

"Somebody?" I can sense my lip curling in a sneer and I spit my next words out. "My husband Dominic, born on a Sunday, is such a religious man, that he gambles for a living. How do you square that with your sudden hell and damnation?"

He falls silent and then looks to Maggie, the regular churchgoer, but clearly she knows better than to embroil herself in this. And his search for reinforcement, when it's *me* who's always been his ally, knocks me over the edge.

"Is it your so-called religion that's stopping you? Or is it that you hate being the cause of our infertility?"

"My sperm goes up and down. You've got polycystic ovaries too, remember? It's a joint problem."

In the brittle silence that follows, the iron candelabra seems to swing with menace above our heads, the flame shadows flickering off the walls. Maggie gently pushes her chair back, while Billy also jerks to his feet and reaches for yet another bottle, even though our glasses are still full.

The sudden Big Ben chime of the front doorbell defuses the tension. Dom escapes down the hallway to let Daisy in, then he makes a nifty diversion into the living room, muttering something about *Match of the Day*. He can't escape home because we're staying the night. My niece strolls into the kitchen looking directly at me for evidence of betrayal, but I stare through her, her dilemma now eclipsed by my own.

"How was the film, love?" Maggie resumes normality, allowing Daisy to regale us with the storyline in ragged detail, while we cluck around her with mechanical questions.

When finally she makes for the stairs, Dom emerges too and hovers in the hallway, with a yawn and a vapid stretch, like some tottie in an aerobics video. He calls his thanks in the general direction of the kitchen and he too heads upstairs to the guest room. Our silence falls upon the room, punctured by the clattering of plates and cutlery, while Maggie fusses with the dishwasher. Then she too goes off to bed, with a light kiss to Billy's head and a tender stroke of his cheek.

Billy takes his time opening the fourth bottle of red, this time the Saint Emilion which Dom and I brought with us, then he smiles gently, pulls his chair up to the table and waits for me to speak. The candles above our heads have burnt down low, casting a shadowy glow about the room.

"I'm so worried about us, Billy," I whisper finally.

"He's not himself Cat, it must be the miscarriage."

"I'm scared though. I'm scared we're going to split up if we don't get there."

"It's only been a few months, you need to give yourselves time."

"I thought he'd come round, I thought I'd persuade him to have another go at it. I know that if I could just get pregnant, we'd be OK again. But you saw him tonight, he's adamant, no more IVF."

My brother tackles me gently. "He will come round, Cat. Why don't you take a break from it, just for a while?"

"No, we need to press on. I'm nearly *forty*."

I grasp my wine glass and watch Billy taking a swig of his own, while I wait for him to reassure me further. But he stares into his glass, swirls it round, drawing us both to watch the streaky legs he creates on the sides of the glass, something I taught him to do long ago. He swirls back and forth for a long time then sets his glass down and fixes his eyes on mine.

"Cat, don't take this the wrong way, but why is having a kid so important to you?"

"What?" For a moment he's thrown me, and then angered me in equal measure. "Oh not you too! Everybody expects you to justify why you want a child if you're having problems, don't they? Did *you* ever have to convince everyone why you wanted kids? I bet you didn't even think it through in your own mind, did you?"

In my agitation, I shunt my chair in closer to the table and begin fidgeting with the place mat, aligning its edge with some gold threads in the tablecloth.

"No." He acknowledges my discomfort with a dip of his head. "But I didn't mean that, sorry. It's just that, well you were always so determined never to have them."

"When?"

"In your twenties, early thirties even, when you were flying high."

"I never said I never wanted them." I shrug. "Just, when I was ready."

He waits for me to continue.

"Look, I know it's late. But I am ready now, nothing else is important to me now. It's got to the point where nothing anybody says excites me, or even interests me anymore. I mean, the other day I was in a café and I overheard a guy telling his mate about this great new holiday destination he'd found, where you could ski in the morning and lie on the beach in the afternoon. And I knew instantly where this was."

Billy raises his eyebrows at my ramble, clearly lost.

"It was the Spanish Pyrenees."

"OK. Not sure what you're saying to me, sis."

"Well, don't you see? I've been there, done that."

"Not really, no. I've never done anything like that."

"I'm just saying that I know most things and I've done most things. In my twenties it was all about newness – meeting new people, trying new experiences. And now, I'm bloody exhausted by it all, I've got no energy to meet, or know, or do anything *new* anymore. I just want a baby."

229

My brother contemplates me from across the table, absorbing what I've said, his large brown eyes have welled up, and now mine have too.

"I'm empty inside, Billy." I clamp my palm to my chest. "There's nothing in here. Except inertia."

He reaches across the table for the hand, pulls it down between his, and we sit silently. One of the candles snuffs itself out and the room darkens.

"He will leave me Billy, if we don't have kids."

"No, he won't do that."

"Maybe not now, maybe not even in the next couple of years. But when it's way too late, he'll go off in search of a younger model. What's to stop him?"

"Because he loves you, Cat."

"Not much evidence of that tonight, was there?" I grit my teeth and focus on lining the placemat up against a more distant thread in the tablecloth.

"Where's my feisty sister?" Billy dips his head conspiratorially. "She's in there somewhere. Where's the girl who used to pin me down on the carpet when I took the piss out of her?"

As he speaks, I hear the toilet flush upstairs, then the creak of floorboards and throw Billy a questioning look.

"It's just Daisy," he says, with a shake of the head.

If it is Daisy, then she probably thinks I'm spilling the beans and, for a fleeting moment, I consider again whether to tell him. Would he be upset if he knew his daughter was about to lose her virginity? But I'm far too caught up in me. And I do no more than muse that he and Maggie were probably only fifteen when they first did it, before I submerge any further thoughts for my brother deep inside my own misery.

23

I'm waiting for Ash to call. We're to meet for dinner at the Cinnamon Club round the corner. Ellie went home ages ago, but given that Tim and I are still at our desks most of the account managers are here too, though these days I'm well aware that nobody comes near unless they have to – don't wake the sleeping ogre.

I'm doodling again, mulling over Dom's outburst on Saturday night. I know full well that it wasn't grounded in religion at all, that it was just another sidestep to evade more IVF. He's been talking it over with his mum, Peggy. I hear him most evenings on the phone upstairs speaking in a low voice, and I can sense her laying him with kindle to torch more brimstone and fire. When Dom and I first met, we did discuss religion, of course, we did. And I told him then that I was doing an excellent job of controlling my own destiny, thank you very much (ha – how ridiculous that now sounds). I said I doubted those believers who lose loved ones and are amazed that God has not protected them from personal tragedy. As if they made that leap of faith hoping for impunity from heartbreak, as if it was some kind of fake insurance.

Dom, meanwhile, always insisted that his faith had helped him through the death of his Gran. He'd explain it in fantastical ways that were opaque to me, just as when my mother had once described the effects of LSD. In those days, Dom was still packed with mystery, and much of what he said promised layers of wisdom which in time would unfurl themselves for me, and which back then caused me frissons of anticipation about our life together. I

231

wonder now, though, if they were actually layers of wisdom. Or something else.

Yesterday morning, I even found myself seeking out Maggie's view. Dom had left for his hockey match, Billy to fetch Scott from his sleepover, and Daisy was still asleep. Alone with her over croissants, I asked what she thought of Dom pulling the faith card on me. It was akin to tugging the string on the back of a talking doll – I engineered the words I wanted to hear and knew I would.

"Seems to me that Dom's happier spending his Sunday morning playing sport than where I'm off to," she said, dipping the very tip of her knife into the blob of jam she'd allowed her plate.

So I reeled out my recently cooked up ethics test for her. "The way I see it, IVF is perfectly ethical for desperate couples, as long as they're in loving relationships, aren't too old, and use their own eggs and sperm. Don't you think?" I yanked that string in her back again.

"Totally ethical," she agreed, after seeming to consider the words but without asking for more.

Then she'd rushed off to church, I assume to listen to God, when she can't or won't listen to her own daughter. Perhaps I should have raised the issue of Daisy with her, but my own problems weigh more heavily.

In the office now, I consider my doodle. No white space remains on the paper, it's splattered with spikes, fanning into a flower, crossing into rows of teeth, splaying out into swords. I can, of course, tick off each of those criteria I invented for Maggie (with a provisional shadow over the bit about loving relationships). Dom would probably call it expedient, but I know that I'm right and I've got to tackle him.

The phone rings and I reach for it with a smile – tonight, however, I need some respite from this life.

At the Cinnamon Club, I am calmed by the white temple flowers bobbing on the pool inside the door and I make for our usual table beside the wood panelling, where Ash is waiting for me with a languid smile. My heels click across the wooden floors of this listed building, once the Old Westminster Library. I inhale the scent of cinnamon candles and pungent spices, enjoying the odd head turning to follow my progress, nodding at MPs, journalists, or other lobbyists. This is where Billy will find that feisty girl who used to pin him to the carpet; my reputation remains unscathed by my present state of being, and tonight I will again play the great pretender to perfection.

"Good evening to you Ms Black." Ash stands and kisses my cheek, lingering a hint too long. "You're looking lovely, despite your no doubt gruelling day at the office."

"Thank you." I catch the aftershave as he pulls back; he is looking lovely too. The candle between us casts a golden hue onto his features, smudging his skin to perfection.

"I'm going to have to shoot off to vote at some point – very briefly though – I hope you've set the whole evening aside for me?"

My nod may be too eager, I'm altogether too keen to lose myself in his presence, but his look is seductive, drawing me in, and I pull away from it, turn to the mirror beside our table and fuss with my hair. Ash turns too. We contemplate each other through the gleaming patina of silver glass, and a memory explodes into my head; the first time we had sex. It was just two weeks after I'd arrived in Brussels, we'd been to a meeting at the European Commission together and Ash had introduced me to some of his contacts, breaking me in, as he cheekily called it. In the lift back down, I'd looked up into the mirrored ceiling, where his eyes had joined mine and he'd grinned. "You could have some fun in here, couldn't you?"

And that was that. In the office there'd been sideways glances, bending at the photocopier for a stray sheet of A4, a brush of shoulders on the stairways; no further preamble was necessary. We'd crunched across the snowy pavements back towards the office, I'd turned in at my apartment block and he'd turned in with me. In the tiny lift to my penthouse we'd stood like soldiers on guard, the tension jumping up a notch with each flash of the buttons; by the twelfth floor he must have been able to hear my heart thumping. And then we were in the apartment, peeling off winter coats, pulling at shirts, finding warm flesh beneath.

In the mirror, Ash is smiling at my glazed expression. "Penny for them?"

"You couldn't afford them – even on your warped expenses." I throw him a brazen smile. Ash apparently has no notion of the way I'm unravelling inside. With him I am as I was before. Strong. Sexy. Valid.

A waiter arrives with menus and slides an amuse-bouche of lentil and potato fritter between us. Ash orders more beers, then tears the fritter apart, while I avert my eyes, even if the lentils are a world away from the green mush of my mother's stews. I choose the chicken in pomegranate and spices, and sit back with a sigh.

"So what's the vote on?"

"No idea, find out when I get there."

"Busy day?"

"Labelling, packaging, traffic lights – the usual riveting Ministerial stuff."

He speaks through a half-full mouth and the smile he's seeking from me comes readily to my lips. I have no wish for this to lead onto a discussion about Stewart though, so I change tack.

"Any good nutters lately?"

He groans. "Had one come flouncing up to me yesterday, just outside the House, no introduction nothing, just launches into me. Wants a new private shop off the High Road closed down."

"What's that got to do with you?"

"Precisely." He sinks some beer. "Local issue. In any case, it's down a side street, so you'd have to literally track it down – and I bet he has done, the pervert. Got nothing more smutty in the window than basques and negligées."

234

"You've checked them out then?" I narrow my eyes at him and pour myself more beer.

Ash gestures at me with a piece of torn off fritter. "Your size probably."

His lips close with smooth perfection over teeth he's had whitened since he's been a Minister. I ignore him, smirking down into my napkin and shaking it out flamboyantly, but I sense his observation of me, and I know there's more.

"You'd think it was crammed with Rampant Rabbits, the way he was ranting on at me." It had to come, of course it did; we'd used those things together oodles of times, all more than a decade ago now, though.

Just as our waiter brings over a series of small steel bowls bubbling with sauces, the division bell resounds through the restaurant. It chimes with Ash's pager. A stack of Sticky Toffee Puddings heave themselves from their seats and bustle off to vote; a commotion which always reminds me of one of those supermarket trolley dashes between fat housewives. They seem to bounce off each other in their haste to get out of the door.

"Sorry, back in half an hour, tops." Ash lays his folded napkin on the table, winks at me, and saunters off at a stride, patting his own taut stomach muscles as he weaves in and out of his colleagues.

The waiter removes the dishes to keep them warm for us in the kitchen. I order another beer then turn again to the mirror, my smile fading. In reality, I look so tired. It's now October, three years since I made the decision to get pregnant, and each one has taken its toll on my face; the crow's feet are deepening, my cheeks show a hint of sag, and my skin's greasier after the drugs. This face will be forty next year. Tonight, however, I'm on holiday from all of that, I'm here to change my ideas, as the French would say, so I restore my smile.

While I'm settling it in place in the mirror, a figure catches my attention, sweeping into the restaurant, stopping by the pool to survey the room. A lithe woman, with caramel skin and black tresses, she reminds me of Harinder in Vietnam. It takes me a few seconds to focus on her, then momentarily she catches my eye. I swear she flinches and I swivel round in my seat; it is her. But the woman has also turned, her thin legs brisk, her long hair swinging, as she clips to the door and out. I stare after her, surely it can't have been her? She's fourteen years older now and must have aged, but this woman looked just the same as Harinder did back then, so it can't possibly have been, she must just have been a younger version of her. My beer arrives and I sip at it, finding myself reminiscing about that holiday, the first time I set eyes on Dom, the surprise of our love at first sight. A world apart from Saturday night.

When the MPs return, Ash is first through the door – he must have jogged it back, although he's not breathless – and the waiter bustles out with our dishes once again. I've not eaten since breakfast and the Indian beer has now gone to my head.

"Your route back was nutter-free then?" I smile at him.

"Oh you know, bit of ducking and diving." He gestures with his head. "Met Teddy in the division lobby though."

"The Health Secretary?"

"Yep. Full of praise for you, says you're the only lobbyist in London worth talking to, the rest are scum. Well you know we all think that, don't you?"

"Bite the hand that gave you a leg up, why don't you?"

"Oh come on, Catriona Black is the one respected name in the business. You do your research, you give as well as take, you've got squillions of credit in the bank, throughout the whole House. You must know that by now?"

His eyes are locked on mine, his forehead creased into fine lines to bring home the message I so need to hear at the moment. That I'm still valued somewhere, by someone.

"Oh, and you're still so hot, too," he adds.

"Teddy said that?"

"No, I just did." His smile is loaded as he chews his meat, then his eyes drop to his plate. "Teddy's lent me the keys to his flat in Dolphin Square. Don't think I'll bother hoofing it home tonight, got an early start in the morning."

His words blast me in the chest. Then they whizz round like a Catherine Wheel on a fence, sparking and flashing. Ash pretends he's having difficulty forking meat into his mouth and faffs around, pressing it in with his fingers, head bent forward, his eyes still intent on the plate. So I do likewise, make as if I have a problem swallowing the chicken, mashing it to a pulp on my tongue. And I give it a good minute, allow that firework time to wind down, to fizzle and finally peter out, until the point when I can muster the blandest possible response.

"That's handy for you, isn't it?"

*

On Friday, I sent Dom an email at work, asking him if we could get together and talk over dinner that evening. But he arrived home having drunk excessively at lunchtime and came mooching downstairs to the kitchen yawning – wide, rude, hissing yawns, which he knew would irritate me. Dragging an open palm across his pink face and blinking emphatically, he claimed to be too tired for the fish I'd marinated. Then he took a pint glass from the cupboard, filled it to the brim with water from the tap, and turned face on to me as he drank it down in one greedy draft, his eyes goading me to snatch it from him. I had to fiddle around with the monkfish to prevent myself from doing just that; tap water has been verboten in our house for a long time now.

Today, Sunday, I come down to find Dom already tucking in to toast and marmalade at the kitchen table, buried expansively in the newspaper. On the radio, *Parkie* is playing Frank Sinatra. I can't bear Radio 2 on a Sunday morning. It reminds me of my childhood, the mushy songs

Lizzie used to sing along to while she cooked her nut roast, with Norman crooning all over her. Dom says it reminds him of his childhood too – that's why he loves it.

I sit down opposite him. He still has two slices of toast to go, and I have him trapped. "Dom, we need to talk. Please."

"What about?" He continues to read, feigning attention to the double-page spread on the Middle East.

"I know you're still hurting. So am I. Infertility is too big a burden for any couple to have to deal with." This is pathetic, I'm sounding like that counsellor. So I try again. "Dom, why won't you agree to do another cycle, just one more?"

"Drop it will you?" He refuses to look up at me.

"Do you still want a baby?"

He shrugs and takes a bite, which I assume means yes, so I continue.

"Well it's not going to happen naturally, is it?"

He considers for a minute, munching toast placidly, then he sighs as if I'm a tiresome child, smooths the paper out on the table and throws me a condescending look.

"You're so obsessed with getting pregnant, *that's* become your goal, hasn't it? Not the baby at the end of it."

His voice is now menacing, soft and quiet, causing a chill to skitter up my spine. And the difference is not at all clear to me.

"What do you mean?"

"You don't even know why you want a baby, you're just driven. Like you've been driven all your life, to get what you want, to control everything and everybody. You just see me as a provider of sperm." He pauses. "In fact, was I ever important to you? I don't think I ever was, was I?"

Dom's words strike me with the delayed pain of a stubbed toe, at first they seem innocuous and then they become excruciating.

"Dom, I love you."

238

"Do you? Do you really? Then why did you make me wait so long before you deigned it was the right moment to have children?"

His clarity now smacks me full on, and it ignites my fury. "Oh, here we go again, it's alright for you isn't it? You wouldn't have had to give up your job, would you? You wouldn't have had to risk missing out on everything you've strived to achieve. What if Geoffrey had decided to make someone else managing director?"

"Who? Tim, nice but dim?"

"For example."

"Little Miss MD, it's so important to you isn't it?"

"Yes, you're fucking right it's important. It gives me my self-esteem, which is something my parents failed to do. I've told you that millions of times, but you wouldn't understand, would you? You were drowning in the stuff when you were a kid, with your beach life and your homemade parkin. You were wrapped up in all that praise, all that gooey life, all safey-safey. You had self-esteem oozing out of every pore!"

We both stare at each other mouths agog, as if it's some kind of game, where the first to speak loses. Then I realise I haven't finished.

"So blame me. Blame God too, if you think he's punishing you for submitting to IVF because it's 'unnatural'." I finger the quotation marks. "You run and hide behind your newfound Catholic values, little boy. And meanwhile it'll be your fault, it will be *you* that's preventing us from having kids."

The radio blares out cheerily, saturating the silence that follows. Dom presses his finger into toast crumbs on the table and rubs them off against his thumb onto a plate. Transfixed by the minute movements of his skin brushing against itself, a finger and thumb that haven't touched me since that night in August, I find the moment excruciating. Calmly then, he looks up at me, his eyes inscrutable.

"I don't like being with you at the moment."

"What's that supposed to mean?"

"What it says."

"I don't get you." My heart is jumping wildly, the blood surges to my head then drains instantly. "Dom, what are you telling me?"

"Oh I don't know, maybe … well, let's just see."

He gathers his plate and mug, places them with ominous care in the sink and leaves the kitchen, calling for Silkie so he can get out of the house. Away from repulsive old me.

I slump onto my elbows staring into the table, while the void he leaves in his wake crashes like cymbals. Is he going to leave me? Already I feel as if a protective layer has been whipped off me, leaving me exposed and alone. And is he right? Do I really want a child, or am I just obsessed with getting pregnant? It's true that I am now desperate for that final spoil, when you've got marriage and career sorted and you raise your head in anticipation of the hat trick. Something which comes to others so readily. The chubby pink warm bundle at the end of it all is an image I don't dare visualise, a feeling I won't allow myself. But then I think back to that moment I had to peel Emily from my chest, to the momentary pang of loss, and the ache catches me again.

With a sigh, I stand and shuffle over to the patio doors, gaze out into the garden and watch next door's cat jump down from the fence. It slinks behind a bedding plant and arches its back at me. I can't think clearly what I want anymore. My mind is fatigued, befuddled by all that thinking and thinking and thinking, none of which has brought any solution. Do I even still want Dom? If I'm honest, I've recently found myself attempting to isolate what it was – what it is – about him that I love. At first I was smitten, of course, but it was his presence, his sense of self that remained after the flurry of daily sex had subsided. Dom was kind too, and I envied him that. It's not that he suffered fools any more than I did, but his Northern warmth embraced all those he carried with him. I wonder, however, if once you start analysing a marriage, once you set about deconstructing it, having to wheedle out just what makes it happy, I wonder then if it's the beginning of the end.

As for how Dom feels about me, I've heard people say that you always love your children, even if you may not necessarily like them at all times, but for married couples I don't see a distinction between the two shades of affection. You can't love if you don't like. It's obvious to me, therefore, that my husband is falling out of love with me.

24

The clocks go back at the weekend. This has always been my most difficult time of year, as if the world is closing in on me. Outside my office window it's a murderous day. Barely light and squally, the wind wrenching the leaves and driving them down to the pavement puddles. Dom and I are barely speaking now, and I feel naked, undone. I keep thinking back to the evening with Ash, to the way he flirted with me, and I feel cloaked again, he's the one layer left upon me.

I turn back to my desk. There are things to do, people to meet, as they say. Stewart is due in around mid-day before his lunch at No.10 and we need to run through the issues he plans to raise. It's an industry-wide affair, but Stewart chairs the food retail trade association, so he'll be at the head beside the PM, who nowadays is a fellow Scot, if grouchily heterosexual.

Before that, I plan to tune in to Jackie's programme, *A Letter from Home*. This week the whole hour is to be devoted to secondary infertility, and I'm curious to hear what she has to say. We're not speaking either at the moment, not after her insensitivity about the miscarriage. But I miss her. And I'm somehow hoping that she's planning a sympathetic approach to infertility generally. Even that perhaps she's produced this show with me in mind.

I head down to the kitchen (I make my own coffee these days) and find the room empty – no doubt they've all scurried to their boltholes on hearing me emerge. Back upstairs, I ask Ellie not to disturb me and roll my eyes at her grunted response – oh, if life were as simple as you in your fluffy pink angora sweater. I tune in online, the hourly news just finishing, and bring up Stewart's briefing note to begin a final scrutiny of the bullet points.

Jackie's voice rings out, honeyed as always for the opening lines of her programme. The grit sets in towards the end when the issues become embroiled, particularly as she herself piles on the polemics. This is why she's so popular.

"When people think about infertility, they often imagine it only affects couples who have no children at all. But secondary infertility, the inability to conceive a further child, after having had a first one, is a growing problem in Britain. And the experience can be just as harrowing."

Just as harrowing? Surely she doesn't mean that? She's got dinky little Emily at home.

"We want to hear from you, if you have experienced, or are suffering now from secondary infertility. But first, let me introduce Dr Olu Akande, a leading fertility expert who joins us today from the Knightsbridge Fertility Clinic."

I gawp at the PC, my heart racing. She's got Olu on. She's invited *my* consultant onto her show.

"Good morning Jackie. Yes, we are treating more and more couples who are unable to conceive a second time, even though they had no difficulty the first time around. And they often find that their family and friends are not sympathetic, nor do they find understanding from couples who are completely infertile."

You're damn right we don't sympathise. Hackles up, I try and focus on Stewart's briefing note, listening to some caller wittering on about how she doesn't feel complete with just one child.

"Now, let's hear from Wendy in Macclesfield," Jackie says. "You describe your life as hell, Wendy?"

"It is hell, yes. You think you can't be infertile, because you've already got a child." The woman's voice is a whine. "And you keep asking yourself, why isn't he enough? And then you realise that there'll never be another *first*. First word, first steps, first day at nursery ..."

I let out a shriek. "I'll tell you what hell is, you stupid cow. I'll never have a first anything!"

On my screen, the briefing has become a blur. Olu offers a soothing 'mmm' and then Jackie's in there again.

"Do you find that you can't focus properly on your first child because you're so desperate for bairn number two? I know that's how I feel with wee Emily." Her usual tactics – add a hint of Scots, show weakness, reel 'em in. My knee is jiggling beneath the desk

"Yes that's exactly what it's like," Wendy says.

"Well we wish you the very best." Jackie's done with her, wrung out the interesting bits, keen to move on.

The next caller also has one child, and says she feels left behind, because her friends are all onto baby number two. Then she comes out with this. "What *I'm* going through is much worse than totally infertile couples. They don't know what they are missing out on. They have no idea what it's like to have a baby, but I do. I *know*."

At that something clicks inside me, the fury sears me and my fingers storm the keys, typing, YOU FUCKING FUCK WIT!!!!!!! For additional satisfaction I stab at SAVE and CLOSE too and kick my chair back from the desk. Pacing the room like a caged raptor, I find myself actually shaking.

Olu is holding forth now. "Many couples might think they cannot be infertile because they already have a child. But of course they are older, so it is best to seek treatment at an early stage."

Then Jackie's back in there, eager to step it up a notch. "It is distressing for those of us who are aching for another baby. And traumatic to think you might now be infertile."

"I can't believe this," I scream at the PC.

And nor can the next caller, Helen from Leeds, the first to speak some sense. "I'd like to know what planet these women are on? They should be happy they have one child!"

"Yes!" I cry.

"And that last woman, how dare she claim that it's worse for her than for me? She can never know what it's like to long for a baby. I've been through six IVF cycles, and I'm still childless. You should all count yourselves lucky. You too Jackie if you don't mind me saying."

Jackie's voice is now razor sharp. "Oh, I don't think anyone should belittle the anguish of longing for a baby, whether it's the first or second. The desire can be just as agonizing."

I shake my head at the bloody-mindedness of my erstwhile friend, sink back down to my desk and pull up the website image of Jackie in her studio – today not a live one. "How can you be so callous?"

She asks Helen to stay on the line. "Dr Akande, do you wish to respond?"

There's a pause before Olu speaks, almost as if he's wondering how he's got himself mixed up in this debate. "I do sympathise with that lady. I have seen much despair among women who will endure IVF many times for their first child, and sometimes they do not succeed. There will always remain a sadness in their hearts."

"Yes, I'm sure."

Jackie's terse reply pricks me. And I sense Olu too, who falls silent again.

"Now, we go to Nottingham, where we have Margaret on the line. I understand you wish to take issue with Helen?"

"Six IVF cycles?" The sanctimonious voice belongs to an elderly woman. "You're talking about IVF as if it's some right, and yet it is completely unnatural. Only God gives life, and if he sees fit not to bestow a precious new life upon some couples, then so be it."

"You old crusty!" I snap. "Just hang up."

"Too many women think they can go swanning through as many IVF cycles as they like. We live in the society which says, I want it all and I want it now."

"What precisely is your problem with that, Margaret?" Jackie whips out the aitch in 'what' – she's reached her tipping point now.

"It's tinkering with human life, that's what the problem is! Have they no moral or religious misgivings about the thousands of embryos which perish during the IVF process? Those which are destroyed or discarded for research, because they're not of a high enough quality? And what about those introduced into the womb which die soon afterwards? I know full well that several embryos are inserted, in the hope that just one may survive. The Catholic Church teaches us about the dignity of *all* human life from the first moment of conception."

"Thank you. Margaret, I'd like you to stay on the line while we bring Helen in again, but Dr Akande, I think you would like to add something at this point?"

"Yes. I feel it is important to understand that the majority of natural embryos created through sexual intercourse do not survive either. They are discarded in the womb and will perish at an early stage, usually unbeknown to the woman. In nature too, only a few lucky embryos will develop into a foetus."

"You could say then that IVF is just a mirror of natural conception. Is that your view too, Helen?"

"My view is that Margaret should focus her hateful anger on the real human suffering in the world, instead of harping on about the *perceived* suffering of embryos."

I find myself nodding at the screen and my ally forges on. "Yes, it's different when the embryo becomes a foetus, certainly when it develops a nervous system, when it can feel pain. But, at the very early stages, in those first few weeks, it is just a cluster of cells. It has no feelings, no consciousness. It has no soul."

While she's speaking I'm visualising an embryo. My embryo actually. My six-week old cluster of cells on the ultrasound screen. I close my eyes and see the white blob, in which a pinprick of pulsing heartbeat should have been. Prickles of emotion spring onto my back. Slink around my shoulders, across my breastbone, up my neck and onto my face, with a creeping awareness. No feelings? No consciousness? No soul? Then why did I grieve? Why do I still find myself weeping now?

My tears threaten while Jackie's voice continues to swirl around me, baiting Margaret for her reaction. And the old woman's disgust rings out again, as if from the pulpit. This time I listen carefully.

"How does she know that an embryo has no soul? With modern science we're falling over ourselves in the rush to discover *what* we can do, but we forget to ask ourselves if we *should* be doing it. We should be humbled by nature, not deceiving it for our own selfish means..."

Jackie cuts the woman off and the tension finally engulfs me. Logging out, I let the tears roll and slump onto the desk. She's right, isn't she? I nurtured that cluster of cells no bigger than a grain of rice. I connected with it, and am still infused by the bond now, I can't let it go. Of course it had a soul. It was my baby. Memories of Emily wash over me. I can see her body clamped to mine, feel the comforting weight of her, smell her milkiness. I need an Emily of my own.

I've no idea how long I've been sitting there, when there's a rap at the door. I jolt myself upright, smear hands across my face, tuck hair behind my ears. Stewart enters the room. I sense his agitation and the panic hits me. I need to alter his briefing.

"Aren't you a tad early?" I bring up the document and click to the end. Today he sports a tie which is various shades of red, bona fide Labour. He sits down and leans over the desk, his breath fuming with last night's whisky.

"Catriona, I believe our contract's up for renewal soon?"

There's a menace about his voice, but I remain composed, nod vaguely as I delete the offending text from his briefing notes. I'm aware that he can see I've been crying, but also that it has no import for him.

"You see, I fear I may not be enjoying the service from you I once did."

As the document comes off the printer, I turn to face him coldly, exhausted by my morning and riled by the tenor of his comment. "I think you'll find perfection in this briefing, Mr Dinwoodie."

"Oh, the briefing? It's OK, I've got that already. Ellie's been super helpful and printed it off from the network for me." He stands and taps a rolled up document on my desk, his own eyes steely now. "However, I think you'll find that fuckwit is one word, lassie."

"I didn't mean you!" I stand to snatch the document from him.

"I'd put it down to PMT, but these lapses are far too frequent."

I gasp and feel myself welling up again.

"Oh spare me." With a withering look, he shakes his head and turns for the door.

25

Dawn breaks into the first day of November just before we reach Stockport. A blood-orange glow leaches from the hedgerows and impinges on the blackened sky, which readily cedes the way. My reflection in the train window, a face that would elicit envy from a hangdog, fades equally gratefully into the beauty of an English landscape. This year, our annual conference on 'Influencing Government' is in Manchester, and I'm to make the keynote speech.

This morning I was up at five, with Dom. Unaccustomed to finding ourselves together at that hour, we stood side by side at our basins, he shaving, I moisturising. In silence. Even if the signals bouncing off him were deafening; the splash of razor too brisk, the hand at his chin too jerky. I wondered if I should speak, if I should utter some words, but I could think of nothing to say – nothing whatsoever to say to my own husband. Even white rabbits came to mind; after all, our good morning grunts had hardly counted as the first words of the month. But then Dom might well have misconstrued the rabbit connotations as an attempt by me to bring up the subject of sex or IVF.

Despite our standoff, I did prolong the moments beside him, because still it comforted me to feel his presence, to engage in a simple husband and wife routine. So I lingered over the foundation, the blaze of lipstick, the dense eyeliner, creating the persona who will play to the gallery in Manchester.

"Shit day ahead of me." That was Dom's parting shot as he shunted on his jacket and left the bedroom, without so much as a backwards glance.

After he'd gone, I dabbed at the smudged mascara, then stabbed the blusher brush at my cheeks, watching the tawny particles cling to my flesh. Done and dusted. I think we are too.

Outside the red brick terraces begin to build up. My phone rings: Daisy's number. I consider ignoring it, but the guy opposite me is glaring above his newspaper, clearly irked by my breaking glass ring tone. I smile an apology and answer it, slinking down into the seat with a whisper.

"Hello?"

"Cat? Cat I think I'm pregnant."

"Daisy!"

I might forever con myself that my instant reaction was concern for my niece, but a flash of envy is straight in there. To be pregnant! To have conceived naturally. Well, it's unfathomable.

"Daisy, are you sure? How do you know?"

"I'm late." Each syllable is a gulp.

"Have you done a test?"

"No. Hoped I'd come on this morning, but I haven't."

"How late are you?"

"Think it's about three weeks."

"Three weeks! How ...?"

I stop myself – but how could she have left it so long before wondering if she might be pregnant? I would have pounced on the first day missed.

"What do I do, Cat? You've got to help me."

"Oh Daisy."

Help her? What can I do for this fifteen-year-old child with an unwanted life in her belly? Spirit it away? My way?

"Look, you might not be pregnant, you're under a lot of stress with exams coming up, aren't you? You have to do a test, sweetheart."

"Can't. Mum knows the chemist."

"Not the one round the corner. Get on a bus down the high street and find another one, use the loo in a coffee shop, doesn't matter if you're late for school."

"OK."

I can hear her calming now, and close my eyes. "Come on, deep breaths, let's not worry unless we have to."

If she is pregnant, then she's already five weeks gone. I know full well that the embryo within her will already be the size of an apple pip, that the chambers of its heart are already forming and that next week there will be a heartbeat. Her breathing slows as she regains control.

"Do it now, Daisy. Call me when you know. OK?"

"I'll have to have an abortion, Cat."

I've been expecting it, but still the word pierces me – maybe it's the ice in her clarity now – and I'm back in that room after the D&C.

"It'll be alright, don't worry, I'll take care of you Daisy."

When she's hung up, I open my eyes and sense a flurry of other eyes darting from me, the spell I've cast broken by the sudden rustling of papers. After a general scowl at the carriage, I look out of the window at the passing houses. Of course she'll have to have an abortion. She can't have the baby, miss out on her GCSEs, on university, to raise a brat with no father – 'cos Jack won't stay around. She's been so stupid. She must have only done it once, maybe twice, how could she possibly have got pregnant? There's a piddling two-day window in every month, and she was trying *not* to conceive, so what are the odds on that? I find myself calculating them, knee jiggling furiously, but my mind insists on swerving me round to where it needs to go. What a fluke. Imagine if Dom and I had sex and I fell pregnant. It'd feel unnatural, bizarre even. The natural way, the expected way for me now is IVF, not sex. What an absolute fluke.

Gradually I'm aware of a steward standing over my table, asking for rubbish as we pull into Manchester, and I fling my empty cup into the plastic bag.

Two hours later, I'm on my feet before the cream of the North West's business community, going through the motions about the need for clear communication when lobbying government. On the white board behind me I've written two words: Pubic Affairs. It always raises a laugh, today fruity Mancunian chuckles, although some of them don't notice the typo at first. Throughout this charade, I'm thinking only about Daisy. I've left my mobile on vibrate and I check each text, each call, with an impolite fiddle. I'm still unable to tie my thoughts down into any logical progression and they come at me from all sides. Will I take her to the clinic if she is? I will have to put her on the pill if she isn't. Flitting alongside these is the preposterous notion that I could even take the baby myself. What's more, I realise now that she's lied to me too; from her timings it's clear she'd already had sex when we talked that night.

Despite such rude attention to my mobile, I receive applause and am collared over coffee by the bankers, publishers and pharmacists I have deceived. They think I would be fun to work with, possibly even sexually available, judging by the innuendo of my opening gambit. In reality, as I work the room together with my juniors, I am a clown, whose joy will be effaced when I leave the ring after chucking this bucket of foil sparkles at the kids.

While they return to the conference hall for the next session, I disappear up to my hotel room, which overlooks the centre of Manchester. It must be around Daisy's break time, she still hasn't contacted me, so I sit on the bed, inhale, count to ten, exhale. Then I punch in her number.

"Hi," she answers.

I can feel her smile, but still I ask. "So?"

"Not pregnant."

"Thank God."

252

It's my turn to stifle a sob. The relief is tinged by an anger that she hasn't bothered to call me, and even by a dismay I cannot begin to explore.

"Have you done both sticks?" I ask.

"Yes, both sticks, not pregnant."

"Fantastic." I resist the urge to reprimand her – for not using a condom, for not being honest with me, for not realising my investment in her.

"We'll make an appointment at the family planning clinic, shall we, Daisy?"

She laughs. "Jack's here, gotta go. Thanks Cat, speak to ya soon."

She's gone. I stand and make for the window and realise that not once this morning did I mention her parents. I look out over the city, a headache thrumming at my temples, and allow my mind the time it needs to unscramble the last few hours. Predominant now is my frustration with her, although it's tempered by my relief, and also by a creeping awareness that it was me who cajoled her into this mess.

At some point, the buildings outside come into focus, together with a clock face, and I realise that I've been standing by the window for nearly an hour. My gaze sweeps the city. I used to be a student here, nearly twenty years ago now, but I barely recognise the place; there was no Harvey Nicks, just the scrappy Arndale Centre, where even in winter the teenage girls scuttled about in mini skirts, their bare legs a mottled blue.

In the bathroom, I splash my face and re-do my make-up, even though I can't imagine that my eyes will be anything but she-witch red for the rest of the day. I look presentable enough in the mirror, but I really can't face going back down. Ash has always taken the pre-lunch slot, but he's too busy being a Minister this year, so the session will be led by the local MP, who will spurt only drivel.

"Bla, bla, bla," I watch my mouth speak the slack words. And hearing them out loud underpins my decision; it's ten years since I last went back.

253

I set off on the chilly pavements just before noon, raising my face to the cobalt sky, which lulls me for the short walk to Oxford Road. When I reach the university, I look up in surprise at the memories which strike me: the Manchester Museum where I used to linger when I craved solitude, the Whitworth Building where our graduation ceremony was held. I hover outside the entrance to the Old Quadrangle, with its iron gates and stone archway. Students are strolling through into the square, scarves wrapped importantly, a new term's files bundled at their chests. So I join them. I step through the archway and emerge, from the back of the wardrobe, into Narnia, into my youth.

I stand and take in the Quad with its grand Victorian buildings. It is smaller than I remember, dinky even; back then it seemed to swamp me. Perhaps my memory has bestowed more magnitude upon it, so formative were those three years spent here – the escape from home, the political awakening, the sexual binge. This is where the metamorphosis took place.

A sense of excitement bristles. The term is barely one month in, and many of these kids will be Freshers, oblivious to me, as I begin a nostalgic lap of honour. Autumn has made its glorious scarlet stain on the creeper swathed across the Beyer Building, and the boulder is still there, of course, swept south during the Ice Age. Next to it, a bench beckons.

I sit down beside two students and sneak a peek at them kissing. Primed for life, they have that air about them, a mix of trepidation and swagger which I remember so well. I feel like a maiden aunt in their midst, but they should know that I too was eighteen once. That I had a clear and comprehensive plan for my life – one which certainly didn't involve getting hitched on graduation, unlike some of my peers. But then it didn't involve being childless at forty either.

Unbidden thoughts of Daisy wash over me again. How could she not have thought about the consequences? So unconscious of the power within her own body. I'll still be reeling with the shock for days, but I bet she's moved on already, cavorting with Jack outside some chip shop. I would never have been so irresponsible at her age. And, let's face it, fifteen's more like eighteen today. I was on the pill at eighteen, popped it meticulously for nearly twenty years and never once had a scare. Ha, how ridiculous that now seems.

Both heads beside me veer my way, and I realise that I've said, "Ha" out loud. I throw them a sheepish smile and heave myself up from the bench. At the archway, I turn to absorb the Quad for a final few moments before leaving. I've always denied any regret about how I've lived my life. Where others have referred to some career blip, or love affair that set them back a couple of years, I have remained silent, hand on Dom's knee, smug that my own existence has been carefully crafted, perfectly honed. But in this time warp I wonder if any of it has really mattered. Perhaps my life should have been lived at random, rather than devised. Perhaps I should have put it on shuffle, surprised myself with unexpected melodies, instead of programming the tracks to play in sequence. Instead of being able to hum the next tune before it began.

I finally return to the conference hall just before afternoon tea. Tim, who is chairing the session, throws me a glassy stare from the podium. Later he'll whinge at me for missing lunch and all its lucrative potential, but I return his look blankly and take a seat at the back. I watch him nip a paper between his teeth, letting it hang there while he flips through the others on his desk, lending him the air of an office junior. As if Geoffrey would ever have promoted him to MD over me. I've always known that haven't I? Holding out until I received the grandiose title was just one tactic on my part to delay what I'll now never have.

Before he's finished summing up, I sneak out the swing doors to the lobby and make for the tea table. I pour myself a cup and eye the sofa longingly, but that would be an unprofessional step too far. Behind me, the lift opens, and the sound of a familiar voice makes me catch my breath, spinning me round on my heels. Ash emerges, together with his entourage, beams at me and makes smartly for my side.

"Am I glad to see you." We both know that my voice is overly effusive as I lean in and kiss his cheek.

"Couldn't break with tradition, could I?" He draws me into him and returns the peck. "Although in truth, I've been visiting a local meat processing plant and thought I'd come by for some free nosh tonight. Not that I'm hungry after what I've had to witness today." He gurns, but that face remains enchanting.

"I'll see what we can rustle up for you then. In return for a few choice words."

As the buzz goes round that he is present, I watch Ash preen himself for his public. These days his suits are handmade, his ties are woven silk, and they're not from M&S. I never thought I'd see him succumb – such a far cry from his days of selling *Socialist Worker* outside the tube at Brixton.

In the early evening, I am in my room zipping up the little black dress I'm pleased to have packed, when Ash calls my mobile. He invites me for a drink in his suite, a prospect far more heartening than a pre-dinner round with the other delegates. Mini-bar wine and a long soak in bubbles of Molten Brown Gingerlily have both taken a soothing toll, and a dose of drops has whitened my eyes. I switch my mobile off, place it in the safe and leave the room.

Ash opens his door with a bottle of Bollinger in hand and beckons me in. When we clink glasses, the fine crystal rim and tiny prickles against my lips are the resounding tonic I need. I savour the champagne with closed eyes for several moments, before I sink onto the sofa, curl up and tuck my stocking feet beneath me.

"You seem preoccupied," he says.

"Just busy day." I smile brightly at him.

"Pull these things off effortlessly these days, don't you?"

I shrug. "Been nearly twenty years now. Sometimes wish I still did get that adrenaline whoosh before speaking in public."

"Ah, that feeling I share. Very little adrenaline at all these days." His hand drops loosely to the sofa between us, the wedding ring a thin band of gold. "Did I tell you I saw Dinwoodie at a Number 10 lunch last week?"

"No?" I feign nonchalance and wait. I've heard nothing from Stewart since that day.

"Have you two had a run-in?"

"No."

"It's just that, while we were waiting for the PM, he was slagging you off, really gunning for you, Cat. Said he's thinking of sacking you."

"Oh?" The panic hits me, Stewart still represents half our business.

"But Lord Grainger was there, whose supermarket chain I believe enjoys 70% of the UK market – *slightly* bigger than Dinwoodie's – and he stepped in. Said he'd snap you up for himself then."

I see where he's going and the dread subsides. "He is a wanker, Ash. Your word, by the way."

"The man is a gobshite. Glad you've finally seen the light. Anyway, thought you'd like to know that you have nothing to worry about. He won't dump you, of course, but if ever he does, you know where to go."

"Thanks Ash."

In acknowledgement, I reach for his hand on the couch between us and clasp his fingers with mine. A jolt streaks through my arm. I'm paralysed by the action, and so it seems is he; no message from either my brain or his will withdraw our fingers. After several moments, I give his hand a sisterly squeeze and release it.

257

"So how are you going to entertain us tonight?" I ask him.

"Thought I'd tell a joke."

"Not *that* joke?" I let out a mock groan, at which he runs a swift fingernail up the sole of my foot, making me yelp and jerk it away.

"Still ticklish then." He grins.

At dinner, the dessert plates have been cleared and we're on coffee after a lavish five-course meal. Tim and I have homed in on the chairman of a Northern bookshop chain, who sits between us, and I've laughed at his copious anecdotes. Giggled deliriously actually, because I'm giddy with wine, with the lightness of being at the end of this odd day. Opposite me, Ash has caught my eye many times; of course really I am flirting with him.

At 10pm on the dot, Ash throws me a quizzical look and I nod back. He stands and clinks his glass, announces the joke, and the collective glow of appreciation around the room sets him off.

"This little tale is all about the need for good policy-making, which is crucial for a man in my position." His expression lightens as he begins. "There was a family of mice living in a field ..."

I smile down into my napkin. Ash first told this one in Brussels over ten years ago, and I've heard him roll it out on several occasions since then.

"... And a big fat cat kept gobbling them up. So the mice asked the wise old owl sitting high up in the oak tree what they should do. 'Put a ribbon with a bell on around the cat's neck so you'll hear it coming,' he said."

Looking down at my narrowed eyes, Ash takes a breath, and the very tip of his tongue appears briefly between his lips. To anybody else watching, the Minister is wetting his lips, but my stomach flips itself over.

He goes on. "So the mice find a ribbon with a bell. But when they approach the cat to tie it on her neck, she gobbles them up."

Once again, Ash looks me in the eye. And my subconscious dangles the makings of a thought my way – your husband no longer loves you, there will be no more IVF, this man has only to sit on the edge of the bed and his wife falls pregnant.

"The mice race back to the owl. 'It didn't work! Please tell us what should we do now?' they ask. And the wise old owl says, 'Oh, I just make the policy, I don't implement it.'"

Beside me, the bookshop owner actually smacks his thigh and I clock similar hilarity on the neighbouring tables; we did right to offer unlimited wine at dinner. Ash sits down with a smug smile at me and we hold each other's look for what we both know is a beat too long, a beat too far; my decision is made. I stand to make my thanks for a successful conference and wish everybody well on their journey home, thinking, now get the hell out of here, all of you. When there are just small-fry stragglers left, I throw Ash one last look, fold my napkin, place it serenely on the table and stand to leave.

In my room, I sit on the bed facing the door and wait, hands placed on my knees in an effort to stop shaking. After a few minutes, I begin to count the black flower sprigs on the wallpaper around the doorframe. Maybe he's waiting until Tim has come up, his room is next to mine, and our juniors are just along the hall too. And then he knocks. When I open the door, Ash is standing against the wall opposite, arms folded, one leg draped over the other, his head cocked on one side Hearing the lift ping at the end of the corridor, I pull him into the room.

He shoves me against the closed door and we go at each other like savages, our mouths breaking off for stabs at newly bared swathes of skin. I am startled by the pleasure which infuses my body, as if I've never before craved

259

another being; my thighs pulse, my nipples ache, my belly is taut with lust. Ash pushes me back onto the bed, sinks to his knees and I await the sensation of an exquisite memory from long ago.

It is not quite light when I awake, to the sound of a Manchester rush hour below. My very first thought is of impending doom. When I realise why, I scramble out of bed pushing away from Ash, who is spooned behind me. The bathroom light is cruel, exposing my skin as yellow, and so it should be. I cannot believe what I have done. There are bruises on my arms, red beads of a love-bite on one breast. In the shower, I scrabble to sponge it all away, douche it out of me, expunge the fact that I have just screwed a man who is not my husband. It didn't begin to factor last night, not even while I was sitting on the bed waiting. I just needed to have Ash.

How absolutely stupid; I could be pregnant. But then it's only been a few days since my period and, after all, I am not a fertile woman. Through the haze of our frenzy, he did ask if I had a condom and then insisted that he'd pull out. He didn't of course, and I didn't care that he came inside me, because I still hadn't shuddered to a halt myself, and nothing mattered more than that one last thrust, one last surge to take me where I needed to go.

When I emerge from the bathroom Ash has gone.

26

To stamp some sense of normality on the start of day, I take my mobile from the safe and switch it on. Whilst it's coming to life, I'm swamped again by shame, and I think back to what the counsellor told me after the miscarriage – that infertility is one of the toughest challenges a couple can ever face. Well throw in a dose of infidelity, and let's see, shall we?

As expected, the phone swarms with messages and missed calls, but I'm alarmed to see also several from Dom. An instinctive glance at the flashing hotel phone on the far desk confirms that something's happened. The first message, left yesterday late in the evening, is doleful enough. *Cat, call me.* Gradually, with my progress through each voicemail, I piece it together. The Japanese technology conglomerate, in which he's invested the lion's share of his fund, is embroiled in a corruption scandal. Its directors have been accused of concealing debts, lying about profits and skimming millions. Shares in the company have plummeted, and with them his fund. By the fifth message, left just after 3am – the darkest hour, the hour when apparently most suicides happen – he is desolate. *I need to talk to you, Cat.*

On the train home I'm stricken. When I finally spoke to him, Dom told me that they've frozen the fund, that he'd spent the night trying to determine the extent of the damage, which will be colossal. His investors will have lost millions, many of them small businesses, canny individuals, and pensioners whose private nest eggs will be wiped out. Just before dawn, his company's CEO had arrived at his desk and advised him to go home. I'm still absorbing this, with the *FT* on my lap, nursing a coffee and staring out at the passing cows. Whenever I shuffle in the seat, my bottom jags me, reminding me of just what capers we played out last night, probably at around 3am when Dom was trying to call me. And I despise the fact that my body, then so self-obsessed, is today even sentient at all.

When I step out of the cab, I see that our living room curtains are closed. I enter a world of dusky mourning, punctured by the yowl of a bass guitar reverberating around the house. A cardboard box sits in the hall, a wedding photo of Dom and I wedged between the notebooks and files. Silkie scuttles up to draw me into the living room, her head turning like Lassie leading the rescue party to the injured. I drop my *FT* onto the hall console – the front page is splattered with the scandal, and he doesn't need to read his name in the related article on page seven just yet – and I follow my Golden Lab into the room.

Dom is flat out on the sofa, eyes closed, smoking a joint, while Pink Floyd resonates off the walls. The scene makes my legs buckle.

"Oh Dom." I sink to my knees beside him and cup his cheeks. He opens his eyes, the blue gleaming through tears that have only just dried and now bubble over once more. His face is grey and peppered with silvery stubble, as if he's aged overnight. It smells unwashed, fusty.

"It's all over, Cat."

For one dreadful beat I think he means us, a narcissistic thought, which will stay with me forever.

"Dom it will be OK, these things work themselves out, it's only business."

He actually laughs, a demented, high-pitched, one beat laugh and shakes his head, seemingly wondering where to start. "It's billions of pounds, thousands of investors, some of them utterly ruined. I'm dead in the water."

He inhales on the joint, exhales, and his body falls slack. The tears spill down his cheeks and, as I rub each one out with my thumb, another discharges itself like gel oozing from a tube.

"I can't believe it. I cannot believe what I've done. Why did I keep going? It felt so safe, a no brainer, but I'm better than that." His voice cracks. "Well, clearly I'm not."

"You're amazing at your job, Dom. It's not your fault, those bastards duped everyone, their accountants, the public, the government."

He throws me a grateful smile and grips my wrist. "I really need you, Cat."

"I'm here. I'll always be here."

I take the joint from his fingers and stub it out in the ashtray on the floor. Then I climb onto the sofa, stretch myself out against his body, clamp each part of my clothed flesh to his, suffusing maximum comfort, even though my tiny frame leaves swathes of his body without succour. My bruised breast is compressed hard against his chest, in a gesture that only I will understand; this breast is yours, this pain is fitting. Dom flops his free arm over me, pulls me to him, and I feel him relax, sense anxiety flowing from him. For him, I will make everything all right.

As I sink against him, however, I know that I'm unworthy of this trust, this guileless belief that I am his saviour. Already, through the fug of darkness, a pinprick of light pierces, and it beckons me. An opportunity. Then my guilt screams at me, like the groaning woman in the Pink Floyd track, who's been building up and is now reaching her crescendo, shrieking at the world. Before the smooth rich bass obliterates her and takes us all off to a more soothing place.

PART THREE

27

It would be all too simple for me to claim that I'm not sure how we landed back in Olu's office. The past few weeks have been a blur – of recriminations by Dom's former employer, of meetings with lawyers, and of reprisals in the gutter press about the flimsy constraints on fat cat fund managers. I stepped in to manage it all for him, it was me who found him an employment lawyer, someone I worked with years ago, and it was me who fielded the calls from reporters. I even hauled in the PR outfit we use for press coverage to support a lobbying campaign, and had them issue a counter attack, reeling out Dom's untarnished history. There's some evidence that this may have helped, unless the natural way of things was for it all to die down anyway.

The tabloids have not bothered with his photo, barely even with his name. Rather they're incensed by the whole city culture, delirious to witness this bonfire of the vanities, even though many of their readers have suffered. The fund attracted armchair investors who dabbled with small portfolios and were enticed by financial advisers to opt for Dom's pot, with the assurance that he was one of the best managers at the game, that his fund had yielded year on year. The *FT* has been kinder, exploring this as a lesson to all, recognising that Dominic Wyatt was a shrewd player for over a decade, wondering what flipped in his mind to invest beyond sensible levels, to keep them there after the initial whiff of scandal.

In a couple of the red tops there have been references to the unfair dismissal case against Dom too. Hints at sexual harassment. While I can tell by the way they've couched them with the word *alleged* that it's probably just spice, still the words leap out at me, black and bold. But I will not mention them. Perhaps Dom senses my suspicion, but my own misdemeanour – which is how I've watered it down – floats at the edges, even if I have ignored Ash's efforts to contact me. At present, Dom and I are enjoying a fragile truce, so we'll leave it there. For now anyway.

My public take on our return to the Knightsbridge is that Dom suggested we have a final stab at it, in one of those moments where we lay clinging to each other. On that first day, our Black Friday, I tearfully refused his plea for sex, lying that my period had just started and hoping that he hadn't registered the yellow tampon wrappers in the bathroom bin a few days before. With time and make-up, the bites and bruises disappeared. Yet when I offered myself up in a fluffy towel, discarded on the bedroom floor to reveal my vulnerable and ready self, the moment had passed; Dom was impotent. They say that can happen in times of extreme stress.

If it was Dom who proposed a last attempt, of course I went along with him. Over cosy dinners, I assured him that a baby would see us through, that work was a minor part of life's balance. Hilarious that, coming from me, but I was desperate to shake him out of his stupor. If we had a family, I insisted, then we could always move to the country – imagine hiking with our little one in a backpack, welcoming friends with a log fire. These were the best images I could conjure up, but in truth, none of that mattered, I just wanted one more go. At any cost. I feel he owes it to me after all I've done to bring him through his crisis.

And, in my further defence, if more is needed, I'm not exactly sound of mind myself at the moment. I am the little girl lost, stripped of her remarkable armour, apologising to people who knock against me in the street. At work, being Catriona Black affords me a welcome anonymity, because

268

most clients and contacts are unaware of my husband's surname. The staff seem to have warmed to the weakness in me. Like spring animals, they emerge from their dens and sniff around me to sense if I am no longer a danger. I watch myself with them, as if from two paces to the side, and I listen to my voice, sadly conscious of the listless shape and tenor of my words.

Yesterday, I sat alone in our study, gazing out into space. A spider's web has spanned the top corner of our window for some weeks now, and I often find myself watching the spider poised at its edge. As I stared through it yesterday, a fat bluebottle flew into the web. Instantly ensnared, it floundered there, wings beating. The spider scurried along the threads and wrapped its spindly legs around the fly, embracing it as if with reassurance – it's OK I've got you. The fly was soon dead. I watched the spider encase the insect in gossamer thread, then haul it like a rucksack over its back, before making a sudden dash up to the corner of the web. And I found myself in tears.

*

At the Knightsbridge, the waiting room has welcomed us back warmly. Soft leather oof sounds puttered from those expensive sofas as we sank into them and took up the usual starting position, eyes glued to newspapers. Now, Olu is at the doorway, his smile broadening. My consultant's presence on Jackie's radio show had me wavering, but I see today that I really am special to him. In his office, he orders tea and biscuits. It's as if we are old friends now. No, it's as if we are to be given greater security clearance, to enjoy more intimacy with him after the miscarriage and have progressed up to the elite – those who nearly got there.

"As I have told you, Cat, because you have already been pregnant, your chances of conceiving are now higher than before."

I'm not interested in his percentages, or his charts. When we started out, Olu told me my chances at thirty-eight were significantly higher than they would be at forty. I can still see his wide eyes, his furrowed brow, imbuing this fact upon me. Well, I am now just four months shy of my fortieth birthday. He should be able to fit us in, he says, before the clinic closes on Christmas Eve – depending on the date of my next period. This is due imminently, but again I'm hoping that Dom's observation of my cycle is poor. Needless to say, if that period doesn't show up then I'm in a far greater fix.

Downstairs at the cash desk, a couple are ahead of me in the queue. When the cashier announces the total amount owed, the man lets out a low whistle and his partner nudges him with an embarrassed shift of her head towards me, but I drop my eyes just in time. With the reluctance of a child handing over illicitly gained sweets, he offers up his credit card, for a sum of £4200. I wonder if he knows that this won't cover all the drugs they need either, the clinic drip-feeds you with those and they'll be back next week for another few hundred quid's worth.

When I've paid, I turn and smile over towards Dom, who's sitting on a chair staring at the floor. Lost in another world, his hands are clasped loosely, his elbows resting on his knees, scuffing the tears in his jeans. Today we're embarking on one last attempt at a happy future together, but somehow he's not looking forward, he's looking into his past. I take his hand, like a nurse might that of an old gentleman, to raise him from his chair and lead him through to the sitting room, where Molly the Spaniel will make her weekly therapeutic appearance to cheer the old folks.

"We have lift-off." I try to rouse the optimism we felt before our first IVF cycle.

The sole conviction that remains with me is childlike, if we can just get there this time, then it will all be OK. It's like running up thousands of pounds on credit cards, juggling them with the minimum monthly payments, but at

270

that last moment before you're hauled up in court, you win the lottery and pay them all off in full. Life resumes. Life would resume if I could only get pregnant. And of that, in view of my age, we now have just a one in six chance.

I squeeze my husband's hand. "Dom, will you ask God if he'll roll us a six, first go, this time?"

28

It's Sunday night, sometime deep in December. Yesterday Dom and I put the tree up and decorated the living room. Later, at 10pm on the dot, I injected myself with the HCG drug which will ripen my six eggs ready for tomorrow morning's collection. Previous cycles have yielded more, but six is somehow now a lucky number for me. I'm curled up on the sofa waiting for the news to come on before bed. Dom's gone on after hockey for a few festive drinks. Not too many, I cautioned, given his one last gala performance in the morning.

I catch a waft of fresh pine and inhale deeply, glancing up at the tree. Dom chose an enormous one, in the hope perhaps that the foliage would invade the room, stretch its way out to plug the hollowness that resonates at home. There's no tension now. It's more of a lull. As if we're hanging in time, suspended on threads, careful not to snag them lest we might smack against all that surrounds us. He went for purple and amber decorations. Next year – I have to believe it – there will also be one of those tacky baubles printed with, *Baby's First Christmas*.

The BBC Christmas filler is up on the screen, a gigantic snowball, built by beautiful children and their radiant parents, rolling past a chocolate-box row of dinky cottages. Then the headlines come on, the usual nothing much of a Sunday evening, something about Iraq, and some MP up for corruption. And then a third item. The newsreader's puffy grey face looks out gravely and tells me that an animal testing laboratory on the outskirts of Derby has been firebombed. What he says next appears to mutate while it

272

spouts from his lips, as if an alien has hijacked his voice. He doesn't say that activists have been apprehended, that the zealots responsible for this arson attack have been arrested, as you'd expect. Instead, he tells us that two elderly women at the scene have been taken to hospital, one of them with severe burns. There are images of firemen, of water arcs from hoses, of an industrial estate, of blackened windows. He moves on to expand the first headline. But I know. I know, even before the phone is ringing, that that's my mum.

"Have you seen the news, Cat?" Billy's voice booms at me, his panic bringing forth a rush of my own.

"It's Mum, isn't it?"

"Has to be." He's waiting for me to decide what to do.

"I'll get the cab to pick you up on the way." I hang up and dial again.

The drive up the M1 takes us two and a half hours. By the time I got to Billy's we'd both been on the phone to the Derby Royal Infirmary, and yes, two elderly ladies had been admitted with cuts and burns. One of them was badly burnt, but neither woman had ID on her. Well of course not, it was a covert operation. What did she do? Forget to chuck the firebomb they'd given her? Hold onto it, so that it exploded up her arm, into her face? I see a flash of my mother screaming, hands thrown to terrified eyes, her mass of wiry hair in flames, the grey wisps consumed by a vicious orange. Her cheeks are blistering, splitting open, spilling muscle, bone and blood.

"What the hell was she doing in Derby, Billy?"

"No idea. Only saw her last week ..."

I'm staring into my reflection in the darkened window, spinning my rings furiously. I want to weep, but the tightness in my chest has me clamped down, and in any case I must try and hold it together for Billy. Please, don't let Mum be the one who's badly hurt, please don't let it be her.

273

"If it's that Maureen, I'd say Mum can move quicker than her." I recall the large woman beside my mum at the police station.

"Yes." Billy reaches across for my hand, resting it with his own on the holdall between us, which he's packed with a toothbrush, toiletries, and one of Maggie's nighties.

When I call Dom it goes to voicemail, so I text him: *Mum in accident, on way to Derby.*

He calls me back. "What happened?" His voice is distressed and, I have the presence to note, not slurred at all. Not that it matters now; I'm no longer going to make my egg collection tomorrow.

"She was trying to fire bomb an animal testing lab." I feel Billy's annoyance, but what other explanation could there be?

"Come on, Lizzie's not that stupid." Dom says.

"Well, she's been badly burnt, they said so on the news."

"The news?"

I nod at the phone. "BBC."

There is silence while Dom decides what to do.

"Do you want me to drive up there?" he asks finally.

"No, it's OK, Billy's with me."

"Alright. Keep me posted though, will you? I'm sure she's in good hands. Take care." Though distant as always now, his voice does linger. Why can't he tell me he loves me?

"Call you later." It's me who ends the conversation.

At the hospital, I thrust a cheque at the cabbie and we sprint into A&E reception, yelling the name of my mother at the nurse behind the desk. She holds her hands up as if it's a heist, but then also swiftly acknowledges the photos we both thrust at her, showing each of us with Lizzie. My snap is ten years old, a wedding photo, but Billy has a recent one taken this summer. With a pang of envy I watch him hand over an image of the two of them, sitting in his back garden, raising glasses to the camera. A summery jug of orange cordial sits on the table, and the shot has even captured a spangle of light playing off its handle, enhancing the warmth of this mother-and-son moment.

The nurse also takes ID from each of us: my House of Commons pass and Billy's passport which he's packed especially, and then she confirms that one of the women is indeed our mother, Elizabeth Stevens.

"It's not her who's badly hurt, is it?" I ask, my tears brimming now. "They said on the news…"

The nurse responds with a calm, close-lipped smile and reaches for her phone. "I'll get somebody to take you to her, now."

While we wait, I'm tapping my fingers on the desk, scuffing my foot on the lino, and bearing down visually on anybody who emerges from between the swing doors. Billy, meanwhile, informs the nurse that the other woman is most likely a Mrs Maureen Titley.

Finally, a male nurse pushes through the doors and approaches us in his pale green scrubs. "Come with me," he says with a gentle smile, "I'll take you to your mother."

"Is she badly burnt?" My voice cracks and the tears bubble, why can't this man put me out of my misery?

"Not too badly, but she's suffered severe cuts. Just through here."

We follow him along a labyrinth of corridors and then finally off into a room, where my knees buckle at the sight of my mother in the bed. Billy grabs me and manoeuvres me to the chair beside her, then he stands with his hand on my shoulder. I feel its grip shaking. Lizzie is sleeping. She looks so fragile, so winsome, the covers stretched beneath her tiny chin across the white gown, binding that slight body as if it's newly born. Only her arms are exposed, the right one heavily bandaged. But the flesh on her cheeks has not blistered or split, it is waxy with rosy patches, you might think it was lightly rouged. Across the pillow, her hair is splayed like a fan of delicate pearly lace against the crisp white linen. While singed in places, it has not been engulfed by flames. Overcome by emotion for that wondrous hair, I reach out to stroke it, my fingers smoothing it gently from her crown and out over the pillow. Her eyes open, she smiles at me and at Billy behind me.

"Hello you two," she says.

It must be around 4am. The policewoman sits in the chair, which Billy has vacated for her and she speaks gently, albeit a conspicuously strategic form of gentle to extract maximum information. I'd put her in her late twenties, her short black hair is parted in the middle and her lips are like a pair of crimson slugs clinging to her face. Visibly, this woman is repulsed by my mother's actions. She has cautioned Mum that anything she says will be taken down and used as evidence, and has asked if she wants a lawyer present. Mum has replied that she'd like only her daughter there, and I resist the urge to insist on a legal presence, allowing her wishes to the fore. After Billy has left the room, I sit down on the other side of the bed and hold her hand.

The policewoman begins. "Tell me, in your own words, Mrs Stevens, exactly what happened last night."

Mum is only too ready, her eyes focused on the foot of her bed as she speaks. "There's this man, an activist, he's been to the stall on the High Road before on a Saturday."

"Which stall is that, Mrs Stevens?"

"Our 'Animals Have Feelings Too' stall. We help man it every week, Maureen and I. He's only stopped by a couple of times, but I've seen him speak at meetings too, he always wears a baseball cap, pulled down."

With difficulty, she lifts her right fingers to an invisible cap and pulls it down, wincing at the pain in her bandaged hand. Her left one is holding tightly onto mine.

"Last Saturday, he asked us, would we like to contribute to the cause? To take part in a rescue operation?"

The woman is noting it all down. "How long have you been part of this... Animals Have Feelings organisation?"

"Fifteen years. On and off."

I smile quietly to myself. On and off with the multitude of other sentient beings that 'have feelings'. I squeeze Mum's hand, she squeezes back.

"And did this man say what that rescue operation was?" I watch the lipstick slugs part and meet again while this officer reels out her flat Midlands vowels.

"Yes. He said they had proof that four chimpanzees were being used in testing."

"Chimpanzees," she says.

"It's illegal, you see, in this country. You can't use great apes for experiments anymore, you have to test on macaques or marmosets."

"I see." The woman scribbles more notes. "And did you see this man again before tonight?"

"No. No, he told us to be at Derby Railway Station at 6pm tonight, two other men picked us up there in a van."

"Did you know these men?"

"No, don't think so, they both had balaclavas on."

"You got into a van with two complete strangers wearing balaclavas?"

Mum gives an imperceptible shrug. "They were clearly there for the cause."

"Did they at any point tell you their names?"

"They both had codenames: Feckless and Gormless, the cows in Cold Comfort Farm. It was supposed to be a joke, I suppose." My mother's voice is so earnest, but as these names are being noted, she turns to me and adds, "Told me I could be the third one, Pointless, if I wanted." Then she winks at me. Is she making this up?

"Can you describe the vehicle?" The policewoman's voice hardens; she's caught the smirk I've given Mum.

"White transit van. Didn't get the registration. We sat in the back, it was empty, there was carpet on the floor. They planned to lift the cages directly and put them in the back,

277

told us they were going to take them to Twycross Zoo, just down the road."

"Twycross Zoo." The woman rolls her eyes, and I feel the need to stand by my mum.

"Awesome publicity stunt," I say.

"Be quiet please, or I'll have to ask you to leave the room."

Mum continues unperturbed. "It smelt of animals in the back. I think they'd used it for rescue operations before."

I have a vision of my sixty-four-year-old mother sitting on a tatty scrap of carpet, which reeks of primate pee, hugging her knees as she is sped, sideways on, to the outskirts of a provincial city, in an old rusty can of a van. When she should be at home embroidering a tapestry, or pickling fruit, or something. A sudden rush of pride engulfs me – at her spirit, at the wonder she still finds in the world, at her guts in wanting to get up and change it. I squeeze her hand and smile. She turns again and holds my eyes with her own.

The woman finishes her page and flips it over, takes a couple of frosty nasal breaths and observes her blank page, seemingly wondering where to go next. Obviously, there is only one way, we need to know the rest of this story.

"And when you reached the site of the laboratory, what happened next?"

Mum shifts around the bed, gathering her thoughts and her strength again. "They said there would be two females, two males. Maureen and I were each to take a cage, then keep them calm in the back of the van on the drive to the zoo."

"Drive. To. The. Zoo." The officer raises a withering eyebrow, one that has been plucked out of existence then sliced back in with black crayon.

"They weren't bothered by the alarm, it was well outside the town and they said we'd be in and out within two minutes." Mum pauses for a moment. "And what they

278

were up to at that lab was illegal anyway, so if the police came, we were completely within our rights."

The woman writes, shaking her head as if to an inane child, and I want to slap her.

"So they broke in, and ran inside, all hell for leather, and of course the alarm was going off, wasn't it? We ran in after them, well Maureen was limping a bit, she's had a bad foot lately."

She pauses, perhaps to see if this policewoman cares about her friend's bad foot, but the only thing she patently does care about is getting to interview Maureen, who is still in theatre.

Mum continues. "It was only a small laboratory, just three doors leading off from the reception area. They switched the lights on and began racing about from room to room, trying to find the chimps. And then they were shouting, swearing. Well they were obviously livid about something, but we didn't know what." She pauses, and I realise that she's doing so for effect. "Something was wrong," she adds.

I hide a smile of surprise at my mother, she is telling a tale, forcing suspense on this woman. It's working too; the officer sits with her pen poised, head bent slightly forward, forehead creased in anticipation, and Mum actually waits. Until she asks, "And then what?"

"Then Feckless, I think it was – or it might have been Gormless – he screamed at us to go into the first two rooms they'd just been in and to open the cages. So, Maureen and I dashed into one of the rooms. And, well there were no chimps in there, no monkeys at all. The only animals in there were …"

"Yes?" The policewoman stops writing, looks up, and I'm reminded of Basil Brush. I too am on tenterhooks.

"Rats. White ones. Scores of them. In cages stacked up against the walls. We could hear cages clanging in the other rooms, the men throwing the doors open. So we did the

279

same. We ran along the shelves, unhooking the catches, flinging the cage doors back."

Mum has hiked her legs up underneath the sheet, as if to escape the torrents which we all know are coming.

"And then, well it was horrible ... I mean white rats are better than those massive brown ones you get, but they were everywhere! The floor was swarming with their vile tails and paws, all scuttling over our boots." She shakes her head at me. "I was petrified one would run up my leg."

"What did you do next?"

"Well, there were counters, workstations you know. One at the window and one in the middle of the room, like an island, and we hoisted ourselves up onto them, only Maureen chose the one by the window. Eventually, most of the rats found the door and out they streamed." She gestures with a stiff sweep of her hand across the bed. "Then the room was empty."

"And then what?"

"Well we had to get out of there, didn't we? I'd heard the men scarper back to the van, and I didn't want us to get left behind, so I started to climb down. Then it came flying through the window. I felt the glass hit my arm and shoulder as I ducked behind the counter, but poor Maureen took the brunt of it, of course. It must have exploded right up her back. I helped her out of there, used my coat to try and stamp out the flames." Her eyes well up again. "You're sure she's alright, Catriona?"

"She'll be OK, Mum." I haven't told her the truth yet.

She nods. "No sight of the men, or their van, of course. And then the police came."

The officer is writing again. "They actually found no animals on the site, Mrs Stevens."

"Yes, well they'll be half-way to Blackpool by now, won't they?"

I stifle a chuckle, as the woman glares at me and flips her notebook shut. Standing to leave, she tells Mum that she'll be back later in the morning to inform her whether they are to press charges. As soon as the door is closed, I smile down at my mother.

"Did all of that really happen, Mum?"

"Few embellishments here and there."

"You were so courageous."

"Well, I'm relieved there were no chimps there, if truth be known." She begins to chuckle.

I lean in, laughing with her "We'll give her another run for her money when she comes back, shall we?"

The fluorescent hospital lighting has left me with no notion of dawn, but I catch glimpses of its gloomy arrival from the canteen window. I stuff a bag with coffees and bacon sandwiches. Billy and I have caught an hour slumped in the chairs by Mum's bed and the police will be back soon.

I needed to get out of that room for a moment of solitude. To imagine what's going to become now of those six eggs inside me. Will they float, unhinged like astronauts, bouncing off each other around the ruby warm cavity of my belly? Will they pop, like sherbet sweets? Release magic dust into the ether? Fertilisation is now no longer an option, because I can't leave Mum. I've asked Dom to let the clinic know that it's off.

On my approach to the room I can hear my mum and Billy talking, and I frame my face into a bright smile before entering. "Bacon butties all round."

Mum frowns at me. "You must go, Catriona."

"Go where?"

"Billy's told me what you've got on today. Please don't miss it for me."

"You shouldn't be worrying her like that." I slap his takeaway coffee down.

"You've said yourself that this one's your last chance."

I shake my head at my mother. I'm not going anywhere, when the police return she'll need somebody strong by her side.

281

"I'll be absolutely fine, Catriona. Won't be my first arrest will it?" Her eyes are twinkling. "Billy will stay with me."

Billy hurls me a don't treat me like a kid look. "I can handle this, sis."

"Please go, Catriona."

A glimpse at the clock tells me I should have been well under the knife by now, but a quick mental calculation brings me also a glimmer of hope.

I sit on the bed and take her hand. "I have been going to reflexology, Mum, and I'm on homeopathy too."

"Then you'll be well on your way to success, Catriona, now off you go, please, skedaddle."

I squeeze her hand, holding her eyes with mine. "Thanks, Mum."

When the cab has pulled away I first phone Olu, and then Dom.

"Dom, I'm on my way home. We can still go ahead, I've spoken to Olu and he believes the eggs could still be viable."

He lets out a strange whoop. "You are an absolute star! What time will you get here?"

"Couple of hours."

He pauses. "OK if I go strut my funky stuff now? Remember I've got that meeting with Ben later this morning?"

Outside the tarmac speeds past my window. Dom did tell me some days ago that Ben had lined up a meeting with the lawyers about the feasibility of a new fund, but I knew that we would have been out the other side of the op by mid morning, so it hadn't mattered to me then.

"Yes, of course, I'd forgotten," I mutter. "You go down there now then. I'm so knackered I'll sleep for hours afterwards, in fact they probably won't even need to anaesthetise me."

"I'll come back as soon as we're through, OK?"

"OK. And Dom? Make sure they label it correctly, won't you?"

He laughs. "Will do."

I smile back. "Love you."

"Yeah, good luck, Cat."

I arrive at the clinic just before noon, a good thirty-eight hours after I took my HCG shot, having the whole journey uttered silent pleas (to whom I'm not sure) that the eggs won't yet have deteriorated. Alone and nervous, I'm processed, prepped and wheeled to the basement theatre. And whilst I lie flat, submissive to the anaesthetist's needle ripping through the skin on the back of my hand, I am conscious that if this cycle works our baby will have been created without its parents having so much as kissed at its conception. We weren't even in the same building.

Then the drugs take hold and I smile woozily up at those Latin dancers painted on the ceiling, savour the vibrant fabrics they wear, the energy in their limbs, the passion in their faces. And I sink under that ripe moon into a final, grateful slumber, for what I know will be my last moondance.

29

Dom and I are sitting on a white powder beach in Barbados, rubbing shoulders with celebrity. Neither of us wished to spend the festive season at home, to endure the burden of other people's hope – both our families are twittering. Mum has recovered well and I settled her in at Billy's house for Christmas, while Maureen has been moved to a hospital near her family. They are both due in court early next year.

Out here, Dom and I can reinvent ourselves, pretending we are a normal couple in a holiday routine. We are, of course, simply waiting. Not only to see if it's worked, but also what will become of us if not. Back in London I'd catch him watching me and I'd find myself watching him, wondering what happened. It's as if we'd lost the memory which was Dom and Cat. As if we'd been switched off and back on again, to find our shared history wiped out. Did I really think that I could exploit his weakest moment without resentment setting in?

But here, each morning we amble to our spot on the sand under an almond tree, away from the umbrellas and gold lamé. Our days are spent reading, lazing to iPods, anything that drones in the mind. And I'm content to go with the flow, not to press him for interaction, so I remain quiet, giving him time. It isn't difficult, I'm pretty subdued myself and am quite content to skim the days. In two days time, on New Year's Eve, I will pee on a stick and see what the dice have rolled for my future. While full of hope, I'm also full of dread.

The beach is splattered with blood red leaves, large rounded pointy scoops, the way children draw them. An almond plops onto the sand between our sunbeds, mottled yellow into brown into red, causing us both to glance up from our novels, as if we've been waiting for some chance to make eye contact. Our smiles are tentative, shy, still distant, but I do perceive a slight change in Dom, I feel he's beginning to relax again. Dare I hope that he's coming round? Professionally he's bounced back somewhat. He's hopeful of getting his new fund off the ground, with Ben and another mate. They've checked out the legals and plan to hitch up with an outfit in Hong Kong.

He returns to his novel, but I sit up and scan the beach. The locals saunter their languorous way across the sand, their smiles contagious while they dupe us with fake gems or artwork. A girl with a perfect body struts past in her thong, and I shuffle myself down into the cushioned lounger. I've read that Caribbean women inject chicken hormones to plump up their bottoms, and mine now feels like it's received that same treatment.

A commotion rises further up the beach. A monkey has broken free from its dreadlocked owner, who's been touting it for a photo opportunity. It scampers onto a beached catamaran and dances on the canvas, with a can't-catch-me look, whilst its master strolls towards it.

"You come back here girl," he mutters.

The monkey makes a dash for an umbrella, snatching the sunglasses from an old woman in a silver bikini, before scooting up to the pinnacle of the shade. The woman shrieks, scrambles to her feet, and Dom and I begin to laugh.

"Mabel, you get down from there." Her master is now straining to mask his panic, but the beast screeches her laughter in his face.

At that, several guys jump up to help the man, and I'm startled to see Dom spring from his lounger too. In the mayhem that follows, there's much mirth and the barking of instructions as they try and trap Mabel, who zips jubilantly between them. Hamming it up, the men trip over sunbeds or flop on the sand in near misses, with the whole beach now looking on. Comedy is a great equaliser. Finally, Mabel sits chattering on a beached Jet Ski, her back turned and Dom is able to creep up with a towel. He makes a dive, smothering her head and body. Her owner is onto the confused animal, his indolent grin returning as he fastens the chain, and a cheer goes up. My husband has achieved again.

Dom sits down by the water's edge with his new friends, while Mabel parks herself behind them, sulking. A reefer is passed around. In his baseball cap and sunglasses, Dom does look the part of beach bum despite the greying hair – his torso still lithe, his legs thick and muscled. He scoops at sand, joggles it as one might a pile of coins. I smile to see him throw his head back laughing. It's been a while.

When he moseys back up the beach an hour or so later, his face is tranquil and he's smiling at me from behind the dark glasses. "You like a foot massage, lady?" he asks in a deep Bajun accent.

I stretch my legs out for him, exhilarated by the prospect of skin contact with my husband.

That afternoon, in relaxed mood, we take a boat trip out to swim with the turtles. Hand in hand we jump in, breaking through the surface into another world of shimmering beauty. When the skipper scatters broken crackers into the water, we're set upon by a feeding frenzy of tiny, iridescent fish, and marvel at each other through our masks. Down here, we are cushioned even more from our reality, by the glassy walls of water, by the muffle of our breathing, by the slow motion of our actions. I peer into the turquoise, catching the shafts of light with splayed palms, sweeping open fingers through this magical backdrop.

Then, from the underwater mist, a turtle approaches me, mouth down-turned, its eyes settled on mine like a grumpy old man. Swimming ever closer, it seems to be making for me and a panic hits me, has me breaking the surface, wrenching off my mask and kicking wildly. A jolt from my flipper lands on its shell and I scream; it's bound to come for me now. Its hooked beak cuts the surface right beside my face, and it considers me with prehistoric eyes, before gulping for air and dipping back down under the water. Then I'm thrashing towards the boat, flinging kicks at the unknown depths beneath me. Dom is beside me in seconds, lifting me, holding me up beneath the armpits like a child.

He fixes his eyes on mine. "It's OK, Cat, it's OK."

"Do they bite, Dom?" I cling to his neck, wrapping my legs around his body.

"Of course they don't bite. I'm here, you're fine."

Once back on the boat, Dom folds a towel around my body and holds me to his chest, while I sit there shuddering and wondering what happened. Have I engineered this moment? Or am I really now so pathetic?

The following day, I suggest we take a trip around the island. We spent the night spooned together, my husband's naked torso pressed contentedly against my back, his arms around me. Even as I drifted off to the sweetest slumber, however, my subconscious was well aware that this was most probably a temporary state of being. That these hours were more likely the makings of the poignant end, rather than inklings of a new beginning.

At breakfast, we're poring over the map, when Sidney, the British joker who's attached himself to us, saunters up in his scarlet shorts and black knee-length socks. I must have been polite with jet lag, because I seem to have become his foil. But I have played along – if only for the jolly aura it's lent Dom and me in this public setting.

"What's Bajun for bacon?" Eyebrows raised, mouth ajar.

"Don't know Sidney, what's Bajun for bacon?"

"Beer can!"

Despite his pitiful local accent, even Dom allows him a mock groan.

Our tour driver exudes the intimate friendliness we've come to love in the locals. North Point, he says, is a must for any tourist, so we set off up the west coast.

"You leave the children at home?" His white teeth flash in the mirror.

"We don't have children. Not yet." My reaction is now a reflex, not at all painful, even if an instinctive hand reaches for my tummy.

"You gotta have children man, it's God's way."

"We're working on it."

My voice carries a cheerful innuendo, implying that we're shagging like bunnies, and the man lets out a throaty black chortle, while Dom continues to gaze out the window.

We travel inland, across hilly country. The driver knows the territory well enough to take the bends a little too fast, and we sweep past brightly painted wooden houses, solid and happy with neat gardens of vivid shrubs and blue plumbago. On rounding a corner, we hear singing ahead and he slows down in reverence to the tambourines and harmonies, which ring from the open windows of a squat, whitewashed building.

"Can we stop?" It's the first thing Dom's said since we left the hotel.

"Sure, man."

Clearly grateful that Dom has stirred, our driver pulls over. Dom gets out and shuffles across the road to a window, stands peering through into the church. I hesitate, then follow him, brushing up against the wall a few respectful feet away.

He turns and smiles at me. "Beautiful isn't it?"

It is beautiful. The voices are in such rich harmony, with perfect timing and rhythm, but it's the happiness that strikes me. This is the sound of joy. I lean back into the wall, my body rippling to the music, and turn my face up to the sun, which infuses me with heat. The sweet voices wash through my whole being, and it's as if they're cleansing me, ridding anxiety, restoring contentment. Fleeting it may be, but for the first time in months I feel at peace. When the hymn ends, I open my eyes and see tears on Dom's smiling face. He reaches for me and I slide into his embrace.

While we hold each other, rocking gently, silently, the connection between us is palpable. I sense his thoughts seeping through me, his yearnings, his fears, as my own secrets flow back into him like an exchange of gases in the lungs. I yearn to hold onto it. And yet, even locked together like this, intimate and exposed, we both know that the moment is simply a mutual recognition of where we're at. It's not a reconciliation. Too much has been stripped away for a simple kiss and make up now. Eventually, Dom pulls away, and the moment is broken.

The happy worshippers spill out of the church into the road, its sticky tar glistening in the sunshine. Dom and I stroll back to the car while our driver moves forward to shake hands with a group of men; polite men, who are wearing suits either a little too large or a little too tight. In their sunglasses they could be gangsters secreting knuckle-dusters in pockets – only these are God-fearing men. The women sport hats, and their bodies are clothed in taffeta of dazzling purples or greens, which pinch at corpulent waists and thick black arms. Every face is smiling.

We arrive at North Point, where the Atlantic Ocean meets the Caribbean in a clash of aquamarine. Hands locked, we stand alone on the cliffs and watch the frenzied froth pounding at the rocks below us, smashing them, as if with just one last effort the waves will break through. Back they come, and again, battering the rock, spraying Dom and me standing high above them on the yellow fuzz which grips the flinty ground. The wind whips our hair. I'm struck by an odd thought; how easy it would be for Dom to launch me over that cliff. I used to believe that I knew him intrinsically, but now I wonder if anybody really knows another. Perhaps we should jump together. I study his face, is he thinking the same?

"Sucks you over doesn't it?" he says.

"It's just vertigo." With a hand drifting to my belly, I turn and make for one of the simple blue benches set well back from the edge.

That evening, a moonless night, we dine out. Tides restaurant is at the water's edge. The blackened sea laps below the wooden deck, and long flames roll from steel torches spiked into the sand. My curry is served in a coconut shell, and Dom's jumbo prawns are swathed by a giant banana leaf. While our conversation does not rise to the expectations of such a splendid setting, flitting as it does from the heat of the night to the exceptional food, even taking in a text from our dog-sitter, still we do manage to end the evening laughing together about our latest encounter with Sidney. He sidled up at happy hour with his rum punch, its turquoise umbrella picking out nicely the parrots on his shirt.

"It's the way he's so tickled by himself," I say now to Dom.

"Yeah. Always funny when people laugh at their own jokes though, isn't it?"

"But his poor wife ..."

"At least I don't humiliate you." He pauses, smiles. "Not like that anyway."

I smile back at him. "Not in any way."

We hold eye contact for several moments, and I see my chance.

"Dom –" I begin.

"Don't Cat." He shakes his head.

In the silence that follows, he stares out into the darkness and sighs heavily. I follow his gaze and struggle to rein in one of my own. Against the black water, there is the odd flash of surf, a streak of white when the waves roll in beneath us, but mainly there's just the darkness.

This really could be the end, couldn't it? I've battled to slow down time, perhaps even we both have. This afternoon, we lingered in the hushed forest of a nature reserve, eking out the day until dusk. We sat silently, listening to the snuffle of snout on leaf, the patter of paws on earth, and I longed to remain there like that forever. Alone with Dom, suspended in time. But the dusk finally caught us, seeping in between the trees; the darkness was bound to arrive.

I take his hand across the table. "I'm going to test tomorrow."

He nods briefly. "Yeah."

There is no more to say.

30

I wake at dawn to hear the birds singing on our terrace. I am swathed over Dom's chest, which is sticky with my spittle, but beatific on his back he's oblivious to both this and my hair tickling his face. There is no duvet and the air is warm and luxurious, so much so that I cannot ever imagine it being cold again. I disentangle my leg from between his and sit up. When I slide out of the bed, Dom curls up on his side.

The blood is a neat patch on the starched white sheet. It is only the size of a ten pence piece, and very pale, as if it will wash out. It will all come out in the wash. How many times have I reassured our new graduates with that when they've been fretting about silly mistakes. Fixing my eyes on the pink smudge I know, however, that if there was ever a time to fret it is now. Instead, I make for the bathroom, sit on the loo and and hum my way through a pee, averting my eyes from the toilet paper when I wipe. My hums are aided and abetted by the deafening deluge released by the showerhead and by the extractor fan, which joins in the brouhaha. I work up a foam, scrubbing my body, washing my hair, averting my eyes from the porcelain tray. As I dry myself, I up the ante, singing la-la-la, the tactic I'd goad Billy with, fingers in ears, *Can't hear you*.

While I'm dressing, Dom, already in shorts and T-shirt, sits silently on the terrace with his back to me, staring out over the sparkling Caribbean Sea. I know that he's seen the blood, but to speak would be to acknowledge it as reality. I am still chirpily tuneful. When we leave the room Dom takes my hand but I tug it away before the surge of emotion can produce tears. We are among the first to breakfast, along with the very young families. A calypso band is playing, as if pre-arranged to help blank out my thoughts, and the room bustles with the preparations for tonight's New Year celebrations. The waitress serves us coffee. I watch the birds flitting around, nabbing crumbs from our table. The one-legged blackbird, with which we've made friends, hops onto my plate and pecks away at the untouched toast, and I gaze at the repeated jabs of its beak.

"I'm so sorry, Cat." Dom's voice is too gentle.

"Yeah."

"I really thought, this time …"

"Me too. Look, I'd rather not …" I shoo the bird with the back of my hand.

Sidney enters the breakfast room – he gets up at six to bagsy a sun lounger – and approaches us with that delighted glint, wetting his lips with today's anecdote. When he reaches our table Dom and I speak in unison.

"Fuck off Sidney."

Mutely, we play out our daily routine, fetching fresh beach towels, scrunching across the sand to our usual spot beneath the almond tree. Dom sprawls on his lounger with a tabloid newspaper while I, in need of solitude, amble to the water's edge and sit down, staring at the sea, hugging my knees in comfort.

The tide is coming in. Under the influence of an invisible moon, a moon which has now left me desolate. So many of its phases in my life, so many cycles natural and otherwise where I should have fallen pregnant. I simply cannot believe that this is the end for me. Behind my dark glasses, finally I allow the tears to spill. They come fast and furious while I stare into the waves, lulled by their flow as they break, retreat and break again. Further out, a swell of blue crinkles when it rises, sprinkled with mosaics, before it clouds over with golden sand to be dragged down onto the beach; the hope, the promise, the dashing. All because of the moon. So much pain, so much damage. Irreparable now.

My trance is broken by Dom's voice behind me. "King Canute believed he could control the waves, didn't he? But you can't control nature, do you see that now?"

His words spike the back of my eyes and I swallow fresh tears. "You're wrong," I say, without turning around, "it was Canute's subjects who told him that. In fact, he stood by the sea and showed them that he couldn't stop the tide coming in."

Behind me there is silence. The next wave splashes over my toes.

Only once the water has reached my bottom do I feel resilient enough to get to my feet. I drag my sun lounger up the beach and away from Dom's. He's been doing the dragging all week in case I'm pregnant, but there's no need for that now. He stands and pulls his own up, settling it far too close to mine, and I sense his sheepish glances. He may be regretting his cruelty, but I'm smarting too much to even look at him. I pull out a magazine, bury my face in it.

I flick at the pages which are nothing but blurs of colour, and soon become aware of a bizarre noise out to sea. It's a low whine, like the sound of a mosquito in the dead of night. I look up to scan the sea and sky, but can spot nothing.

"It's a kite, look." Dom points at the sky.

Scouring the blue, I finally make out a white string of a tail flipping around. I become mesmerised by the monotony of its wheels and dives.

"Looks a bit like a sperm," Dom adds, as if to rouse me.

"It's moving a hell of a lot faster than yours." It snaps itself out, rewarding me with a generous sense of retribution.

Dom smacks his paper shut, snatches his iPod, and is off the sun-lounger in one leap. I watch him stomp his way off the beach, picking up speed through the gardens and rounding a corner towards the pool bar. When he's disappeared, my gaze lingers for some moments on the space he's just left, and then I flop back onto my bed. I guess this is how it will be from here on in, though I refuse to dwell. I chuck my magazine down and reach for the newspaper on Dom's empty sunbed. Might as well get back into the swing of home. As I flip the paper over and slap it flat, the front page headline jumps out at me: IS THIS MINISTER'S SECRET LOVER?

Below it is a picture of Ash, leaning over to kiss a woman on the terrace of the Houses of Parliament. It's a grainy image, you can only really make out that the woman who offers her cheek up has a black bob. My instant reaction is to shove the paper into my beach bag as if it's stolen goods, but I need to read the article. I do so four times, mercifully clocking the fact that they don't have a name. Still, a jumble of thoughts converge on me. How unjust – this photo was taken before we'd done anything … it must have been one of my staff at the hotel … did Dom read it?

I let out a sudden laugh, staccato and hysterical. I'm the baddie in some amateur whodunit and this is my demise, the moment when the detective gathers everybody in the sitting room and unravels his theory. Then all eyes swing at me, to the backdrop of sharp intakes of breath, as he handcuffs me, locks me up and throws away the key. They've got me. I'll never be a mother, my husband will leave me, my best friend has dumped me, my colleagues have grassed on me, and even my one-night stand of a lover will extricate himself from this.

I rummage through my bag for my mobile and switch it on. Surely Ash must have tried to contact me. Just three messages appear, nothing from Ash, but texts from Billy, Mum, and also one from Olu, sent this very morning. I click on it.

Call me if you need to
I jab my reply.
Am bleeding

I press send. Then the finality of my situation overpowers me. I begin to shake uncontrollably, and flop back onto the lounger, my body convulsed with sobs. My mobile bleeps.

Have you done a test?

Oh for fuck's sake, did I not make myself clear? I'm so furious with Olu that it takes me an age to stab out a correct reply, my fingers fumbling on the buttons.

I AM BLEEDING!!!

I don't care how unnecessary or aggressive this is, to a person who has only ever been kind to me. He is back within seconds.

Always do a test anyway

Always do a test anyway. I can even hear his voice, rich and measured as ever. Shrieking, I snap my mobile shut, and hurl it into my bag, causing several holidaymakers to sit up and raise their sunglasses at me, but I ignore them, sinking back into the lounger. How could I possibly be pregnant if I'm bleeding? The notion is ludicrous and Olu is simply exacerbating the misery. With cruel little prods, I stab at my belly, punishing him, and it, for not producing – and the sensation makes me frown. It does feel quite swollen. My hands stray to my breasts, which I jab away at with the tips of my fingers. Odd, but they are still sore, even though my period's started. Suddenly, I'm aware of that buzzing sensation – those battery-charged dicky-bows are spinning inside the core of each breast.

I'm up from that sunbed as if a pistol has cracked beneath me. Halfway off the beach, I realise I'll need our room key and swing back, kicking sand at faces in my sprint back to the lounger. I upend my bag, sifting the contents crazily. Dom must have the key. Heart pounding, I stumble back across the hot sand and take off across the gardens towards the pool. Then I sprint into the main bar, breaking protocol in my bare feet and cozzie as I scurry past faces which frown up from their newspapers, the only smile from an ageing rock star sipping a cocktail.

Our pavilion is a couple of hundred metres from the main hotel. In case Dom isn't back in the room, I stop at reception to request a second key. The young girl on duty is only doing her job by telling me she'll ask a porter to meet me there and let me in, but I throw her an exasperated frown and mutter, "Jobsworth."

I scoot off, slipping on the wet marble floor which is being mopped, and race through the grounds, making it to our room in record time. For a good minute, I hold my thumb on the doorbell, but Dom is not in the room. In search of a cleaner, I sprint around the pavilion, with an apologetic wave at the woman sunbathing on her private terrace next door. Then, through the scarlet hibiscus bushes, I see a mama with a trolley, standing at a door a couple of blocks away, and hurtle over the lawns to her waving, "yoo-hoo," like some frumpy woman calling for a bus to wait. The cleaner sees me coming and turns slowly back to the door, already shaking her head at my approach. Still I plead with her to unlock my room.

"More than my job's worth, ma'am."

"Please? I'll give you fifty dollars."

Her head turns deliberately and she spears me with a dead eye. "Ain't up for no bribes either, ma'am."

Back at my room, the porter still hasn't shown up. I kick the door with ineffectual bare feet and swear at it several times, then stand back and survey the squat building. The tiny window of our bathroom is ajar, and I reckon I could just about squeeze through it. I reach up and lift the metal arm off its catch and push the window inwards, then hoist myself up on a flower tub and onto the ledge. By shunting my shoulders through on the diagonal, I find I can inch my way into our bathroom and grasp the toilet cistern with one hand. Across the room, my toiletries bag sits open on the sink, the test pack tantalising me. Delirious now, I shunt forwards a little more, and then I find myself immobilised. My swimming costume is caught on the window latch. In the minute space available, I squirm and wriggle, but the

297

Lycra refuses to budge. I am balanced like a seesaw, my bottom and legs flapping in the open air behind me.

"Miss, would you like me to push you in, or pull you out?" The deep voice outside the window is full of fun and I stop dead.

With a final frown at the test pack, I give up the fight and feel myself deflating. My costume has ridden up between my buttocks – I can feel him staring at them – and the thought of him manhandling me in through the window is too distressing.

"Could you unhook me and pull me out please?"

"Certainly, Miss."

He is swift. A flick of his finger releases the Lycra from the catch, and he grips me by the hips, gently threading me back out through the window, as if this duty was a module on his general training. Once I'm on the ground again, I aim to regain a degree of dignity, pinching the costume out of my bottom, adjusting the shoulder straps across my chest. Almost in mimicry, he also tweaks his navy uniform, smiling broadly.

"Thank you, now could you let me into my room, please?"

"You're welcome." He gives a small bow. "Yes I can, Miss."

He saunters to the door, glides in the plastic strip, and I rush inside thanking him, swinging the door shut behind me before realising he'll need a tip. I jab at the safe combination buttons, pull out a twenty-dollar note and usher him away with more thanks.

"All part of the service ma'am." He touches his cap.

I heave the door shut and make for the bathroom, yanking off the swimming costume. It takes both nails and teeth to break into the plastic wrapping of the test pack, but finally I slip the white stick beneath me and pee.

The thick blue line is instant, and bold. It materializes like secret ink made from lemon juice, a magic message appearing on ironed paper. The line jumps up at me, screaming, if you'd only asked me earlier I'd have let you know sooner. I fling it on the floor and take the other strip – I know they can be defective. Back on the loo I will myself to wee again – come on, come on, brain to bladder – and a trickle spills out onto the second test stick. Another blue line appears in its window. Unable to comprehend, I sit and stare at the sticks, one in each hand. My heart is bucking like a wild animal, my body trembling with the makings of joy.

I haul the costume back on, slipping both test sticks into its elasticated front, wrap a sarong around me and race out of the room. Dom's trainers were on the floor, so I know he's not at the gym. I dash back to the pool, then onto the bar upstairs, from where I survey the beach. A hunch tells me he might be in the business centre; he's been emailing Ben and the other guy about their new venture most days this week. I see him through the glass, sitting at a PC with his back to me, and my heart lurches. The room is empty but for him and I fling the door open.

"Dom!"

He tenses up and continues to work, swishing and clicking the mouse.

"Dom."

I'm beside him at the desk before he can swing the chair round. On the screen I see that he has typed only, *Dear Harry*.

"Dom, I'm pregnant. Look."

I slide out the two test sticks nestling at my tummy, and shove them in his face. He examines them and those smudges of flush I know so well appear on his cheeks, along with a flicker of frown, which of course must be bewilderment.

"But you can't be, you're bleeding," he says finally.

"I know, I can't believe it either. But I am pregnant, look they're both blue. Isn't it fantastic?"

"Amazing."

He's still sitting down, so I grasp at something practical to say. "I'll call Olu, shall I? He'll know what to do."

Eventually Dom stands and folds his arms around me, his chin resting on my head. He smothers me into his T-shirt and I sink into him, inhaling gratefully on the scent of my husband, mingled with sun cream. We've made it. Tomorrow is the start of a new year, 2008, the year in which our baby will be born.

31

It's Midsummer's Day. A Saturday, but as usual Dom is at his new offices consolidating the business with Ben and Harry. Jackie's spending the day with me in our garden and we're lounging on reclining chairs, while Emily scampers round the lawn in her white summer dress and bloomers. Immobile behind sunglasses, I lie in worship to the hazy afternoon sunshine, while Jackie is up and down, dragging Emily off the flower beds, her outfit now patched with grass scuffs and dirt.

"She's a wee urchin, this one."

For the sake of our renewed friendship, I feel compelled to be torn away from the sun and watch with empathy as Jackie scoops soil from the child's mouth. "Just mind her with the rhododendron leaves, I think they might be poisonous."

I smile to myself, Dad called this week and he's having the oleander bush by his pool chopped down.

"More drinks?" In need of my tart lemon barley fix, I heave myself to my feet.

When Peggy visited us recently she told us how she ate coal when pregnant with Dom. Alongside her repertoire of other anecdotes, this enthralled him – he loves what he calls the full circle of it all. And we've certainly pulled off our own full circle too; the past six months have restored us. A period of rest for me soon staunched the bleeding too. It was quite common Olu said, and there have been no further scares.

As for Ash, well the day after that photo appeared the press snuffled out their name, together with a new photo –

Kimberley Stratton, his American research assistant. No matter that the bobbed hair in that photo of him kissing me on the terrace at Westminster didn't match the tresses of twenty-year-old Kimberley, it did the job. It helped bring the visual message home; that one of Britain's best loved Ministers, a family man, an ardent campaigner against teenage pregnancy, had been caught with his pants down. Beside Kimberley's photo, the tabloid had gleefully regurgitated the, *Keep Our Youth Young* mantra, and had added, *So I Can S**g Them.*

We still meet for lunch, and there is the odd frisson, but I'm relieved not to have taken it further, to have risked losing the man I have always loved, and whom I nearly lost forever. Dom is completely in the dark about it all. I think he's been pretty much absorbed these past few months by the excitement of us getting pregnant, together with the makings of his new business.

Recently we've been attending birthing classes, sniggering together at the rainforest music and pin-wisps of incense rising in the darkened room. The birthing adviser had us rehearsing techniques for labour, with Dom massaging me, while I sat circling my hips on a rubber gym ball. Dom dribbled aromatherapy oil onto the base of my neck, then splayed his hands across my back and pressed his thumbs into my flesh, slowly sweeping outwards before beginning over again. Breathing in the scent of rose, I soared and sank to the movement of his strokes, felt my body loosening, my mind swimming. And I was eased into a trancelike state.

From the kitchen, I see that Emily has now thrown herself face down on the grass and is kicking like a wind-up toy gone berserk.

"Right lassie, time for your nap." Jackie hauls her daughter under her arm, as if she's a rolled up carpet, and carries her inside. "OK if I put her on your sofa, Cat?"

"Fine," I call after her. Our sofas are cream linen, but pregnancy hormones must be narcotic, because I'm laid back to an extreme.

Back outside, I tip the garden chair flat and breathe in deeply, just as my reflexologist has advised during the weekly sessions which are nurturing me through pregnancy. Mum was right about that. I close my eyes, enjoying the amber glow of sunlight on sealed eyelids and listen out for the hum of bumblebees, for the chirp of our resident blackbird. My mind is constantly in a lazy state these days, dulled and lulled by the simple offerings of life, rather than pole-vaulting over the next hurdle.

The baby kicks and I cup the mound with my palms, brushing gently against my taut swollen belly, its button now a Smartie on a cupcake. It was Stewart's revolted stares, and his comments about sprogs in ovens, that finally brought us to a head. Yesterday, I completed the handover of his account to a new female colleague, a kick-arse manager with two nannies at home. Stewart won't even know her kids exist – nor me now, because I'll slink off his radar and he off mine. Possibly he may move his business elsewhere, but we both know that I'll scoop up Lord Grainger and his food empire if he does. I may even reveal the odd Dinwoodie trade secret too.

After a good half hour, Jackie comes scurrying back out to the garden and slips her bikini top off. "Now for some serious sunbathing."

She shuffles back down onto her recliner and I find myself staring at her breasts, which hang against her ribs like used condoms.

She catches my look. "Ach, these things. That's what three months of breastfeeding does, you wait on. And the pain, it's like slicing your nipples with razors."

"Ouch." I reach out for her hand and squeeze her fingers. The birthing adviser assured us that three months of breastfeeding will provide a strong basis for immunity, so she's done well. She squeezes back, but then neither of us know what to do next, until finally she fakes a sigh, shifts a little, and we drop hands.

I called Jackie as soon as I flew home, and we are building bridges, albeit still awkwardly. At forty-three, Jackie is still not pregnant again, and Emily's now nearly two. She insists she's come through all of that, and she's delighted for me, but sometimes I catch her eyes fixed on my bump and I'm not so sure. We've not yet been able to clinch that closeness, and I feel that we'll never quite get there again.

"Have you had any more hassle from the wife?" she asks.

"No." I refuse to expand, and regret again having told her that Ash's wife had landed on my doorstep a week after Barbados.

I did feel sorry for the woman, and hope I managed to convince her that it had been a one-off, a kind of unfinished business. Possibly the fact that I wasn't a brand new body to him softened the blow. And of course she had more to contend with once the scandal with his intern was out. I was worried she might tell Dom, but it's six months on now and she's clearly not stooped to that.

"So she hasn't pitched up again?"

Jackie's persistence is riling me. She wants to wheedle her way into a part of me that's still closed to her, and I'm not prepared to let her in. It's as if we can fling off the hurt, can seal the gap between us with a plug of hushed confessions, and of course I'm to go first. I'm to confess that I did shag Ash, but that's a secret she'll never extract.

"Do you know what?"

"What?" She lifts her head, expecting juice.

"I think I should sleep in this contraption at night, it's much more comfy than my bed." With a crafty smile, I allow myself to drift into the afternoon slumber that is every expectant mother's right.

I am woken by Dom kissing my forehead, and open my eyes to see him holding a giggling Emily, both of them sporting *Winnie the Pooh* stickers on their noses.

"I found this little bundle roving round our living room," he says.

Beside me, Jackie is still asleep, her breasts squirting sideways, which Dom is pretending not to notice.

"Aunty Cat fancied a change of colour on the walls, didn't you?" He swings Emily around in his arms.

"What's she done?" I grin at him.

"Ooh, I'd describe it as byzantine blue Jackson Pollack. Amazing what effect you can pull off with a biro."

"Ha, this is fast becoming a family home, isn't it?" I do like the sound of that word 'family' and have been using it often.

Dom nods and puts Emily down on the lawn, I think he enjoys hearing it too. "It'll wash off, or I'll paint over it, I'm sure there's worse to come."

"How was the office?"

"Fine. Making progress." Dom is already walking inside. "Fancy a cuppa?"

"Mmm, please." Jackie has woken, slipped her T-shirt on and is scooping Emily up onto her knee.

Dom brings out a tray of tea and sits down on the grass beside me. He places his hand on my stomach and, as if in response, our baby kicks his palm. Gently, he presses against the movement.

"Delectable," I say, drawing his eyes up to mine.

"Yeah." He gazes again at the rippling of my flesh, biting his lip with the emotion of the moment.

When the kicks cease, he beckons Emily over to play *This Little Piggy*, and the toddler shucks her neck to avoid his tickling fingers. She adores her Uncle Dommy.

*

Billy and I are strolling through Hyde Park. It was a challenge to prise my brother off the sofa, away from Dom and the cricket, even though I'm in no rush to reveal the reason I've brought him here. He arrived in good humour, as always, just as I was unwrapping this week's bouquet of roses and peonies. Each week Dom adds an extra stem to mark my gestation in weeks and today there are thirty-three fluffy pink heads in our statement vase.

"Blimey, what you been up to Dom, matey?" Billy asked him.

"Cynic." I dumped the cellophane on him, which he dutifully put into the bin.

In the park now, we sit contemplating the statue of Peter Pan.

"He reminds me of you as a kid, a right little rascal." I say.

"Somebody had to lighten up that dungeon."

"An apt description of our new home."

"No chance of us staying kids forever, was there? You and I both grew up too soon."

"Yeah."

He takes my hands and helps me to my feet. My stomach has grown substantially in the last few weeks and I now sport it like an icon. We amble back towards Kensington Palace. The park has that bright, relieved look about it after yesterday's storm, but inside me the angst is mounting. I have rehearsed how I'm going to say it, and it would be better to get it now out while we're walking, but I'm delaying, lulled by the sweet birdsong, the dappled sunlight. So Billy asks me about the baby, and I chatter on about how I've asked Mum to help me after the birth. He loves hearing about our new togetherness and I'm aware that I'm rambling on about our lunches in order to soften his disposition towards me.

Finally, we reach the Round Pond, which is heaving with tiny motorised boats. An empty bench beckons. We sit down and my chest feels weighted, welding my back to the wooden slats as the inexorable moment arrives. For distraction, I scan the scene of mothers lounging on picnic blankets with their flowery oilcloth bags.

"They seem young for London mums."

"Most of them are nannies." Billy nudges me. "The clue's in their Hispanic skin."

"Oh." I can't find it in me to smile back.

"What's up sis? You've been morose all afternoon."

I take a deep breath, focus on the boats zipping across the pond. "Billy, there's something I have to tell you."

"Sounds ominous. Let me guess? The baby's not Dom's."

"Of course it is," I snap. "Look. Last year, last November…"

"What? Tell me."

"Daisy." I turn and lock eyes on him, here we go. "I took her to the family planning clinic. I had her put on the pill."

Billy recoils on the bench as if I've just stung him with a cattle prod.

"You did what?"

"She had a scare."

"What?" I wait for him to work through my meaning. "You mean, she thought she was pregnant?"

I nod.

"She was having *sex*?"

"A boy at school."

"I'll fucking kill him. And her." He stands to accomplish the job, but I grasp his T-shirt, pull him back.

"Billy… They, they start young these days."

He knocks my hand away and glares at me. "At fifteen!"

"I know …"

"Does Maggie know?"

"No."

"You put my daughter on the pill?" At his shrieks the women are glancing over, even a few of the children have stopped splashing to stare.

"She was going to carry on doing it, Billy, so I thought it was best to sort her out. And she did plan to tell you, at some point."

"At which fucking point was that then?"

"She was scared."

"Of her own parents? You're so full of shit!"

"I'm sorry, I know I should have-"

"You narcissistic cow. You thought you knew best for my daughter, even thought you were more important than her own mother."

"No, it wasn't like that."

"Yes it was, it's always like that. Everything revolves around you, doesn't it? Always has done."

I take the hammering in silence, flurries of shame coursing through me.

"All your life, it's been Cat, Cat, Cat. You're so self-obsessed, you've never once given a thought to anybody else." He jabs a finger at his jaw. "I mean, you never even realised how I got this scar, did you?"

I shake my head mutely; what's he on about?

"You just waltz through thousands of pounds worth of IVF, totally insensitive to my financial situation, we could have had our loft converted with what you spent on getting pregnant. And you've consumed Daisy, haven't you? Did it make you feel better? After what you did to her? Well she's my daughter, not yours, and I'm going to sort her out."

He springs up off the bench with a parting shot. "*And* everyone knows that you tortured our cat!"

My heart pumping wildly, I watch Billy marching towards the distant park gates, and the baby chooses that moment to bat me with a fist. Taking deep breaths, I spread my hands over my stomach, I can feel all eyes on me.

I'm still steadily calming myself when Billy swivels round and strides back towards me. As he nears the bench, I can hear the blood thumping, my palms are dripping, and my throat is parched with trepidation. But then my brother simply sinks down beside me and slumps over his knees,

308

knitting fingers through his matted hair. He grasps his head and shakes it, while I wait for him to speak. Eventually, after several minutes, he begins to sniff. I place a tentative hand on his back.

"So she was doing it without using anything?"

"I should have told you."

"Yes, you fucking should have done."

"I'm sorry, it was totally out of order. Think she only did it once. At least she's careful now."

He slides his face in his hands, muffling his voice. "It's my fault too, I should have been there for her."

"Doubt if many teenage girls talk to their dads about these things, Billy."

With that, I realise I've left an accusation hanging against Maggie.

"Look, I'm telling you because you're right, I did think I knew better than Maggie. I've always drawn Daisy to me, I'm aware that I prised her away from you." I rub my brother's back, fingers splayed on his bony spine. "Billy, I was wrong, so wrong, and I'm sorry. Sorry for meddling in your family. I thought we had a special bond, Daisy and I, but families are much more complex than that, aren't they? And yes it was always about me, not her, I did it for my own selfish needs." I pause, hoping my brother is listening. "Think I was jealous of you too, if I'm honest. Of you being a father, I wanted a piece of what you had, I guess."

I can feel Billy struggling to control his breathing, then he takes the tissue I offer him. "Shit father though, eh? Why didn't I see it coming?"

"She's very smart."

"Always been old for her age, hasn't she?"

I assume he's referring back to the 'accident' but I won't be let off the hook. "I egged her on, Billy, with the boyfriends."

He lets out a soft snort. "She worships you."

"Not anymore. She knows I'm telling you, Billy." I phoned Daisy last night and she is livid with me.

"So, she's having regular sex now is she?"

I shrug. "Nearly sixteen anyway, isn't she? Think she's more careful, though."

My brother breathes in, links the fingers on both hands and stretches the palms out, then he arches his back and stretches that out too. He holds himself static for a moment, before relaxing his body, blowing the air out of his lungs, as if he's just shifted with the world.

We sit in silence, our eyes fixed on the pond. A squirrel scampers up, sits hopefully on its hind legs, before realising it is not our priority and scurries off.

"Billy, she's petrified of Maggie finding out. But that's your decision, you need to talk to her."

He throws me a wan grin. At my statement of the obvious? At the fact that I'm reasserting my dominance over him?

"I will talk to her first," he says. "Guess I'm glad you told me."

From behind a cloud the sun comes out, throwing instant warmth onto our faces. A young boy, fully clothed, steps into the pond to retrieve his boat, and several women jump up from their blankets and launch into a commotion around the edge. He wades back out to receive a smack on his wet shorts, and Billy and I let out soft sniggers. I shuffle along the bench and pull him to me.

"Sorry about the cat comment," he says.

"Didn't know you knew."

"We all did, Mum, Dad, me."

"Oh. They say if you're cruel to an animal as a kid you'll make a crap parent."

"Have you hurt anything living in the last thirty years?"

"Not physically."

"Think you'll be OK then."

"I'm going to love this baby so much, Billy."

"I know."

I squint at him against the sunshine. "Anyway, you got that scar playing football at school."

He laughs. "Try, Norman split my chin open."

I gaze at him, memories of the phone call from Mum that day flashing through my mind. "No?"

"Er, yes."

"I never knew, Billy."

"Could have asked though, couldn't you?"

My brother slides his arm around me and hugs me to him, presses his lips to my temple and kisses the strands of hair clamped by the sweat on my forehead.

32

It's the height of August, and Dom has joined me in the nursery department at Peter Jones. His mum, Peggy, had advised that it's unlucky to buy the pushchair before the birth, and Dom has apparently believed her. He's been reluctant to purchase the cot, the car seat, or any other large paraphernalia we need either, even though, with an amused shake of the head, he's indulged my need to buy an item of tiny clothing each week. However, at thirty-eight weeks pregnant, I need to tuck the final feathers in my nest and I've insisted we shop today.

This particular nursery department I know well; each aisle of vests, of pastel plush rabbits, of baby baths and musical mobiles – we'll need them all. The shop assistant must be worn out by me now, but realising that today's the day she'll make the kill, she's willing to devote two hours of her prime sales time to us, and follows us with a clipboard noting our purchases for delivery. By the time we reach the buggies she's onto her second page. I've researched pushchairs at length, but I want Dom to be involved in the decision, so I ask her to take us through their full range and she humours me, explaining once again the swivel wheels and how to add the car seat. As I'd known he would be, Dom is keen to examine the feat of engineering that is the pushchair and he bends to inspect them, figuring out the levers. He smiles with the shop assistant when she rolls out her patently well-worn joke about how many men it takes to collapse a pushchair – in the same vein as the women and light bulb gag.

"I shall show you ladies, that it takes just one – albeit a highly accomplished one."

Dom rubs his hands together in preparation for a tricky endeavour, grips the handles of a navy blue buggy and shakes them, while his little finger fumbles blindly for a lever on the underside. The pushchair remains rigid.

I let out a soft snigger as he brandishes it again. "Come on Daddy, you can do better than that!"

Dom grins back at me while he has another go, and again nothing happens. "This one must be broken," he says, reaching for a second one beside it.

"Do you plan to manhandle them all?" I say, watching him drop that one too.

He laughs. "What's the secret then?"

"Ah …"

My sniggering escalates to rich laughter, and I'm soon weak with it, helpless and happy. This is what it's all about – me, my husband and the momentous joy that awaits us – I'm shaking so much that I feel the baby kick and my hands brush my belly.

"Does the baby find it funny too?" Dom beams at me and slides a hand onto my bump. "Now come on, young'un, I don't want you siding with your mother."

I exchange knowing smiles with the shop assistant as he returns to his task, dropping to his haunches to examine the handles.

"I think I might just have to admit defeat here."

He rights himself and stands back. I step in, grasp the handles and flick a catch which collapses the buggy.

"Smart arse," he says, laughing. "Come on let's go and get a coffee,"

We pay and head up to the top floor café, where I sit by the window looking out over the rooftops of Kensington.

"These chimney pots always remind me of *Mary Poppins*," I say to Dom as he slides the tray onto our table.

He sits down opposite me. "Yep. And we're going to buy all those Disney films, Cat. Watch 'em again, over and over, just like I used to do when I was a kid."

I smile warmly at him and take his hands across the table. "My dad loved *Mary Poppins*. Think he fancied himself as Bert."

"Cor blimey guvnor." Dom pulls out his best cockney, our eyes meet in laughter and we hold the look for several moments, savouring the togetherness.

Then Dom's eyes spot something behind my head, and the light in them is snuffed. He drops my hands, knocking over a teacup with his, and jumps to his feet.

"Harry," he says.

Even as I turn my head, I know that this moment spells doom for us. My vision sweeps around, in a movement so slow, so all embracing, and yet it takes in nothing, except for the woman reaching our table. I know her, don't I? We met years ago. Clear recollections of those thin brown legs, cycling ahead of me beneath crimson poinsettia trees, Communist banners flying above our heads.

Harinder.

I too am propelled to my feet in shock, but am then surprised by the way I wee myself. It is the worst moment of my life, but still, I hadn't ever thought that I would lose control like this. There is so much pee; I can feel it drenching my jeans, washing onto the tiled floor – of one of the most prestigious department stores in London. I'm vaguely expecting the sting of a hand on the back of my legs, as if I'm a naughty girl, but around me nobody is in the least angry with me. In fact, while we three continue to gawp at each other, a waitress appears and presses me gently back down onto my chair. It seems that my waters have broken.

Dom's eyes are fixed on the floor, while Harinder is glaring at his bowed head. "You never told me she was *pregnant!*"

He shrugs, staring into the vast puddle I've made between us – into his past or his future, I can't tell which.

"How long?" I hear myself asking, in a voice that is soft and measured.

He shrugs again.

I'm aware of the hush that has fallen on the café. People are bowed over their cups, but I can feel all eyes upon us, and I hear a child's voice. "Look, mummy, that fat lady's weed herself." Deep inside, I feel the onset of a period pain, a dull ache beginning to unfold. I wrap my arms around my belly to cradle my little one. This is all that matters right now.

Harinder shrieks at him again. "*You* are a liar and a cheat."

Yes that about sums my husband up.

The pain pinches, but this is good pain, and I take a deep breath in, struggling to focus on the exercises I have learnt. When the contraction subsides, I weigh up Harinder. She really has aged well, still the flawless skin, still the glossy skeins of black, but her eyes flash with anger. You'd think it was me who had done her an injustice.

"Fuck off bitch," I say quietly.

Finally, Dom lifts his head, as if he's backing me up in this, as if she's simply appeared all these years on, to hound us. After a final glare at him, Harinder turns, the hair flying, the heels skidding slightly in my amniotic fluid, and heads for the lifts.

In the ambulance, my contractions are coming more regularly, more ferociously. They take me by surprise, my whole belly feels trapped in a vice, twisted round and round into a knot and then abruptly freed to spring back, leaving me thinking I've imagined it. The intermittent pain fuels a vicious fury, which in my moments of calm then uncoils itself at Dom, like a snapped cable.

"How fucking long?"

315

I'm competing with the siren as the ambulance rocks in and out of the traffic; it's only a short hop to the hospital, but Chelsea are at home today.

"She came to London this year." His face is clammy and pale.

"And before that?"

Dom attempts to engage the ambulance man, who is filling in my record sheet with a low hum. "Should I be timing them yet?"

The man purses his lips without looking up. "Could do." He wants no part in this conflict.

"Tell me!" I scream, as the contraction creeps up on me again.

Dom knows better than to speak to me while I'm writhing in agony and simply removes his watch, lays it on his knee with a little pat.

"How many more were there? Don't expect me to believe it was just her! Did you screw that woman you sacked too?"

"Cat, let's focus on the baby shall we?" He's frowning at his watch, willing the second hand around.

"Call Jackie!"

He turns the frown on me. "Why?"

"I want her there."

He hesitates, shifting in his seat, imploring me with eyes filling up now.

"Call her!" I scream.

Dom fumbles for my mobile causing a photo of us in Barbados to slip from my handbag out onto the floor of the ambulance. He bends to scoop it up, but I wrench the phone from his other hand. "Give it to meeeee."

A whirling dervish now, I yank it open and scroll my contacts. The pain has me back in its grip and I gasp, "Jacks."

"Who is this?"

"S'me, s'gat."

"Cat?"

316

I reckon I've still got another minute, during which I will not be able to speak, so I let out a low guttural moan. Canny lass that she is, Jackie waits for me to emerge.

"Jacks I need you at the hospital."

Whether she assumes Dom is not with me, or whether she's just solid gold, Jackie says, "Chelsea and Westminster, yes? I'm on my way."

The ambulance screeches to a halt and they roll me out.

33

It's true what Jackie said about responsibility being the wrong word for it. I am gazing down at William who's suckling me voraciously. Once he's content he mews, his forehead crinkling into lines of rapture like a pianist lost in reverie. Without me he would die, that's what Jackie meant.

After he was born, I didn't leave the house for two weeks, bizarrely convinced that everyone was out to get him. When finally we ventured out to Kensington Gardens, each step was danger, every stranger plotting to snatch my baby. The dreams have been even more vivid, of knives and blood, but I haven't told a soul about them. I've scoured the books for the symptoms of post-natal depression, but I find nothing of what I experienced. No copious weeping, or rejecting the baby, in fact I would lay down my life for him. And with each new week I do relax a little more, begin to accept that the world is not on a mission to harm my son.

Without pressing me to elucidate the full reality of what I've seen – or imagined – Jackie has talked me through it, and from her knowing looks, from her embraces, I sense I am not the first mother to travel this path. My dearest friend spent ten hours at the birth, spraying my face with mist, rooting for me with urgent eyes, while Dom sat silently in the corner. We two are back on the same plane of shared experience, one which is so much more necessary than any we've known before.

Mum enters the living room with a tray of tea and smiles at the bundle in my arms. William is dressed in a cardigan and baggy leggings, knitted from a 1960s pattern, and of a particular blue only to be found in dusty wool shops. Mum has been prolific in her production of outfits for her grandson and I've actually dressed him in them when we've gone for our walks.

"You're doing so well, sweetheart, so well." Her words are much needed. I never thought that I'd buy praise from Lizzie, but we've settled into some sort of harmony.

The doorbell rings and Mum lets Billy in.

"Where's my nephew?" He lifts William from me, leaving me torn by the sudden loss of warmth and weight from my lap. "How about your uncle Billy gets your very first smile then, matey?"

William sighs, snuggles into Billy's shoulder and fills his nappy with a spurt.

"I'll take that as a start, shall I?" Billy grins at me. "Want me to do it?"

"Please." I love to see my brother getting involved.

He drags the nappy bag out from behind the sofa and unfolds the changing mat on the rug, then lays William down tenderly. Mum's Burmese grey jumps up onto my empty lap and, once again, I find myself stroking it; that love has to flow somewhere when I'm apart from my son. I couldn't have expected Mum to leave her cat with neighbours for weeks on end, while she moved in to care for me. So Silkie is confined to the boot room whenever the cat is set free from the kitchen for its occasional run of the house. An awkward arrangement, there has been the odd glitch – of snarls (cat) or yelps (dog) – but then life is a catalogue of the unexpected just now, and I react as it comes upon me.

Mum finds it amusing that the cat has chosen me to sprawl over, but it means she can get on with her knitting. Watching her clicking beside me, I have to smile at her latest creation, a stripy turquoise all in one, with spherical pearl buttons. Yesterday she had to undo a whole section, row upon row.

"That's a shame after all your work, Mum," I said.

"It's worth unravelling to get it right though, isn't it?"

My eyes prickled with her words and I watched her face, gentle and quiet in concentration, until, eventually she glanced up at me and smiled.

We often find ourselves sitting together of an afternoon, Billy, Mum and I. It's sometime in early September, I've no idea what the date is, but the air already has that raw autumn quality, which allows you to slob around drinking tea and chatting with impunity, not to feel pressed by the need to go out and do something jolly. Mum regales us with anecdotes, about Greenham Common, or the fur protests. She's been on good behaviour since her conditional discharge after the lab raid. Billy talks about his family, Daisy has begun her A levels, the sciences she'll need for university. In my case, we focus on the baby, avoiding all mention of Dom and the tatters of my marriage.

As yet, Mum hasn't broached any memories of our early family life, it may be too soon for us all. Today, however, Billy has decided to jump smack bang in there.

"Mum? Do you ever hear from Norman these days?" he asks.

"No. And good riddance, I should say."

She fumbles over a dropped stitch. I watch her jabbing a needle into the thick wool, sip my tea and wait. Billy's going to tell her about the scar.

"How did it end?" he continues. "You never did tell us, he just disappeared into the ether."

"That last affair did it." Mum seems to realise that this is too close to the bone for me. "Well there were oodles of them, not just one. And you know what actually brought things to a head?"

Billy raises his eyebrows in question. But I've known that stifled smile since I was a kid, tongue stuck in cheek, rolling against the inside of his mouth. This isn't about his scar.

"Well, I got this card, must have been from his girlfriend of the moment, cheap floozy. And there were these photos of nipples stuck to it, all of them cut out from newspapers and magazines."

With a sharp breath, I stare at Billy, who winks at me, tongue now working his gums in a desperate bid against that smirk.

But Mum perceives my shock differently. "I know! It was disgusting. Big ones, small ones, brown ones, pink ones."

Billy and I begin to chuckle, which spurs Mum onto a smile. "And it said something like, oh what was it? This is how many tits he's sucked."

I gasp at the words – which my own brother had written. His thrilled eyes meet mine and I choke back my laughter and reach for the teapot, I have to escape this room. Down in the kitchen, I release the laughter in heaves so strong they steadily become silent. Soon, I find myself doubled-up, my eyes blurred with tears – good job I've got those post-partum disposable paper knickers on too.

*

Dom and I are sitting on a stone bench at the Italian fountains in a far corner of Kensington Gardens. He is staying at Ben's place and, even though he's been round to the house each day, we haven't talked, not beyond William's needs. Today though, a cool grey morning somewhere in September, I feel that perhaps enough time has lapsed. Asleep in his buggy, William is only four weeks old. He tends to sleep all day and wake me constantly throughout the night, so I feel eternally jet lagged as Jackie put it, all woolly and surreal. Life surrounds me, gently nudging me on, taking itself forwards in slow motion.

I've been watching a young Mediterranean couple as if they're in a film, walking hand-in-hand between the ponds; he tells a joke, head close to hers, she breaks into laughter, head thrown back. So much want, so much need. How much life has transpired between us since those days.

"How long had it been going on?" As I ask my husband the question he failed to answer in the ambulance, a wave of fatigue washes over me. Do I really care now?

"She came to London in the summer."

"And before that?"

I cannot muster anger, and that saddens me. These days are strange and I'm unable to discern if this is the shock of a new baby or something more profound. We two have been playing at a relationship for such a long time now, and I'm confused by what is pretence and what is real. So all I can rustle up is a modicum of curiosity about the extent of his deceit – and maybe a little more concern about how much of our past life his response will eat into. Whether it will impinge on the good times too.

"Few months," he says finally.

"Since Barbados?"

"Bit before. After I was sacked."

I swallow hard. This I can take, because my own shame dates from around the same time. We sit in silence, and I am fixated by the loved-up couple. The boy is tightrope walking along the raised stone edges of the pond – the male of the species – while the girl's eyes sparkle for him, a concerned hand over her smile – and the female.

"Do you love her?"

"No." He sounds weary himself now. "Never did. Harry was just the rebound after Suzanne."

"Did you screw her too?" It's a sneer I regret instantly.

He ignores me, but uses the moment to present a further offence for consideration. "I did ask Harry to marry me in Hong Kong."

"You proposed to her?" He's floored me now. And yet some sort of grotesque glee creeps up on me; that my husband is still able to astound me.

He throws me a subdued look. "It was before I met you, well, the decision was, I was going to ask her in Vietnam, had the ring and everything. But then I met you."

"Dom you're not being clear, when did you propose to her?"

"After Vietnam. I just went ahead with it. Didn't seem fair not to."

"Didn't seem *fair*?" I glare at him. "And she said no?"

He nods. Well of course she did, she'd witnessed our capers in Hanoi well enough.

"Is that how seriously you take marriage? Is that how seriously you took *our* marriage?"

"No, I – "

"Eleven years, we've been living a lie?"

"Look, I was twenty-six, it felt like the right age to get hitched, but I wanted her to say no, really. I knew she would. You blew me away, Cat!" He's shouting at me now. "You know that."

"Do I?" I shout back at him.

"Yes, you do!"

"What I do know is that you are a weak man, Dom."

"And you are a conniving bitch."

Shocked, I swing round to my husband with a deep scowl, which he returns with one of his own. Eyes locked, we're glowering at each other and I catch a sudden flash of connection. For the first time in months, possibly years, there is a flare of honesty between us, the remnants of that blinding love. Both stunned, we quickly reach for the clouded reserve, pull the toll of our draining relationship back into our eyes, but I did see it. Fleetingly, the connection was made.

"You were the most important thing in my life," he says eventually.

"Were? Not are?"

"Are, still."

We both glance instinctively at William in his pushchair, oblivious to this complex start to his life.

323

I reach for the buggy. Dom gets to his feet after me. I watch the olive-skinned couple take our place on the bench – they will do it more justice. In silence, we set off towards the Serpentine. Above us, the horse chestnut leaves are battling to display their ruddy glow against the gloomy sky, while beneath our feet, they have been trampled in layers to a slippery mush.

Bitch, that's a first from Dom. He's right though, I was at times. Conniving too is a perfect choice of word, but he must know that we wouldn't be here without it. And if he hadn't been so weak it wouldn't have worked on him anyway. He has always been weak. And yet it's not that he asked another woman to marry him, it's the fact that he proposed to her because he thought he was the right age to settle down. Pathetic.

It's beginning to drizzle and I stop to pull the plastic cover down over William, pausing for a moment to observe his luminous cheeks.

"Our beautiful baby." Dom leans in with me.

"If you'd married her instead of me, maybe you'd have had kids sooner. Been able to emulate your parents, recreate that childhood of yours. That's what you really wanted isn't it?"

"I wanted you. Don't take what we had away from us, Cat."

Onwards we stroll. Despite the weather, all the pedal boats are out on the Serpentine and the roller-skaters have attracted their usual mass of onlookers. A dreadlocked guy completes a tricky manoeuvre around a series of obstacles and the tourists cheer, delighted with their day in London, but we plough on, the breeze in our faces.

"Maybe if you'd had my childhood, you wouldn't have been so driven by your career," he says.

"That old chestnut? You mean you weren't driven by your work too?"

"You could have managed a baby as well, Cat. There are nannies ... your mum. Anyway, that problem's not gone away, just because you're older now."

My heart lurches; I doubt I'll be able to leave my son with anyone, ever.

"So are you telling me that you had an affair because we didn't start trying earlier?"

"I had an affair because you shut me out."

"I felt shut out too, Dom." A burning flush consumes my cheeks. "In fact ... well, Ash and I ..."

Our eyes remain fixed on the route ahead, each of our steps rhythmic behind the wheels of the buggy which, plastered with wet leaves, are slopping against the path. We are making for the park gates before he speaks.

"I know you did," he says.

On the small of my back I feel the flutter of his touch.

34

Mum is cooking a sauce to go with the buckwheat pasta she'll prepare for our dinner. Clearly our normal pasta is not up to scratch, but I've let that one pass – and all the others. Stirring the pan, she's humming a nursery rhyme. I can't yet place which one as they all still merge into one tune for me. William and I are wedged into the rocking chair, which Dom had delivered to the house, and I'm savouring the fruity tang of tomatoes, together with the vaporous heat that cradles me. I'm enjoying my mother's company. Increasingly so. She stands in bare feet, her ankle chain tinkling each time she pads lightly to the fridge, and turns to reach for herbs from the cupboard with a smile for me and my sleeping son.

Daisy came to the house again today, and we found ourselves alone in the living room. She sat planted on our window seat, the sun slanting through the shutters casting stripes on her bare shoulders, and I watched her while she cradled William.

"He's so real, Cat," she said.

I had to stop myself from remarking that indeed he was not a doll. I observed the tender curve of her cheek, the strands of her hair back-lit by the sun. She smiled at me, and it was then that I saw something more mature in those wholesome eyes.

"To think, what I might have done, Cat."

"Well you didn't, Daisy, you didn't." I glided over to take her in my arms and hugged her tightly.

I'm thinking of her now, gazing dreamily out the patio doors at the sky as it's gradually washed into an indigo-pink. William awakes, ready for his usual teatime feeding frenzy just as we adults settle down for the evening, and Mum catches my wince as he latches on – Jackie was right about the razors too.

She turns back to the hob and stirs the sauce. "You've done well to go six weeks, sweetheart, it'll get better you'll see, they toughen up."

I throw her a double take. "Did you breastfeed us?"

"Nine months. Both of you."

The wooden spoon continues its rhythmic circling of the pan, but her back stiffens with emotion, and my eyes well up.

"There's so much to talk about, isn't there, Mum?"

She turns and smiles at me; our reconciliation has taken ten years off her face.

"I hope we've got as long as it takes, Catriona."

Some time later, Dom arrives, ringing the bell of his own front door. I smile up at him as he enters our living room and sinks awkwardly beside me on the sofa, pecking my cheek as a visiting uncle might. He lifts William from me, cradling him to his shoulder, and again I am struck by how my husband is a natural, the way he hums in a low register, the way he knows just how to soothe his son.

Mum sits us down in our kitchen with candles and a bottle of wine (she has sanctioned one glass a night) before returning to the living room to watch over her grandson in his bouncy chair. I take charge of the practical, pouring Dom his wine, shaving Parmesan for us both, and wait to hear what he has to say tonight. We've spent the past two weeks dissecting our marriage, pinpointing the moment it began to falter, and I know that tonight we need to move on. There can be no more recriminations.

He picks up his fork and holds it in mid air. "Cat, I do know how tough the IVF was for you."

I wasn't expecting this and I regard him blankly. Was it? Strangely, the pain, the humiliation, the emotional swings, they've all blurred. I make an effort to recall the injections, to summon up the distress of an egg collection, but they've gone from me, I've even forgotten the sequence of drugs. Against the joy of William, the IVF has paled into insignificance. So all I can do is shrug at him.

Clearly surprised, he scans his plate, as if wondering which piece of penne to stab. "It's just that, well it was hard for me too."

"I know it was." I've spent time on this. "We should have been more open with each other right from the start. It's as if we both retreated into ourselves, didn't we? And then it drove a wedge between us."

"Yeah." He's grateful for my honesty. "But we always used to talk. Before."

I hold his eyes with mine, searching for any trace of that connection again. But all I see is sadness, regret, and a tinge of fear.

He goes on. "And you're dead right, I am weak, I've always followed the path of least resistance. But then all my life that's what's offered itself up to me. I was lucky, up until then, and I flunked it. I mean, I know that you tried to involve me, at least at the start, that it was me who pulled away first."

I shake my head. "I shut you out by involving you."

"What do you mean?"

"I asked you to be there for the injections. I knew you loathed having to watch me do them, but I was angry that it was me and not you having to endure it."

"Only physically though. Emotionally, it was just as tough for me as it was for you."

"How could it have been?"

"Jesus, Cat, why can't you see that?"

I flinch at his raised voice, and realise we're being sucked down again instead of moving forwards. It's all too rooted within us, too entrenched. Still, I don't respond.

"I wanted a baby as much as you did, Cat."

I nod, but say nothing.

"And I had all the guilt to deal with too."

Oh come on. "Don't you think that I felt guilty too, Dom?" I smack my palm against my chest. "I felt a complete failure as a woman."

He shakes his head, those benevolent blue eyes now resting calmly on mine.

"You never failed at anything in your life, Cat."

With that, I see that the moment has come to nudge us on and I let it slide out gently.

"Except my marriage."

With a rum smile, I raise my glass to clink his. He observes me in silence for a few moments, and then he does some nudging of his own.

"But marriages are meant to be tested, aren't they? I think we should view this as a challenge sent to try us, don't you?"

"Sounds a bit religious Dom." I swig my wine and roll my eyes at him.

He ignores my comment. "I mean we were swanning along up until the IVF, weren't we?" His eyes are beseeching me now.

"You're right," I say nodding, "If it weren't for that, I think we would have come through."

"Are we not going to come through, then?"

I take a deep breath and soften my face, while Dom searches it, fighting back tears. Finally, he stares down into his wine, fiddling with the stem of his glass. I observe those lashes fanned on his cheek, and the skin around his jaw, which this summer was plump with the makings of a double chin, and now hangs loose. Sorry. That's all I feel for my husband. I wish I felt more. The silence hangs between us.

Eventually he speaks. "Whatever happens, I'll always be glad that you schemed against me. He's so perfect, Cat."

He lifts his eyes with a smile, and once again there is that sudden bolt of connection between us. Like a zip through my heart. In reflex, I beam back at him, reaching across to squeeze his hand before the moment might fade. I look into his face, and wonder if I could find it in me to love him again.

"Who knows?" I find myself saying. "In time, maybe William could meld us back together."

"Yes!" His eyes fill with the hope I've offered, and again a sadness consumes me.

"But William's what matters now. You and I are secondary, we had our chance, our stab at happiness."

"Cat, we're barely forty."

He's right. So I could call it quits with him and move on. But then, even if I can't love him again, perhaps it could be possible for me to stay, to expect less, to breathe more shallowly from this life. I have an inkling that to do so I may even be among the majority, muddling through, the once glorious union subjugated to the child.

My foggy mind plays out these permutations of the future, before I lose myself and give up. On daytime telly, I've seen a children's dance mat advertised. A coloured patch lights up and you have to jump to it, before a different patch lights, and then another – from purple to orange to blue. It's haphazard, there's no sequence. And that's how I believe my life should play out, for the moment anyway.

From the living room, I hear William beginning to cry and my breasts constrict in pain. I fetch him down to the kitchen and Dom looks on while I feed our son, his eyes gleaming at William's twitching cheek.

"I'm so happy you didn't give up, Cat."

"Me too." I smile at Dom then coo down at my baby, "You three, heh?"

At that moment, William's mouth pops off and he smiles up at me. For the very first time. My chest tightens and a rush of emotion flushes my face, flurries down through my body. I never expected this – I never *knew*. I smile back at him and stare deep into his soul, with all the messages I need to convey; that I will keep him safe, I will make him happy, I will be by his side as long as he needs me there. When he smiles, my son resembles my husband so intensely, and I see a burst of Dom's own smile across the table in Vietnam; the magnum force of that first ever connection.

I cradle William to my shoulder, stand and shuffle over to the patio doors. The moon is full, a rich and luminous harvest moon, which has taken up the whole of the sky, as if hanging there to greet my son. It kept me waiting, forced me to slow up, until I was ready, until I really wanted you. As if it recognised that the endless waiting would make you all the more precious.

Your body is clamped to mine, I am suffused by your vulnerability, your need. It's about you now. It is only you.

THE END

ACKNOWLEDGEMENTS

Once again, profound thanks to all at Blackbird, especially Stephanie Zia, my editor, and now close friend. Particular thanks also to those who scrutinised drafts of *Moondance*: Ruth Hunter, Barbara McKinlay, Susie Howells, Cathryn Chadwick, Wilma Ferguson. Thanks too to my kindred souls at Writers at Work, John Elliott, Judith Evans, Jana Ferguson, Peggy Hannington, Cath Hurley, Joy Isaacs, Janice Rainsbury, Barry Walsh. Special thanks to Maddie, not least for her ideas on the cover design. And most of all, thanks to Nick, for everything really.

ABOUT THE AUTHOR

Diane Chandler worked first as a political lobbyist in Brussels, and then at the European Commission for several years, where she managed overseas aid programmes in Ukraine just after the fall of communism. Ukraine soon worked its way into her heart, and she travelled there extensively. Back in London, when Diane married and her daughter was born, she was able to pursue her passion for writing in those few hours she could snatch. Ukraine became the subject for her first novel *The Road To Donetsk*, which won The People's Book Prize for Fiction 2016. This, her second novel, was informed by her personal experience of the emotional and physical impact of IVF. She is currently working on her third novel.

Keep up to date with all Diane Chandler news and new titles, join the Diane Chandler Mailing List

http://eepurl.com/9QUyn

(All email details securely managed at Mailchimp.com and never shared with third parties.).

READER AMBASSADORS

You are one of the very first readers of this novel. If you enjoyed it, please would you consider leaving a review? Word of mouth is so important in the early stages of an author's career. *Moondance* is listed on most major retailers' websites including Amazon, iBooks, Waterstones and at www.goodreads.com. Thank you!

If you would like to know more about becoming a Reader Ambassador for *Moondance,* please email us at editor@blackbird-books.com and we'll let you know how you can become a valuable, visible part of this book's journey to a wider audience.

More Original Quality Titles at
Blackbird Digital Books

Fiction
That Special Someone by Tanya Bullock
The Modigliani Girl by Jacqui Lofthouse
Valentina by S. E. Lynes
The Dream Theatre by Sarah Ball

Nightingale Editions
Dark Water by Sara Bailey

Non-Fiction
I Wish I Could Say I Was Sorry by Susie Kelly
Love & Justice by Diana Morgan-Hill
Schizophrenia – Who Cares? A Father's Story by Tim
Salmon
Tripping With Jim Morrison & Other Friends by
Michael Lawrence
Cats Through History by Christina Hamilton
*A London Steal: The Fabulous On-A-Budget Guide to
London's Hidden Chic* by Elle Ford

Blackbird Digital Books

The #authorpower publishing company

Discovering outstanding authors

www.blackbird-books.com

2/25 Earls Terrace, London W8 6LP
@Blackbird_Bks

blackbird